D0370436

the THREAT BELOW

Brathius Legacy Book 1

J.S. Latshaw

fernweh books

This is a work of fiction. Names, characters, places, and incidents are either a product of the author's imagination or used fictitiously. Any resemblance to actual persons, living or dead, events, or locales is entirely coincidental.

Text copyright ©2015
2nd Edition ©2020

Published in the United States by Fernweh Books.

ISBN-13: 978-0692463598 (Fernweh Books)
ISBN-10: 0692463593

Cover artwork by Daria Brennan

Part One
The Highest Point in the World

1

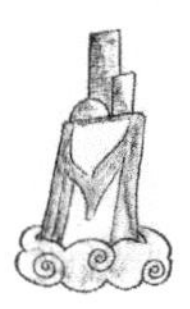

THIS WHOLE TRIP down the Mountain is for squirrels. As embarrassing as that is to admit, it's true.

I've stolen away from my job at Waterpump. Rincas doesn't love when I do this, but he does love me (not with untoward intensity, but in the way someone loves honey-soaked acorn cakes or when a friend tells a funny joke), so he won't complain. He'll keep my secret. He knows how I enjoy spending time with Adorane and how that time has grown scarcer and frowned upon by those who don't deserve to have an opinion.

When Adorane meets me at Waterpump, he's bursting with excitement, like a child with a secret too big to keep hidden. I love catching these glimpses of him, where he forgets how badly he wants to be seen as a guarded, tough man and becomes the Ad I've known since we were babies. Babies! How many people get to be friends with someone since the day they're born? I don't understand why people think Ad and I need to start spending less time together.

Adorane won't tell me where we're going (and I ask many times). "You'll see," he teases. "We're almost there."

"There." He points toward a tree. It's not any larger or prettier than any other tree I've ever seen. Maybe Adorane is easily impressed.

"It's a tree, Ad." I giggle. Whether he's joking—or, even better, is actually made glad by the sight of this typical tree—it's hilarious.

He rolls his eyes. "Look closer. At the base. There." He crouches near a small hollow in the bottom of the trunk. I peek inside, wondering what treasures I might find. Gold and gems from the Apriori? An undiscovered (or, more accurately, rediscovered) creature? A portal to a different world?

I see a pile of nuts.

"That's great, Ad. Should come in handy if you want a snack at some point."

Ad reaches in, grabs an acorn, and holds it out to me. "Look at it."

I examine the acorn, turning it slowly. Then I stop and blink. Neatly fashioned letters carved into the side of the acorn spell the word 'ICELYN.'

"Why is there a nut with my name on it in this tree?" I ask, looking at him suspiciously.

"Grab another." I do, and my name is on that acorn too. Every nut in the pile is labeled ICELYN.

"I don't understand—"

Ad shushes me. "Oh! Quiet!" He pulls me away from the tree and into the nearby brush. "Look," he whispers.

A squirrel scurries across the forest floor, carrying more ICELYN acorns. The small creature deposits its collection into the tree, then rushes away to find more.

"How…" I trail off, confused. Are squirrels writing my name on nuts? That's not possible.

"Here, I'll show you!" Ad proclaims, and he takes off downhill.

I freeze. He's running down the Mountain, in the direction we are forbidden to go.

But I have to follow.

The air is thinner in Mountaintop.

That's what I'm told, anyway. I wouldn't know; it's the only air I've ever breathed, so how am I supposed to compare? I've never been able to understand what thick air would feel like. Maybe like walking through a block of water, currents pushing against you, slowing your progress, but without the wetness?

These thoughts run through my mind as I struggle to keep up with Adorane. I swear, that boy moves through the pines like an ultralion. Me—when it comes to running, ducking, dodging, and jumping, I'm a hell of a scholar.

"Do you need me to help you?" Adorane calls back with a grin. "Maybe carry you for a spell?" He loves exposing weakness in me, as much as I try to conceal it.

"Your Latin tenses were a mess last I checked, so I'm not the only one who could use a boost," I huff as I strain over a fallen log. Why am I wearing my puffy ultralion skin parka? It seemed so chilly earlier, but now I might as well be dipped in lava and rolled in burning embers. I do need help, but I'm loath to admit it.

"You must wish you hadn't worn that parka by now. I knew you'd regret it!" Not for the first time, I wonder if he can read my thoughts. More likely, he's reading the drops of sweat I subtly try to wipe away from my eyes.

"It's good to be prepared. Father expects a frigid streak sometime soon. Those can come out of nowhere."

"Your father expects a lot of things, doesn't he?"

"Much that he expects, he gets."

This friendly back and forth between Adorane and myself is not new. It's as familiar as the threadbare wool blanket Mother uses to tuck me in every night. It's been going on, I guess, since we met—so seventeen years now. I fancy our repartee flirty, but I keep that to myself for many reasons.

All this loss of elevation is making me nervous. I've never been this far down the Mountain before. I wish I hadn't mentioned Father. Now I'm thinking about the rules we're breaking and the consequences for breaking them, and my face is growing even hotter, if that's possible, at the thought of getting caught. "Do you think they're looking for us?"

Adorane (pronounced ADD-OR-RAH-NAY! Some Veritas girls call him ADD-OR-RAIN, which annoys me to no end) shakes his head. My concern doesn't merit one word in reply.

"But if they did catch us down here, technically the Code calls for us to be..." I can't finish.

Disbursed. The very word makes my chest flare up in panic. What was I thinking, following Adorane down here, risking my place in the Kith? Disbursement doesn't happen often, but it does happen.

"Oh please! They'd never disburse you. Now me, forcing you down here? That's another story. Let's be honest, I'm the only one in any peril."

Is that supposed to make me feel better? I shiver at the thought of life in the Kith without Adorane.

Even the trees are different here. I swear I see a Manzanita, which

I've only read about in books before today. Everyone knows that Manzanitas only grow lower on the Mountain. I shouldn't be anywhere near them.

"So anyway, I've been leaving acorns all over, down here, with your name on them…"

Sure Adorane, that's a normal thing to do in your free time.

"Hey, that's a Manzanita, right?" I feign calm, but Adorane knows me too well. He laughs and stops to lean against the glossy red tree. He's so casual, as if it's not terrifying that we're seeing a Manzanita. At least we are still above Cloudline, I think, trying to calm my racing thoughts.

"I wanted to see if the squirrels that use that cache in Mountaintop come down this far when they're foraging for nuts. And guess what? They DO!"

Great, Ad. The squirrels forage for acorns here. That precious knowledge is definitely worth risking Disbursement.

"Stop acting like this isn't incredible. I can drop a nut here, with a message on it, and they carry it up to the village. Like the letters and mail system the Apriori had—only using squirrels instead of people."

Sure—look at it from that angle, and it's impressive. I mean, at least it's interesting. But why? I don't understand, and I don't want to stay here and try to figure it out any longer. "How far down the Mountain are we, anyway?"

"Oh, you still believe all the old myths?" I can't tell if he's serious or joking. I don't think he knows, either.

"They're not old myths! They're history. You've just never studied enough to know the difference."

Ad grabs a green leaf off the Manzanita and chews it. I stare. For me, the tree represents terror, a harbinger of the deadly danger that decimated humanity all those years ago. Ad just chews up the leave, spits it out, and grins. "When you're thirsty, these can be a godsend. Bet your textbook never told you that. Why spend all your time studying history when you can go outside and make it?"

He dashes ahead. I guess he thinks that's all the rest I need. Sometimes I wonder if he's made of different materials than I am. While I huff and puff, my skin flushed and my brow sweating, he glides along like this is the easiest thing in the world. I recently learned that birds have hollow, lightweight bones that make flight possible. I suspect Adorane is part bird, while my skeleton is packed solid with rocks, metals, and other heavy things.

"I saw the nuts. Why are we still going downhill?" I shout after him, exhausted.

"Oh—I figured since you're this close, you might as well see it."

"See what?"

He looks back at me. "Icelyn, you know what I'm talking about."

I hope I don't. I stop in my tracks.

"You've seen it? Not just pictures or drawings, but…Ad, you've actually seen it? How is that possible? "

He sprints away again, calling over his shoulder: "Forget pictures and drawings! It's always better to see things with your eyes." Then he looks back with a wicked smile. "Catalandi loves it down here."

Why did he mention Catalandi? He must know it bothers me. Is he ignorant, or is he being cruel? Perhaps he's just being frisky, as we always are together. Mother always tells me that "Adorane was born with a gleam in his eye, and I'd be wise to remember it." Whatever that means.

I pretend I'm not upset by the thought of Catalandi. I'm sure she has no problem keeping up with Adorane. As a Cognate, I'm not supposed to want or even admire lithe legs and tautly muscled arms, but it's hard for me to see Catalandi and not feel envious. Since she's promised to Adorane, I've cause enough to be envious anyway—although I know the adults would tell me that's unreasonable.

Why do Adorane and Catalandi spend time alone down here? They're only seventeen! We have years before betrothals morph into marriages. Adorane must realize how sickening it is when he's acting like some musclebound character from the Apriori's tawdry mating novels. I'm queasy just imagining them running through the woods together, laughing.

It's too early. We're still only children.

Adorane slows long enough to peer back at me while I dodge to avoid the scratchy underbrush. "C'mon, Ice—I saw it just up here."

I'm frozen in place again as a new wave of anxiety, washes over me.

"How far down are we, exactly?" I ask, because now I think I do know what thick air feels like. As if the sky is pressing down on me from all angles, pushing me to the ground to keep me there. It'd be easier if I could cut this air into pieces before I tried to breathe it in, because it doesn't feel like it's making its way down to my lungs anymore. It doesn't fit through my nostrils.

Adorane doubles back and grabs my hand. If I weren't busy choking on this dense air, I could pay attention to that. We don't usually touch;

after all, physical contact between unmarried people is forbidden among the Kith. But hey, being down here isn't allowed either, so it looks like we're both living in Ad's own state of anarchy right now.

No. I dig my heels into the ground hard. "We should head back—"

"Ice! You can't come this far only to turn around. Please." He pulls me and I tumble forward, shocked, because it's so strong. Lightweight yet still a force of nature, like an ox. That's Adorane.

Ox: a large muscular mammal that the Apriori used in manual labor while farming, then slaughtered and ate. I read about them the other day in a dusty book I found in Belubus' library. Isn't it incredible what you think about when you're afraid?

Suddenly we break through the thick underbrush. Adorane stops short.

I'm not sure if it's the heavy air, the exhaustion from the trip, or the shock of what I'm looking at, but one thing is for sure—now I really cannot breathe.

2

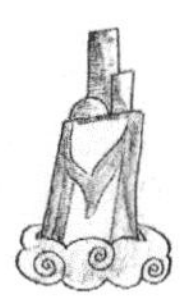

NICHOLAS BRATHIUS SURVEYED Mountaintop from his rooftop courtyard atop Brathius Tower, the highest point in all the known world. (Granted, much of the world was now unknown.)

Brathius Tower, all polished stone and hand-hewn pine, stood at the peak of Mount Savior, the center of the hamlet of Mountaintop. At sixty feet tall, calling it a 'tower' was a stretch, but any other label seemed farther afield. It was not a castle and certainly not a palace. So 'tower' it remained.

Talmer Brathius, Nicholas' great-grandfather, had tried to build an actual tower, 200 feet high, 87 years earlier. The ruins stretched down the steep north side of Mount Savior's peak and were now referred to as Talmer's Folly. Sixty feet tall was now the limit; in this loose ground, anything grander would topple over. Forget the skyscrapers, cathedrals, and castles that were common in the Apriori cities.

Comparing life in Mountaintop to Apriori civilization, Nicholas knew, could result only in heartache and jealousy. The world had changed. The Apriori way of life was no more possible now than life on Mars or at the bottom of the ocean.

So he compared Brathius Tower to the rest of Mountaintop instead. Especially the east side—where the Veritas lived in rounds, low-slung domes cobbled together out of wood and mud. Some Cognates called the east side 'Brutaltown' and derisively referred to the Veritas as 'Brutes.'

Compared to Brutaltown, Brathius Tower *was* a palace. It wasn't that those on the east side lived in squalor. The Veritas were capable of quality workmanship; they had built everything on the Cognates' side of town too, even Brathius Tower. But the Veritas were rationed smaller lots that were closer together. They were only provided materials like wood, leaves, and mud to build their homes—certainly not stone. But this was only fair. There were more Veritas, and they were accustomed to close quarters. They didn't require solitude for reflection and study, as the Cognates did. Also, the Cognates were a less sturdy people who couldn't handle the extremes of cold and heat that seeped through the mud walls of the rounds.

Cognates lived in two-story stone homes called labs, the name a tribute to the buildings where their ancestors made majestic discoveries when they lived in grand Apriori cities long ago. All straight lines and right angles, the labs lined the western streets, creating a stark contrast to the organic Brutaltown rounds just beyond.

Nicholas discouraged the Cognates from using the name 'Brutaltown,' or from calling the Veritas 'Brutes.' He wouldn't add this prohibition to the Code; it was more of a gentle suggestion than anything else. But he knew that insults could only damage the Kith in the long run.

"How long are you going to take? I could fetch the water myself if you'd rather."

Nicholas turned to see his wife, Marjan, stumble toward him. She was still in her bedclothes, hardly presentable should any Kith citizens below glance up toward them. He turned her back toward their bedroom.

"Darling, the sun is too bright for you. You need your rest."

"What I need is *water*."

"I was on my way out."

Silently, Nicholas again cursed the decree—his own decree, by his own pen, no less—outlawing the pipes that carried water into personal homes, even Brathius Tower. But the pipes the original Ascenders had brought to Mountaintop had corroded, and with no metal or plastic to replace them, water had begun to leak through the cracks. There were many things in short supply in Mountaintop, but water was the most precious. *I'd rather something else, but this had to be.* It was a Brathius family proverb for a reason.

Nicholas hated how often his progressive ideals ended up costing him. He'd love to send a Tarlinius—the Veritas family who had served the Brathius for generations—out to do these menial chores. In his weaker moments, Nicholas understood why the Brathius had always had servants. Why waste Brathius effort lugging pails through town? A Brathius shouldn't have to lug anything.

But Nicholas had recognized that it was unfair that the Tarlinius were forced to serve the Brathius, so he had put an end to it. Marjan had told him to reconsider, but Nicholas had been stubborn.

All the same, he wasn't looking forward to a trip to Waterpump. He didn't feel like talking to anyone. As soon as he stepped outside, he'd be overwhelmed with requests. Martinique's daughter had taken ill and needed her nutrient ration increased. Trillian thought his son would make an outstanding match for Icelyn and was willing to sweeten his offer. Lunarnis wanted to know when the next meeting of the Ultracognates would be, because he had a proposal he wanted the committee to consider.

But Nicholas' darling Marjan was not getting better, and he didn't care about anyone else's anything in comparison. He craved the kind of silence that could only be found at the top of a tower. (Even if the tower was a meager sixty feet tall.)

Nicholas pulled on his ultralion skin cloak and fastened an ultrabear head covering to obscure his face. It wasn't cold enough to warrant this outfit, but he hoped it would provide anonymity down on the ground.

Those hopes were dashed soon after he left the building. Despite his mood, Nicholas plastered a smile on his face and tried to push through the group of Cognate and Veritas that had quickly surrounded him. Nicholas wanted to be liked, and he considered himself a beloved ruler. The truth was, he was neither loved nor hated. Some appreciated the changes he'd made to the Code. But nothing about Nicholas was inspiring—and what his subjects wanted most, whether they realized it or not, was inspiration.

Nicholas suffered through three awkward conversations, made two half-hearted promises, and told one outright lie, a promise to attend Jonas Crowses' prowess event. Anyone should know that Nicholas would never show up to a lower level Veritas' coming-of-age ceremony. But he couldn't say that to Barl Crowse, who was irrationally proud of his son.

Nicholas arrived at Waterpump. At least he'd have a chance to see his daughter Icelyn, who was working there today. That was another one of his progressive initiatives. Brathius children, and all Cognate children, had begun working apprenticeships around Mountaintop in addition to their schooling, just as the Veritas children had always done.

The Cognates hated this reform, and the Veritas didn't seem to appreciate it as much as Nicholas thought they should. He regretted the decision now, but at least Icelyn appeared to enjoy working at Waterpump. As she should—the place was in her blood.

Waterpump, the dramatic stone and metal edifice that reached taller than anything but Brathius Tower, had always been a source of pride for the Brathius. Brathius brains and leadership had conceived and designed it. It was the second most important thing Sean Brathius had done almost three hundred years before, the first being figuring out how to escape the Threat Below and lead his people here. That's why a Brathius was now, and would always be, Chief Cognate of Mountaintop.

Nicholas skipped the line that wound down the dirt road. No one would mind; they all knew he likely had important business to attend to elsewhere. He reached an overworked, harried Veritas who was barely managing to keep his cool while attending to irritable Veritas and Cognate alike.

"Rincas, I thank you for your contribution to the Kith today." It was the traditional, expected greeting a Brathius made to a worker in Mountaintop. Originally meant to show gratitude even in the harshest times, it now only annoyed Rincas—and truth be told, Nicholas too.

"How many Gallons, Chief Cognate?" Short and to the point. Rincas had no time. The Veritas behind Nicholas sighed, having no patience even for that. Nicholas had taken their place in line.

"Oh, I'd rather Icelyn fulfill my ration, please. Fetch her for me?" A groan floated up from the line behind Nicholas. He turned around, raising an eyebrow, but he couldn't tell who'd issued it.

"I would love for her to help you. And me, for that matter. But she's been gone all morning."

"Gone? Oh, no. She isn't at home. She told me she was working."

"Trust me, I would know. She isn't here."

This wasn't like Icelyn. "Then tell me, where could she possibly be?"

3

I'VE HEARD ABOUT it before. Every child in Mountaintop has. But dear God—I never expected to see it. *What the hell am I doing down here?*

A heavy wind kicks up as soon as I see it. For the first time today, I'm glad to be wearing something warm. I pull my coat tightly around me and try to wish away what I'm seeing. I realize suddenly that I'm not as brave as I've always thought I was. I've simply never seen anything truly scary before.

The Wall.

Ancient and imposing. Built 30 feet high, out of tree trunks bundled and bound by cords made of (I'm guessing from the rusty coloring and rough texture) metal.

A warning is plastered on the Wall, repeated in multiple languages. I recognize a few of them as obsolete tongues the Apriori spoke—one called Japanese, another called French. One word—ACHTUNG—I can't place as any language I've heard of before. Then there are some markings that I assume are words and letters, though I doubt anyone could tell you which language they are.

I'm reminded that the First Ascenders spoke many different languages and even split themselves up into factions based on petty matters such as eye color, shade of skin, outdated concepts of gods and goddesses, and food preferences. That was before the Ascenders had to pull together into the Kith, embrace one language, and accept the leadership of my ancestor, Sean Brathius.

ATTENTION! BEYOND THIS WALL LURKS THE DEATH THAT WE HAVE ESCAPED. DO NOT PASS. YOU WILL BE HUNTED. YOU WILL DIE.

Below these dire words someone long ago painted the terrifying silhouette of a monster—just in case anybody was not yet suitably scared off.

I realize I've read the warning out loud when Adorane answers with a smirk, "You say it like you believe it."

Believe it? I have a difficult time believing *him* anymore. My fear boils over into anger.

"Goddamn it, Ad! Are you really going to pretend this is nothing? Doesn't this GIANT WALL prove it's not all a myth?"

"*Goddamn*, Ice? I love it when you dip into the Apriori superstitions. You, of all people!"

I hate when he acts like I'm an exception, like an action is *especially notable* when I perform it. As if I am held to a rarefied standard or judged by a separate set of rules. Most of the time, what I appreciate about spending time with Adorane is the exact opposite. He treats me as I want to be treated—like I'm his oldest friend, and we're nothing more than the two kids we've always been. But sometimes he acts like all the others—pointing out that I'm *special*. And not the good kind of special. *Me, of all people*? Why did he have to say that? For a best friend, Adorane didn't always act his best, or even particularly friendly, toward me.

"They built this Wall for a reason, Ad." I'm trying—and failing—not to think about that reason right now.

"292 years ago, Ice. Yes, I know the history. What we're told of it, at least."

"Just because we're told something doesn't mean it's not true."

"Doesn't mean it *is* true either. So it doesn't mean anything at all. But even if it were true, all of it, it's been 292 years! Do you know how much can change in that time? Everything. That's a hundred lifetimes!"

I know he's exaggerating, but I have to correct him. "If you take the latest life expectancy statistics from the Commission on Life and Living, it's actually only seven lifetimes."

Adorane treats me to an amused yet disappointed expression. I'm used to it. I probably deserve it.

"Look at the Wall, Ice. You think that pathetic barrier is going to keep anything *out*? Anything set on getting in? Anything strong and deadly?"

Now that I'm past my initial shock and have a chance to examine it with clearer eyes, it does appear dilapidated. Rotted wood, whole tree trunks eaten by worms and turned into horizontal pillars of mushy sawdust. Adorane approaches the Wall and touches one of the metal cords; it crumbles apart, pieces falling to the ground. I'm tempted to agree with him, but conceding when Adorane is right and I'm wrong never ends well. It goes straight to his head, and I don't hear the end of it for months.

He still mentions the time that I misunderstood an essay question and he outscored me (purely out of luck) in our Year Three schooling mid-term. I couldn't make him understand that it's because I overthought my answer, while he viewed it simply, and that my incorrect reply was actually a result of greater intellectual rigor. I had insisted that fish could fly while birds swam underwater. (Point of fact is—though I wouldn't expect Adorane to know this—that there *were* fish that could fly and birds that swam underwater. They were called flying fish and penguins, respectively, and I read about them in Belubus' library.) Adorane still laughs at my expense over this unfortunate event more than a *decade* in our past, back when we were young enough to be taught in the same classroom even though he's a Veritas and I'm a Cognate. As a result, I never, ever allow him to think he's right.

"Of course it's weathered. What would you expect? It was built ages ago."

"If it's really meant to keep things out, why wouldn't they maintain it?"

Another good point. I don't reply. I look past the Wall, further down the Mountain. Another thousand or so feet and I almost feel as if I can see Cloudline, where the thick mass of clouds that obscure our view of the valley below begins. When I was younger, I'd sit with Father at the top of Brathius Tower, and we'd look at Cloudline—thick and white, with fluffy hills and valleys made up of what appear to be magic and happiness. I didn't believe him when he told me that walking on the clouds was impossible. They looked so substantial. I'd beg Father to let me try. *Has anyone ever tried? Then how do we know? Please, just let me try.*

He told me that if I tried, I'd fall right through the clouds and land Down Below. *What's it like down there, Father?* I'd prod him for answers, clues, anything about Down Below, but he'd just joke and laugh at me until I gave up. (Father is always good-natured about questions that other adults would frown upon.)

But one time he did give me an answer.

"It's dangerous, Icelyn. That's what it's like down there. You must never go down there. Never."

The sky above Cloudline is the lightest blue. Father always says it reminds him of my eyes. *Brathius blue eyes,* he calls them, though his are nowhere near the same shade. I close my palm around the special necklace he gave me long ago, which bears a brilliant shining stone the color of Brathius blue eyes.

I wish Father was here. What am I *doing* down here?

It's dangerous, Icelyn. That's what it's like down there. You must never go down there. Never.

Ad is still talking. "You know what I think? I think it's here to *keep us in.* They want us in Mountaintop, where they can keep tabs on us, keep us docile. Trapped, yet thankful for their protection."

Oh, wonderful. Adorane will now share his ridiculous conspiracy theories, which he keeps sharpened and aimed squarely at the Cognates—and my family most of all. He does this often, and I hate it. Veritas aren't supposed to think these things. And even if they do, they certainly aren't supposed to speak them aloud. Especially not within earshot of a Cognate. Adorane is my dearest friend, but I can't help but wonder when he will gain the common sense the Veritas are supposed to be known for and take his place as a decent member of the Kith. He certainly hasn't yet.

"The 'they' you speak of includes me. You know that, right?"

He chuckles. "Come on, Ice. You're a Cognate in name only."

But I'm not. I'm Icelyn Brathius, heir to Brathius Tower and the next Chief Cognate of Mountaintop. Far from being a Cognate in name only, I'm working toward the day when I am the Cognate all others must defer to.

As comfortable as I am with Adorane, and as brash and blunt as many accuse me of being, I can't say this to him. Although he might not see it, I understand that a wall exists between us—silent, invisible, erected by those distant Brathius before us, always there. Everywhere else in Mountaintop, I am assured of my position, comfortable with my status—but every time I try to speak of it to him, I falter. So I just smile like I agree with him and inwardly curse myself for doing so. Someday we'll talk this out. Just not today.

"So now I've seen the Wall. And you're right, it's astonishing. Exhilarating. But we should head back. Our absence has probably been noticed. We should figure out a cover. What have we been doing?"

Adorane lifts an eyebrow, and I blush.

"Adorane Hailgard! No! As if that's a suitable excuse, anyway. We'd still get in trouble. You most of all."

"I didn't say anything. Your dirty mind must have conjured up thoughts deserving such a deep shade of crimson blush."

All this... whatever this is (flirting?) is becoming more frequent in our exchanges. I love and loathe it. A dangerous thrill that I know can kill me, but I hope never subsides. Soon I'll have to end it. Not today, though. I hate that I'm storing up all these unpleasant conversations.

I'm shaken from my thoughts by a crash. What *was* that? I hear a loud shuffling through the bushes and the snap of breaking tree branches beyond the Wall. *Beyond the Wall!*

I want to bolt back up toward Mountaintop, but my limbs stage a rebellion, and I'm paralyzed. What's the point of having good sense if your body won't follow your mind's commands?

Adorane draws the beloved bone knife he received from his father after completing his prowess event. Finally, it seems he's taking our predicament seriously.

"Wait for me here! This is going to be fun." Before I can ask what could possibly be fun right now, Adorane darts from my side and, with grace and strength, scales the Wall. As I watch frozen in disbelief, he drops over and disappears on the other side.

I am alone.

4

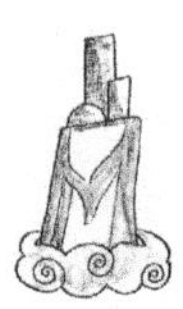

NICHOLAS HURRIED TO Brathius Tower with the three-gallon tin of water in tow, ignoring the jealous looks from others along the way. Metal was a status symbol. The tins had been in his family for nearly three hundred years. Of course he was going to use them for water. Was he supposed to use ultralion stomach bladders like a Veritas?

He would have been better off carrying the water in a stomach bladder, he thought ruefully. The status derived from the metal tin came at a heavy price, and Nicholas struggled with its weight. He needed to rush the water to Marjan before he could search for Icelyn without letting anyone else know she was missing. What would people think if they knew the daughter of the Chief Cognate was unaccounted for? At best, it would be shameful; at worst, people might start reconsidering their leadership options.

Nicholas' legs threatened to buckle, and his lungs resisted with fierce agony. He pushed through, psyching himself up by imagining that his speed would prove his love for his wife and his daughter. The thought motivated him, and he felt weightless. But the effects soon wore off. He'd have to find less physically taxing ways to demonstrate his passion.

Aclornis Hailgard, busy sealing the roof of his round in anticipation of the imminent cold streak, tried to ignore Nicholas' struggle. It was bad form for a Veritas to call attention to a Cognate's physical weakness. But Nicholas needed assistance. Aclornis leapt from atop Hailgard Round and approached Nicholas just as the heavy water tin slammed into the ground.

"Not that you need it, of course, but I'd be honored to assist the Chief Cognate with his water." Good, trustworthy Aclornis. Always looking to help, yet making it seem like *you* were the one doing *him* the favor. It was a skill that Nicholas appreciated.

"It would be my honor to have the Chief Veritas by my side."

Aclornis lifted the water tin with ease. "Where are we headed?" He wanted to add *in such a hurry, and why?* to the end of his question. Aclornis was curious, along with the whole village. No one had seen Marjan in months, and rumors were spreading. He controlled himself, though, as prying into a Cognate's business wasn't proper.

As soon as Aclornis asked where they were headed, Nicholas realized his mistake. If Aclornis accompanied him to Brathius Tower, he might see Marjan. Marjan's illness was a well-guarded secret known only to Tranton, his closest advisor. Even Icelyn had been kept in the dark about its severity.

Nicholas grabbed the tin back. "I just needed a moment of rest. I can take it." This proved immediately to be a noticeable lie, as his fatigue returned and he had trouble lifting the tin.

"I'm happy to help."

"Let me be on my way," Nicholas answered abruptly.

Aclornis relented. "If you need anything, I'm never too busy for you." Aclornis meant it—he meant everything he said.

As Aclornis watched Nicholas plodding toward the tower, he wondered if Nicholas was exceeding the exertion level allowable for Cognates in the Code. The Chief Cognate was sweating like a Veritas in training. It was shameful, and Aclornis hoped no one else witnessed it.

5

"AD! YOU…WHERE…Ad!" My vocabulary is stunted. "Ad! Ad!"

Unlike my brain, my emotions haven't been numbed by his departure. I'm hit with vivid fear and anger. They're more color, sound, and smell than feeling—red, hot, loud, heavy and earthy.

How could he bring me down here, within feet of this nightmare, and then abandon me? I'm going to collapse under the weight of my fears. Then, finally!—my body moves once again.

But in the wrong direction. Toward the Wall and Adorane.

I follow Adorane's steps and climb the same portion of the Wall that he scaled. Knots in the fallen trunks and metal cords form a ladder. *If it's meant to keep things out, don't you think they'd work a little harder to maintain it?* Ad's words race through my head. It does seem like this Wall is more a symbol than a barrier.

If *I* can get over it, who—or what—couldn't?

From the top of the Wall, I spy Adorane racing through the thick woods, pursuing something.

"Adorane Hailgard!"

He grins at me. "Ice! I'm impressed. I've never fancied you a hunter, but if you're desperate to try, I'll wait."

"You ass! I have no desire to join you out there—come back with me to Mountaintop right now!"

Adorane laughs as if I told the funniest joke he's ever heard. He's testing our friendship today. I pace on top of the Wall.

"Adorane, I am begging you. I'm scared. I need to leave. And I need you to leave with me when I go." It will take me a long time to forgive him for forcing me to utter this embarrassment. But there are times when pride must yield, when you must admit that you're terrified and can't bear to be alone for a second longer.

It seems to work. Adorane walks back toward me, and I recognize compassion in his eyes.

"Ah, Icy. When you put it that way, how can I say no?"

I take another step toward the edge of the wall. It's a mistake. The tree trunk beneath me, rotted from time and worms, crumbles away.

No more than a moment elapses as I fall thirty feet, but I feel frozen a hundred times longer as I tumble downward. *I'm going to die.* Father and Mother will be heartbroken and confused. What was I doing here, they'll wonder? Where did they go wrong? How will this tragedy reflect on Father as the Chief Cognate? I wish I could talk to them one last time, assure them that none of this was their fault.

Adorane will be disbursed. He probably won't care, though, because apparently he spends his free time scampering around outside the Wall anyway. He will, of course, miss me terribly. He'll suffer from intense loneliness, along with a lifetime of crushing and deserved guilt. Poor Adorane. He'll probably spend the rest of his days wishing he had fallen along with me and died by my side. Hopefully my passing will serve as the jolt he needs to become a full, productive member of the Kith.

Who else will miss me? My thoughts race on. Torrain Pannous will feel relief, that waste. Who knows what my mother sees in him or his crud-encrusted family? Oh! My beloved teacher, Belubus. I am his life's work, his greatest investment. He'll never recover.

Now the ground is coming. I wonder if death will hurt.

I crash into a thick bed of briars. Even though thorns rip into me, it's a blessing because it cushions the impact.

Far from dead, I'm only a little scratched up. I lift my bloody hands to my face and stare at them in disbelief.

"Ice! Say something! Are you hurt? God, say something." Adorane crouches over me, his eyes misty. "I'm so sorry. I've been down here a thousand times—I swear I thought it was safe. Say something. Please. You're bleeding!"

I'm tempted to milk this moment, I enjoy it so much. But seeing Adorane's desperation, I'd be cruel to let it go on. He's being so tender and careful with me, all my anger from earlier has evaporated anyway.

"I'll survive."

Relief floods his face. He squeezes my hand. "I guess you're made of tougher stuff than we thought."

"Or I fall into thicker, more cushioning bushes."

He takes a closer look at my forearms. They're crisscrossed with lines of blood. "We have to dress this."

I sit up. Moving hurts less than I thought it would. I am going to be fine.

Except maybe not. I feel my panic rise again. I'm outside the Wall.

"Tranton can attend to it. Please, let's get back to Mountaintop."

"Tranton will want to know how you were cut. As will your Father. There are ferns about two hundred yards from here; they're all I need to fix you."

I grab Adorane, fearful that he'll abandon me again. "I'd rather bleed out every drop than be left alone here." Part of me, the smarter part, is telling me I'll regret these unrefined and unfiltered words. But when your blood spills to the ground as you watch, rawer speech seems appropriate.

Adorane helps me to my feet. "We'll go together."

"But…we're outside the Wall."

"I've been hunting out here for years. All the young hunters do. The ultralions and ultrabears have grown sparse inside the boundaries of Mountaintop. There's nothing to fear out here. I would know."

I prefer Adorane when he's sincere, like he is now. I trust him more, too. I limp beside him toward the ferns.

"Do you really think I'd let you run free, exposed, if the Threat Below was lurking nearby?"

I don't want to believe he would, but I don't know *what* to believe today.

"Icelyn, sometimes I think you don't know me at all."

We reach the ferns and Adorane attends to me. I watch his muscled arms as he cracks the stems and applies soothing aloe to my wounds. He gingerly pats the leaves up and down on my skin. "You'll have to wear long sleeves if you want to avoid any questions from your parents."

I nod. Now that the pain is subsiding, I realize how much I've been hurting.

"Do you really journey here?" I ask softly.

Ad nods his head yes.

"Often? Outside the Walls? Does your father know?"

"Certainly not! He's part of the old ways and still believes in the Threat Below. He wouldn't understand." He says this last part as if I *would* understand, but I don't. I didn't know that believing in the Threat Below was considered an *old way*. Apparently I've become antiquated without even realizing it.

"Maybe you should stop coming down here, though. There's a chance you've just been lucky so far."

"A hunter knows what's in the woods, Ice. Ultralions and ultrabears are the most fearful creatures prowling here—and I *hope* to find *them*." He finishes applying the balm in sure, confident strokes. "There! All clean. How do you feel?"

"Better, thanks." Much better. I never even knew that Adorane had this skill. Wall or no Wall, it's certainly better than anything Tranton has ever been able to do for me.

We head back in the direction of the Wall. "Adorane…" I trail off, trying to phrase my words perfectly.

"What is it?"

"Really, don't come out here anymore. You shouldn't. Even if you think it's safe—it's forbidden."

"I hear you, Icelyn."

I hear you? What a mysterious reply. I'm not asking to be heard. I'm asking him not to scale the Wall anymore. "Does that mean you'll do as I ask?"

"It means I hear you."

"But I wasn't asking to be heard. I—"

"You're asking to be obeyed. I know."

"That's not fair. I'm just worried about—it's not as if I'm your mother, nagging you like a naughty child."

"No, it's not. I'm glad you agree. That's why, right now, I only hear you. I need some time to think about what you've asked."

I clamp my mouth shut, my irritation rising at his easy smile.

Suddenly something catches his attention. "Oh, it's Jarvin! Jarvin!"

Jarvin is another Veritas and the closest thing Adorane has to a friend other than me (and, unfortunately, Catalandi). Apparently he's also another hunter who has no regard for the Code, if he's out here. Is there *anyone* who isn't gallivanting outside the Wall these days?

"Where? I can't see him," I ask.

Adorane lowers his voice to a whisper. "See how he isn't moving? He must be tracking something. Come with me." I peer into the darkness, following where he points, but I still can't see anyone in the thick forest.

Adorane darts through the underbrush with a grace I don't possess. With all the noise I'm making, I'd be amazed if whatever Jarvin was tracking hasn't already retreated.

By the time I catch up with him, I see that something is wrong.

"What's going on, Ad?"

Adorane's face pales as he stares upward. His voice is weak. "You should go, Icelyn. Turn around—go back." He's desperate to keep me from seeing something.

I follow Adorane's troubled gaze and look high in a tree. There I see Jarvin, where he had tied himself in with leather restraints, bone-tipped spear by his side. His head hands down, as if he's asleep.

"Dear God." The ancient superstitions once again escape my lips as I see what has scared Adorane.

Jarvin's not sleeping.

I can't understand what I'm seeing.

His chest, or where a chest normally would be, has been scraped out, like when the Veritas women empty a gourd to make their Harvest Pies. He's *hollow*. I can see the inside of his ribs, which are oddly white and gleaming, as if they've been polished and bleached.

Looking at Jarvin, I feel like I am outside of myself, disconnected. Adorane's hard grasp on my arm brings me back. He's shouting and pulling me after him, but I can't look away from Jarvin.

"We have to go! Run with me!" His voice is gruff, desperate.

I've never heard him like this before. I sprint to keep up so he doesn't have to slow down to pull me along.

Then I hear it.

A hunter knows what's in the woods, Ice.

Does Adorane recognize that breathing, that bustle through the underbrush growing louder and louder? Is that why he's so afraid? Or does he, for the first time, *not know* what is in these woods? The idea fills me with fresh horror.

Jarvin thought he knew what was in the woods, too. But there was something here he didn't know about. And whatever it is, it's chasing us.

We reach the Wall, and I'm grateful because the climbing here is as easy as it was on the other side. Adorane pushes me ahead, ensuring that I reach the top before he does. I drag myself upward, hands grasping desperately for trees and wires, driven by panic. The horrid sounds—short ragged breathing, crashes through the underbrush, and the snapping and crunching of twigs and branches—have grown terrifyingly close.

An unearthly howl emerges. It's like nothing I've heard before. I cannot turn around; I just pray the sound will end. Then it does end, and I'm seized by the fear that I'll hear it again. I'd give anything to have the memory of that sound blotted out. I reach for the final handhold, desperately hurling myself onto the top of the Wall.

"What is that, Ad? What is that?" I shout.

"Quiet!" he shushes me from behind.

The screech is two-toned, high and low notes that clash with each other, creating a dissonance that I feel as much as hear. It cuts through me. There are sounds that I've heard that shake me deep inside, like they have direct access to stoke my fears without any thoughts filtering them first—an angry warning from a threatened rattlesnake, the low rumbling roar of an ultralion. But nothing compares to this howl. I clamp my hands over my ears, my eyes desperately searching the ground below. I can't see the beast anywhere, but I can feel its howl everywhere.

Where is Ad? He hasn't joined me here at the top of the Wall. He is just below, peering back toward Jarvin, as if he could still help his friend in some way.

"Adorane, *climb!*" What good is being safe up here if I'm forced to watch that thing eviscerate Adorane like it did Jarvin? I'd rather die along with him.

Adorane looks pained, but he obeys and scales the Wall in seconds. We scramble down the other side and bolt back up the hillside toward Mountaintop.

The howl is replaced by a louder, more piercing cry that sounds like terrible pain, which is followed by a heavy thud and then silence. As I run, I hear slow dragging noises begin, moving further and further away. Something terrible, I imagine, is stumbling and limping.

"Ad…what *was* that?" I gasp.

Adorane doesn't slow his pace. He seems as intent on returning to Mountaintop as I am.

"I have no idea, Ice."

6

WHEN HE FINALLY reached the Tower, Marjan's parched and sallow appearance made Nicholas forget his own exhaustion. She didn't resemble the vibrant, brash soul he'd loved for the last twenty years. He pushed away his worries. She'd recover; she had to.

Nicholas brought a cup of the water to Marjan's lips. "Can I get you anything to eat?" he asked.

Marjan shook her head.

"You need more than water, dear," he said gently.

Marjan continued to shake her head while she drank the water. No use arguing with that.

"I'm sorry to leave, but urgent matters need attending—"

"Stay."

Nicholas couldn't explain that Icelyn was missing. He had to look for her, having delayed too long already. Yet he knew Marjan needed him. It was a riddle that had no answer. "I'll send for Tranton."

Marjan shook her head in disagreement.

Nicholas spoke quickly: "You're looking very unwell. We need his guidance."

Tranton Nilsing, Nicholas' most trusted advisor and Kith Chief of the Healing Arts, had been treating Marjan. An examination with Tranton allowed Nicholas to leave Marjan's side without leaving her alone, which was the real reason Nicholas wanted him there.

As Nicholas walked quickly toward the Pannous Family Lab, having arranged a visit from Tranton, he felt a heavy guilt at abandoning Marjan to Tranton's care. But Icelyn was missing, and Marjan wasn't remembering half of their interactions lately anyway. Hopefully he'd find his daughter and all this would be forgotten.

Nicholas knocked at the door, willing himself to appear calm.

"Oh, my. Whatever is the problem, Chief Cognate?" Marcel Pannous was surprised and concerned as he greeted Nicholas. He even forgot to deliver a traditional greeting.

"Nothing's wrong. I'm here to see Torrain. It's been too long."

"Let me fetch Nando and I will arrange a joint sit-down with all of us together."

Nicholas had no desire to participate in a tedious and regimented joint sit-down, where parents and betrothed children gathered together —all four adults and two youths—and learned about each other's family histories and stories. Nobody enjoyed them.

"Just me and Torrain, if you will."

"Chief Cognate, I'm sure you're aware that your request is unusual." The Kith were adept at making accusations without becoming accusers. Nicholas knew Marcel was unhappy about this surprise visit and smiled widely to diffuse the tension.

"The Code does not prohibit the Chief Cognate from bestowing honor on one of his favorites. I only wish to bless him."

Marcel was not placated, but he'd made his reluctance known, and Nicholas had pushed forward regardless. There was nothing to do but politely comply.

Nicholas closed the door behind him. The teenage boy sat at a desk carved out of a tree trunk. He sketched on rough, thick paper. (The art of paper-making had only crudely survived the trip up the Mountain; the paper Mountaintop's residents used more closely resembled tree bark.)

Nicholas greeted Torrain in the customary way. "I am grateful for your presence in my life."

The boy continued his drawing of Apriori technology. Cars, rocket-ships, skyscrapers, and airplanes. Diagrams of the innards of ancient machines, with gears, wires, and other pieces that Nicholas didn't recognize.

Nicholas grew annoyed. Torrain wasn't responding in kind. "And are you even more grateful for mine?"

Torrain's smile said *not at all,* though he said nothing.

Nicholas tried another approach. "What are you working on here?"

For the first time, Torrain seemed interested—not polite, but at least mildly engaged. "A reverse combustion mechanism, a process where you take carbon emissions, like the air we breathe out, for instance, and convert it into energy or fuel. It could be used to—"

Nicholas clucked quietly. "I question whether this is a productive use of time. Do not deviate from your prescribed studies. When you're ready, perhaps you can return to this line of innovative thinking."

Torrain knew he'd never be encouraged to return to this line of thinking. Nothing new (or even old but unfamiliar) was ever studied in Mountaintop.

Nicholas sighed. "I hoped Icelyn would be here."

Torrain spoke without looking up. "As have I. Every day."

Nicholas wondered why the boy still hadn't bothered to acknowledge his presence. "I've been meaning to ask, how are the Bonding Sessions proceeding?"

Torrain only laughed.

Nicholas sat on the boy's spartan bed. Vines and saplings groaned under his weight. "I presume they are going well, then?"

Finally Torrain dropped his stick of charcoal and turned toward Nicholas.

"Are you so ignorant?"

Nicholas coveted more deference from this one. Not for the first time, he questioned Marjan's choice. "I'm not here to answer riddles, Torrain. Tell me plainly what you mean."

"Icelyn's yet to show up for a single Bonding Session. Unless you count the time she stopped by to tell me they weren't going to happen, which I don't think should count."

Nicholas was shocked. This couldn't be true.

"Why wouldn't you tell us earlier? Marjan and I have been under the impression that the Bonding Sessions have been happening for nearly a year now."

"Ratting a girl out to her parents isn't the best way to win her heart."

Nicholas didn't know what to believe, but he knew without a doubt that he'd grown tired of talking to this boy. His lack of respect was horrifying.

"If she's not here, then where could she be?"

Torrain chuckled to himself. It was as if he didn't care that he had the leader of all of Mountaintop in his bedroom.

"Tell me, Chief Cognate, have you lost your darling Icelyn?"

"Not at all. I'm sure she's somewhere sensible. I've had so much on my mind lately. She probably told me, but I've forgotten. I thought she told me she'd be here."

Unsatisfied with Nicholas' explanation, but not interested enough to respond, Torrain returned to his drawings. The boy was talented, Nicholas had to admit. Unfortunately, artistic talent had no practical worth in Mountaintop. Hopefully his parents would steer him away from the wasteful dalliance soon.

"Did you really think Icelyn would be here with me? I barely know her, and even *I* know where she probably is. You only have one child. It can't be so hard to keep track of her interests." Torrain was not as skilled at masking accusations as his father.

"Careful, Torrain. Upward accusations are not tolerated."

"Not an accusation, I promise. An honest question. I've got an awful lot to overcome if I'm to win her over, you know. I thought everyone knew that."

For the first time, Nicholas felt sympathy for him. Betrothal to Icelyn could not be easy. She was stubborn and made herself difficult to know.

"I'm sure things aren't as bad as you think."

"She called me a self-absorbed, hollow-headed bug. She said she'd rather face the Threat Below than spend one more minute with me."

That sounded exactly like Icelyn, and Nicholas didn't doubt that she had said it.

"Tell me where she could be."

Torrain's vulnerability retreated quickly. The boy smiled and shook his head. "But she's not lost, right? Not lost at all."

"Answer the question without commentary. Where should I search next?"

Torrain looked at Nicholas as if the answer was the most obvious thing in the whole world. "Well, let me ask *you* something, Chief Cognate—a question you can hopefully answer without commentary, because it needs none. Has anyone seen Adorane Hailgard lately?"

7

WE RUSH UPWARD toward Mountaintop. My lungs and legs aren't conditioned for the climb. I feel melted from the outside and torn apart from the inside at the same time.

But I'm thankful for the distraction my ragged body provides. Otherwise I'd focus on what I saw, what I heard, and what just happened outside the Wall.

Jarvin.

When we were much younger, he gave me a piece of wooden jewelry he'd snatched from his mother's collection because he thought it would look pretty on me. Then, as if to confuse me, the next day he played a cruel trick. He shared his acorns, which I thought was kind, as everyone loves the crunch of acorns. But they were newly collected bitter acorns, not yet leeched of their acids! Though I spat them out right away, I suffered a nasty aftertaste for the rest of the day.

Why would someone be so kind one day and cruel the next? Mother explained that he acted this way because he liked me.

That left me convinced that Mother was even more confused than I was.

But now, poor Jarvin, up in a tree, hollowed out in a manner I'd never imagined a human could be. I wonder if maybe Jarvin hadn't been hunting up in that tree? Maybe something had tethered Jarvin up there, on display, for people to see.

For us to see.

Somehow, even more haunting than the grisly memory of Jarvin's body were the sounds that followed—the howls, the crashing, the breathing, and the lightning-fast footfalls through the woods. We were being hunted.

"...He deserves at least that."

I realize that I have no idea how long Adorane has been talking to me. I've been lost in my own thoughts.

"I'm sorry, deserves what?"

"To not hang in a tree like a picked-over scarecrow for all of eternity," he answers bitterly.

I know that Jarvin won't hang up there for all eternity. There are any number of elements that will take him out of that tree in time—animals, insects, wind, rain, snow, even whatever killed him. But the thought fills me with dread, and I see the pain on Adorane's face, so I keep my mouth shut.

"I should have gotten him down, brought him back to Mountaintop, to his parents. But I ran like a child."

Only Adorane could find shame in managing to evade the nightmare lurking outside the Wall.

"You *saved* me. Isn't that something?" For now, I'll leave out the part about how he was the one who got me into danger in the first place.

"Jarvin was a good Veritas."

"One of the best in Mountaintop." I decide to never again mention the business with the bitter acorns. Nobody needs to be reminded of that.

My lungs need a break. I begin to wonder about water, and why we didn't bring any. It's astounding how my thoughts go back to primal, base needs—air, water, rest—even in the wake of what's just happened. I motion to Adorane to slow down for a moment, and we sit next to one another on a large rock, breathing heavily.

"What am I going tell his parents, Ice?"

It hits me like a wound—unexpected and painful. Adorane can't tell Jarvin's parents anything. Neither of us can. We can't admit that we know any of the details of Jarvin's fate. The only way could would be if we were outside the Wall—and we can't ever admit to being outside the Wall, or we'll risk disbursement.

"You can't tell them anything. You know we can't."

"It's bad enough I had to run like I was some *Cognate.* Now you expect me to hide this from his parents? They'll be terrified when he doesn't return. And I'm just supposed to say nothing?"

He didn't have to throw an insult about Cognates into this. I am looking out for him. The truth is, he was right earlier. *I'll* be just fine if Father finds out I was outside the Wall—if he even believes me. I'm worried for Ad.

"I'm not saying this for me, Ad. You could be in real trouble if anyone discovers we were down here."

"This is bigger than just Jarvin's parents, too, Ice. What about the Quota? People have to know what's happened to Jarvin, if only to replenish."

The Quota. Mountaintop only has enough water, food, and shelter to comfortably support around a hundred people. Previous generations learned this lesson through disease, famine, thirst, and death.

Sixty-four of those slots are allocated to the Veritas and thirty-six to the Cognates. To maintain a population of around a hundred, all births are rationed and planned. It's only when one member of the Kith dies that another is allowed to be born. (It's a little more complex than this, with different rules around periods of population growth and decline, but this is the general idea.)

"Once Jarvin is missing for ten nights, an official inquiry will be launched to determine if he can be listed as permanently absent. If they designate him as such—and they will, because he *is*—then the next prospective parental couple on the Birth List will get the approval they need, just as if he were confirmed dead."

I am quoting. I know the Code in and out, and there's something comforting about reciting it now. "I know it's hard, Ad, but you can't say anything. It won't change what happened; it'll just bring danger for us."

Ad struggles with his thoughts, as if there must be a solution he hasn't come across yet. But there isn't. He picks up a stone and tosses it. "I'd smash all this to pieces if I could. But I can't."

I've won the argument. This is what Ad says when he disagrees but admits defeat. It's a phrase he's learned from his father, passed down through the years. (Every family in Mountaintop has its own set of proverbs, along with a crest and societal position. Ad may hate it, but at least he recognizes the wisdom.

"I'd rather something else, but this had to be." That's one of my phrases—one I've inherited from Father, which he learned from his father, and on and on.

I doubt Ad could appreciate it now, but at least we'll have another baby Veritas in Mountaintop soon. There hasn't been one in more than a year. The thought brings me a pang of joy.

But just as quickly, I remember Jarvis—the small boy with a shy smile offering me a wooden necklace, the tangle of bones strung from the branches above. Angry tears well in my eyes as we stand to resume our ascent; I hurry to brush them away before Adorane can see.

8

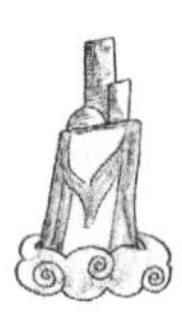

NICHOLAS HATED BEING harsh with Aclornis, who'd shown him kindness only an hour before. But a Veritas boy taking his Cognate daughter to an unknown location for who knows what purpose? Unacceptable.

"If you're covering for your son, no Brathius will trust a Hailgard ever again."

If Aclornis had any idea what Nicholas was referring to, he was a skilled actor. "Nicholas, Adorane is hunting to fill Mountaintop's food supplies. Has been since this morning. I swear it."

Nicholas was not satisfied. "If my Icelyn has even one hair on her head out of place, for whatever reason, I will scour the Code to find the most unpleasant consequence possible for Adorane, his future child, and that child's child."

The door to the Hailgard Round—livable as far as rounds went, though still modest compared to a Cognate's lab—swung open. Icelyn rushed in and crashed into her father. "I'm sorry I've caused you such concern! I brought water to the hunters today in the Southside Wood."

Adorane followed Icelyn in. His expression was blank—but for one who knew him well, as Aclornis did, it bordered on dark. Aclornis hoped that Nicholas wouldn't be able to pick up on it.

Nicholas looked hard at Adorane. "Adorane, did Icelyn bring the hunters water?"

"We put in the order yesterday." This was actually true, and the reason Icelyn had settled on this story as her excuse. Both knew Nicholas could check on this easily.

"Who signed the Water Resource Request Form?" he asked.

Icelyn cringed. *Who* signed the request? She knew. She'd seen the form, but only now remembered. She had to spare Adorane the indignity of answering, having to say the name out loud, so she jumped in instead. "It was Jarvin, Father. He signed the request."

Icelyn felt Adorane's eyes boring into the side of her head—*not only do we have to hide his death, but now we're using him as an alibi?*—but she pressed on. "A thousand apologies, Father. I even wrote a note for Rincas before I left my station at Waterpump—but silly me, I left it in my pocket."

Nicholas' affection for his daughter was strong enough to cover this sin. He nodded at Aclornis. "Please forgive me."

Icelyn was flooded with relief. Her father believed her. This was followed by shame because—well, her father believed her.

Aclornis placed his right hand on Nicholas' shoulder, as Mountaintop citizens did to affirm a bond. "You did what any protective father would do."

Sometimes Icelyn wondered how Aclornis, so trusting and true, could raise a son like Adorane, who suspected Nicholas and the Cognates of sinister motives at every turn. She knew Adorane wouldn't be uttering encouraging words while placing his hand on her shoulder anytime soon. Even when she became leader, she knew she could trust him to temper any kind words he said with some kind of insult about Cognates.

Nicholas nodded back at Aclornis, thankful for his graciousness. "Icelyn's mother desires our presence." Icelyn had no time to check Adorane's attitude before she was whisked out of the Hailgard Round by her Father.

As they walked back to Brathius Tower, Icelyn could hardly believe her luck. She decided to make one more gesture to smooth everything over. "Thank you for understanding, Father. I won't disappoint you again."

Nicholas took her hand in his and squeezed it reassuringly. "Far from disappointed, I'm proud of you."

Icelyn winced. She was glad to avoid his wrath, but she didn't deserve his acclaim. "Father, please."

Nicholas leaned toward her confidentially. "I mean, really. You think I believe that silly water ration story? Hunters pick up their supplies in the morning. They don't rely on deliveries."

Icelyn's cheeks reddened. Her ploy hadn't worked.

"I know what happened, Icelyn."

How could he know? Did someone see them? It was probably a member of the Family Tarlinius. They were always looking for ways to ingratiate themselves to Nicholas, desperate to recapture their previous role as servants to the Brathius family.

"You must understand, I never intended—"

"A father always knows. But don't worry, I won't tell Mother."

Won't tell Mother? Was he intent on keeping this whole affair a secret?

"Look, Icy, I know how boys can be. I was one myself, not so long ago. I've no doubt Adorane hit you with the best he had to offer."

Oh God, Father thought that Ad had tried to—

"Father, please!" Icelyn interjected, hoping to cut him off before he said anything else, but he continued.

"But I took one look at Adorane's dejected face, and knew that you rejected his advances. Just as your Mother and I have trained you to do."

A Father always knows? A Father had no clue. Any satisfaction Icelyn felt at eluding him again, though, was swept away by guilt at not restoring Adorane's good name. "Well, yes—of course, nothing like that would ever happen."

"You will be glad that you are saving yourself for the Pannous boy."

Icelyn was overcome with disgust. She wished he hadn't mentioned that worm. She still had years before that would be her life.

"I know you're not fond of him, but he's rounding into an ideal Cognate. Your mother has never steered you wrong."

Icelyn was overwhelmed by the many things she wanted to say. She needed to cry and confess to Father exactly what she'd seen—about poor Jarvin and the terror that had chased them. She wanted to ask about the feelings she had for Adorane, and how to get rid of them—she knew as well as anyone that a Cognate could never be with a Veritas. She wanted to beg him to make Marjan reconsider Torrain Pannous, because she couldn't imagine a day when just the mention of his name wouldn't make her stomach turn.

Mostly she felt like a small, young girl who wanted her father to tell her he'd handle everything, and that it would all be made right.

But *just because you want something doesn't mean you should have it.* Another Brathius proverb, and one she had learned well. Marjan had practically printed it on Icelyn's forehead when she was a child.

She hoped to visit Adorane soon. He'd lost his friend. She pushed away thoughts that he might not want to see her. He had to forgive her, given enough time. It was the only possible answer.

Her father's face had settled into a mask of sadness, and she realized that he was troubled beyond their current conversation. A new worry struck Icelyn. She almost didn't want to ask, but she did: "How is Mother doing today, Father?"

"She's not well."

Icelyn leaned over her mother, who slept fitfully. She'd gotten worse. "How can it be that ladling roots do nothing to make her better? Should we try elderberries?"

The Apriori had had medicines so great that Icelyn suspected they were only legends. Pills for every malady—clogged-up lungs, feverish sweats, and even dark thoughts and sick hearts, which were incurable to the point of disbursement in Mountaintop. Yet now all they could do was scrounge through the bushes hoping something might help abate her mother's suffering. Progress!

Icelyn wondered how in almost three hundred years, the combined power of all the Cognates in Mountaintop hadn't been enough to learn the secrets behind the pills, balms, and treatments the Apriori had used. She understood the excuses. In Mountaintop their resources were constrained to only those raw materials that were available within the Wall, while the Apriori had had access to the whole world. Still, it seemed that a people as brilliant as the Cognates claimed to be would have more technology by now, especially when the blueprints were available in the books they'd brought with them when they ascended.

"Tranton is doing everything he can, Icelyn. I trust him," Nicholas reminded her, his voice clipped.

As if summoned by the mention of his name, Tranton entered. "Icelyn, it's so nice to see you back in the Tower. How was your shift at Waterpump?"

He asked the question in a way that made Icelyn suspect he knew she hadn't been at Waterpump. She wouldn't give him the pleasure of her discomfort.

"Uneventful." Icelyn paused a moment, then added: "Tell me, are you pleased with the way my mother grows worse under your care?"

"Icelyn!" Nicholas scolded. Direct questions, especially insulting ones, were frowned upon in Mountaintop. High-level Cognates like Tranton should never have to suffer attacks like this. "Apologize."

Tranton pursed his lips and waved off Nicholas' command. "No, no. She's lively. Never squelch it. Icelyn poses the questions that ought to be asked."

As was often the case, no one in the room knew whether Tranton meant what he said. Icelyn suspected he didn't.

Nicholas persisted. "No, Icelyn. This is how you speak to the Veritas if they've worked in your living quarters and items have gone missing. Or children if you've caught them being naughty past bedtime. But never a Cognate—and certainly not the Chief of the Healing Arts."

A thousand rejoinders sprang to Icelyn's mind.

I've seen neither healing nor arts, so forgive me if I forgot his title.

I'm sorry if I assumed such a great Cognate could handle an innocent question from a child.

But why bother? This battle wasn't worth fighting after all she'd seen today.

"Blot out my words, Tranton. They were misguided and impetuous."

Tranton bowed slightly to acknowledge the apology. "The truth is, I have discovered the cause of Marjan's illness. My worst fears have been confirmed. I bear bad news—not just for Marjan, but for all of Mountaintop."

A change had stirred in Tranton. It had started in a trivial way, as most important things do. He had been cleaning behind his bed. Like everything else in Mountaintop, the bed was hundreds of years old, and Tranton hoped to find a particular book of anatomy that his grandfather had famously misplaced decades ago. (Things were often so dull in Mountaintop that even a lost book could send the rumor mill into overdrive.)

Tranton never found the book. He stumbled across a fragment of paper instead. Written in faded ink, its cryptic message awoke a hunger in him.

Tranton had never had any real problem with Nicholas' leadership. He'd never thought Nicholas was particularly smart, of course, but he didn't mind serving him. After all, geniuses were often tethered to fools. And as far as fools went, Tranton could do much worse than Nicholas.

Tranton wasn't as bad as he appeared in the shadow of Icelyn's judgments. Though something about her did tend to bring out the worst in him, he wasn't evil. But he also wasn't good to the degree that he deserved the naive trust Nicholas placed in him. He was somewhere in the middle, like most—with enough space between good and evil to eventually become one or the other, or neither.

Now, in the words scrawled on this ancient scrap, Tranton found a destiny he hadn't known he was looking for.

We are the true leaders of Mountaintop. –T. Nilsing

Remember, his mother had always told him, *Nilsings are great. So it has always been, and so it always will be.* Tranton never knew what she meant when she said that. Being a physician seemed 'good' to him at best, not great—especially given how little he could do to heal anyone with the meager resources at hand.

We are the true leaders of Mountaintop.

He put the note aside, brushing it off, refusing to bestow any more importance than a scrap of paper deserved. But the words stuck with him. Tranton didn't even want to believe the words were true, but he heard them whenever Nicholas made a verbal gaffe or proposed a ridiculous amendment to the Code.

What did the words mean? Who had written them?

Tranton had to learn more.

Marjan opened her mouth, wincing in pain. She was thirsty, but too weak to tell them.

Nicholas poured water into a leather-bound goblet. He raised it to Marjan's lips, and joy flickered across her face as she anticipated relief. But before she could take her first sip, Tranton reached past Nicholas and knocked the goblet away.

The goblet crashed to the ground, and wasted water splashed across the room. Marjan fell back into bed, discouraged. Icelyn grabbed Tranton's hand, as if she could stop him from doing what he had already done.

"How dare you deprive her!" Though the accusation was clear, and direct, Nicholas was too shocked to reprimand Icelyn. Why had Tranton done this?

"You'd be wise to let go, Icelyn. Physical contact between male and female is forbidden. People may get the wrong impression—or perhaps you nurture a silent affection for me, and this is how you choose to make it known?"

Icelyn wanted to take the fallen mug and smash Tranton's smug, satisfied face with it. Instead, she let go of him, her face flushed. She had noticed his lingering gazes and how he often accidentally brushed up against her. If anyone harbored hidden feelings, it was Tranton, but she was sure they didn't consist of anything so innocent as love.

Nicholas retrieved the mug from the ground and refilled it. "Icelyn, I'm sure… it was an accident. Tranton, what is the meaning of this?"

"It wasn't an accident," Tranton said loudly. "And if you bring that water to Marjan, I will knock it from your hands again."

Nicholas didn't understand. "She needs water!"

"Not this water. Fetch her some from the Winter Rain reserves. This water is the reason Marjan is sick. The water flowing up from the valley below into Waterpump is…" he paused for dramatic effect, "poisoned."

Nicholas had always insisted that Icelyn drink Winter Rain water, not the water from Waterpump like the common Kith. Marjan had considered it a needless luxury and refused. But if this were true, Nicholas was thankful for the indulgence.

Now it was Icelyn who was offended by such an accusation. "That's laughable. I know everyone at Waterpump! All good, trustworthy people. None would poison the Kith's supply."

Tranton tutted. "Listen to my words. I've tested the water many times, there is no doubt – I'm happy to show you the proof, but Marjan's illness is proof enough, I would think. She'll get better as soon as stops drinking it. But I didn't say the water was poisoned at Waterpump. It's being poisoned before it gets there. Down Below. In the valley."

Impossible. Poisoned Down Below? By whom? And why? None of them even wanted to think about what this would mean for the Kith and Mountaintop, if true. They depended on Waterpump. The Winter Rains reserve wouldn't last four months.

Questions raced through Icelyn's mind. She finally broke the silence. "How is that possible? If it's poisoned, why is only Mother sick?"

"It would appear she's just more susceptible. But I'm starting to see sickness in others, too. Everyone must stop drinking, or we'll all get sick."

"What can we do?" Icelyn asked, her voice rising in fear.

Tranton placed a hand on Icelyn's shoulder condescendingly. Icelyn glared at him. What of the prohibition on physical touch now? "Icelyn, I hate to tell you this," he said in a way that sounded like he did *not* hate to tell her this, "but these are matters better left to your father, myself, and the other members of the Council of Ultracognates. Though bright and precocious, you are still a child."

Icelyn drew back, enraged, twisting her shoulder from beneath his grip. "My father trusts me, and I'm sure he is comfortable with my continued participation in this conversation."

Tranton turned now and placed his hand on Nicholas' shoulder. "Nicholas, your faith in your daughter is touching and well earned, but this is a matter for the Council of Ultracognates alone."

Nicholas avoided eye contact with Icelyn. "Icelyn… all things considered…it… would be better if you left us alone. For now."

"Father, please! This affects Mother. This affects us all—every member of the Kith."

"A child's obedience is proof of a father's ability to lead." Tranton recited one of the Nilsing family proverbs to Nicholas, as if it would help.

"Damn your oppressive family proverbs, Tranton. This is between my father and me."

"Actually, it's between your father and *me*. Isn't that correct, Nicholas?"

Icelyn looked for the support she was sure would come. She waited for her father to put Tranton put in his place, but instead she saw only indecision and weakness on his face.

The beast stumbled into a thick grove of gnarled trees, desperate to coat itself in dirt and darkness. It loosened itself on the inside and a roar filled with anguish and rage rattled the ancient oaks. It couldn't care that the other creatures, mindless in their own hunger, may hear him.

Though it could still taste bits of its unfortunate human prey stuck between its fangs, it was hungrier than it had been before it had feasted on its prey. *The other two,* was all it could think, not with words but with searing desire filled with regret and fury. *They were so close, they were mine. I savored them in my nostrils.*

How had they escaped? Losing out on them made the trophy the beast had hung high in the tree worthless. It made the sweet human blood it had tasted bitter.

The creature dug into the ground with its sharpened talons and tossed fistfuls of rock fragments and leaves into the air until all it could see and smell was the earth. It lost itself in the soothing mess it made until it found an uneasy, temporary calm.

It would learn from this. This would not happen again.

9

I BOLT TO the exit because I'd sooner have my skin peeled raw than have Tranton see tears in my eyes. I won't let him collect my tears as his trophies! He'd think making me weep was his achievement. This anguish comes courtesy of Father and no one else.

I hope Father knows this.

I can't decide which dagger plunges more deeply into my heart: Father's agreement with Tranton in those quiet words—"Icelyn, you have heard my decision"—or the fact that he hadn't even bothered to look at me while he said it. His own daughter! Like I was some Veritas that he was ordering out after I cleaned the windows, swept the floor, and lingered a little too long making conversation. I was half tempted to bow and quietly mumble, "Forgive me for assuming your time and mine are of equal value," the standard apology given when Veritas service workers presumed to chat with a busy Cognate. But I needed to leave the room before the tears fell.

I scold myself. *Icelyn, grab hold of your thoughts.* Yes, Tranton is a rotten pail of roach dust and Father has betrayed me. But I should put all that on a shelf to be dealt with when I have the luxury. The real worry right now is Waterpump. If what Tranton claims is true, then I wonder how Mountaintop will survive.

The water from Winter Rain is meted out carefully, an expensive indulgence for wealthier Cognates who require something more rarefied and exclusive than common valley water for their special occasions. If the Kith depended on the Winter Rain store for all their water needs, it wouldn't last.

I've never seen the appeal of spending a small fortune on water that fell from the sky as opposed to water that was pumped up from below. Father insists I drink only from Winter Rain, but I don't care either way. Long ago, I snuck sips from Waterpump, and so I can compare it to Winter Rain. It all just tastes like...water. I suppose Winter Rain is considered valuable because it is rare, and the wealthy need valuable things to collect and consume, if only to have a way to set themselves apart from the poor.

Now I'm sounding like Adorane.

My thoughts migrate to Ad, and my feet do the same. This wasn't the plan. I had intended to visit Waterpump to check on the water situation myself. Instead, I'm headed toward Hailgard Round.

Once again, the question I haven't heard anyone raise floats to the front of my mind. Who, *or what,* exactly, is poisoning Waterpump from Down Below?

I knock on the front door of Hailgard Round and hope that Adorane will answer so I can avoid small talk with his father. Though I like Aclornis Hailgard, I don't want to see anyone but Addy, who I'm confident will know exactly what I need—though I'm not sure what that is myself.

Aclornis opens the door. It's customary in Mountaintop for the father to answer the door and offer his family's unique greeting. "You could enter our home a thousand times, and we'd still miss you when you leave."

Aclornis' welcome is delivered with less verve and more stress than usual. I nod to acknowledge it and look past him, searching for Adorane. Instead, my heart sinks.

Torrain Pannous and his greasy, feckless father, Marcel, are seated at the table. This is the worst day among all days.

How difficult it must have been for Aclornis to share his traditional greeting with them. That's the thing about these customary greetings—eventually they force you to lie. The Pannous family renders every friendly greeting in Mountaintop deceptive.

Torrain approaches and holds his hand toward me, as if I might take and nestle it to my heart. I don't care if that's what Intendeds do with each other by custom. I walk right past him.

"You see, Father? She is here, no doubt to see that Veritas!" Torrain spits the word 'Veritas' bitterly, like there's no curse more vile one could utter.

It doesn't seem fair that Torrain knows why I'm here when I'm in the dark as to why *he's* here. "What are *you* doing here, Torrain?"

"Your presence is more cause for concern than mine." There's an edge to his voice that frightens me. The mood in the room shifts; the air grows icy and silent. *Tread carefully, Icelyn.*

I decide to placate him.

"Torrain, please. We're all just kids. Adorane and I are childhood friends, as the child of the Chief Cognate and the child of the Head Veritas have been since the Ascension. Nothing more."

Torrain appears not to hear me at all. "I'd like to lodge a formal Accusation." He enunciates every syllable with precision. The words chill me.

I relinquish any pride. If he wants me to beg, I'll beg. Anything to ward off what he is threatening—a course so far over the line, it's like using fire and acid to clean your hands after playing in the dirt. "No, Torrain, there's no need. Say no more. If you value our Intention at all, you will speak no more of an Accusation against Adorane."

An Accusation is a serious matter. Only a Cognate may make one, and only against lower station Cognates or, obviously, Veritas. Once an Accusation is made, it cannot be undone. Often they end in Disbursement. It's a nasty business.

Not completely terrible, of course. Logically, I know that this is a well-reasoned and beneficial tradition. Living under the threat of Accusation, Veritas are kind and respectful to Cognates. The arrangement breeds an atmosphere of peace, generosity and goodwill. That's written into the Code, and of course it's true. The Apriori struggled with rebellions and uprisings, constant strife from their lower classes. Not in Mountaintop. Everyone is almost always well-behaved here.

But forget about what I know in my head. In my heart, when poised to strike at Adorane, Accusation is the ugliest monster I can imagine. Torrain is letting me know that he holds a noose around Ad's neck, one he can tighten whenever he wishes.

Torrain studies me. I've overplayed my hand and betrayed how much I care for Adorane.

"I'm sorry, Icelyn, but interfering with an Intention—especially between two eminent Cognates—is a serious offense. Our courtship has been difficult. We've yet to enjoy one Bonding Session."

"That's not Adorane's fault, Torrain. It's mine." I know what I should do now. I should take all the blame, maybe even soften up a little, take his hand in mine, promise to be a better Intention partner, smile the way that girls do when they want boys to think they like them. I've seen other girls do it. As much as I'd detest it, I could do it too.

Instead, I think about why I don't want to attend Bonding Sessions with Torrain—about how arrogant, self-centered, and thoughtless he is. I think about our Intention party, and a shudder runs through me. As was custom, we'd presented each other with our Intended Gifts. Each gift is meant to be an object suited to your Betrothal Partner; you are supposed to study their interests and their personality, then give them a unique gift that displays how you understand and appreciate them. I gave him a rare set of pens and paintbrushes, along with reams of paper. He gave me a painting he'd had commissioned *of himself.*

So I know I should stop, but I can't resist adding, "Well, it's mostly my fault, but it's partially yours, too."

Torrain does not like to accept fault, even partial portions of it. His face twists into a smile. "Well, since I cannot lodge an Accusation against *you*, my hand has been forced."

Torrain's father is beside him. I'm also in attendance. Two Cognate witnesses. This Accusation will be legitimate, legal. Real.

"I, Torrain Pannous, of the great Pannous family, experts in the studies of Rocks and Land Forms, do now make an Accusation against —"

I can't let the words be said. "Wait! Shouldn't he at least be present? You wouldn't want to make a *cowardly* Accusation."

I've targeted the only two things Torrain cares about—himself and how people view him. When a Cognate makes an Accusation, the Accused should be present. Face to face. If word got out that you'd made an Accusation without the Accused in attendance, you'd never live it down.

Torrain nods appreciatively. I've spared him a measure of shame. "Yes, fetch him."

I bolt to Adorane's door and pull it open, my mind reeling through options, hoping to figure out how to use this meager ration of time I've managed to buy. Perhaps I'll whisper what's happening to Ad and we can escape through the window together, into the woods. Perhaps Ad could fake an illness, so he'd be in no medical state to receive an Accusation. Perhaps—

Dear God!

I can't breathe. The solution has presented itself, unbidden—but it's a terrible solution, worse than the problem itself.

When I open the door, I see—we all see—Adorane and Catalandi, lying together on Ad's swinging bed. They are kissing and hugging, acting like *lovers*—not like proper citizens of Mountaintop, but like characters I've read about in stories written by the Apriori.

I didn't think anyone actually did these things anymore. But here I see, before my eyes, proof that people do carry on with such practices. Slithering against each other with enthusiasm and great enjoyment.

I feel like someone's punched me in the stomach. I know I should feel relief for Adorane, but instead I feel only pain.

Torrain smiles. "Oh, my. I suppose I'll withdraw my Accusation for now."

Before I can confront Adorane, or even look him in the eyes, a sustained musical tone washes through Hailgard Round. It's familiar but disorienting. The sound repeats insistently. I feel more than hear it. The vibrations cut through me.

"Why would someone ring the Summoning Bell?" Aclornis murmurs, concerned.

Ah, that's what it is! The Summoning Bell, saved only for emergencies, not rung for more than a decade. It had been used frequently in the early days of the Ascension—more than once a week, they say. But those were desperate times.

I remember when I last heard the Bell. My grandfather, Chaser Brathius, had died in the night. Mother had cried; Father hadn't. Father was anointed new Chief Cognate. I was confused at the time—sad because I'd never again sit on Chaser's lap and listen to his tales of the Ascension, but also proud, for now Father was the leader. I remember asking Father if this meant he owned Mountaintop, if the town at the top of the world was now his. He had laughed, held me close, and whispered, "Something like that, yes."

How many children got to say their father owned the whole world? Just me.

The decade that followed tarnished that joy. I saw Father's premature gray hair, heard the worried murmurs that Mother and Father shared at night. I'd suffered through countless lectures from

Adorane about how everything would be much better if someone else could own Mountaintop. I began to wish Father had never become the man who owned the whole world.

Adorane and Catalandi manage to untangled themselves and join us. *How proper of them.* Both are smiling, unashamed, as if nothing has happened. Catalandi tries to greet me with a quick nod, but I won't return the gesture. Why pretend everything is normal when absolutely nothing is?

I try to remember how I arrived outside Belubus' Lab, but I can't get the events into sequence. Adorane had flashed his best smile, as if everything between us was as calm as a moonlit autumn night. We had an understanding, right? He'd writhe around and slobber all over Catalandi in my presence, and I would take no offense. Deal?

No deal.

Ad suggested that we should all walk to Kith Hall together. I couldn't bear the thought of traveling as if we were a happy group of first-year students at school heading out to recess.

I fear I said something regrettable, though I'm not sure. I think I bolted for the door, and someone might have tried to grab my arm, and I probably kicked whoever it was. I hope it was Ad.

Now I find myself outside my beloved teacher's lab. I pull at the front door, hoping Belubus hasn't already started his walk toward Kith Hall. I need to see him. As soon as I open the door, I'm flooded with sensory relief. The scent of ancient books and antique scientific equipment brings me joy.

I would never admit this to Adorane, but I too suspect that most Cognates, Father and Mother included, are not actually interested in knowing much. There is a stagnation embedded into most of their intellectual pursuits—born of obligation, but empty of interest or passion.

Not Belubus. His every breath depended on what he could learn next. Sometimes, as we researched something together, I would fear for him. His inhalation would grow ragged, his face would flush, and he would sweat through his robes. He could feel the impending discovery approaching, fast and unstoppable. He'd suffer the pain of dead ends, agonize as we hit an unscalable cliff in pursuit of more knowledge. He enjoyed every second of it. So did I. I couldn't help but catch his fever whenever we chased such treasure.

"Belubus? Are you here?" I step in through the door and see his impressive collection of glass tubes and microscopes, all arranged mid-experiment. My hopes soar; Belubus would never abandon the pursuit of knowledge halfway in.

He shuffles into the room, a tiny man. He carries fur pelts, leaves, and vials of water. His sharp eyes fix on me. From pictures I've seen in ancient books meant for children, I believe Belubus has the eyes of a fox—piercing and sly.

"Darling! To what do I owe this pleasure?"

"Do you hear the Bell, Belubus? The water is poisoned! Adorane is... and Jarvin. Tranton and Father..." My thoughts collapse into a murky dark stew. The more I try to focus, the less sense I make.

"Child, of course. We all have days like that." Belubus is kind to pretend I've communicated anything understandable, when even I can tell that I haven't. "Now, what is this about the water being poisoned?"

"Waterpump, the water, it's killing us! Mother! But Father is listening to Tranton, and I fear what they have planned. Please talk to him. He cannot listen to Tranton."

Belubus may be easily shaken into emotional unease by scientific endeavors, but situations that would stress any normal man leave him calm. "I see," he nods, as if we are merely talking about what kind of tea leaves I prefer in my drink. "The water is killing us. Poisoned Down Below, I imagine?"

"Yes. But I have a feeling...I feel that Tranton has something dark planned." As soon as the words leave my mouth, I know they are true. This is what's upset me, even beyond Father's betrayal—a dark sense of foreboding." I tried to talk to Father, but he sent me away. You taught him, like you teach me now. I know that he trusts you."

The Summoning Bell's ringing grows in intensity. I look toward Kith Hall, not wanting to miss whatever is about to happen.

Belubus tidies up his experiment. "You go ahead. I'll be along. And as far as your father is concerned, I'll do as you ask. I could never say no to you."

For the first time today, some good news.

10

THE TOPS OF Kith Hall's spires stretched above Icelyn. Set against a sheer granite cliff, the structure was one of the grandest in Mountaintop.

It was built shortly after the Ascension with a level of craftsmanship and artistry that had been lost to time. The construction of the Hall had used many precious materials—strong stones and metals—before anyone knew how rare they would become. At the time, they had been sure that their mining efforts would strike troves of resources below Mountaintop; but you cannot strike something that isn't there.

Some still grumbled that the Hall should be dissembled and the resources redistributed, but Nicholas held fast against that notion. A town needed tradition, and people needed something beautiful to inspire communal pride.

All members of the Kith, Veritas and Cognates alike, converged on Kith Hall. They passed below the grand entry arch, beneath the words inscribed upon it, the belief that bound the Kith together: '*Not children of God, nor subjects of Lords. Solely what we know, becoming greater through what we learn.*'

The Summoner Bell had spooked them all.

"What do you think this is about, Ice?" Adorane joined Icelyn with Catalandi by his side. *Damn!* Icelyn was sure he'd already be sitting inside Kith Hall, far away from her. Instead, here he was, acting as if Icelyn hadn't just seen the two of them entwined like a couple of ultralions in heat.

And he called her *Ice*!

Icelyn didn't know exactly what she expected from Adorane right now, but after the undermining of standards she'd just witnessed, he could at least try to restore a *hint* of order and formality by using her full name.

She led by example. "Adorane, firstborn of Aclornis Hailgard, I do not know." She used his full name, all four syllables, plus his formal title, making sure to crisply enunciate her words. These were serious times, and deserved serious behavior.

Adorane appeared hurt by Icelyn's stiff response (and Catalandi smirked at it, which only made Icelyn feel stranger.) While Icelyn had hoped Adorane would take her solemn cues and fall into line, she felt a stab of regret. She wanted to give him advance knowledge of the crisis facing Mountaintop. He was unusually bright, in his own practical, Veritas way. If anyone could figure out the problem, he could. But then the scene she'd witnessed in his room flashed before her eyes again, and her pettiness won out. "I suppose the Kith marrieds got wind of the passionate example you and Catalandi were setting. Perhaps they're hoping you two can put on a demonstration—to improve their private goings-on, should they be called upon to initiate the next birth."

Catalandi stole a quick glance at Icelyn and suppressed an urge to smile, instead staring straight ahead and trying to appear tuned out of the conversation.

A light dawned in Adorane's eyes, as if he hadn't realized that Icelyn might not like what he and Catalandi had been doing. As if he hadn't betrayed something unspoken between himself and Icelyn by doing those things. "Oh, come on, Ice. You're telling me that...you and Torrain... don't ever—"

Icelyn cut him off before he could finish the thought. "Please! Ugh. *Torrain?* Anyway, you know that physical contact is forbidden." Did Adorane think she and Torrain did *that*? Did he pay attention to a word she said? She never held her tongue when it came to her opinion of Torrain.

"Not among Intendeds."

"*Permitted* Touch is allowed between Intendeds! That was not, by any measure, Permitted Touch!" Touch was only allowed in a limited, supervised capacity among couples who had entered the later stages of betrothal. Certainly nothing like what Icelyn had witnessed between Adorane and Catalandi. "And in any case, that was beyond mere physical contact."

"My goodness, Ice. We were clothed, you know."

Icelyn checked to make sure Catalandi wasn't listening before continuing, now whispering. "If you think I'm about to commend you for avoiding complete nakedness, you're wrong." That she and Adorane were even having this conversation was disgraceful.

Icelyn brushed him aside and entered through the large open doors of Kith Hall. The cavernous space was packed, but no one spoke. The mood was the complete opposite of that of the normal Sunday marketplace—the customary use for the grand Hall these days—where people loudly greeted each other, laughs flowed freely, and children shouted, ran, and played games.

Adorane walked quickly after Icelyn. "Ice, you don't need to make so much of this."

Icelyn didn't want to hear what she did or did not need to do. "You go sit and enjoy the meeting with Catalandi, Adorane Hailgard."

Icelyn left Adorane behind in the Veritas section, which was situated in the rear of the Hall. Adorane had always resented this tradition, claiming it was discriminatory. *Well, thank God for oppression,* Icelyn thought now, grateful she'd be sitting where Adorane and Catalandi weren't allowed. She progressed past the lower level Cognates until she reached the front, where the Brathius family sat.

She didn't want to sit here, either. She'd expected to see Father and hoped to see Mother, too. However, she found that Marjan was not in attendance—and in her seat was Tranton, his lips stretched wide and thin in a ghastly smile. Not in the Brathius row! This was improper. Yet there he was, patting the open space next to him and grinning at her, as if he'd saved her a seat in the lunch room.

Icelyn noticed that Tranton and Father kept looking at each other. Both bore the expression of two men who shared a guarded secret.

Icelyn took a seat on the far end of the Brathius row—away from Tranton and Father, away from Adorane and Catalandi, trying to look proud in her isolation. She wondered what the secret could be, and why it was that she feared finding out.

Thick yellow liquid fell from the jar into the shimmering water currents of the great river which had formed this valley thousands of years earlier. It was picked up by the ancient waterwheel and lifted into a smooth stone channel.

Ah yes, go and do what you were made to do. Flow to the top of that mountain and lay waste to all who live there.

Every single one.

In all these years which had passed, they'd not heard from anyone who lived above the clouds. In all these years which had passed, they'd simply accepted that their enemies continued existing up there, their hearts still beating, breath still in their lungs, still terribly, horribly alive.

But no longer. Something had changed. Something had awakened. And soon, those who lived high above, comfortable in their evil and hateful perch, would be wiped away. Blotted out. Finally. And forever.

Nicholas dreaded what he was about to do. He had fought against it, hoping to find a way out. He hated admitting that someone else was more intelligent than himself, but after today's discussions with Tranton, he felt outclassed. *Probably just the lost sleep and worry as a result of Marjan's illness,* he comforted himself. *Tough times dull the intellect.*

He'd made strides toward a freer, more equal Kith society. While keeping the lines between the classes defined, he'd at least made them softer, and less aggravating for all. Structured but comfortable. Organized but free.

Today was going to undo all of that and more.

"We're facing a threat second only to the Slaughter Below, Nicholas!" Tranton had hissed. "Now is not the time for niceties, well-mannered chit-chat, and sociable grins. We won't survive by being polite."

Tranton had remained steadfast, trapping Nicholas in a checkmate. Every argument was denied. No matter how Nicholas directed the conversation, it led to the same terrible conclusion.

Nicholas approached the elevated podium, his footsteps the only sound in the large space, and it occurred to him that this was a moment of great importance, the kind schoolchildren would be forced to study for years to come. (If there were, in fact, going to be any years to come. Or schoolchildren, for that matter.) He'd always thought he'd relish leading his people through historic times. But now he realized how foolish he'd been. He'd give anything to avoid this. Moments of great importance are many things, but they certainly aren't enjoyable.

Another set of footsteps sounded beside his own. Tranton had joined him. This wasn't planned. Nicholas couldn't direct Tranton to sit down. Such a confrontation, while every eye in the Hall followed his every move, would project chaos. Nicholas pretended this was pre-arranged with a grateful nod.

Tranton stood beside the ornately carved podium, grave and serious, as Nicholas ascended and faced the gathered Kith. Nicholas scanned the familiar faces. Yesterday these people wrestled with lightweight concerns—preparing for prowess events, debating the finer points of gravitational theory, hoping their permit application for a son or daughter would be reviewed favorably. What he was about to say would overshadow everything they thought mattered most. He felt the immense gravity of what he was about to do, and wished more than anything that he could avoid it.

Nicholas scanned the audience until he reached Icelyn. He tried to draw strength from her, but she looked away.

Icelyn seethed. Tranton! Standing beside Father like he was a co-leader. Couldn't Father have asked *her* to accompany him? *She* was the one who was to lead the Kith in the future; she was every bit as bright as that meddler.

She hated when Father pushed her away while pretending they were still close. His look just now did that, and she wasn't about to return the favor. *You can't twist the knife you've plunged into my back and act as if we're simply embracing, Father. That's not how it works.*

Nicholas broke the silence. "We find ourselves in a dire position in history. We are descendants of the only ones hardy enough to survive the Threat Below. The universe has entrusted us with a great responsibility—as the sole representatives of humanity, the guardians of our grand species' survival."

Icelyn groaned on the inside. It was clear that Tranton had written Father's speech. If asked, she'd have composed something far more elegant than this verbose tripe.

"In my time as Chief Cognate, I have made it my priority to blur the stark boundaries between our classes. It has always been my belief that near-equality between Veritas and Cognates would result in a stronger Kith."

Father, enough with the prologue. These people want to know why you've called them here.

"But we must all be aware of our history. When we were threatened, the ancestors of the Veritas protected humanity. With their weapons and their warriors, they fought. And while their efforts were praiseworthy and brave, they were also futile. They could not stop the massacre Down Below. No amount of physical training could stem the onslaught. They failed."

Murmurs arose from the Veritas' section. While this account of their past was taught to the children in general terms, it was not often discussed outside the classroom. Nicholas himself had appointed a committee to rewrite the historical curriculum, to emphasize the Veritas bravery and sidestep their shortcomings.

"While the Veritas failed, the Cognates did not. They held the light of knowledge that led us upward. They discovered that the Threat Below could not survive—could not breathe, or even remain conscious —at these great heights. The Cognates created the technology and developed the strategies needed to ensure humanity's survival.

"And this is fitting, because intelligence and knowledge alone set humanity higher than all other beasts and place us firmly on a pinnacle above all living things. No matter how much a human athlete trains to run faster, he can never outpace a cheetah. Years of building muscle cannot produce a human who is stronger than the weakest bull, or one who is able to out-jump even the smallest mountain goat. We cannot fly high above in the skies nor survive deep beneath the waves. In matters of physical ability, we are overmatched by the smallest bird or the humblest fish. We can delude ourselves into thinking we're fast and strong while we struggle to build up these meager skills, and yet we are faced with one unavoidable truth: Human physical prowess can never supersede, or even compare to, that found among the dumbest beasts in the animal kingdom."

Father had tied the word prowess to the image of dumb beasts! He'd insulted the Veritas' most cherished value. *God, the things Adorane must be thinking right now.*

"This is why the Cognates were held in the highest regard way back then. Every time we compete, our intelligence, insights, and innovations are why we win. They are our salvation. And because of this, the Kith have always honored Cognate above Veritas. As we still do."

All this was true, historically, Icelyn mused. But why was her father *saying* it? Weren't certain unpleasant truths better left assumed and not proclaimed? There were a couple of Brathius proverbs about this, which Nicholas seemed to have forgotten: *Better to hint at something than say it outright,* and *A hard truth need only be said once, quietly, and then merely remembered.*

Back in the Veritas section, the low simmer of whispers boiled over, causing Aclornis to stand and face Nicholas directly. He remained composed and polite, but the mere act of standing during the Chief Cognate's speech constituted an act of rebellion.

"Toward what purpose do you share this *historical review*?"

While Nicholas had another three pages of prepared comments from Tranton, he decided to answer Aclornis' question in his own words.

"I've had to make difficult decisions. They will not be popular. But I need to remind everyone why my orders must be followed without question. This is the only way we will survive this crisis."

From the back of the room, a Veritas—Nicholas was never able to figure out which one—shouted in an exasperated voice: "What the hell is the crisis? Will you deign to tell us?"

Nicholas held his breath. No turning back. Everything was about to change.

"Waterpump is poisoned and making us all sick. We cannot drink from it anymore."

Nicholas' words set off a wave of fear and shouting.

"Please! Silence!" No one paid any attention to him, so finally he roared: "Silence, or I will drain the waters of Winter Rain and we will all die together! Do not test me! Sit and listen!"

This had the desired effect. The threat to drain the remaining water had been Tranton's idea. If the Veritas decided to overthrow Nicholas and the Cognates, they could. Emptying the water supply was his only leverage against rebellion. Nicholas had been sure he wouldn't have to threaten them; but once again, he had been wrong.

"Aclornis will gather a group of Veritas to find the source of the poison. And he and his team will fix it."

"Such a thing should not be ordered from on high, as if you are some sort of god! You must ask for volunteers!"

Icelyn recognized the clear, confident voice.

Adorane.

Fiery Ad. He's bound to get himself in trouble at some point. Could she ever be so brave? No. And *she* wouldn't even face actual discipline. But people like Adorane had been disbursed for less.

Aclornis put a calming hand on his son and whispered so that only Adorane could hear, "He's right, son. His request should be fulfilled by the Veritas. It is a chance at redemption."

Icelyn wished she could hear what they were saying. Everyone did.

"But Father, that was no request," Adorane growled in a low voice. "To be commanded, like pack animals? He could have *asked* us, but he chose not to. He insulted us, and then he ordered us."

"His personal failings don't change the fact that this is the right path for us. It is a weak man who lets mistakes made by others rob him of his destiny."

Adorane nodded and took his seat—not convinced, but satisfied for now. Icelyn studied his expression, hard and angry.

Aclornis turned to face Nicholas again, this time with a question. "Have the esteemed Cognates determined where the source of the poison is?"

Nicholas paused, knowing the panic his answer would set off. "The water is being poisoned…Down Below."

As Tranton had predicted, the meeting at Kith Hall melted into disorder once everyone realized how bad their situation was. The water was poison. They'd need to send a team Down Below, who could only restore their water source if they survived the Threat Below, which had slaughtered all of mankind centuries ago. That's what had sent the last survivors fleeing to Mountaintop in the first place. It seemed impossible.

Nicholas was disappointed that the Cognates acted like mindless animals driven only by instinct. They rose to leave Kith Hall shouting and panicking, children and adults alike crying and screaming. He'd expected this from the Veritas, but they exited the hall calmly and quietly, following the example set by their leader, Aclornis.

Despite the reminder that it was reason and logic that had saved them in the first place, the Cognates rushed toward the Winter Rain Supply in a beastly stampede. The Veritas, not wanting to be left without any water, followed quickly behind.

A large crowd gathered outside the Winter Rain Supply, which was a small stone structure, nothing more than a windowless cube above ground and a lidded hole in the stone floor below.

Nicholas was thankful that metal had been rationed long ago to create a tall fence surrounding the supply. Winter Rainwater was a luxury, so it had to be protected. Nicholas had always thought this an unnecessary relic from Apriori civilization, as Mountaintop suffered little crime. It was virtually impossible to get away with stealing anything in such a small town, and when someone did, their disbursement deterred any further crime for a long time. No one had tried to steal Winter Rain since Yardile the Veritas was caught with a vat hidden in his round. Yardile's disbursement had been example enough; no one else had dared try again.

That changed today. Cognates and Veritas alike shoved their way toward the front gate. Many held stones in their hands and banged away at the lock.

Members of the Tarlinius family stood inside the fence, defending the supply. Tranton had arranged for them to take their places even before the gathering in Kith Hall in preparation for the onslaught.

If the whole scene hadn't been so surreal, and the undercurrent of fear running through the crowd so visceral, Icelyn would have been tempted to laugh. Seeing the Tarlinius men prowl about like they were highly trained soldiers was strangely hilarious to her.

A Tarlinius scaled a stone wall and perched atop the main entrance to the supply building. He shouted: "Back away from this building! Nicholas is devising a comprehensive plan that will ration water to all families! Your efforts here will only harm you!"

His words made no difference. "Surely it will not be fair! Are we to believe he will divide it up equally? What shall we do when it runs low? Water will flow toward Brathius Tower before it goes anywhere else!"

Icelyn strode forward into the crowd.

11

I PUSH THROUGH the mass of people. These are Kith members I know, and who have known me since I was a baby. Good people who yesterday understood the proper order of things, who would have stepped aside politely and allowed me a drink of water first, as protocol dictates. Now they struggle against each other, and me, as if their lives depend on thwarting their newly minted rivals. I don't recognize any of them!

I keep my head low and try to escape detection. Someone yells something about water being diverted toward Brathius Tower. What did people expect? Of course the Chief Cognate and his family will have enough to drink. But so will they. Everyone just needs to trust Father, and we can get through this.

Then again, who am I to judge? I have a hard time trusting Father right now too. More accurately, I have a hard time trusting Father when Tranton is never further than ten feet away. I wish Father were stronger—more like Adorane. I'd even settle for more like me.

I'm shoved off my feet. Time freezes, and I'm seized by a memory. When I was a child, I once played beside a Waterpump channel, ignoring Mother's warnings, and fell in. The current grabbed me, and I was plunged into a dark world of panic. Finally Mother pulled me out, and I welcomed her embrace, even if it came with a stern scolding.

I feel the same way now, but even more afraid. Instead of faceless water, I'm overrun by the people I know, the people I thought were good. I cry out for help, but no one hears me. I try to shield my head, catching glimpses of the world flashing around me. I'm not the only one struggling to rise from beneath the crowd. There are many of us down here being trampled underfoot.

There is no light. There are only different sensations of pain everywhere—crushing pain, grinding pain, stabbing pain. Then, just like all those years ago, I feel a hand reach down and grab me—strong, but caring. In my confusion, I feel as though I am young again—my mother has come to save me. I cling desperately to her hand. I am a small child once again, cold, dripping wet, being yanked up from the darkness.

The hands pull me to my feet, and somebody shelters me from further damage. I collapse into strong arms, grateful and spent.

Adorane whispers: "You're going to be all right, Ice."

I want to stay in this moment forever. This is what I've needed to hear all day. It doesn't even matter if it's true—and I suspect that it is not, which is why I needed someone to say it.

You're going to be all right, Ice.

I want to cry like a child, but the tears don't come; I am still frozen in fear.

Adorane carries me out of the crowd and toward a higher vantage point, where we watch the bedlam below. *This* is the Kith I know? Were we always so close to mayhem that a few drops of poison could stir up this maelstrom?

Adorane removes his outer tunic and sops up the blood on my arms and legs, which I'm noticing for the first time.

"This isn't us, Icelyn. The Kith are better than this." Adorane puts words to my thoughts.

"I'd like to think so."

"We've lost trust. After the way Nicholas…" Adorane pauses to see how I react to my father's name. Maybe it's the blood loss, but I don't have any energy to argue with him, so I take no offense. Plus, I probably agree with whatever he's about to say. He continues, "…After the way Nicholas handled this, no one is going to believe that he has the entire Kith's welfare in mind above his own, above the other Cognates."

I hate to face it. Instinct screams for me to disagree with Ad, just to bury my own sense of shame. But I can produce no alibi for the crime we've all seen Father commit. I am suddenly angry with Father for putting me in this position.

"I make no excuse for him, except to say that this had to be Tranton's plan, not Father's. He is...not strong. Tranton overpowers him. If I can break through, make him realize the cost of handling things this way, maybe we can change something."

Father appears inside the Winter Rain Supply fences and shouts for attention. Nobody listens. I can't make out his words, though I pick up on bits and pieces. I hear *drain* and *supply,* and before I can piece together what he's saying, a rushing noise breaks through the chaos.

A wave of drinking water pours from an opening in the Winter Rain Supply building, crashing to the ground and flowing downhill toward the crowd.

Hundreds of gallons of Winter Rain. Enough to stave off thirst for several families for months. Father has wasted it just to get their attention.

The crowd screams and falls to the ground, trying to scoop up the water before it seeps into the dirt. Some take muddied sips, as if it'll be their last gulp.

Father's voice rises over the chaos. "You all heard me declare that if we cannot maintain order, I will drain what water we have and we will perish together. You see now that I meant it." Father's cursed action works. Those gathered grow deathly quiet, afraid to even breathe loudly.

"We are creating an equitable plan that will ensure every person's survival. We need you to wait as we finalize it, and then listen respectfully while we communicate it. Now is the time to return to your labs and rounds and resume your normal lives."

Nobody moves.

"From now on, the area around Rain Water Supply is forbidden. You must leave!"

None do. No one wants to be the first to follow the rules, just in case the case the rule-breakers get an advantage.

Tranton joins Father. *Of course.*

"Nicholas Brathius is a good man, with no desire to strike as hard as is required to maintain order. But *I* have no such reservoir of compassion, so I will dirty my hands on his behalf." Tranton lifts a piece of paper and reads from it. "By order of the Chief Cognate, you must turn and leave this place immediately. Anyone who remains in the forbidden area around Rain Water Supply shall be conscripted into the expedition Down Below to cure the poisoned Water Supply. There shall be no exception made for age or gender."

Gasps rise, though I can barely hear them over my own. *My father* would send women and children Down Below? This can't be true.

Tranton faces Nicholas. "Nicholas Brathius, do you affirm that this is your decree?"

Father struggles with his words. "For the good of the Kith, and to protect our survival, it is so."

The crowd begins to back away, and the area outside of the Supply clears. People keep their distance, still watching.

Tranton smiles. "Good. We knew we could trust the Kith. As you can all see, reason prevails."

His grin angers me deep inside. Who has he turned Father into? The Brathius *save* children from the Threat Below. They don't sacrifice them! This is not who we are.

I must show Father the folly of his actions so that he can repent and return to being the leader he was yesterday.

I slip away from Adorane. He reaches toward me, whispering, "Icelyn, what are you doing?"

"What I must." It's my turn to be the brave one.

I stand tall, like Adorane would. I stride toward Rain Water Supply, emerging from the receding crowd. I attempt to walk faster, ignoring my limping left ankle, trying to project the confidence and courage I do not feel.

Father sees me. "No, Icelyn! Not now. The decree applies to all. Turn back!"

I'll force him to revoke the decree and end this now. This isn't the way of the Kith, or the way we live in Mountaintop, or the way Father rules. This isn't the work of a Brathius. He will relent, and civility will be restored.

I continue my advance, bloodied and bruised from the trampling. Adrenaline courses through my body. I ignore the pain; it does not matter anymore.

I stand before Tranton and Father, just the fence between us. The rest of the Kith, speechless, watch me from a safe distance. I turn to them and invite them to join in my defiance. "Will no one stand with me? Do you all agree this is the way we should live in Mountaintop?"

But those I thought would support me drop their eyes to the ground. Not a single person steps forward. They are either too afraid—or, I realize, they assume that though I will be pardoned this transgression, they will not.

Tranton speaks. "Icelyn Brathius, do you understand the decree that has been signed by your father?"

"I do. And I understand that there are *no exceptions.* Not even for age or gender. Isn't that right, Father?" I stare directly at Father, my eyes blazing with challenge.

He stares at me dumbfounded. I hope he barely recognizes me, in the same way he has made himself unrecognizable to me today.

12

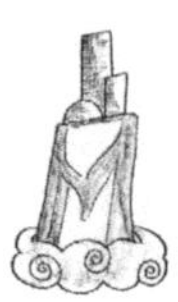

UPON FINDING THE first hint of his destiny, Tranton had made a more thorough search of the Nilsing ancestral lab. In another ancient dusty volume, he found a hand-drawn map. It went into great detail about Mountaintop, but also areas outside the Wall, far enough down to include parts of the Valley Down Below. Areas all over the map had been marked, but there was no explanation or key.

He recognized the handwriting from other books and journals he'd found in the lab. His great-great-great-great grandfather, Travis Nilsing, had created this map. But why?

He would have to go outside the Wall to find out.

Icelyn had been sleeping for more than a day. Nicholas watched her, disturbed by her fitful slumber. He wondered how her body could be getting the rest needed to recover from her injuries. Her troubled sleep exhausted him.

He suffered a surge of guilt. The thought of her being trampled in that crowd ate away at him. To his shame, he'd been too focused on everything else to notice.

Icelyn wasn't being disbursed, and she wasn't going Down Below. That much was obvious—even if Tranton had tried to remind him, more forcefully than Nicholas thought was proper, of the "no exceptions" part of the decree. Sometimes Tranton held ridiculous opinions. This was one of them. What was the point of being the Chief Cognate if you couldn't overrule your advisors to save your own daughter's life?

Nicholas insisted Icelyn recover in Brathius Tower, instead of at the Kith Health Arts Lab. Tranton thought this would look bad to the citizens of Mountaintop—the Chief Cognate not trusting the common facilities where all others were expected to recover from their illnesses. Especially at such a sensitive time, when the divide between the Cognates and Veritas was more dramatic than it had been in centuries. But it was Tranton and his harsh policies that were responsible for this divide, so why should he worry about mending it now? He seemed to care about equality and peace only when it suited him.

Cognates with any personal wealth infirmed in their own labs. This was nothing new, and Veritas understood. Cognates could afford to pay doctors to make regular visits, and Veritas could not. This was not controversial or unjust—it was just the way it had always been, and he was just doing the same.

Marjan shuffled into the room. As Tranton's discovery had predicted, she'd been doing better since she stopped drinking the poisoned waters, but she was far from well.

"Darling! Return to your bed. You need rest."

"Am I to pretend our daughter was not battered underfoot yesterday? How is a mother supposed to rest, Nicholas?"

Nicholas understood; any good mother would feel this way. But he didn't want her to see the negotiations that were about to happen.

"Trust that I am looking over her, Marjan. Let that be the comfort you need to rest."

And what of yesterday, while I slept? Who was looking over her then? Marjan thought bitterly, but a loud knock at the door told her that now was not the time for this discussion. She lowered her head in submission.

"Thank you for defending our family." Marjan teared up as Nicholas held her close. She knew who was coming and what Nicholas had to do—and she was grateful she didn't have to be a part of it.

It was Tranton at the door. When Nicholas had refused to send Icelyn Down Below, despite the decree, Tranton had declared that they needed to determine the "exact cost of your decision, per the Code that governs us all." He was here to accomplish that task.

Torrain waited for the summit to begin in the Brathius sitting room, equal parts apathy and attitude. The whole matter inconvenienced him terribly. As Icelyn's betrothed, his presence was required, but Torrain acted as if this was an unfair imposition on his life. *Less time to sit in your room and mope?* Nicholas judged him. *How awful that we force you to lazily grouse here instead!*

Nicholas had also requested that Adorane attend, believing that his testimony about Icelyn's state of mind after nearly dying in the mob would help.

Tranton started, his voice grave. "As we are all aware, a decree was made, carrying the full force of the Chief Cognate's authority. We are in unstable times, and defying direct orders destabilizes a delicate house of cards."

Nicholas interrupted. "Let's back up. There is a Brathius saying that I would like to serve as a foundation for our discussion: *Better a broken law than a broken heart*."

Tranton chuckled. "Some sayings are better left stitched into pillows. Not all have practical application."

Adorane's hot blood got the better of him. "She was not thinking clearly. She wasn't five minutes removed from being trampled beneath the mob! Blood still flowed down her temples as she defied the decree." Nicholas was grateful for Adorane as he read the room. Adorane and himself sat on one side of the long table, Tranton opposite them; down at the end sat Torrain, who seemed to pay no attention to any of it.

Tranton was unaffected. "Icelyn inspires fierce emotions." He glanced at Torrain before adding wryly, "For most, at least. But as someone interested in the survival of humanity above all, I cannot care about individual loyalties. I'd rather see a thousand hearts broken than one law violated. Laws protect—and often what they're protecting against are the hearts of men and women, weak as we are. Nicholas, you'd feel the same way if the heart in question weren't your own."

Nicholas felt his face heat up. Tranton was proposing they hold to the decree, as if Icelyn joining the expedition was actually a possibility.

"I understand that when you first saw your daughter collapse, you were overcome with a flood of feelings, like mud mucking up a pool of water. But as time has passed, and the water has cleared. You should be able to see that asking the Kith to make such a sacrifice seems hypocritical when you won't make it yourself."

Nicholas' mind raced. He turned over his thoughts, examining each carefully but finding that most were half formed. He cursed his luck.

Good thoughts weren't built through hard work; they came to you unbidden, like a butterfly landing on your shoulder. Indeed, genius seemed to be the ability to attract as many butterflies as possible. And Nicholas knew that he was not a genius.

Then one thought, with the potential to solidify his allies in the room, came to him. "Torrain, are you prepared to journey Down Below alongside Icelyn?"

This jolted the boy out of his faraway gaze. "What? Why should I be?"

"The rules of Intention state that the male shall do all within his power to provide protection for the female once they are promised to one another."

"That's nothing but a fanciful romantic gesture," Torrain scoffed. "Poetic musings written into the Code!"

"Regardless, it *is* written in the Code. If Icelyn goes, so do you."

Nicholas' diversion had the desired effect—for once, Torrain was fully engaged. Nicholas watched as Torrain attracted his own brilliant butterfly. The boy sat up straight, and Nicholas noticed that when he stopped slouching, he seemed taller and more powerful. Torrain stood and approached Tranton.

"Tranton, Nicholas has a point. The Kith would be horrified if we sent a *girl* to face the Threat Below. This alone could ignite rebellion! Icelyn is the most popular member of the Brathius family, and many look forward to the day she leads."

Nicholas knew this was meant as a slight to himself, but he couldn't disagree. He'd never resented her magnetism; rather, he was proud of it. Plus, if people liked Icelyn, they indirectly liked him more too.

Torrain continued, "You wouldn't know, since you haven't been out since the showdown at the Winter Rain Supply—but the sentiment is twenty to one against Icelyn joining the expedition. If you force Nicholas to follow through on this silly decree, you'll have a revolt on your hands. The decree never should have been made in the first place. You don't fix an error by masking it with a larger one."

Nicholas was impressed. He knew Torrain was only arguing in defense of his own skin, but he'd put together a better argument in under a minute than Nicholas had been able to muster over the past two days.

Tranton was taken off guard. "What, then, would you propose? Wash our hands of it and tell everyone we were joking?"

Torrain paced back and forth behind his chair, then stopped in his tracks as a new thought came to him—a brilliant thought, though this time laced with danger. A venomous butterfly.

"What of a substitute? Let's be honest—a girl would be useless on this journey anyway. But what if another volunteered to go in her place?"

Nicholas thought that perhaps he'd misjudged the boy. Was he volunteering to take Icelyn's place? "Torrain, you'd go in her stead?"

Torrain laughed. "No! What would I do against a dangerous threat?" He reached forward and snatched up the sketches he'd been making earlier. "Doodle it to death? I'd be less valuable than Icelyn down there. But there *are* others who are better equipped to serve as proxy."

All eyes settled on Adorane as it became clear what Torrain was proposing. Torrain couldn't believe his luck; he was finally going to get this infernal Veritas out of the picture. Either Adorane would volunteer to join the expedition and be ripped to shreds by the Threat Below, or he'd decline and Icelyn would know that he'd been too cowardly to save her.

Nicholas knew what Torrain was doing, and he was filled with revulsion. But the idea did possess an elegant logic, however twisted, and solved many problems at once. Icelyn wouldn't have to go Down Below, but the decree would remain intact, and Nicholas' fragile authority along with it. Nicholas despised the choice presented to Adorane, but he wasn't going to speak up and stop it.

Even Tranton supported the idea. "Well, Adorane, what do you say? Can you think of anyone who might volunteer to take Icelyn's place?"

The two deer glided through the clearing, breezily nibbling at wild blackberries and white sage. Now and then, out of instinct and an abundance of caution, they'd lift their heads into the air and listen, assuring themselves that they were safe from any predators. Then they'd return to their simple existence. Grazing along the thick briars, lying down in soft heather, chewing on twigs. They grew comfortable in their assurance that they were safe from being hunted, and forgot, for a moment at least, they were ever prey.

They were wrong.

With unbelievable swiftness, a swarm of shadows and stealth diced the deer, opening their sides with surgical precision, and hungrily consuming their viscera, entrails, and organs until all that had been inside was picked clean.

It was merciful. The deer passed before they could even feel any fear.

13

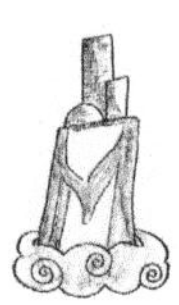

EVEN WHILE ASLEEP, I realize this is not real. There's a heavy sensation to every movement, a slight delay to every sound and action.

I've always envied the fantastic, imaginative, and vivid dreams other people have. I never dream. I've chalked it up to the fact that my life is constricted—confined to this small space at the top of the Mountain, seeing the same people doing the same things every day. Nothing happens to me in my waking hours that needs to overflow into sleep for processing. There's nothing to work out or decipher in my subconscious, no mysteries that required overtime to be solved.

But I've read that everyone dreams—the only difference is whether you remember it or not. Perhaps my dreams are simply too dull to register, not notable enough to be committed to memory.

The past few days have been the exception in my uneventful life—and so now, I must be dreaming. Adorane makes an appearance. Father is there, too, and Mother. They're talking. I can tell they're discussing me, but I can't make out a word they say.

A sound echoes, pulling me toward waking. I fight it. I want to stay asleep. But the sound grows louder, distantly familiar, unsettling—and impossible to ignore. Suddenly I am awake. I find myself back in my bed, disoriented. I feel like I've been sleeping for ages. I can't remember going to bed. I don't know how I got here.

"Father! Mother!" I spring from my bed and instantly regret the decision. My body aches, and the pain brings back the memory of being trampled by a flood of people, of Ad pulling me to safety. I collapse back into bed.

"Icelyn, you're up!" Mother appears at the door, concern creasing her face. Other than that, she looks much better than she has in some time.

I stand again, slowly. I'm sore, but I can move. Something about Mother's overall demeanor is not normal. She's trying too hard to *not* disturb me—so hard that it's actually notably disturbing. "What's going on? Where's Father?"

"Sit down, please. You need your rest. We all do! Let me get you some tea."

Mother hasn't offered me tea since I was eight years old. I know this because I've missed it. "How long have I been asleep?"

Mother approaches me and takes my hand. She looks me in the eyes, the way she used to when I was a child. Back then, she was a young mother who worked hard every day to convince me that I was loved. At some point, she must have grown convinced that I learned that lesson and required no further reminding. I guess this is true. I'm no longer an infant in need of constant reinforcement.

But still, it's comforting to be reminded. Physical contact has lessened as I've gotten older. I know this is only right—a parent should not embrace a teenager. However, I realize that I've missed it. And yet —though I hate to ruin this moment, something feels wrong.

I pull my hand away. "Mother, what is it that you're working so hard to conceal?"

Mother looks flustered. "Only that we've been concerned about you. Father's made a trip to fetch our week's ration of Winter Rain. He'll be happy to see that you're awake. He's been sitting beside your bed just waiting for you to recover. You scared us."

Her words make me remember my challenge to Father's decree. That's the last thing I remember. "Mother! At Winter Rain Supply, when I approached Father despite his decree…"

Mother knows what I am asking. "Taken care of, darling. You needn't worry about it anymore. Your father worked to sort it all out. You should be proud of him." Mother doesn't add *like you used to be,* but we both know she's thinking it.

A high whistle sounds from outside my room. "There's the tea! Let's drink some together, and then we can both get back to the business of resting our weary bodies." I collapse backward on the pillow; I don't understand what's going on, but I like that she refers to us as *we*. I've been alone for so long.

Mother carries over a tea tray, just as she did when I was younger. I'm tempted to rummage under the bed, find the dolls we'd set up back then, and turn this into a proper tea party. I look away and bite down on my lip, lest Mother see tears forming—unbidden, unwelcome, and unexpected—in my eyes.

"I've missed you, Mother." I didn't know how much until now. I haven't even had time yet to let myself enjoy the fact that she's no longer getting sicker.

This cozy interaction between Mother and me is exactly the kind of dreamy sequence that I imagine others enjoy while they doze.

My dream! I'm reminded of it once again, and how it ended. That strange sound pulling me out of my sleep. Now that I'm awake, I'm able to match conscious thought to subconscious memory, and I know exactly what I heard.

It wasn't my dream. I was awakened by the Summoning Bell.

I have to go.

I leap forward off the bad, rushing from the room as my mother cries out after me.

By the time I enter Kith Hall, the ceremony has already begun—and I realize that Mother was not being loving. She was only trying to distract me.

This is an event they wanted me to miss.

I think of Mother and feel a flash of bitterness. I can now see what a cruel trick growing older is: watching this person who used to happily tend to your every need slowly turn into someone who merely tolerates your presence. I'm not sure when she changed, but the mother I remember is a different person entirely than the one I now know. When did she become someone who lies to me with ease? Anyone who would attempt to fool me into thinking I am loved for her own selfish reasons cannot possibly love me at all. My face burns, and I'm not sure whether it's caused by anger or sadness. I believed her, fool that I am.

Strangely enough, Adorane stands at the front of the gathering, as if he's somehow become a member of Father and Tranton's exclusive club. He stands between them—Father on one side of him, and Tranton on the other—as he addresses the Kith.

Adorane's voice is calm. "I had my doubts about the way our leadership handled the poisoning and the Winter Rain rationing. I have since discussed matters with Nicholas and am satisfied that his plan is a good one." While Adorane projects confidence, I can tell he doesn't agree with anything he is saying. A friend can tell. *What is he doing? How did they ever get him to do this?*

"The time for critique has ended. Now is the time for action. Nicholas Brathius has my unquestioning support." I almost laugh out loud at how ridiculous the words sound as Adorane forces them from his mouth.

I slip toward the front of the hall, staying in shadows untouched by the torchlight. I am a Brathius; I should be sitting in the Brathius row. I catch glimpses of Veritas faces as I pass by. It looks as though their concern is being eased by Adorane's speech. The Veritas respect Adorane almost as much as the Cognates look up to me. I can't blame them; there is much to admire about my friend.

I reach the Brathius row and curse myself because Father notices me. He motions toward me—a brusque, wordless gesture ordering me to turn around and leave. It's the kind of command you'd give to a dog or an infant. I stare at him, my eyes blazing, as I sit slowly in my seat.

"To demonstrate my support for Nicholas' plan, I will personally—" Adorane stops, stunned silent by the sight of me, now sitting directly before him. This is no accident. It's exactly what I wanted—and what Father apparently wished to avoid.

I mouth to Adorane: "What are you doing?" Whatever deal Tranton and Father made with him for his support, I am hoping that Ad won't be able to press forward with my eyes locked on his. With me, he has no choice but to be who he truly is.

He shifts his eyes away from me and swallows, as though he hasn't had water in a week. I wait for him to look at me again, to draw strength from me, and then to resume being Adorane—bold and confrontational, even when it's difficult.

Instead, Adorane looks everywhere I am not.

"...I will be joining the expedition that goes Down Below."

What? I feel like I've been knocked in the head, like the time I slammed into a tree when chasing Mother through the eastern alpine grove. Pain, and not a lot of conscious thought.

I realize that everyone is looking at me, some of them gasping and shaking their heads. One hurries to cover her child's ears. I realize that I have spoken out loud. I don't know what I said, but it must have involved salty, intemperate words if mothers are shielding their children from my outburst.

But I can't believe it. I continue, shouting, "No. Adorane! What are you thinking?"

Adorane carries on as if I hadn't just pierced the silence with my plea.

"We will find the poison, and we will make Waterpump pure again."

Father nods at a couple of Tarlinius Veritas and they flank me as if they're attending to my needs. But I know better. They are handling me, taking me out of the meeting so I won't be a distraction.

"There, there. We need to get you home for some rest," one says to me loudly, producing a flask from her pocket. I try to bat her arm away, but she touches it to my lips. A dark haze of exhaustion passes in front of my eyes, and my body slumps forward. *What is happening?*

The last thing I hear is Adorane saying, "We leave tomorrow morning. We will succeed."

I want to die. I wonder if I already have.

14

TORRAIN CHUCKLED AS he strolled past the rocky crags toward Brathius Tower. This plan to defeat his rival hadn't been a long-term plot, carefully executed using patience and care, but it might as well have been. It had worked perfectly.

He tried to figure out how best to reframe events. If anyone asked, should he admit it was a last-second idea—and thus make himself look like a genius without even trying? Or should he pretend he had been plotting Adorane's demise for months, maybe even years? The tactician who thinks twenty steps and two years ahead could be even more intimidating.

Torrain didn't have to make up his mind now. Let them guess! Couldn't he be both? Either way, people would be forced to acknowledge his brilliance. He didn't have to say a word, but everyone would know.

Icelyn was the one sour note in his otherwise flawless symphony. The heartbroken look on her face when she realized that Adorane was going Down Below made Torrain want to take it all back, just for her. But the move had already been made. As the Pannous family motto stated, *There is a reason we do not walk backward*.

Torrain was disturbed by what he felt for Icelyn. It began when he'd been forced into defending her. Torrain had never thought much about

Icelyn prior to that, outside of annoyance at her for treating their Intention as if it meant nothing. She'd called him such horrible names! Grub, louse, worm, tick, creeper—what had he done to deserve any of that? Perhaps now that Adorane was gone, he'd graduate to a level above invertebrate. Perhaps she could even learn to care for him.

It had occurred to Torrain that since Icelyn was going to be the Chief Cognate, he, as her husband, would *actually* be the Chief Cognate. Cognate women submitted to their husbands in all things (except the choice of Intended partner for their children, of course). This appealed to Torrain, and he caught himself thinking about Icelyn throughout the day. Now that he'd been in the great decision rooms, he was beginning to realize what an opportunity his Intention to Icelyn was.

When he'd seen her enter Kith Hall—even though Nicholas and Tranton had assured him and Adorane she would not be there—he was surprised by both her appearance and his reaction to it. He wondered if she had always been so attractive. He chalked it up to excitement over his own achievements, a glowing halo that made all within its radius luminous.

Now, late into the night after his victory, Torrain found himself still thinking about her. Finally, he decided he should talk to her. With Adorane dispatched, she was officially the spoil of a war he'd waged and won.

As he neared Brathius Tower, he was amused to see members of the family Tarlinius patrolling. What did they think they were now, guards? These were common untrained servants and assistants. Torrain hid behind a boulder, determining not to dignify their ruse by asking for permission to pass.

He waited until they'd marched toward the western side of Brathius Tower and crept by in the darkness.

That was when he first heard her. "Please! Someone help me. Someone. Don't ignore me!" She sounded like a little girl who'd fallen and scraped her knee, scared and betrayed.

Torrain's stomach flipped. What was this feeling? *Perhaps I'm sick,* he thought. He had experienced so little compassion in his life that he didn't recognize it; he guessed it was only a bad reaction to his mother's ultralion pie. Torrain's mother had rushed to make the pie in time for the ceremony at Kith Hall, and it had tasted terrible. She often left out key ingredients or added others that no sensible cook would consider. He reminded himself to discuss her lack of cooking skills with Father when he returned.

Icelyn appeared in her window, tear streaks staining her face, her eyes tinged red. She sobbed, "You cannot keep me prisoner in my own home!"

There was another sound, a metallic clanking that Torrain couldn't place. He felt sicker, even feverish, as he watched her. His face blushed in the darkness. He desperately wanted to talk to her, to make her feel better.

Torrain stepped from the shadows into the moonlight and whispered, "Icelyn!"

As she saw him, her face twisted. He was the last person she'd hoped to see.

He wasn't sure what reaction he'd wanted, but it wasn't this. Torrain felt awful, his heart burning, his stomach squeezing and stretching. This sensation was unfamiliar to Torrain; he'd stopped letting people hurt his feelings a long time ago. But one look from Icelyn tore him apart.

"What are *you* doing here?" She choked the words out through her surprise.

Torrain realized he didn't know *what* he was doing there. He'd just wanted to talk to her—he hadn't thought of what he'd actually say. "I thought maybe you could use some company," he said haltingly.

"Not yours." Her voice was flat and hard.

Torrain wondered if Icelyn had realized that it had been his idea for Adorane to go Down Below in her place. His blood pounded in his ears, terrified.

"I heard about your ruse—how you pushed Adorane to volunteer! I know what you did. You used him! You coward!"

Well, that answered that question. His mind raced to come up with an excuse.

"I only wanted to see you spared. The thought of you going Down Below hit me as terribly wrong. I couldn't bear to have it happen. I was desperate. I came over here because I realized I would miss you if you were gone, and I wanted to sort things out between us."

The words hung in the air, and neither Icelyn nor Torrain knew what to do with them. Friendly words in Torrain's mouth were so foreign it was almost as if he'd spoken one of those obsolete tongues that the Apriori used. Icelyn didn't know how to comprehend it.

Did Torrain actually *care* about her?

His words gave Icelyn an idea. It wasn't kind to Torrain, but what kindness did he deserve? He was probably lying about his feelings in hopes of getting something from her anyway—she was only matching his deceit with her own.

Icelyn felt dirty, but she let the words escape her lips anyway. "Torrain, hearing you say that…I feel the same way but feared it would never be reciprocated," she lied. Icelyn was acting like a character in the Apriori novels—women who used their beauty and charm to manipulate others. Icelyn felt neither beautiful nor charming—but from the look on Torrain's face, it seemed to be working. She tried to hide her surprise, plastering a smile across her face.

Torrain was shocked at how her words cut through him, causing his heart to pound and his face to flush. She felt the same way?

"Well, then," he stammered, "when all this nastiness blows over, you and I can get a fresh start on our Intention Immersion. It's not been the experience either of us wanted so far."

As uncomfortable as the role she was playing made her feel, Icelyn pushed further. "Why wait until then? I'm free tonight." She twisted a lock of hair between her thumb and pointer finger, mimicking something that Catalandi often did when talking to boys.

A broad smile crossed Torrain's face. "But you're locked in there," he laughed. "Should we have a picnic though the bars, dodging these Tarlinius guards?"

Icelyn joined him in laughter. "That the Tarliniuses even think they can pass as guards is ridiculous!"

Were they both acting, or was it only her? Icelyn couldn't be sure, and it confused her. She grew serious, with a hint of flirtation woven through her voice. "You're a smart one. Figure out a way to get me out of here. I want to spend some time with you—alone."

Icelyn had never asked to be alone with him before. *No* girl had ever asked to spend time with him, alone or otherwise. Torrain's mind raced. *She's right. I'm smart enough to get her past a few Tarlinius guards.*

He thought for a moment, then he beamed up at her. "Stay there. I'll get you out."

"Stay here? Where am I going to go?" They shared another laugh, and he darted back into the shadows.

God, he looked so genuinely happy. Icelyn caught a glimpse of what Torrain must have looked like as a little boy, before he blossomed into the pompous bore he was now. She was tempted to feel sorry for him. Either he was a better actor than she was, or he actually *liked* her. She shook off the thought. Torrain only ever cared about himself and what he could get from people. He was simply a man falling for a woman's trap. She felt a small thrill at her newfound power. It had almost been too easy.

She waited in the window for him to return. After the Tarlinius passed on another one of their rounds, she heard Torrain approaching out of the darkness again.

Well, let's hope he's as smart as he thinks he is.

Torrain strode past Icelyn's window. Without slouching, he looked like a different person. He appeared to be carrying a bouquet of flowers. Icelyn wondered how he could have found them so quickly. *Does he carry a spare all the time just in case?*

He rapped gently on the front door and waited. He figured his odds were fifty-fifty that the next step would be easy. Marjan, not Nicholas, pulled the door open. Relief flooded Torrain: a stroke of luck.

From the way Marjan anxiously scanned the darkness behind him, Torrain could tell she didn't feel safe in Brathius Tower. The scene at Winter Rain Supply had been terrifying, and the Tarlinius didn't really count as security.

Torrain held the flowers out to Marjan and beamed. "I wish to honor the source of my Beloved's beauty." He bowed his head slightly.

Marjan accepted the flowers with a tight smile, but it was clear she was in no mood for a visit. "Torrain, this night of all nights..." she trailed off, lacking the energy to finish the sentence.

"I'm only here to help, I promise. I wanted to speak to Icelyn."

"I'm not sure how that could help at this point."

Torrain lowered his voice, as if there were someone else in the room who could overhear him. "Given recent events, I believe time is of the essence. Surely Icelyn could use a pick-me-up? The circle of people who can make her happy seems to be growing smaller by the day."

Might as well let the boy try. He seemed eager enough. At worst, Icelyn would accuse him of betrayal and vow never to love him, as she'd done with Nicholas and Marjan.

Marjan sighed to herself. Even as an adolescent, she'd never been as dramatic as Icelyn. Then again, Marjan's parents had never locked her in her room while her best friend was sent to his death—but still.

Marjan pointed toward Icelyn's room. "Please secure her door when you leave. Unfortunately, it's necessary." She slumped back toward her own bedroom, her body and soul depleted.

Torrain marveled at his luck. He hadn't counted on Marjan being so inattentive. He slid the heavy plank of wood that secured Icelyn's door aside, and it creaked open. Icelyn crashed into him with a warm, tight embrace.

Acting or not, Icelyn was grateful for what he'd done. This room in the Tower had gone from being one of her favorite places in the world to a desperate trap. She needed to leave—by any means necessary.

Her rational thoughts caught up with her, and she broke from the embrace. "Ah. Unsupervised physical contact is forbidden, even among the Intended…" she mumbled as an apology, an explanation for the sudden change. The truth would have been harder for Torrain to hear. Icelyn had simply realized she was touching *Torrain* and drawn away in disgust.

"I promise not to tell if you won't." Torrain had a gleam in his eye.

"Okay…well, let's get past the Tarlinius, and then see how closely we hew to each letter of the Code." Icelyn's cheeks reddened with embarrassment at how well she played this role. She was better at pretending to be Catalandi than Catalandi herself.

Torrain took the blush as a sign of passion and firmed his resolve to make this clandestine courting session a reality. He snuffed out the candle and waited at the window, watching.

"Come here!" he whispered. Icelyn joined him. "Look."

Icelyn couldn't see anything. "What am I supposed to be looking at?"

"Here, closer. Out there." Icelyn had to scoot toward Torrain until she was basically nestled into his side. She waited for her eyes to adjust to the moonlight outside. She could hear Torrain's breath and feel his rapid pulse. Torrain was more nervous than he had been letting on.

Icelyn felt a sudden flash of compassion and wanted to put him at ease. "You know, even if we're caught leaving, it'll just be greeted with a smirk and a knowing look." She knew this wasn't really true. A week ago, probably—but now everything had changed.

"How would you know? Are you often caught sneaking into the woods with boys?"

Icelyn felt offense swell up inside her, but she muzzled it. She laughed airily. "Oh, yes. At least once a night—and twice on Saturdays."

Even though she was close to freedom, and she knew staying the course was the best way to get there, she couldn't help but set the record straight. This was her honor at stake. "Of course, I'm joking. I am untouched in every way. Both heart and body." Not exactly flirtatious, but it had to be said.

"Oh...well, good," he responded awkwardly. "But you don't think I risk...disbursement if we're caught?"

"Of course not! You're a Cognate, and we're promised to one another."

She could tell he wasn't put at ease. The conversation had made her more nervous, too. The stakes had grown higher; this was no longer a game. And what exactly was she going to *do* after he sprung her from Brathius Tower?

She wasn't sure—but she was about to find out. As the Tarlinius guards passed by on their ineffective rounds, she beckoned Torrain toward the doorway.

Torrain followed Icelyn through the woods. Though whispering, he was chatty. It wasn't as though Torrain had never talked before, but normally Icelyn found most of what he had to say either boring or annoying. Tonight he was doing a better job.

"Someone needs to reassign Tranton. He can go study mold spores —it's all he's fit to do. He should stop meddling and let a Brathius lead."

Icelyn knew he was only saying what he thought she'd want to hear, but she enjoyed it anyway. Wasn't that the definition of kindness—saying something because someone wants to hear it? Ad could learn a lesson from Torrain.

"He's made a mess of things for Father," Icelyn replied. "Not that I have any sympathy for the Chief Cognate," she continued. "He should be strong enough to say no to Tranton. That's what I would do."

"That's what you did. You said no. Do you know what people are saying about you around Mountaintop?"

Icelyn blushed. She hadn't thought about it, but surely the Kith were buzzing about what she had done. "What are they saying? Tell me."

Torrain played the tease. "I probably shouldn't. It'd only inflate your ego. I know how you hate arrogance."

"I only hate it in you. I tolerate it in myself just fine."

"Vices are like that, aren't they?"

"That's the difference between virtue and vice. What I consider a virtue in me is definitely a vice in you."

Icelyn found herself actually enjoying their repartee. She couldn't speak like this with many people. Father, once upon a time. Adorane, often. Belubus, of course. Torrain had never seemed a candidate for membership in this club, but he was making his case.

They arrived at the ruins of Talmer's Folly, the great Tower her ancestor had tried to build decades ago. Icelyn scaled the fallen remains of the Folly. Every bit of metal had been stripped from it long ago, leaving only great hunks of eroded stone. Icelyn had always loved it here, even though Father acted as if she should be ashamed of it. She liked what it represented. Talmer had failed, but he had reached beyond what anyone could have dreamed. Such courage was much better than the safety that everyone now preferred.

Icelyn had always thought of herself as brave, but she didn't think she had the courage to attempt anything so foolish, which made her appreciate it even more. Talmer's Folly seemed like the kind of failure Ad would be responsible for—and then he'd laugh, before trying again on an even grander scale.

She could see the graves of her ancestors not far from the base of Talmer's Folly, in a private Brathius-only graveyard wedged between two large boulders. Her parents thought it macabre, but Icelyn had always loved this little space. She thought she could *feel* the fallen Brathius resting here (though she knew they weren't actually here at all; they weren't anywhere).

Icelyn especially liked looking at Sean Brathius' grave. It was almost 250 years old, with the carved epithet: *The greatest pain is the love you leave behind***.**

No one had ever told her what this meant (though she had asked many times), but it was so poetic and deeply melancholic that Icelyn knew she and her great-great-great-great-great Grandfather Sean would have gotten along well.

"I'm surprised your parents let you explore down here. I'd think they'd want the whole thing cleaned up and hauled away," Torrain observed.

"Well, that would be a waste of Kith labor, now wouldn't it?"

"I can see that. I'd just think the Brathius family would want to erase this from our memory."

"It's nothing to be ashamed of."

"Nothing to be proud of, either," Torrain replied bluntly. He meant it as a joke, but Icelyn didn't take it as one.

The playfulness drained from Icelyn's face as she hopped from the ruins to the ground. "I don't remember asking your opinion on my family history."

The chill hit hard and made him woozy. Fortunes had turned so quickly. "No, of course not. Ice, I only meant to—"

"It's Icelyn." She moved back toward the darkness of the thicker woods. "Not Ice."

"Wait! I just sprung you from your house. I thought we were going to—spend time together. You can't just take off. Everyone will wonder where you are!"

"Let them wonder."

"I've broken the Code to free you! You can't leave! I thought I'd be able to stay with you, to keep you safe."

"Keep me safe? *You?*"

Icelyn continued her retreat through the woods. She heard him attempting to chase after her, but she knew the area much better.

"What did I do? We were having such a good time."

Icelyn stopped in the darkness. She felt a twinge of guilt, but she suppressed it. The plan had always been to ditch Torrain after she escaped from her locked room; they'd simply been getting along so well that she'd delayed. Regardless, her next steps—whatever they were—couldn't include Torrain. She needed to abandon him, either by cold calculation or hot-headed emotion. No reason to draw it out.

"It didn't come from anywhere. I don't want to be around you. This is nothing new."

"Icelyn, please! Don't leave me. This has been…I don't want this to end." The pain in his voice made it obvious. She was hurting him.

Icelyn didn't know what she owed Torrain. Suddenly the last two days crashed down on her—the poisoned water, the imprisonment, losing Ad, finding Torrain. He had tried to push Ad to his death. He was cowardly and mean-spirited and arrogant. Still, she suddenly realized that she'd never given him a chance. Perhaps this could have been something more, and she'd ruined it. And what's more, he actually cared for her, even after all she'd done. This could be the last time they ever saw each other. She shifted from one foot to the other in agony.

"If you go, what should I tell everyone else?" he called out, sounding defeated.

"Tell them…tell them, you're not as bad as I thought you were. And…I'm sorry."

She darted into the darkness.

The winds shifted and brought the scent of those things that lived inside the wall into the faraway creatures' nostrils. This was an accursed treat, one that didn't occur often. Heavy and sweet, the scent enraged and enticed the beasts, heightening their already mindless hunger until they could only ram into and claw at the deadened trees which had been bound together to keep them away from what they desired.

They bashed against the wall, fueled by instinct more than thought, until blood poured from newly formed wounds and drenched their ratty fur. Finally, exhausted, slippery crimson and dizzy, they fell to the ground, moaning in quiet. defeated desperation.

Just a taste, just a sip. Just a taste, just a sip.

They would gladly die for less than that.

15

ICELYN HAD BEEN telling so many lies and cloaking herself in deceit more often than not. It worried her. She'd been saying things that didn't match up to reality. That's what crazy people do—that's how you know they're insane. But she knew she wasn't mad, because she was aware of what she was doing. Crazy people (the kind that got disbursed!) weren't. She was doing it by choice.

Not a crazy person. Just a rotten one.

She'd reached her beloved mentor's lab. "Belubus! Belubus!"

Icelyn kept her urgent calls to a whisper. Torrain wouldn't report her disappearance to anyone—after all, he'd get in trouble as soon as the others found out—but it wouldn't be long before people came looking for her. There wasn't a member of the Kith who didn't recognize her, and everyone knew that she wasn't free to roam Mountaintop at night after what she had said and done. Even if the Kith agreed with her defiance, she knew too well how obedient the people of Mountaintop were.

She tried the handle and found the door locked. Her heart skipped a beat. Belubus never locked his lab, night or day. He didn't even own a key.

She stood outside his bedroom window, rapping softly on the wall. There was no flicker of fire inside. Icelyn peered up at the position of the moon. By her reckoning, it was only a little past midnight. It wasn't like Belubus to go to sleep this early—he often did his best learning in the later hours.

The locked door. An aborted night of experiments. Icelyn tried to push off the slow feeling of dread building inside her.

"Belubus! Belubus!"

Heavy footfalls broke through the night, and Icelyn fell to the ground. She pressed herself against the outside wall of Belubus' lab, hoping for invisibility in the shadows.

The orange light of a torch approached. Icelyn felt relief surge through her. Belubus had probably been on one of his late-night trips through the woods in search of specimens and supplies. She'd be sure to tease him about locking his doors; recent events no doubt had everyone on edge.

But as the torch grew near, Icelyn's heart fell. Illuminated below was not the short, stout figure of her beloved mentor. Instead, it was a Tarlinius—now outfitted in a black uniform that seemed inspired by the spiky back of a boar.

Icelyn crept behind a rocky outcropping, fearing that he was looking for her. The Tarlinius continued his steady advance.

Now that he was closer, Icelyn could see it was Raistin. He always presented himself as a brute, with his chest puffed out, his voice unnaturally gruff and low, his facial hair unkempt. But Icelyn saw this masculine posturing and felt like she knew his true secret.

She had once come upon Raistin near Yellow Meadow, alone and sobbing. In his hands, he held a lizard frozen in death. The lizard's name was Glenn, and Raistin had kept it as a pet for years. But that morning when he checked on Glenn, well… Raistin had trailed off as he explained. He couldn't bear to say the word *dead.* They'd dug a grave for Glenn, fashioned a coffin out of tree bark and leaves, and then shared spontaneous tributes. Icelyn thought that no lizard had ever enjoyed such a touching funeral. She felt that she had looked into Raistin's soul that day and caught a glimpse of something gentle, fragile, and good.

She almost called his name. Anybody who'd properly send off a reptile wouldn't betray her into a locked dungeon. *No. People can change,* she reminded herself. *Sometimes from one moment to the next.*

She watched as Raistin neared the front door. He pulled a slip of paper from his pocket, and, with the blunt edge of his torch, pounded a nail into the door. Then he turned and stalked off into the darkness.

When the light of the torch was far enough away, Icelyn emerged from her hiding place and ran to the front door.

This Lab is property of the Kith.
Belubus has been disbursed due to violations of the Code for Common Good
By Order of the Chief Cognate.
Let us all agree:
We are stronger with him away.

Icelyn strained to read through to the end, her vision blurred with tears.

Belubus had only done what she had asked! He'd tried to talk sense into Father about Tranton and the decrees. It was all her fault. He'd been thrown outside the Wall—where the shrieking, howling thing that had carved up Jarvin was still waiting.

Cognates were almost never disbursed! Veritas who broke the Code were sent away—and of course, Veritas with physical infirmities such as poor eyesight or weak lungs were disbursed too. But that was a mercy, not a punishment. Strength was all the Veritas had. A weak Veritas would suffer such shame that it was better to allow them to leave.

The thought reminded Icelyn of something. She slid in through Belubus' back window and crept into his private quarters. She found lab equipment shattered all over the floor, pages scattered everywhere. There had been a struggle. Poor Belubus, trying to fight back. At least he hadn't gone peacefully. Good for him.

Icelyn searched below Belubus' meager straw mattress. She located a box and pulled it out. She flipped it open: empty.

She hoped Belubus had his spectacles. Disbursed was one thing—but disbursed and blind, he stood no chance. Hopefully he'd hidden them in his clothes when they came for him. There were few sight-correcting glasses in town, only those brought by the original Ascenders long ago. They would have been confiscated and saved for another high-ranking Cognate, not wasted and sent outside the Wall.

Icelyn knew that everything had changed. She had no one left now. She had to get out.

The match burst to life and cut the darkness, illuminating the plaintive faces of those gathered. All eyes were closed tight, downcast, or bleary with tears.

Charnith Hailgard, tall and taut, eyes rimmed with red, dropped the fire into a long, thin clay pot. Lazy plumes of smoke rose, filling the air.

Charnith eased into a note, high, soft, and clear. The others joined, each hitting their own note, creating harmonies and overtones that swirled through the air. It was almost as if, in addition to seeing and smelling, you could hear the smoke—ephemeral and temporal, sweet and thick.

She pulled the smoke toward her with strong, purposeful waves of her hands, letting it wash over and through her.

"For Aclornis we plead for mercy. For Adorane we beg for grace. Fill them with your strength, and grant them your wisdom. Send your angels before them, prepare their path, and guide their feet."

Charnith dropped to her knees. The others laid hands on her for comfort and strength. They mirrored her. When she cried out, they cried out. When she sang, they sang.

"They are all I have! I'd sooner survive the loss of my own heart. Take my lungs—I won't need them anymore, anyway. Aclornis and Adorane are the reason I breathe!" Charnith dropped her head in anguish, her tears falling down onto the hard packed dirt floor.

16

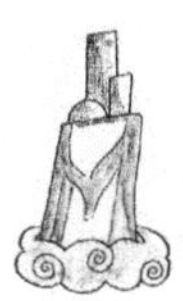

I RUN ALONG on the outskirts of town. Adorane would be proud.

I stand, all alone, in the still night, and take stock. The tight burn in my chest, the sweat dripping from my brow, the ache in my legs—this pain reminds me of Ad. I've only ever felt this way when I've been by his side (or struggling to keep up with him). All the times I've chased him and felt these things! I used to think I was miserable. I realize now that I'd give anything to be trying to keep pace with Ad's smooth, steady stride again. As painful as the burn is, it reminds me of him, and that feels good.

I am alone. Father has betrayed me. Mother manipulated me, taking me for a fool. Belubus has been snatched from his lab, Adorane sent Down Below to die. And I've just burned whatever rickety bridge had formed between Torrain and me.

I wander, allowing myself to cool down, my breath to slow. I forget my sadness—I simply feel the ache in my body. I feel strangely free.

That's when I hear it. At first, I think it's a ringing in my ear. But it's not the same—this sound is soothing, appealing. It almost sounds like an animal, like the howl or wail of a beast. Yet it's more beautiful, like a bird's morning song. Instead of wishing it would stop, I am drawn to it.

I follow the sound east.

Should I be afraid? Is this the beguiling call of whatever killed Jarvin? Did it tempt him to follow it and find the source? No—I am sure it is not. There is nothing threatening about it, even though (I'm realizing) it is filled with pain and sadness.

I follow the sound into the Veritas' part of town. Brutaltown, I've called it in jest. I feel a pang of shame. Had I known how truly brutal things would become for the poor Veritas, I never would have said such a thing.

The sound draws me to a destination that should surprise me but doesn't: Ad's house. I know Hailgard Round well, and I circle the perimeter until I reach the rear yard. I slide under a part of the fence where Ad and I would frequently sneak in and out of his home.

I'm trespassing on something intensely personal. Part of me knows I should leave, but I cannot ignore the desire to stay.

I peek in through a barred window and see inside Hailgard Round. Ad's mother Charnith kneels before a crude wooden X. Other Veritas women rub her back gently, whispering and murmuring. The beguiling sound is coming from them!

I remember something Belubus once tried to teach me. It was a practice the Apriori indulged in, which we've given up in the years since Ascension. The practice used to be much beloved, but it was stopped because it appealed to our baser animal side. *Singing,* he called it. His description perplexed me—though he'd never heard it himself, he said it was like talking, only mixed with an eagle's call and an ultralion's howl, or the sound of the wind at night. It was what birds did in the morning sun, but with people's voices and words. I could never understand what he meant. I begged him for an example, but his throaty squeaks only made me laugh. Why would anyone love doing *that?*

Now I understand why.

Perhaps the Veritas had never given this practice up. They seem quite good at it, though I have no experience to judge. (This is certainly better than Belubus' attempts!) It seems they are all singing different tones, and yet they form one unified sound. It's unlike anything I've ever heard.

I listen to the words drifting from the room, and it dawns on me slowly.

"Be their shield, be their light. Comfort the hurting, and heal the broken. Hear our cries, God."

God! Not said as a casual expression, but as if they were speaking to an entity that could hear them and maybe even speak back. To a god.

They can't be—no. There has to be a reasonable explanation for what they are doing here. Perhaps they are participating in a living history exercise, acting as the Apriori would have in order to better study ancient rites and rituals?

But this is no act. I can tell. I can always tell when something is real. Are they partaking in the Old Ways, the beliefs of the Apriori? It's too terrible to consider. But here I am, seeing and hearing it. What more proof do I need?

Is this something they've dusted off and resurrected because times are tough? Or have they believed this all along? Could they have been hiding it, conducting secret meetings here in Mountaintop for decades, for centuries, while the Cognates slept in their labs unaware?

Has Adorane's family always believed in these religious superstitions? Did *Ad* believe in this? Did Ad sing, kneel, cry, and *talk to God*?

I'm repulsed by the thought. How could he hide this secret from me? Religion is forbidden in the Code. Even its mention has always seemed unnecessary to me, because I've never met anyone who could possibly want to indulge in such things. Or at least I *thought* I hadn't.

I can barely stand to think of it—but somehow, it doesn't feel wrong. I can see why they would be doing this, now, facing the loss of their husbands and their sons. The singing, the tears, the words, the smoke, the wooden object, the closeness they all share. I want to hate it, and half of me does—but the other part of me, a deeper part, craves the comfort I see in the firelit room before me.

I feel something. I'm not able to give it a name, but I've felt it before—back when I read that in Apriori times, human babies were cuddled close and given milk directly from their mothers' breasts. Like animals! Back before the Kith organized child-rearing functions communally and assigned them to certain Veritas for efficiency. I laughed at the thought—my Mother, cooing at me, holding me!

But then, I felt a deep sadness for that moment of closeness—me a baby, Mother holding me close and feeding me. I mourned something that had never happened. I wanted to return to a part of my life that had never been.

I suddenly envy the Veritas. I will never know what this is like. I will never feel what those women feel as they kneel before the X, hands on one another, voices raised as if by magic. That makes me sad. I know it's foolish, just as it is foolish to want to go back and be a baby again with Mother, but still—I feel it.

Damn it, now the tears. I haven't asked for them. I felt alone before, but now I am desolate. I no longer have a place with the Cognates, with Mother or Father. And now, having seen the true face of the Veritas, they are also strangers to me. Any hope I'd harbored of slipping in among them and fitting in is dashed. I have no one, no one in the world.

Mountaintop is barren. It's filled only with lies and empty promises. Everyone who matters to me, and everyone who I've ever mattered to, is outside the Wall. My stomach suddenly seizes with a dreadful certainty.

Why didn't I realize it sooner?

Outside the Wall. That's where I must go.

Part Two
Leaving Mountaintop

17

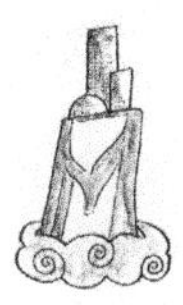

I'VE NEVER BEEN this far from home alone—only with Adorane, and never in the dark.

What role should I play in the disaster my life has turned into? A hero? Should I find Belubus, stow him somewhere safely, and then—what? Challenge Father and Tranton, get the Disbursement reversed? That's never been done before—and anyway, I'm an escaped prisoner myself.

A fighter? Should I join Ad's group on their quest Down Below? I could be an asset for them, with my wits and morale-boosting presence. But Aclornis would insist that I return to the safety of Mountaintop. He wouldn't bring the daughter of Nicholas Brathius along on a mission fated to fail.

Every scenario ends with me locked away again—back in my prison bedroom in Mountaintop.

A survivor? Maybe I should find a cave, sharpen some sticks, and try my hand at hunting. Not the life I envisioned for myself when I scored the highest on the Cognate Potential Test at the age of thirteen, but better than being a prisoner in my bedroom, at least.

I could even live in the Lost Labyrinth, the vast unmapped mines that the Kith dug over the centuries in their fruitless quest for metals and minerals. I could be a lost soul aimlessly wandering, and they seem like they could use a good haunting.

I crack a stick on the ground until it has a sharp point. I'm no warrior, but I feel better holding my homemade spear. I can do this. I run faster, imagining that with this weapon in my hand, I could fulfill all three roles—hero, fighter, survivor.

I tune out the sounds of the night. The woods aren't like this by daylight, with shuffles through the underbrush, branches cracking, chirps, and howls. Last week's Icelyn would grow afraid and turn back. But not me. If the makers of any of these sounds dare show themselves, I will run them through with my mighty spear and make them regret it.

I wish Ad could see me. He'd be proud. I feel light, as if my bones are hollow like a bird's. Is this what running is like for him? It's effortless. It's fun. No wonder he enjoys it!

I see the Wall.

I'm amazed when I think back on how much I've learned since I last saw the Wall. The concerns I harbored then seem trivial now. My biggest worry was that they'd realize I was missing at Waterpump and Father would give me a scolding. Now I am an escaped prisoner, my homeland poisoned. I am being forced beyond the Wall and into the danger beyond, hoping to find my exiled mentor and reckless best friend, who are both likely already dead.

I want to point my spear in the direction of the unknown, unseen terror that lurks beyond the Wall, in hopes of somehow defending myself. But I no longer have the weapon with me; I realize I must have dropped it when I first saw the Wall. Curse my coward's instincts.

Everything inside of me wants to stay away from the Wall, yet I climb up the side, hand over foot, every moment taking me further from safety. The safety I relished just a week ago I am now forced to leave behind.

I reach the top. I've read in books written by the Apriori that people used to jump from buildings and bridges, on purpose, and die. This act of killing yourself, which they called *suicide,* had always seemed like fiction, something they'd written into their stories to add drama. After all, who would ever willingly throw away their life?

But now I stand on the border between everything I've known and the mystery beyond the Wall—a place about which I know only one thing, that it's lethal. I imagine myself a suicidal Apriori, standing at the top of a bridge, the swirling waters far below. Making my choice.

I understand now, crouched atop the wall, my breath the only sound in the vast darkness, why a person would choose to jump. When there is no place for you in the world you know, what choice remains? Other than to close your eyes, take a deep breath, step into the beyond, and hope that something better is waiting there?

So that's what I do.

18

ALL THROUGHOUT THE alpine woods, in thick bramble where they rested, beneath piled up boulders, and even in the soupy mists of Cloudline, the hungry creatures lifted their heads suddenly, involuntarily. A shift in the atmosphere passed through them, an invisible magnet pulling them to their feet.

Confused, they stumbled one way, and then another. What had changed? A new flavor had been mixed into the air in the forest. One that attracted and frightened them.

And, as always, made their unending hunger grow.

This feeling was familiar to them, but old. A second chance at something they'd missed out on long ago. Finally, they would be filled.

Torrain pulled his legs close to his body. Panic washed over him like he was drowning.

Normally his mind could clean up any mess, sort it all out, and put everything away in its proper place. But now—now he struggled with thoughts just as messy as his feelings. He could no longer tell where his intellect ended and his emotions began. He felt like an abandoned baby, a jumbled mass of raw nerves, tears, and pain.

She'd betrayed him. How had he blown it? Or was this her plan all along—to give him a hope that he didn't even know he could harbor, and then dash it, all so she could be set free from her bedroom prison? How could she see through him better than he could see himself?

How long until Nicholas came to see him? He would notice Icelyn's absence soon. Torrain watched as the dawn broke, the sun rising ominous red against a slate sky. How could he have been so stupid as to talk to Marjan? He hadn't been stealthy, and now they would suspect he'd helped Icelyn escape.

Torrain had to devise a story he could deliver without emotion, one that made perfect sense, while exonerating him in this messy Brathius affair. How unfair that he'd gotten caught up in this petty spat between father and daughter.

He gave himself up to his tears. Might as well get it all out now. What good was trying to deny that your heart was broken? It wasn't as if his heart would play along and hold together to maintain the illusion.

Tears fell in Brathius Tower, too. But here, they were not born of betrayal. Marjan's tears were angry.

"This is on your shoulders! You *had* to be Chief Cognate first. You couldn't just be her father!"

Marjan's accusations gave voice to the nightmares Nicholas had tried to ignore since he first discovered Icelyn's disappearance. "What choice did I have? All of Mountaintop teeters on the edge of destruction. This was not the time to focus on the ever-changing whims of our daughter."

"I wasn't asking you to give in to her whims. But what good did locking her in her room do? Making our home her prison?"

Nicholas knew this was his fault. He sunk into a chair, cradling his head in his hands. "How could she have slipped away? Her doors were locked. Bars on her windows." The question came out forcefully, laced with more accusation than Nicholas intended.

Marjan's voice caught. "I thought he only wanted to visit with her."

Marcel and Nandor made their best attempts to ignore their son's sobs and eat breakfast. Nandor wanted to break into Torrain's room and hold him while he confronted whatever demons were haunting him.

Marcel put that plan aside with a subtle shake of the head. "You can't stop a storm. You can only clean up the aftermath."

"Maybe Torrain handles such things differently," Nandor argued. "He was a sensitive child, his eyes often brimming with tears, his heart ever open, his face quick with a smile or frown."

"Until he grew up and exerted control, as an adult must. When's the last time his eyes brimmed with tears?"

A loud sob from Torrain's room answered his question.

"Could you fetch some ultralion from the market?" Marcel asked.

"I'll not," Nandor answered firmly. Just like Marcel, to try to end a conversation by diverting rather than resolving. She wouldn't let him send her away from her crying child, simply so he could ignore Torrain in peace.

"You are defying me?"

"I've found that when one has a craving, it is better for their character if they work to achieve its satisfaction. Relying on others—that's the way of the child, of the feeble one."

Marcel hated when Nandor argued with him by quoting his own words back to him. Context mattered, and Nandor rarely understood enough of it to see why things were appropriate for him to say, while inappropriate for her.

"I see," he replied, exasperated.

They returned to their acorn cakes.

Tranton and his Tarlinius goons joined Nicholas and Marjan as they headed toward Pannous Lab. Marjan despised their company.

"This should be a quiet matter between our two families."

"Matters involving the fate of humanity and the life of its next rightful leader cannot be kept quiet," Tranton declared.

"Dampen the drama, Tranton. Rebellious, willful children, pushed too far. Nothing more."

"You'd better hope that is the case. But we both fear it's not, don't we?"

Marjan suspected that Tranton was enjoying himself, and she hated him for it.

Tranton sighed. "Let's hope the Pannouses are in an agreeable mood."

Nicholas noticed Tranton and a Tarlinius nod toward one another, as if they knew something that no one else did. Normally Tranton saved his secrets for Nicholas; he felt a twinge of envy. "Of course they'll be agreeable. Why wouldn't they?" Nicholas stammered.

"Best to be prepared for any number of outcomes."

19

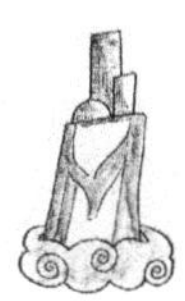

WHEN THEY HEARD the knock, Marcel and Nandor panicked. What awful luck, a visitor! The one time Torrain was an unstoppable geyser. Manners dictated that they invite their guests in, but it was difficult enough for the two of them to sit there and pretend Torrain wasn't sobbing. How could they uphold the ruse while entertaining? Nandor approached the door and lingered behind it, hesitant to open it.

A voice called softly through the door. "Nicholas Brathius, requesting just a crumb of your most precious possession, your time."

Nandor bristled at the request, her eyes opened anew to its hypocrisy. The phrase acknowledged that their time was valuable and theirs to spend, while the one speaking it knew full well they had no say in the matter.

She decided to take Nicholas at his word. A request? By definition, a request can be denied. Politely, of course.

"Our humblest apologies, Chief Cognate. Marcel and I find ourselves indisposed."

Nicholas was taken aback. "We'll give you a moment to gather yourselves," he spoke in a low voice through the door.

"We will not be available today."

Marcel rose to join Nandor. "What are you doing?" he scolded. "You are being improper."

"To entertain the Chief Cognate while our son blubbers like a child would be more improper."

Marcel whispered, "But to deny him at our doorstep?" He raised his voice and spoke to Nicholas through the door. "Perhaps we could meet outside of our house. In the Center Green. Alongside the pools near Waterpump."

Nicholas and Marjan sensed Tranton's displeasure at the exchange. Marjan took the lead, with an edge to her voice. "You are proposing meeting in public, like two nervous Intendeds during their first Bonding Session? We must misunderstand you."

The Tarlinius skirted the edge of the lab. He pointed toward a high window—Torrain's room. Muffled cries escaped from it.

Tranton nodded his head, as if he had figured it all out.

Marjan shot him a nasty look. "Let us handle this."

"So far, this is very much out of hand," Tranton cooed.

Marjan tried a pleading voice. "Marcel and Nandor, as the parents of your son's Intended, I ask that you let us in. We need to discuss something with you."

They waited for what felt like forever, but finally the door opened.

As soon as Nandor saw Tranton she held the door firm. "No. We will open our doors to you. Not him."

Tranton placed a strong arm on the door and pushed against it. Nandor couldn't hold it against his weight.

"Nicholas trusts me. We're here to see Torrain."

Marcel helped Nandor with the door and held it firm. "The boy's in no mood to talk to anyone."

Tranton continued to push. "I care little for moods. Open immediately, by order of the Chief Cognate."

Nandor didn't like what she saw in Tranton, and the way he said Torrain's name sounded like a threat. "I'm not familiar with the section of the Code that allows the Chief Cognate to force himself into a Cognate's lab. You will not be seeing Torrain today. I'm sorry, that's final."

Marjan tried to lighten the confrontation, which had grown tense quickly. "Tranton, leave us. We'll handle this with Nandor and Marcel. Nicholas and I no longer require your help."

Nicholas nodded, to Tranton's disappointment.

"That is not your decision to make," he hissed at them. "Torrain must be held accountable!"

Nandor had heard enough. "Accountable for what? Leave. He is suffering, and he doesn't need you to add to his misery. Get out!" Nandor shoved Tranton toward the door. She struck him three times.

Nicholas and Marjan gasped, frozen. Such violence! This was beneath the behavior of even the lowliest Veritas. It was angry, passionate, and beastly.

Marcel attempted to restrain his wife, but she could not be reined in.

"Nandor, my dear friend, what has become of you? Calm your heart!" Marjan could barely get the words out.

Tranton remained placid despite the barrage. "Consider this a final warning, Marcel and Nandor. Grant us access to your child or suffer the consequences. We may even need to take him away from you."

His calm threat ignited Nandor. She dug her nails into Tranton's arm, leaving deep scratches behind, drawing blood.

Nicholas did his feeble best to placate Tranton. "Tranton, I'm sure Torrain's involvement was an accident." None of them had ever been in a situation like this before. Nandor continued digging her hands into Tranton as he winced, never breaking eye contact with him. "What we all need is to step back and breathe, take a quiet moment to reflect before—"

An unearthly crack split the sky and silenced Nicholas. His ears rang. They coughed and blink their burning eyes at the cloud of smoke that engulfed them.

Nandor slumped against him and grew limp.

Marcel was the first to notice. "Nandor?"

Nicholas and Marcel sank to the ground, setting Nandor down as a crimson circle grew outward and stained her robe. Everyone was silent, stunned in the wake of the blast.

Marcel looked up at the Tarlinius in horror. "What have you done?"

Tranton crouched down beside Nandor and examined her. Blood dripped from her onto Marcel, pooling beneath them.

"Mom?"

Torrain swung open his door, drawn by the unnatural sound. Marcel looked at his son with tears in his eyes.

Nicholas could not believe it. Had the Tarlinius been holding *a gun*? How was that possible? Guns were a relic of the past; as far as he knew, none had even made the trip up to Mountaintop.

Tranton stood over everyone, wiping his hands carefully, as if they were covered in blood.

Torrain ran to his fallen mother's side. "Mom! What's happened?"

"Unfortunately, she's been wounded." Tranton held his arm up, the angry red scratches on display. "Brower was protecting me against her attack."

Nicholas shrank at the sight of the gun. "I didn't ask for this. Where did you get that…that…"

"It's a gun, a great weapon, Nicholas. If you think none had been brought to Mountaintop, you underestimate just how much the Apriori loved them. But don't worry, I assure you that only those loyal to me, and you, have any in their possession."

Their eyes all turned to Nandor as she gave her last gasp. She didn't tell Torrain and Marcel that she loved them. She didn't say or do anything other than quietly pass. Torrain crouched beside her, watching as her reddish skin lost color and settled into an eerie gray. He knew she was gone.

Torrain stood and faced Tranton and Brower's gun, his face twisted in pain. "What evil have you brought into this lab?"

Tranton breathed a tired sigh. "She was a wonderful woman, and my heart aches for your loss. But I implore you, back away, lest any more blood be spilled."

Marcel restrained his son.

Tranton smiled, satisfied. "Now let's talk about what happened last night."

20

I RUN FIVE hundred steps downhill. Away from *him,* hoping not to see *him.*

Jarvin.

I know, though, that I have to turn around. Even if it means struggling through the difficult upward trudge to make up the distance I foolishly fled down the mountainside, I must see what's become of him.

I dread seeing him again, lashed to the tree, his body broken. I feel the outer edges of terror close in as I recognize the area. This is the place. He's near.

I pretend that a noble impulse drives me toward Jarvin. I must pay him the proper respects. Perhaps recite funeral words taken from the Code, over his body, as is tradition.

I know myself well enough, though. Nobility alone could not drive me back up a steep path toward ever-growing terror. In looking for Jarvin, I really hope to find Adorane, or hints of his being there.

I suppose I've made my decision about what I will do next: Find Adorane. And I know that Ad would have taken the expedition to Jarvin as soon as they scaled the Wall. He's the one with the noble impulses. I'm just the one trying to find him.

Jarvin no longer hangs in the tree, exposed. Instead, in the moonlight I find a freshly dug mound of dirt, intricately decorated with twigs and leaves and stone. The Veritas and their love of beauty! Though I know, logically, that such things are a waste of time and effort, the sight of it takes my breath away.

I leave Jarvin's grave exactly as I found it.

I notice that some of the twigs are fastened together to form the same X shape I observed during the Veritas secret singing ceremony. It's a sure sign that Adorane has been here. But the sight of the ancient symbols makes me uneasy—a remnant of the past, dark and beastly, beyond my understanding.

I find no other indication of where Ad and his team could be. My face grows flush as I realize the depth of my naiveté. I'm no tracking expert. How am I supposed to figure out where they went next? What am I doing out here, without even my makeshift spear?

I am seized by the urge to run blindly into the darkness, but I surprise myself. Jarvin deserves at least this, I decide, as I return to his grave. I will recite the appropriate portions of the Code over him. Coming from the Chief Cognate's daughter, this would be an honor no other Veritas could dream of receiving.

I kneel beside the grave, the somber tone of my voice surprising me. "A speck at the edge of the cosmos. A blip on the backdrop of eons. Yet among the Kith, you found meaning. In our thoughts, you will continue. The best any can ask for, and precisely what all are granted."

I wish Adorane were here. In the darkness, I raise my eyes to the X shape before me, and I shiver.

21

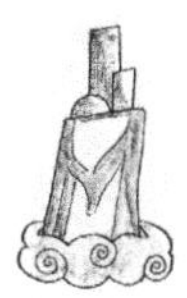

THE MAP HAD been detailed and accurate, and Tranton felt a glimmer of pride at his forefather's cartographic skills. Most of the marked areas were too far down the Mountain for Tranton to dare go, but the one that was near enough was astonishing.

In a cave just above Cloudline, nearly completely obscured by thick brush and dense fog, Tranton found a battery of mysterious machines that *were still running*. Electricity, up here! How was this possible? What could their purpose be?

Also, a cache of weapons—enough guns to arm all the Tarlinius. But all this was overshadowed by Tranton's larger discovery: scrolls. A hidden library. He learned a history of the Nilsing family that he'd never known. As he read through, he grew to understand the role he must play. Humanity relied on him, as it had on his ancestors hundreds of years ago.

He finally understood what his mother had meant when she'd said *Nilsings are great. Nilsings have always been great. And they will always be great.*

Tranton now knew. The Nilsings were not only great. They had always been, and should still be, the true leaders of Mountaintop.

Tranton regretted Nandor's death. Casualties were unavoidable in this battle he'd been forced to wage, but Nandor's had been unnecessary. It served no purpose. He was furious at Brower Tarlinius' eagerness to use his gun.

Tranton hated where this was headed. A heavy darkness had fallen over the room. Even he was affected by the profound sadness that weighed on Torrain and Marcel, still seated on the floor beside Nandor. But he knew he had to move forward.

"I wish there was some other way. No man should have to lose his entire family in a day."

Marcel's face drained of color. "What do you mean?"

Torrain grew frightened. "Father, what is he saying? Nicholas, Marjan, what is he talking about?"

Marcel rubbed Nandor's cold, still hand, over and over, as if doing so could bring her back to life. He barely looked at his son.

Tranton, for once, remained silent. Nicholas couldn't look anyone in the eyes. The Tarlinius slipped out the front door, signaling to his kin to dig a grave for Nandor.

Marjan saw that it fell to her to explain. She put an arm around Torrain. She couldn't have known her action would be a trigger, but this reminded him of his mother, and brought a fresh batch of hot tears.

"Your Intended, Icelyn, is endangered. You are bound by the Code to find her and save her."

"Outside the Wall?"

"If that's where she is. Is that where she is?"

"I don't know. I have no idea. She left me. We shouldn't even qualify as Intended anymore. She wanted nothing to do with me." More tears —for his mother, for his broken heart, for the fear of what lay beyond the wall, for his wasted future. It all blurred together in a cacophony of pain.

"Even if you were no longer Intended, there's no practical difference. You'd be disbursed for kidnapping the Chief Cognate's daughter. Either way, you'll end up outside the Wall. At least this way you can leave Mountaintop a hero." She tried to keep her voice soft and encouraging, but as she said the words aloud, she knew how futile this was.

Of all the things Torrain had hoped to someday be, a hero had never even been on the list. Rage flared within him. "Kidnapping! She asked me to help her out, and I did. That's it! We spent a half an hour together, if that, and then she left me. How is that *kidnapping?* I thought she had finally started to love me. The only crime I committed was being stupid and pathetic."

"The Code is clear."

Torrain ached for his mother. She would have fought for him. She wouldn't accept this as inevitable. She'd push until something broke, even if the thing that broke was herself.

"Father, will you sit there in silence and allow this to happen? Mother would have done something." Everyone looked at Nandor's body. She was dead precisely because she had fought for Torrain. But Marcel was frozen, shocked, silenced by what he knew was inevitable.

Torrain grew cold as he realized there was no one left to fight for him. Nobody who would take a risk to defend him. He was alone.

"The Code is clear, son," Marcel whispered.

22

I AM THIRSTY. Water is what got me into this mess in the first place, and I forgot to pack even a drop when I fled Mountaintop.

My mind races. This kind of mistake causes people to die. I'm sure that Ad and his team brought enough water with them. I am supposed to be the smart one. Yet my mouth grows drier with every step I take.

Ad told me that Manzanita leaves can quench thirst. I grab a fistful and eagerly shovel them into my mouth, chomping down on them, only to spit them out right away. They're more bitter than anything I've ever tasted. I've probably poisoned myself.

I'm not equipped for life outside the Wall. I've always known that in an academic way, in a way that never had any consequences because I always thought I'd be *safely within* the Wall. But now I realize what my lack of knowledge means in the real world – a bitter taste, a dry mouth, a desperate thirst, increasing dizziness, and eventually death. I'd feared running into a monster and being devoured, but instead I'll die in the jaws of nothing but my own ignorance.

In long periods with no rain, how do animals get the water they need? I know I've read it, or heard it, but forgotten. Such things never interested me much. How your interests change. Now I care about nothing else.

My heart pounds in my ears and I sit to gather myself. I visualize the great pump in my chest, working away, as it's done for seventeen years now without taking a break. If I had any other belonging that was seventeen years old, I'd consider it ancient and worn out. But hopefully my heart has many years left in it. *Pump, pump, pump.*

Blood. Blood is liquid; it must have water in it. Of course. I could drink blood. That's how some animals do it—they eat other animals. They steal their water by sucking the life right out of them. Humans are made up of primarily water; I wonder if maybe I could figure out a way to drink just a bit of myself.

I lick some sweat from my forearm. It dampens my sand-dry mouth, but that's about it. This won't save my life.

I spy a bright yellow slug inching across a fallen log. It leaves a thick trail of iridescent slime in its wake. Slime is at least part water. I know what I must do. That slug is filled with water. I'd seen cruel boys squish them when I was younger. (Jarvin did, now that I think about it.) They'd leave behind a pile of ooze. I'm thirsty for the ooze.

I grab the slug, glad that it doesn't wriggle against my touch or make a noise in protest. I bite down on it, messily gnawing it in two. It is tougher and chewier than I expected. But despite its fortitude, I chomp through and am rewarded with a wet, gooey center. It tastes awful, but better than the leaves, at least.

The goo makes me feel less thirsty.

I set out to find another slug. A smile twists across my face at the horrid absurdity of the moment; look what I've become on my first night outside the Wall. Icelyn Brathius, Slughunter! But it feels like a plan, a step toward survival.

I stumble through the thick woods, squinting for a glimpse of yellow, but find none. Was that the only slug on this side of the Mountain? I laugh desperately. Will I die by failing in my hunt for a slow and stationary slug?

Despite the bright morning sun overhead, my vision is darkening, as if I'm entering a tunnel. The edge of my sight grows blacker, and I really I am losing my peripheral vision. I imagine that dangerous beasts hide on my right and left, just outside my shrinking field of vision. I turn my head to the left, then snap it back to the right. I imagine something is toying with me, dancing just beyond what I can see, ready to pounce whenever it grows tired of this game.

I've stumbled my way to a rocky edifice marked by multiple caves. These caves are not natural; they look to be cut by human hands. This must be the entrance to the Lost Labyrinth. Below me, miles of caverns, dug by my ancestors who were hoping to find metal, water, silicon—anything they could use to make life on Mountaintop more like what they had enjoyed Down Below. Miles of darkened emptiness that came to represent only dashed hopes and unfounded optimism.

My eyesight continues to fade, and my pulse pounds in my head, bringing searing pain. *Pump pump pump.* I may die, but at least my heart is still beating; I listen, fascinated. As I give myself over to the blackout, it seems fitting that I should die here, at the mouth of this monument to disappointment.

I fall to the ground. It's so comfortable here. Why didn't I do this earlier? The last thing I see before my sight fails is confirmation that I wasn't imagining the shadowy figures on my right and left. As I fade, they come to stand over me, peering down on me. They are just blurs to me now, and I know I should fear them, but I don't.

I hope it will all be over soon.

23

ADORANE PRETENDED NOT to hear his father. He wanted to stare and lose himself in the fire. The flickering flames shifted from one shape into another, and Adorane had always enjoyed pretending there was a message to be gleaned from what he saw. Fire was vibrant, and otherworldly. Couldn't it be a messenger bearing mysterious communications?

Adorane believed that familiarity with fire had robbed it of its mysticism. Legends had long maintained it was a gift from the gods, or even a stolen treasure. If one were to imagine what the world of the gods spilling over into the world of man would look like, fire would be a pretty good guess.

If you had never seen it before, wouldn't fire be magical? Wispy yet powerful, it has no mass, yet it fills whatever space it occupies.

"How should we prepare the men to journey through Cloudline?" Aclornis' voice rang out again through the darkness. All Adorane wanted was to be left alone, but he supposed he should take it as a compliment. Father was treating him as an equal, a trusted advisor. And he knew he'd find no messages in the fire tonight.

"Do they know?" Adorane asked.

"They've heard whispers," Aclornis replied.

"But do they *know?*" Adorane insisted.

"Only we know what lurks within Cloudline, son. They have only fear and rumor."

Adorane grabbed a knife and transformed a branch into a spear. "It's worse than anything their minds' eyes could conjure, I'm sure of that."

When Nicholas had shared Mountaintop's ancient history with everyone gathered at Kith Hall, he had left out one notable aspect of the shameful part the Veritas had played.

It was true that the Veritas, many of them descended from those humans entrusted to keep society safe from harm (known to the Apriori as the military, the police, firefighters, and the like), had failed when the Threat Below arose. But there were heroes among the Veritas, even if Cognate history omitted them from the record. Aclornis and Adorane knew because their ancestor, Oliver Hailgard, had written extensively of the journey up the mountain and the sacrifices many Veritas made to ensure humanity's survival. They guarded these documents in their round, the greatest treasures they owned.

Gallons of Ascenders' blood spilled in Cloudline, that foggy boundary between the lower and higher mountain. Oliver wrote that twenty-five thousand Cognates and Veritas set out on the trip up the Mountain, but fewer than five hundred survived.

The Threat Below, the horrors that had slaughtered humanity, cannot breathe above ten thousand feet in elevation, Oliver had written. They die from lack of oxygen, just as humans drown under water. They can survive up to about seven thousand feet, but with terrible side effects. At that elevation they grow desperate and succumb to a condition early Cognates described as *mountain madness.*

It bore many of the hallmarks of the disease formerly known as rabies. Creatures afflicted by mountain madness were highly aggressive, even more than they were Down Below (where they were already lethal) and showed no inclination to back down. Most attacking animals will retreat if you demonstrate that you are a threat to their life; but mountain madness robbed the creatures of this logic, making them even more deadly.

Cloudline, a thick, soupy patch of fog and mist, circled the entire Mountain between five and eight thousand feet of elevation. A two-mile journey as the crow flies was required to pass through it. Though no one had checked in the last three hundred years, Oliver Hailgard claimed it had been filled with desperate, hungry creatures—relentless, fast, and terrible. These were like the sickened animal that leaves its home in the wilderness and starts foraging through garbage; the mad beasts were rejected by their own and had grown even more dangerous because of it.

Oliver had drawn sketches of what he had seen. His drawings looked like mostly shadows, motion. Adorane had studied Oliver's detailed rendering of a human body after the creatures had torn through it.

Adorane shook off the chill. He wasn't sure he even believed in the Threat Below anymore—the only hint that something lurked there was what had happened to Jarvis. "We don't know that there's still anything in Cloudline. It's different now, we know that."

This was true. Originally, by all accounts, Cloudline had been a seasonal phenomenon. It seemed to happen in June, when a heavy marine layer would blow in from the ocean and collide with warmer inland winds. But shortly after the Kith had ascended, Cloudline became a permanent fixture. It grew thicker and murkier. Many early Ascenders made note of this. There hadn't been a day in almost three hundred years when Cloudline hadn't been thick. No one in Mountaintop could see the valley floor. All you could see in Mountaintop was the top of the mountain breaking through the clouds, like an island in the sky.

Aclornis could sense the danger waiting for them beyond. "Make another twenty of those spears, and we'll warn the men later tonight. We enter Cloudline tomorrow morning at first light."

24

I OPEN MY eyes, but everything is so dark it's as if light had never existed. Am I dead? Is this it? Some low-level perception, but nothing left to perceive. Only the thoughts in my head, the memories of the life I lived.

I adjust to the oppressive darkness, and my other senses awaken. I hear a faraway drip. The echo makes me feel as though I'm in a large room. It's chilly. I'm lying on small pebbles, dirt, and stone.

Am I alive? Am I in the lair where the Threat Belows drag their prey before they have a meal? Terror courses through my body. I won't give them the satisfaction of hearing me scream.

I've awakened to my thirst, and the sound of that drip makes my mouth drier. When I try to get to my feet, I'm jerked back to the floor.

Someone (*something?*) has restrained my waist and chest. Cords tether me to the ground. I begin working against them, frantic to free myself.

My thirst isn't going to kill me. Something else will first. I hear it coming now.

25

WHEN ACLORNIS' EXPEDITION had left Mountaintop, the Kith crowded together and cheered. Torrain knew he wouldn't receive that kind of send-off, but part of him entertained visions of a weak imitation. The official story was that he was off to save Icelyn. Didn't he deserve a crowd?

The rest of the Kith believed that lie as much as he did. He was being punished, sent to die. No one showed up to say goodbye.

Not even Marcel.

Torrain thought about how Nandor hadn't been able to say goodbye before she died. Now Marcel wasn't going to either—he just lay uselessly in bed inside the darkened room he hadn't left in the past day.

"Here's a spear. The tip has been hardened in the fire. It's already slain ultralions, so it's a proven weapon." The Tarlinius rambled on about the supplies Torrain had been given. In the back of his mind, Torrain knew he should pay attention. But he'd be facing more than just ultralions, and he couldn't see how this spear could do much against the Threat Below.

"Here's three days' worth of water. That should be enough to get you through Cloudline."

Cloudline. Torrain shuddered. He was a Cognate. He should be learning about the conditions that made Cloudline possible and the vegetation that sprouts there. He should be writing a paper about that thick ring of mist and fog. He shouldn't be *passing through* the place.

It was hopeless. Even if he somehow survived, he wouldn't be welcome back into Mountaintop without Icelyn, and she was probably already dead.

The Tarlinius heaved the heavy leather pack and crashed it down on Torrain's shoulders. Torrain could barely stand under the massive burden.

"It weighs more than I do."

"It's a shame you're not a Veritas."

For the first time in his life, Torrain agreed with this sentiment.

"Well, that's it." The Tarlinius nodded toward the Wall. "Go."

Torrain looked back at Mountaintop. He didn't know what he was waiting for. Marcel wasn't going to come crashing through the forest to give his son one last embrace. But Torrain did see movement in the underbrush.

Marjan emerged from the thick shrubs. Her eyes were red, her face streaked with sweat and tears.

She embraced Torrain.

"You're a smart boy, Torrain. Your mother lives on in you."

Torrain nodded silently, his eyes downcast. He didn't know what to say.

"You've always been more Nandor than Marcel. Even if you don't realize it yet. Even if they branded you a Pannous. Remember that."

Torrain stood up straight under his pack.

"She was a fighter, Torrain. This is not a death sentence, because you're a fighter too. Find Icelyn. Return a hero."

The supplies didn't feel as heavy now. Torrain gripped the spear in his fist.

Marjan had given him his mother again.

26

CALM, ICELYN. BREATHE. Calm. I will not die panicked. If these are my last moments before I pass into the ether, I will infuse them with meaning.

Mother. She betrayed me, but she loved me. I hope she knows I loved her. The times we spent exploring the ruins of Talmer's Folly. She'd pretend to be an original Ascender, Sean Brathius' daughter, nicknamed Lovely. One time as a child I pretended to be a Threat Below, chasing her, snarling and growling. She didn't correct me or tell me not to speak about such things (even though imitating a Threat Below was forbidden in the Code). No, Mother ran away, acting terrified, screeching. I had roared with laughter.

When I caught her, I gave her a hug. It was hot, sweaty, and so wonderful that it almost felt wrong, though nothing in the Code forbids that kind of contact between mother and daughter. It's just something that Cognates seldom do—unlike the Veritas, who are always wrestling, tickling, and rolling around like beasts.

I hear sounds. *Thump, drag. Crunch, crunch.* Something is coming. *Do not listen, Icelyn. Think about your life.*

Father. He is weak, but I can't hate him for it. One day I hope to be strong enough to overcome his weakness and make him a real leader. I know he could be great. I have always adored him; he has always shown me kindness, especially for a Cognate. Expectations placed on Cognate fathers are low. Most give their station to their children and invest nothing else. Father gave me an excess of his time. We walked through town together at least three times a week, him putting up with my silly, probing, annoying questions.

"But how, Father? How do we know there aren't other villages, other groups of people? Other Kith?"

"Don't you think we'd have met them by now?"

"Maybe they live on another mountain, far away from here. Or at the bottom of the ocean. Or in the middle of the desert, where the Threat Below don't bother going."

"I think it's better to concentrate on what we know for sure. The Kith who live here. That's it. They are our world."

"Well, and the animals."

"True—the ultralions, ultrabears, slugs, lizards, and birds. All the living things that share the Mountain with us."

"I mean the animals that live below, too. Tall creatures called *giraffes* that look like they walk on stilts. Burly beasts with horns called *buffalo*."

"Yes, you can think about them if you'd like, but you'll never see them. They might as well be imaginary. It's better to learn about the things you might someday see."

"Shouldn't we know more about the Threat Below?"

"We will never see them, Icelyn."

Thump, drag. Thump, drag. Louder now.

I wish Father had been right. I have always wanted to learn more about the Threat Below. But now I am about to learn way too much—and not in the way I'd prefer.

I pull against my restraints, but it's futile. Instead, I force my thoughts onto Adorane, the deepest wellspring of happy memories. What better way to make the transition from life into ether than by dwelling on the times I spent with Ad?

Thump, drug. Crunch. I hear breathing now.

One time I fell while chasing Adorane through the woods. I tried to shrug it off, because that's what he would do. (I never once saw him acknowledge any physical pain, even when he broke his arm falling from the Big Boulder when we were seven. He'd only winked and said he was happy because now the bones would grow together stronger. Oh, Ad.)

I had fallen and my ankle was already twice the normal size. I could feel my heartbeat in the swollen mass that was turning red and purple before my eyes. I blinked hard, but tears rolled down my cheek. I prepared for Ad's ribbing. But instead, he took my leg gently in his strong hands and elevated it.

Despite the pain, his warm hands felt good on my skin.

And then—it seems silly, but in my memory, *Ad started singing*. I know this can't be—I've never heard the Veritas sing until yesterday. But I ache to hear him sing now, and he does in my memory. I've never been happier than hearing his haunting, trembling voice. Every one of my senses was overwhelmed in that moment, the sight and scent of Ad, so close. His touch on my skin, the delight I took in the song. In my memory, I felt I would die from sensory overload.

I miss Ad. I hear his song in my imagination, and when I do it washes away the coming thumps, drags, and crunches. His song makes me think of the sun that shone overhead that day when he lifted me and carried me back to town. The Code forbids physical contact between unbetrothed juveniles except in the case of emergency. I was thankful for that sprained ankle for creating an exception.

I blink, confused. The sun is not in my imagination. But the sun is not the sun, either.

It's a torch. Steadily approaching me.

I wait for the first searing flash of pain. I clench my eyes shut and in my mind's eye see Jarvin, hollowed out. I know what to expect. I'm not here, I tell myself. I'm being carried through the woods by Ad. He's singing. His warm skin is damp with sweat. My heart is happy.

"Another one disbursed—and so young. A pity."

The voice is kind and warm. Even if the Threat Below could speak, which they can't, they'd never sound like this.

An elderly woman crouches beside me, gently loosening the tethers. She hands me a heavy mug. Confused, I drink. Water. I've never appreciated it enough. My mouth and throat are full, yet I wish I could drink more.

"We didn't want you to awaken and go wandering through the mines, so we secured you to the ground. I hope that didn't give you a fright."

The woman is joined by four others. Each of them bears some deficiency. The woman who has done all the speaking is elderly. (So curious to see an actual *old woman!*) There's a young boy with his left leg missing below the knee, replaced by a gnarled piece of oak. A man wearing a patch peers at me with his one good eye. A woman with a bright red stain covering half her otherwise beautiful face holds a hand out to me. I grab the hand.

She lifts me to my feet and puts a comforting arm around my shoulders. "Whatever horrors the Kith have subjected you to, be at peace now. You are safe, hidden away with the rest of the rejected, here in the Mines."

27

TORRAIN STOOD AT the top of the Wall. The sun had set, and the forest below teemed with the frightening sounds that accompanied oncoming darkness. The noises would have scared him less had he be been able to attribute each to a known source—that noise was just a quail, this one a lizard, that just a frog. But everything blended together in a soft haunting roar, alien and unknown.

He glanced back at Marjan, whose eyes were wet, and the Tarlinius, who appeared bored. He delayed the inevitable, looking back over his shoulder, giving his father one more chance to appear even though he wagered it wouldn't happen.

He was right. Bitterness rose up in Torrain's throat, and he jumped.

For the first time, his feet touched ground outside of Mountaintop. It felt untamed, wild, and foreign. He gripped his spear as he made slow progress over rocky outcropping and through scratchy thick foliage. There were no paths—just walls of obstacles telling him which way not to go.

Inside the Wall, the Tarlinius grunted to Marjan and turned back toward Mountaintop. She stared at the point where Torrain had been. She knew that she had witnessed a slow-motion execution. Outside the wall, Torrain would find only death.

* * *

Mountaintop had changed.

Even just last week, members of the Kith had gathered on the Village Green all day and late into the night, exchanging stories amid laughter. Now the streets were empty, the rounds and labs closed tightly, the community members in hiding. Except for the occasional Tarlinius proudly displaying his shiny rifle while patrolling, it appeared to be a ghost town.

Being the ruler of this is worse than being no ruler at all, Marjan thought to herself.

"You'll stand still until you're checked, please!" A Tarlinius pointed a rifle at her. Marjan's first instinct was to protest, but memories of poor Nandor stopped her. What was the use of standing up for yourself if you end up bleeding out on a desolate street?

"Your business, please? You need clearance to wander Mountaintop past dark."

This was a new regulation. No doubt Tranton's brainchild.

"I was seeing Torrain Pannous off on his quest to save my daughter," she said proudly.

The Tarlinius startled as he noticed who he had stopped. "Uhm—good, you are conducting legitimate business. We have to stop anyone we see. We've heard of schemes to steal from Winter Rain Supply, which would hurt us all."

"No need to apologize."

"Please do not mistake my explanation for an apology. No one is above the Code."

Despite her misgivings, Marjan couldn't let that go. "Restrictions on our normal freedoms are not part of the Code. We are, after all, not children."

"Tranton and Nicholas have added to the Code."

"There is a process for adding to the Code. One that involves all Cognates and the Veritas leaders."

"In Tranton's words, a crisis doesn't allow for the luxury of a *process*." The Tarlinius stroked his gun, sending fear flaring within Marjan's chest. "Or the luxury of debate, either. You ought to get home to your husband."

As Marjan entered Brathius Tower, she felt Tranton's dreaded presence. She wasn't surprised at all to see him pacing through the great room as Nicholas scrambled to write down his every word. The Chief Cognate, reduced to a subservient scribe!

Tranton appeared to savor the taste of his words leaving his mouth. "For the good of the Kith and the survival of Humanity, we grant the Chief Cognate and those who operate under his authority permission to act vigorously on behalf of community defense and exoneration for any action that must be taken to defend Kith safety."

Marjan stayed in the doorway. "Tranton, I'd like to speak with my husband. Alone."

"When we're finished."

She approached Nicholas and put her hand on his weary shoulder, reading over what had been written.

"I believe you've done enough for today. I know when Nicholas needs rest."

Tranton bowed his hea, acting the part of a gracious servant. "Of course. I'll return when Nicholas sends for me."

Marjan closed the door behind Tranton, and pulled a thick wooden bolt to lock it.

Nicholas rose, unwilling to look at her. "I believe I will take that rest —"

"All these weapons, rifles, and bullets that now patrol our streets— the expedition that went Down Below could have used them."

Nicholas sighed. He'd hoped to avoid this conversation. "We need to protect the Winter Rain Supply—"

"So you think the weapons are better aimed toward frightened members of the Kith than the vile beasts that roam down below?" Marjan's voice rose in anger. "And why didn't you *tell* me we had a store of guns and ammunition?"

Nicholas hesitated, and she sank into the seat next to him.

"Oh, God. You didn't know, did you? Tranton hid it from you. Who is really in charge here?"

"I am! Without a hint of doubt I can tell you that."

"Then you need to relieve Tranton of his duties. He's steering you off course. If we follow his path, the Kith may survive, but only by betraying what the Kith are."

"I couldn't. I can't."

Marjan knew why. "Because the Tarlinius are loyal to Tranton, aren't they? And the guns belong to Tranton. He controls it all. You didn't even know they existed."

Nicholas looked at Marjan, a moment of honesty between long-time allies. "I don't know, Marjan. And I don't want to find out. I'd rather wait until I have viable alternatives, if it turns out that Tranton is the one in charge."

Marjan said what they both knew. "He *is* in charge." Marjan held Nicholas close to her. "We'll come up with those alternatives together. For now, continue as you were."

Nicholas chuckled darkly. "As his lapdog?"

Marjan smiled ruefully. "As a *mighty* lapdog. Exactly. I just needed to know that you're a lapdog by strategy, not out of weakness."

Nicholas placed his head on her chest gratefully, exhausted. Marjan stroked his back, calming him. "In the meantime," she said, "let's figure out what to do with those guns."

28

THE LOST LABYRINTH. We'd been warned about this place as children: that it was haunted, cursed. Our ancestors had dug for centuries and found only deadly accidents and empty holes.

I've always been told that the souls of dead miners roamed these darkened corridors—which was easy to laugh off at the time, since the Kith don't believe in souls, ghosts, demons, or hauntings of any kind. Still, down here in the dark, there is a difference between what I know and what I feel—and feelings have the advantage.

I follow the elderly woman, Jalda, through the twisted, narrow passages. Everything is dark to me, and I trip over roots, stony outcrops, and long-discarded machinery. Jalda knows her way around, moving unnervingly fast for an older person, making turns without hesitation. Embarrassment keeps me from asking her to wait, so I hustle to keep pace.

"The Kith are a hollow people! That they would leave a tender, young thing such as yourself alone, vulnerable to whatever may lurk outside the Wall. They've done it to all of us, you know." While Jalda is kind to me, she possesses nothing but vitriol for the Kith.

I decide not to reveal my identity.

"Nicholas Brathius! He pretends to have a compassionate heart, and yet he shoved me out into the Wilderness just because I fell and snapped my hip."

Father would never disburse someone for being injured. "Oh, you must have been mistaken. Kith doctors heal those with injuries. They take great pride in it."

Jalda snorts. "Not if you're a Veritas on the wrong side of sixty years! Then they just disburse you to your death. Didn't you know that?"

I shook my head. I don't believe it.

"Well, it's true. I'm sure they told you that they transferred me to the Elder's Lodge. That's what they tell people. But I was left outside the Wall to die, just like everyone else who lives here now. Finly, whose test scores weren't high enough to remain among the Cognate. Persopile, who was from a Veritas family famous for their beauty yet born with a mark on her face."

It must be the Opal family. They are known for their deep brown almond-shaped eyes, high cheekbones, and statuesque figures. I'd heard that they suffered much grief just before I was born when their daughter did not survive childbirth. Had that baby actually been cast aside because of the stain on her face? I shiver in horror.

Jalda leads me through a small opening I would have missed on my own. I squeeze and push until I enter into a four-foot-tall cavern. I crouch to avoid hitting my head on the sandstone ceiling.

Jalda produces a mug from her coat and holds it toward me.

"Drink, my child."

I lift it to my lips and wince at the cruel trick. The mug is empty.

Jalda erupts in laughter. "You have to fill it first!" She points to the corner of the cavern, and my eyes take a moment to adjust to what looks like a darker stain running down the rock wall. My ears pick up on it first—the drip. A natural spring down here would be a miracle; I've always been told that no springs exist up here on the Mountain.

I run to it and put my mug against the wall. It takes a long time to fill even a quarter of the way. This is not a gushing waterfall.

"It takes a full day to fill one barrel—just enough to keep all of us who live in the Mine from becoming dehydrated," Jalda explains. "In the summer it slows to a trickle."

"Thank you for letting me have a drink." I gulp it down, wondering if I can ask for more.

"Of course, child! If you are thirsty, we let you drink—no matter who you are. We don't believe it's a waste of water as long as someone gets to drink it. You see, a spirit flows through all of us, and to treat any one of us with cruelty is to tear a hole in that spirit."

Blast, what is happening with this madness? I can't walk three feet without running into someone blabbering about spirits and souls these days.

"Hurting others damages everyone, even yourself. We have an opportunity to strengthen that spirit by caring for those that the Kith toss away like garbage. Even if you're old, weak, damaged, or..."—she examines me carefully—"...whatever it is that's wrong with you. You look like you might be at risk of fainting spells. Or maybe fits of hysteria?"

I'm not sure what that looks like, exactly, but I don't think it's a compliment.

"Um—no, nothing as odd as all that, I promise you."

"Then tell me: Why did they abandon you, child?" She holds her torch close enough to my face that I can feel the heat of the flame. I feel like a bug under a magnifying glass.

She starts at the realization.

"Why would they abandon...Icelyn Brathius?"

I want to run.

Jalda shoves me ahead of her. I'm glad I didn't run when she realized who I was, because in the dim light I can see drop-offs and open pits and my certain death had I attempted escape. Instead, Jalda is joined by Persopile Opal, the woman with the stained face, and they bind my arms and feet with thick, black roots.

"Please! You don't understand. I fled Mountaintop—"

"Silence now, Brathius! We'll see what Beloved Leader has to say about your story!"

"No, you don't understand. I left because I didn't agree with what was going on there!" I try to wriggle my hands free, but Jalda pulls the roots tighter, glaring at me.

"You are a spy," she hisses. "You came to take our water, didn't you? Invading a kind, defenseless people—a people that you've already cast out? You should be ashamed of yourself!"

What good would I do as a spy? I'm too easy to recognize! I wonder how she calls herself kind while treating me this way. Is she blind to irony? Or maybe she didn't score well on her proficiency test, and that's why she had been disbursed. (The injured hip story sounds suspect to me.)

I stumble and fall, which only enrages Jalda. "Can't stay on your feet, Brathius? How is that possible, considering you're young and healthy? I'd expect that of the old, the broken."

Jalda has unresolved issues with the Kith and the Brathius family, I tell myself, and I am simply the instrument through which she has chosen to work them out.

Persopile sneaks a look at me, and I can tell she is embarrassed by Jalda's behavior. God, she is beautiful. Clear brown eyes, almost amber in color. High cheekbones and a finely sculpted mouth. Except for the stain, she looks just like Hares, the younger sister she's never met. Once Persopile "died," Hares had been born to take her place. I wonder suddenly, painfully, if Mother and Father will have another child to take my place.

How terrible to be replaced. I hope Persopile never has to find out about Hares. Yet—what luck to have a sister! Families in Mountaintop are fortunate to have even one child; multiple children are not allowed. (At least in my generation. Back about fifty years ago, the Kith numbered well over a hundred. It was the tail end of a period of population growth caused by some unpermitted births and general optimism. The one-child policy had been enacted to gradually decline the population until we had to grow again.) To have brothers and sisters—I can't imagine what that must be like.

"You're beautiful, Persopile." I can't help blurting out the words—they are true.

Jalda pulls me to my feet. "Flattery won't change your fate. Beloved Leader will determine your punishment, and Persopile's appearance will have no say in the matter!"

"I just thought she should know."

Persopile speaks softly. "Thank you."

"She knows," Jalda replies, cutting Persopile off. "No thanks to you and your kind. If you had your way, that pretty face would've been eaten by beasts or frozen in the cold!"

"If I had my way, we'd be friends." It's true. I like Persopile—without effort, right away, which rarely happens to me with anyone.

"I've half a mind to think you're mocking her, Icelyn Brathius. Oh, I've heard about you—yes, I have. Rumors float down from Mountaintop and collect here, deep underground. You're a proud one, they say—you think you're better than everyone else."

Is that really what people say? I'm no more arrogant than is appropriate to my station.

"Down here, under the dirt, you're just another shadow. We'll let Beloved Leader decide whether you're better than us!"

I fall again. Persopile helps me to my feet. "I know you aren't mocking me," she says quietly.

Jalda keeps us all moving. "You've never lived among them, Persey. You've been raised by the accepting, the loving, the kind." I fall again, gashing my knee. I feel the warm stream of blood run down my leg and bite my lip to keep from shouting out in pain.

Jalda hauls me to my feet once again. "Move it. We're almost there. Beloved Leader will set all things right. We're fortunate that he's here with us now to resolve this crisis. It's rare that we are blessed with his physical presence."

We arrive at a massive, rusty steel door. Guards are posted at either side of it, holding spears. They look past me as I stare. Then they pull the steel door open, and Jalda pushes me through.

The air is stiflingly hot. A bonfire thirty feet tall dominates a cavern that stretches as high as Brathius Tower. Stalactites of different lengths and colors hang overhead in bunches. It's the first time I've ever seen them outside of books, and even in my terrible situation, I am struck by their beauty.

"Approach me!" The voice booms from a stone throne carved into centuries of calcium deposits and stalagmite formations. I walk quickly toward the throne to get away from the blistering flame.

The voice belongs to a dark figure, who wears a cloak obscuring his head and face. To his right and left sit others, presumably a court of some kind.

I walk toward him with as much poise as possible with these stupid roots tied around my ankles.

"So the whispers are true. Icelyn Brathius, daughter of Chief Cognate Nicholas Brathius, great-great-great-great-great-granddaughter of Sean Brathius, leader of the original Ascenders, has deigned to pay us a visit. Tell me, Icelyn, how did you find yourself down here among the sick, weak, and twisted?"

I consider his question. My first instinct is to say that I fainted outside and was brought down here into the Mines, but I know that is not the answer they want to hear nor the one I want to give.

I roll over a thought that's been flitting about the edge of my mind since I'd met the people who live down here. These disbursed were expelled from Mountaintop in order to keep the Kith strong, and yet—look now!—the Kith are weaker than ever, on the verge of dying, and not as strong as those in the Mines. I can't fail to appreciate the irony.

Beloved Leader loses his patience. "Will you speak, Icelyn Brathius?

Your reputation would indicate that you will, even when you shouldn't." Laughter from the court. I am struck with uneasiness at being teased by people I've never met before, as if they are family or old friends.

I clear my dry throat, wishing I had been able to have another drink of water, and choose my words carefully. "If you have found a place where men are *not* sick, weak, and twisted, please share your secret. At least down here there is no falseness, and all is out in the open. In Mountaintop, they hide their imperfections in their hearts. Concealed flaws are the worst of all."

Beloved Leader chuckles, and I'm struck by a wave of warm nostalgia. By the time my thoughts catch up with my feelings, I'm too shocked to believe it. He lowers his hood and smiles. "See, I told you all—I trained her well. Welcome to the Mines, Icelyn Brathius."

Belubus—dear, wonderful Belubus!—holds his hand out to me. I grab it, and I make sure to catch Jalda's eye as my tutor pulls me into a strong embrace.

"You're still thirsty."

Belubus claps his hands and a servant limps into the opulent, well-lit chamber we've entered. The cave walls are covered in maroon velvet drapes, artwork, and tapestries from before the Ascension. They portray subjects the Apriori found interesting, like horses, kings, and soldiers.

Belubus' chamber is extravagant compared to his spartan lab in Mountaintop. A servant carries an ornately carved pitcher, made of a metal I'd never seen before, lustrous and yellow as the setting sun.

I hold out my mug, and the servant fills it. Despite the relief I feel while I drink, and the initial rush of joy at finding Belubus here in these dark mines, I'm struggling with something foreign to our relationship. As he speaks to me, I find that I want him to be quiet. I've only ever wanted to hear more of what he had to say, so this disturbs me.

"I imagine you are surprised, Icelyn, and have a thousand questions. I promise you will get the answers you seek."

I don't understand. His voice has always been a source of comfort and wonder to me; now I cannot listen to another word.

"I'm angry at you, Belubus." I say at the same time I realize it myself. "Living this life, hidden from me, when I thought you were dead."

"I have wanted to tell you, dear Icelyn! But how could I risk you telling your father—or worse, Tranton?"

Another facet of Belubus' deception dawns on me. He's an enemy of Father. He's secretly ruling over this community that despises Mountaintop. How could he care for me, a Brathius, as he leads those who harbor vile thoughts about Mountaintop? Simple—he cannot.

"Still thirsty?" Belubus summons the servant, who refills my mug. My former tutor is too eager. He knows I'm upset and hopes it's only dehydration. I am tempted to dash the water across the ground.

Water. *Wait, water! This solves everything.*

"Belubus! We must let Father know you've found another water source! It may not be too late to call Ad and his team back before they pass through Cloudline. This could be the solution to the crisis."

Belubus shifts uncomfortably and clears his throat. "I've considered this carefully. Icelyn, we cannot let Mountaintop know we exist."

He knows the fool's quest that Ad and his team have undertaken, one that will end in death. All to secure clean water. Yet he sits silently on a spring! He'd rather watch Mountaintop wither, and my best friend die in vain, than let Father in on his secret. *He's considered it carefully? How big of him.*

"Reconsider, dear Belubus." I struggle to keep my tone even. I've never once spoken harshly to my tutor. "Your decision will lead to the death of the Kith."

"In the same way their decisions promised death to every person who lives in the Mines."

Again, that grating voice, every word he speaks like a gnat buzzing in my ear.

"This is about revenge, then? You would choose to be petty, to condemn them to death to get back at my father?" I bite my tongue before I say anything more, even though I have words, sharp and pointed, stored up and in great supply. The nerve of Belubus! Sitting in this gilded chamber, more luxurious—and ridiculous—than anything found in Brathius Tower. Carved, polished mahoganies and precious metals, jewels and gems. Does he think he is a mythic king? He's nothing but a pitiful pretender, hiding in this hole he calls a kingdom, waging his own pathetic war against my father, the true leader of this mountain! Who launches a war without even notifying the opposing side?

"Icelyn, you've seen the spring. It can barely support the fifty souls who make the Mines their home. How could that water be enough for another hundred thirsty mouths? Tranton and your father would march on us with their guns and claim it for the good of the Kith, disbursing these unfortunate people—who look to me for protection—once again. I'd be powerless to stop it."

My soul flares with hatred, mostly because he is right. I stammer through my reply, embarrassed by my own lack of confidence. "My father would never do something so—"

"Your father wouldn't have to. Tranton would. If Tranton learns of our existence down here, we are doomed."

"So instead you bring doom to every man, woman and child in Mountaintop? It's not only Tranton and the Tarlinius who live there. Most are good, honest, innocent—unaware of how the people who hide in the Mines were mistreated." I have found my voice again.

"Their lack of awareness is a choice." It's not the first time I've heard Belubus say this, but it's the first time it's brought blood to a boil in my veins.

"Then you must make that choice on a daily basis, dear tutor."

He laughs. The condescension!

I cannot stay here. I know what waits for me above ground—thirst, exhaustion, fear, and likely death. But I'll face it all to escape what Belubus has become. (Or has always been, I suppose.)

"Belubus, thank you for your generosity. I'll be leaving the Mines now."

"Icelyn, it comes down to a simple lack of resources. Nobody is killing anybody. It's the same decision Mountaintop made decades ago; you're just on the other side of the coin now. Of course I'd rather everyone survive. But there isn't enough for everyone, and I have to look out for my own people."

My head spins with the logic of it all. What he says makes sense. God, I'm only seventeen years old. I cannot deal with the weight of these conversations, with realities where people die regardless of what choice one makes.

"Take me above ground, please."

Belubus sighs again. "I cannot do that."

Now I realize the truth. While the walls are covered with velvet and the floor lined with precious metals, this is a prison, and I may never get out.

29

TORRAIN THOUGHT HE'D be reduced to a bundle of fear wrapped up in self-pity and sadness once he leapt from the Wall. Instead, he was surprised to find that confidence surged through him.

The worst had come. Icelyn had rejected him. Father had ignored him. Mother was dead. He'd been exiled from the Kith. Everything worth worrying over had happened—and yet he'd survived. There was a freedom in losing everything.

Torrain made slow but constant progress through the overgrown brush. A thick knot of thistles cut into his forearms. The deep red color of blood broke through the fog that had filled his head for the past few days.

Torrain heard birds singing overhead. He climbed over fallen trees and around boulders, wondering why he'd never ventured into the woods before. He was more alive out here than he ever was cooped up in Pannous Lab.

Torrain hatched a plan. He'd travel down the Mountain. That's where Adorane and his team were headed, so Icelyn would follow. He would find her and tell her how little she meant to him. Then he'd leave her and be on his way. He would live Down Below, enjoying the world that others were too fearful to explore. If the woods only hours outside of Mountaintop were this grand, what incredible wonders waited for him below Cloudline?

He hadn't noticed when the birds had stopped singing. Suddenly he realized that the woods were silent. Through a cluster of pine trees, he spied a pile of rocks and pebbles. Curious, he ran toward it.

A grave, marked with a name. *Jarvin.*

Torrain knew Jarvin; he was Adorane's best friend. Had the expedition experienced a casualty already? No, Jarvin hadn't been a member of the expedition. How had Torrain never heard of Jarvin's death? A Kith death was monumental news in Mountaintop, because they were rare outside of childbirth. When had Jarvin died, and how?

And why was he buried out here, where no one could visit and pay their respects?

The woods, which had seemed vibrant and promising, now held dark secrets and whispered threats. People died out here and were put in the ground to rot for a lonely eternity. People his age, but even stronger and better equipped to fight.

Torrain turned back toward Mountaintop. What had he been thinking? He'd slink back, climb over the Wall, and hide on the outskirts of town until the trouble had blown over. Forget about the rest of the world.

He tried to run back up the Mountain, but felt like he was moving in slow motion. His breathing grew heavy, ragged, and loud.

Incredibly loud.

Torrain slowed to a walk and tried to control his respiration. Still, the gasps and wheezes continued.

Torrain held his breath, willing himself to be as quiet as possible.

The heavy rasps weren't coming from him.

30

I MUST ESCAPE. Belubus offers me a second-in-command position as his trusted advisor. No. Playing Tranton in this false monarchy holds no appeal.

I expected them to bind me like a prisoner, but Belubus is intent on catching this fly with honey instead of vinegar. I am given a well-appointed room, decorated with more relics from the Apriori. There's a metal stand that holds many candles at the same time. Heroes are carved into the base—leading their armies to victory over rival nations, slaying dragons, being attended to by women. I have a soft bed and a pitcher of water (what luck!), carpets on the floor, and paintings on the wall. This is the life Belubus hopes to seduce me into. It's tedious. He could have at least given me a shelf stuffed with books; it's like he doesn't even know me.

But I know him.

I knock on the locked door. Tethers or not, I am still held against my will. Belubus doesn't trust me not to tell Father about the Mines. But he's wrong about me. With time to think things through, I've decided that he's right—Tranton would destroy the people who live here, and I'd play a part in their death. I can't let Father know about this place.

Jalda answers through the door. Despite Belubus' instructions, she still treats me with unguarded suspicion, as if I were the one who personally signed her Disbursement Order. "What do you want?"

"I'd like to meet with Belubus. I've made my decision."

"Of course you have, little lady," she says, making no attempt to hide her condescension for me as she swings the door open.

The ridiculousness of this throne room. Grander than anything in Mountaintop. Down below the ground, in fetid darkness, my former mentor plays king with richer props than anything in that true seat of power, Brathius Tower. Who would have ever thought he could be charmed by this ornate nonsense? I swallow my thoughts and project reverence.

As I speak, I wonder how my face doesn't betray my dishonesty. "Belubus, I know you, and you know me too. It was rash emotion, from the shock of learning too much too soon, that caused me to doubt you earlier. I've since seen the wisdom of your words, and I would be honored to serve alongside you."

I detect relief in Belubus' face. I've fooled him, just as I did Torrain and Father. I've discovered a talent for deception, but it brings me no pride.

He extends a hand to me. "You will serve alongside me. Please forgive the lushness of this room. I'm still the humble academic you've trusted over the years—but, as you'll see, the ones who live down here require a show. It brings them comfort, helps them believe they are well taken care of."

"They *are* well taken care of. It is not just show."

He smiles. "No, it's not. I care about them deeply." I believe him.

If I'd been introduced to this situation in a different way, I might be proud of Belubus. He'd seen an injustice and corrected it. But I cannot forget that he's made me a prisoner down here in this musty pit.

"I have just one request, and of course I will understand if you deny it."

"I cannot spare even a drop of our spring water for Mountaintop—"

"No," I interrupt, "it's nothing to do with that. I understand that Tranton can't know. It's just that...you and I, we used to gaze at the stars. When I was a child, you would point out the shapes to me, the constellations, and tell me their stories."

"I remember." I knew he would. This was one of our favorite activities.

"Being down here, I miss the sky. I didn't get to say a proper goodbye to it."

Belubus shakes his head. "Very few are allowed above ground, Icelyn. Just myself and a few commissioned to gather essentials. It would arouse suspicion or jealousy in the others. Plus, it's dangerous out there."

I know that all too well, but I can't stay trapped here.

"Do you remember what I would say about the moon, when it was full, and all the stars around it? I used to say that they weren't stars at all, but baby moons—and one day they'd grow up and set off to light another world's night, just as their mother did for us."

Belubus lost himself in the fond memory. "One time I asked you who the father was, and you laughed and said, 'Silly tutor—why, of course it's the sun!'"

We laugh, as we did when I was ten years old. Belubus has no children of his own. I am as close as it comes for him.

"It's a full moon this week, silly tutor."

My words cast their spell and, despite Jalda's objections, Belubus is taking me aboveground. I will remain unbound. We will make the trip unaccompanied. Unguarded..

I planted a desire to relive our past in Belubus' heart. As I've learned with Torrain, a man in the grasp of desire is an unstable, irrational creature, capable of anything. Even a smart one like Belubus.

Belubus shares more stories from our past as we walk through the darkened passages. But I can't enjoy them because of my growing guilt.

"You used to sing a song, a haunting melody—always the same melody, but the words would change. They'd be about anything and everything or nothing at all, just whatever was going on in your heart and your mind at the time. Do you remember that song?"

He hums a tune. My god. Now that I hear it, I do remember. I'd forgotten singing altogether, but early on, even I would partake. *I used to sing?* Like some sort of feathered bird? How embarrassing.

"Oh, that was long ago. The things we are quick to outgrow."

"I didn't hear a no. You have never been afraid to say no, when no is the answer. Please, sing it for me. Indulge an old man."

I'm surprised as the melody comes to me. I hum quietly, my voice cracking at first, then growing more sure. I'm about to shame this man in front of his followers—and break his heart. I can spare a few notes to soften the blow. He stops and leans against the cool dirt wall, closes his eyes, and smiles.

"That's it. I could listen to that all day."

It's as if he's begging me to lose all respect for him. He's moved by my singing, like an animal soothed by stroking. It's beneath him—and me too. We're both brought lower by this indulgence. (Still, the song sounds pretty. I blush to admit that it stirs something in me, too.)

Once I finish the last lilting notes, Belubus leads me to a large, circular stone door that looks more like a boulder than anything manmade. He works on a number of locks and bars, turning a round dial back and forth according to a special code, pulling on ropes in a particular order, pushing buttons in the right sequence. There is no way I could have escaped on my own. This is my only choice.

Metal bars holding the boulder door closed slide away. Belubus pushes and it swings open, allowing moonlight to stream in. He steps out into the cold air; it rushes over my face, and I have never felt so intoxicated in my life. I follow.

We stand outside the hidden entrance to the Mines. The moon is so bright that it's almost like day—only with no color save multiple shades of blue and gray. I stand an arm's length away from Belubus, and freedom is mine. I'm faster than he is, and stronger too. I could run now, and he'd never catch me.

"I am an old fool, aren't I?"

Out here, so close to freedom, my face has finally betrayed me. He knows I am leaving.

"I have no other choice, Belubus. You forced my hand."

"No other choice? Your choices are valuable, young Brathius—the most valuable possessions you will ever own. Please do not relinquish ownership of them. You are making a choice, and it's *your* choice. Don't pawn it off on me. Claim it."

"I need to find Adorane, to go Down Below, to help save my people." This is a revelation to me. I still want to save Mountaintop? I suppose, now having said it, that it is true.

"It's a noble choice." He knew all along, even when we were in his throne room. I blush at the thought of me exploiting our most precious memories, thinking I was tricking him. "I wish you hadn't felt like you needed to lie to me."

"I told you I needed to leave—" I say, ashamed.

"You asked once. Asking twice is very different from asking once. And telling instead of asking—that's another act all together. Then there's convincing, rallying, inspiring. Appealing to dignity, compassion, reason. You did none of these things. There are many higher paths one can take before resorting to deception."

Still teaching me.

He hands me an ultralion stomach bladder full of water and a bag of roots and leathered meats.

"In order to survive, you may someday be forced to take the form of a worm. But at least *try* to be an eagle first. Always strive to be noble, even when you feel forced into acting lowly."

"Of course. You're right." He is.

"Icelyn, don't condemn us to death. There are good people here."

I nod. "You don't need to worry about me."

"I worry about you every day, as I always will. Now go, run!"

I scramble into the woods, away from the Mines.

Behind me, growing fainter, I hear Belubus humming my melody.

31

THE HUMMING FADES, and I hear the rumble of the boulder door closing. I'm alone. Unruly words that I wish I had spoken to Belubus swirl through my head. They're exhausting because they don't match up. Some are grateful, warm—others angry, annoyed, embarrassed.

He let me go, and he gave me water and food. But why couldn't he just have let me go in the first place, without his moral test? I failed it, and yet he still had mercy on me. I did—and do—feel guilty for lying to him. Yet, he's been lying to me all these years—if not with the words he said, then with the words he didn't.

Living in the Mines like a king, yet pretending to be a humble tutor. Who is Belubus? Is he the teacher I trusted, or the ruler who hoards water and wears plush purple gowns? How can he be both—and if he is, how am I to feel about him? I love the former and despise the latter.

The nerve of that deceiver, lecturing me about relying on deception!

In order to survive, you may someday be forced to take the form of a worm. But at least try *to be an eagle first.*

He's the one slinking around in this hole beneath the ground, playing at being a king. *He* is acting the part of the worm, not me.

Honesty isn't a Brathius value. The Aclornis family holds loyalty and honesty in the highest regard; if Adorane ever lied, he would be shamed forever. But I am a Brathius. We are innovative and clever. My escape plan was both—and it worked, didn't it? I've been true to myself and my family, so I can do without Belubus' hypocritical lectures on deception and the guilt that comes with them.

But this guilt stays with me still. I hate when I feel the weight of opposites so strongly. I feel as though I'm being squished in the middle of two titans bashing each other without remorse, with no safe ground between them.

I am hungry and thirsty. I stop running and take a frugal sip of the water. I break off an inch of root and chew slowly. The simple acts of chewing and swallowing are distracting enough to broker a ceasefire in my head. Gratefulness has won the day; I have always loved Belubus, I decide, and I always will.

The oasis of peace lasts only a few minutes.

A guttural, ragged breathing rips through the quiet sounds of the night forest.

Am I imagining it? I stop walking and force my breathing to be silent. I don't hear it at all now; I hear only my own racing pulse. Fear courses through my body.

I hear it again. It sounds painful, like whatever is making the noise is struggling for breath. But I don't feel sorry for whatever it is; I am afraid. It's getting closer and louder.

I dart between the trees. I'm being hunted. The rasping grows more rapid. Branches crack and leaves crunch behind me; it is making no effort to conceal its movements now.

My steps, fueled by instinct, avoid going further down the mountain. Whatever it is probably came from down there, and going lower would give it an advantage. But I know that if I head toward a higher elevation, I'll start to wear out. Instead, I make my way horizontally across the slopes, ducking under and through thick patches of thistle.

The rasping creature sounds large. Passage through the brush is barely possible for me, so I hope it's completely impassable for whatever that thing is. The noises, while angrier, are finally falling farther behind.

I continue running through the brush, crouched over, ignoring the fresh jabs and scrapes that are the cost of each lunge forward. I'm tempted to stop and hide until the creature grows tired and leaves me alone. But every time I slow, its otherworldly growls propel me on.

I reach an area I'm convinced no animal larger than a rabbit has visited before. A network of wooden branches cage me, creating a dead end.

Rasps echo behind me. Every lunge forward makes the thing angrier and more determined. It's getting closer.

I throw myself forward in desperation and am snared in a diabolical gauntlet of branches and thorny roots. Panic floods my senses. I exhale.

Icelyn, it can't end like this.

I blindly feel the ground around me, trying to find anything that might help. I grasp a few stones. I heave one to my left. It lands far away, crashing through the leaves and branches.

The wheezing stops moving toward me; the creature is confused.

Please follow the sound.

Follow it.

I hold my breath and find another rock. I toss it further in the same direction, creating more noise.

Please let this work.

Waiting feels like an eternity. I wish I could see what is following me. I can hear that it's not moving, but it's invisible in the darkness so I don't know where it is or what it's doing.

I methodically locate every branch tip that keeps me from moving. I snap them one by one, muffling the cracking sound inside my hands, hoping none of them makes too loud a noise.

Snap. Snap. Snap. Each feels like a giant risk.

Through the quiet, another sound. It takes a while for me to distinguish it from the other sounds of the night, but then it's clear.

The creature is sniffing.

No! With the last few days I've had, I'm sure I emit a distinct scent.

Then, progress again. Ragged breathing, wheezing. Coming toward me. I throw another stone to my left, but it makes no difference. The creature has my scent. Noise won't disorient it now.

I grab another rock and bash against the snares that hold me tight. One thick branch breaks with a loud crack. The creature howls and quickens the pace.

The crack attracts the creature, but it also encourages me. I remain trapped, yet I'm closer to freedom. I swing at another branch and break it in two.

The terrible inhuman sound is close now, and with it comes an odor. It's nauseating, like a dead carcass mixed with a sharper, muskier scent. I struggle to tune out the smell and the growing sense of dread that accompanies it. I don't dare look back.

I focus all my attention on the branches that hold me.

I am cornered. I have to do something or I'll die.

I struggle through a minuscule break in the brush, paying the price as the snapped branches slice into me. I won't look back to confirm, but I sense the creature cannot follow me. It screams in rage and shoves against the foliage, but its sounds and scent both fall further behind as I strain ahead.

I break through the thick underbrush, but I'm on the thin, pebbly rim of a steep drop-off. To my right and left are stone outcroppings. About thirty feet below, a layer of thick fog obscures what awaits me.

This seems dangerous. But I cannot go back toward the creature. There is only one way at this point.

I begin my climb down.

32

ACLORNIS DRIFTED THROUGH the makeshift camp on the border of Cloudline—that thick, foggy ring of clouds engulfing the mountain.

He watched Adorane, who was brooding and staring at Cloudline. His beloved son. Adorane was everything he had ever wished for in a child. It seemed to perturb the boy to hear his father say such things anymore, so Aclornis mostly kept silent, but he had to believe Adorane knew.

He observed his men sharpening their spears, chipping away at the stone tips and wooden handles to fashion ever more lethal weapons.

It was good that they had something to hold their concentration, even if the weapons themselves would make little difference once they entered Cloudline. The camp seemed peaceful, but Aclornis sensed the dread that had settled over all of them. So much fear—and no one else in the camp had even seen the descriptions or sketches Oliver Hailgard had committed to paper.

Aclornis knew what they faced, and his hope wasn't that they'd all get through Cloudline alive. That was greedy and foolishly unrealistic. He prayed instead that at least one of them would survive this next phase in their journey.

And he hoped it would be Adorane.

33

HALFWAY DOWN THE cliff, my muscles begin to ache. I can't stop shaking.

I curse the Cognate way of life, which instructs us to scale back physical activity as we get older to concentrate on more academic pursuits.

The theory was: *Why act like an animal if you're human?* This had always made sense to me—until now.

Why act like an animal? Well, maybe you'll someday find yourself in an animalistic situation—being chased by something that wants to sink its fangs into you, for instance, and needing to scale a sheer cliff wall to survive. I'd appreciate the ability to act like an animal right now.

I've reached a point in my descent that requires expert skills. I know what I have to do: There's a small shelf to my left, about three feet down. If I can reach that with my left leg, I can lower myself down, and from there, it looks like the going will be easier. But lowering myself those three feet requires arm strength I don't have.

I point my left foot, hoping my toe can find the support of the ledge while I strain myself as far as I can.

Too far.

My arms give out, and I'm pulled downward. I hit a rock shelf but can't catch myself. I continue to fall, hitting rocks and dirt with tremendous force, like the world itself is bullying me. God, it hurts. Time slows down so I feel each impact like it's its own day.

Suddenly I'm in a thick fog with no visibility. I don't know whether this is better or worse, but at least it's different. I've come to a stop, and the beatings have ceased. The world is silent.

And I'm still alive.

At least, I think I am. Surrounded by white clouds, and surprisingly clear headed (I've heard that pain can do that), everything seems heavenly, to steal a word from the traditions of the Apriori. I have a fleeting silly thought—perhaps I've died, and joined the celestial bodies above?

Only if celestial bodies cry.

Quiet sobbing breaks the silence. I gingerly feel my cheeks to see if I'm crying, but I'm not. I feel bruised and dizzy, but nothing seems broken.

The sniffles are human. I know it's not Ad; he would rather fling himself headlong off the Mountain than be heard blubbering like a newborn. Who would be out here, so far from the Wall, crying? I follow the sounds.

I reach the mouth of a cave. The sobs come from inside.

The fog seems to originate inside the cave, too. I stare in wonder; fog shouldn't come from the insides of mountains.

Odder still, there's machinery scattered around the mouth of the cave: man-made equipment, black, shiny and glassy, facing the skies. Old, maybe, but not abandoned, as something left here from the time of the Apriori would look. The units consist of a black metal support stuck into the ground and a flat rectangle at the top. There are thin, manmade plastic vines that I believe were called *wires*, which carried electricity—the force that powered so many of the Apriori wonders, but whose capture has eluded us in Mountaintop.

On the bottom left corner of the shiny rectangle, a small dot of green light glows for a count and then ceases, flashing over and over. I've never seen it before, but my guess is that this machine has electricity flowing through it.

Whoever is crying tries to stifle the sound, but it doesn't work. The efforts seem to make the echoes louder. My curiosity piqued, I enter the cave.

The cave should be frightening, with fog pouring out of it and the darkness growing as I progress. But what kind of threat could lurk here if the crier is still alive to cry?

Through the mist and darkness, I make out a large metal box that emits a constant hum—then another, and another, a vibrating cluster of six. They're warm to the touch.

My eyes adjust to the dark, and I can now see the purpose of these towering metal boxes—fog billows out of slots at the top of each.

The mist flowing from the cave and joining with Cloudline is *man-made*. With machines that require electricity. My mind swirls around this puzzle I cannot sort out.

The machinery isn't all I find in the cave. There are shelves of canned food and other supplies that I do not recognize. They look like gadgets the Apriori would use. There are also volumes of books and scrolls. What *is* this cave?

A sniffle and then a voice not far from me should shock me, but I'm too wound up in this remarkable cavern to care. "Have you figured it out? Because I don't have a clue."

Emerging from the shadows, his eyes puffy and his skin muddied, Torrain resembles a shoe that's been fought over by a couple of frisky ultralion cubs.

I feel a stab of something—sorrow, guilt, maybe even relief—seeing him here, like this. "Torrain, what in the world are you doing down here?"

He smiles despite himself, but it's a rueful grin, sadder than if he had resumed his muffled sobs. "I came to tell you that I don't care about you at all, and that you can't hurt me anymore."

And then the tears begin to flow again.

34

NOTHING WAS GOING as Torrain had rehearsed. He'd replayed the moment he found Icelyn over and over again in his head, rehearsing. His face a stoic mask, he'd coolly inform her that though he'd come to rescue her, she could do as she pleased, for all he cared. And while they were on the subject of his caring, she shouldn't delude herself into thinking she'd hurt him, because she couldn't hurt him, and he could not care less about what she did or where she was. Then Torrain would walk away in silent triumph, ignoring Icelyn's calls to come back and talk to her.

Instead, he stumbled through a few words, crumpled into tears, and fell back against the stone cave wall. He couldn't breathe. This wasn't going well.

Icelyn leaned over him, concerned, and put a hand on his shoulder. *No,* Torrain thought fiercely, *she's not going to fool me again.*

"Torrain, what are you doing outside the Wall?"

"I'm not a child who's lost his way. You can flush the pity from your voice." It sounded more pitiful than he'd hoped.

"But are you lost? I mean, God…are you out here looking for *me*?"

"Not everything is about you, Icelyn. Just ignore my tears; I'm tired. Let's talk about something else." The familiar chill returned to Torrain's voice. Finally, not so vulnerable.

"That's a relief. You don't have to beg me to ignore your emotions. That's my preference."

Torrain felt a familiar pulse of pain. Though he'd requested Icelyn move past his tears, she'd done it a bit quicker than he wanted.

"Where are we?" Icelyn asked.

Torrain approached one of the large metal machines. Icelyn joined him, and they stared at the humming monoliths. The flow of billowing white was hypnotic, like a rushing river of clouds.

"Someone designed this so that Cloudline would always remain opaque, regardless of the weather. And they're meant to stay on. I tried turning them off, but I couldn't." Torrain was doing a capable job of leaving the emotion behind. This conversation was a welcome diversion from his pain.

"But why? What purpose could Cloudline serve? And there's electricity here—which we've been told wasn't possible in Mountaintop, one of the many wonders we left below."

"Maybe it obscures the view of Mountaintop from the Threat Below." Torrain wished he hadn't said that, because it reminded him of how he ended up in this cave, chased by something fast and horrifying. Tears filled his eyes again.

"A lot of good *that's* done. We're no safer above Cloudline than we are below," Icelyn replied.

"How do you know that?" Torrain asked.

Jarvin—cut open, carved out. So many things she didn't want to share with Torrain.

"Torrain, you should go back to Mountaintop. It's dangerous beyond the Wall. The warnings weren't just stories told by our parents to keep us well behaved."

It annoyed Torrain how Icelyn was acting like a grizzled veteran who'd seen things he could only dream of. He'd run from something monstrous; he'd watched his Mother die. He knew more of the world than she did.

"I'm not some innocent baby rabbit that needs coddling," he said, more angrily than he'd intended.

"I never said you were." Icelyn suppressed a laugh. "I doubt I'll ever accuse you, or *anyone*, of being an innocent baby rabbit."

No, Torrain thought. *We're not going to be playful*.

The humming was getting to him. He'd been in this cave with the droning machines for hours, and he craved silence.

"I've got to get out of this cave." He headed out toward the first gray light of the morning. Icelyn grabbed his arm, and Torrain felt a surge of electricity in her touch. He hadn't been touched by a girl since he was a child playing tag.

"No. It's not safe."

He brushed her hand away, even though his skin still tingled where it had been. Finally, he was getting his chance to play the detached, untouchable tough man.

"You haven't cared one pebble about me before today, so I hardly see why you should start now."

"Torrain! Come on. This is no time for being petty. Torrain!"

He walked away without looking back. It was even better than he'd planned.

35

"I APPRECIATE YOUR summons, Chief Cognate. I am honored to serve you." Tranton entered what passed for the throne room. Rarely used during Nicholas' reign, it was meant for important discussions and formal proclamations.

Nicholas was fidgety. He knew he should maintain eye contact and project confidence, but he couldn't.

"I found a section of the Code that applies to our recent course of action."

Tranton grinned. "You know I love to discuss the finer points of the Code."

"Section Carthene, in the Medeoine Volume, states that 'weapons shall never be carried with the intent, either explicit or implied, of injuring or threatening injury against other members of the Kith, but only for defense against those outside forces that may threaten the Kith.' As you can see, the Code is very clear on this."

Nicholas knew he was reaching. Though this part of the Code *seemed* to apply to the current gun-bearing policy, he knew it had been written as a result of a small farming squabble between two Veritas more than a hundred years ago. Arguing over a ration of water, one had threatened to hit the other with a shovel, which at the time broke no explicit section of the Code. This had been remedied by an emergency meeting in this very throne room.

Tranton was aware of the passage and marveled at how long it had taken Nicholas to mention it. A Chief Cognate without intimate knowledge of the Code was no asset. A stronger leader would have raised this objection the moment he saw the guns, an immediate instinct rather than the fruits of slow, methodical research. Tranton relished his luck. *Be the leader, or advise a feeble one—either way, you're in charge.* This was a proverb that had been in the Nilsing family for centuries, though not shared with others.

"A century-old farming dispute doesn't apply to the grave situation we find ourselves in today—the fate of a stalk of corn versus the fate of all humanity."

Nicholas wasn't in the mood for a debate, and he wasn't skilled enough to win one anyway. "I want the guns, Tranton. Locked up here, with me, in Brathius Tower."

"Disarming the Tarlinius sends the wrong message."

"We have responded to bug bites with a bludgeon."

"Everything I have done, I've done for you, Nicholas. The Kith viewed you as weak."

"Is it weakness to hate what happened to Torrain's mother? Nandor was only trying to defend her son—"

"It is weakness to let that hate put the Kith at risk. This situation calls for strength. Your position calls for strength. History begs for a show of strength. Schoolchildren hundreds of years from now need to study feats of strength."

"Where did the weapons come from?"

The guns, along with Tranton's destiny, had been in the foggy cave he'd found outside the Wall. But he wasn't going to share that with Nicholas. No reason to scare the man more than he had to.

"I received an anonymous tip from a loyal Kith member."

"If you knew of the guns' existence, why didn't you equip the expedition Down Below with them?"

"I didn't find the guns until after the expedition left. I would have given Aclornis and his men the weapons if that weren't the case," Tranton stated.

He knew this would placate Nicholas and give him something positive to tell Marjan, which would help maintain peace in Brathius Tower.

"Let's keep a constant eye on the situation. I need to know that we're monitoring it, and that we're flexible enough to change tactics if need be. That's all I ask."

Tranton placed a reassuring hand on Nicholas' shoulder. "I'm honored to serve a wise, compassionate man. Of course, what you ask is what we need. We are fortunate to be led by you at a time like this."

36

I'M ALONE OTHER than the constant hum of the fog machines, and I'd give anything for silence. Without Torrain, the cave makes me uneasy. I shake off the idea that I'm miserable because Torrain has left me behind. Am I lonely for Torrain?

I might as well go track him down—for his sake, not mine—before he's sliced up and hung in a tree. I stumble to the mouth of the cave. The river of fog pours from the opening and descends to join Cloudline about a thousand feet below. He was right; this must be the purpose of the machinery. To keep Cloudline cloudy.

I wonder if Father knows about this place. If he does, why wouldn't he tell me? I pride myself on my ability to keep secrets, especially when they are given to me freely and not stumbled across.

Torrain makes no effort to be quiet, and I can hear him trampling through the woods above me. He's probably caught up in heady pride from putting me in my place right now. But I know that he was lying. He does care that I hurt him. I care, too.

I scale the modest stone cliff and follow Torrain's heavy footsteps. He's broken branches and kicked aside enough dirt to leave a trail clear even to my untrained eyes.

I see him, but he doesn't know it. He's talking to himself. Slowly his voice comes within earshot, and I am hit with a flash of embarrassment

—first for him, then for both of us.

"You haven't cared one pebble about me before today, so I hardly see why you should start now."

He's celebrating his kiss-off line!

He's reached a high point, a dead-end lookout onto the expanse below, and I know that he can't make any more progress. Now that I've crept closer, I can see that his face is flushed and he seems wobbly. I wonder when he last ate.

He delivers the pebble line again, this time punctuated with laughter. I'm tempted to turn away and forget about him. Let him mock me, alone and pathetic, until he dies from either being eaten or not eating enough.

Instead, I crave the chance to do something right for once. I'll help this boy who takes such joy in rejecting me.

I emerge from the woods, holding roots toward Torrain as a peace offering. "You've got to be hungry, Torrain."

Torrain stops laughing and stares at me blankly. He seems hollow and unhinged.

"Take some. You need it."

"Why are you here? I left you behind. In the cave," he asks, dazed, as if I have materialized in the most miraculously unexplainable way.

"I followed you. Easily, too. You aren't exactly being sneaky."

"But I walked away, never to see you again. I…left you in the cave."

"How long has it been since you've eaten, Torrain?"

"If you're saying that I'm hungry and not thinking straight, well, you're wrong. How did you get here? I left you behind."

"I know you don't care about me, and I know that I haven't cared a pebble about you before today, so why should I start now—"

"Hey! That's what I said! How did you know about that, and the pebble? That's what I was thinking! That's what I said. You can't say *the pebble* too!"

The boy has lost his mind. I push through. "Just take this. A person needs to eat."

Torrain examines the root with suspicion, as if I could poison or strangle him with it if he isn't cautious.

I sigh, exasperated. I'm helping him! Some people make it so hard to like them. I drop the root at his feet. "Anyway, eat it if you want to live. I don't care anymore." I walk toward the high point, away from Torrain. *If we're going to play it cool, you have no idea how cool I can be. My name starts with Ice.*

My back toward Torrain, I peek around to see him circling the root like a curious animal. He picks it up and nibbles it, then catches me looking and drops it. Stupid. I ignore him and turn my attention to the view from the outcropping of rock that I'm standing on. I can see a flat dusty area, about five hundred feet below, then the white haze of Cloudline another five hundred feet below that.

I hear Torrain chewing behind me and am surprised at my relief. I don't want to be his best friend, and never his wife—but I don't want him to wither away and die, either.

"This tastes good. What is it?" A sane stability has returned to his voice. His coloring is better, too.

"Roots—you know, from a plant. How the hell should I know?"

He laughs. "Well, obviously."

"I mean, it's not anything we ate in Mountaintop, and I'm no botanist," I joke.

"Oh, and here I thought you *were* a botanist! I guess I should stop calling you Icelyn the Botanist." He joins me at the high point, looking down on the dusty plain. I take a root and chew it too. Eating is always better when done with someone else, even if it's Torrain.

"It almost tastes minty—sweet," he says, chewing thoughtfully. "I think I'll call it Dessert Root."

If Torrain wants to call it Dessert Root, I'm not going to argue. "Look at you, labeling plants. Maybe *you're* the botanist."

"My mom is dead, Icelyn." He says it flatly, out of nowhere, surprising me.

"What?"

And before he can answer, or explain, I see it. Something so horrible that I hope the roots we've been gnawing on are hallucinogens, because this creature in the dusty field below us cannot be real.

It's hideous, walking first on all fours, and then standing on two legs. Alternating between two and four legs as it moves, it's fast and graceful. It moves with unsettling speed.

It stands, and I can see that it's frighteningly tall—nine or ten feet in height. It's larger than any living thing I've ever seen. It's slender, lean, and well-built, like a Veritas in his prime. It wheezes as it walks. Ratty fur hangs down everywhere, shaggier on the back and head, matted with mud and what I fear is blood. Flies buzz around the creature as it stalks through the field. Though we are far above it, and a good distance away, the powerful smell of death, rot, and decay overtakes me. I can see large talons curling from the beast's paws.

Where there should be a face, there is shadowy red-black darkness.

The only familiar thing about this creature, which makes its appearance more chilling, is its bright blue eyes, shining in the midst of that shadowed face. Forward facing, wide set, like a primate. Like a human's eyes—only larger, rounder.

The Threat Below. I've always been curious what one looked like. Now I wish I didn't know.

I cover Torrain's mouth to keep him from replying to my question and pull him to the ground. I motion to him to get as low as possible, in hopes that the nightmare moving through the field below doesn't see us.

It doesn't work.

37

IT LOOKS AT us with those glacial blue eyes, snorts with recognition, and then explodes toward us with terrible velocity.

I grab Torrain and we sprint down into the woods. We're a good five hundred feet above that thing. Can it scale that distance and find us? Are we safe?

Of course it can—and no, we're not.

As we run (and God, I have to pull Torrain to keep up with me!) my mind scans for anything I know about escaping large predators. When I was twelve I was fascinated by animals that ate humans, and I would read endlessly about them—grizzly bears, great white sharks, saltwater crocodiles, African lions, anacondas. How do you escape when you're being chased? You run. No, you stand still. Actually, you play dead. When that doesn't work, you jump up and down. If that fails, you make a commotion. If the attack continues, you stay silent. When that makes no difference, you fight back.

There was never a consensus. Probably because, regardless of what you tried, if the beast was determined to eat you, you were going to be consumed.

We jump downed trees and dart left and right. I don't want our escape to be a straight line; random diagonals will give us a better chance of escape from the Threatbelow. (That's how you're supposed to run from large reptiles called alligators, because it confuses them.)

I don't know for sure that the Threatbelow is still chasing us. But I know we can't stop and figure it out.

Torrain gasps for air. "Hold on. One second. I need a rest." I pull him for another thirty steps, ignoring his pleas. He can rest later, when we're not in danger—or for a very long time when we're dead. But not now. (I'm the Adorane in this situation; that's how weak Torrain is.)

Whether as a protest or accidentally, Torrain falls face first into the pine needles and dirt.

"Get up!" I hiss, looking behind us.

"I told you, I need rest." He gulps air and ignores the blood on his face. He seems happy to have fallen, because at least he's not moving anymore. I despise his Cognate lifestyle, where he spent most of his time sitting indoors, staying weak. At least I chased Adorane around to build up some endurance.

I don't hear anything following us. Maybe we're safe.

"We can't stay here long, Torrain."

"I'm not asking for a picnic. My muscles aren't working. I need to wait until they do."

"Keep it down," I whisper. He's being too loud, emphasizing and enunciating words as if this were a school debate.

"Just another ten counts," he begs. I take the time to examine our surroundings. Stillness. Torrain's heavy breathing is the loudest thing around. (I wish he'd shut up!) Maybe we've evaded the creature.

"You've had it. That's ten." I offer him a hand. "Now let's get going." But Torrain's face is white, ashen, and he stares beyond me. A horrid stench seizes my nostrils.

No.

I turn to see, just a few feet away, standing completely still, the Threatbelow.

I just looked there! How did it get near without making a sound?

I am going to die.

It's unbelievable up close. I want to look away, but to do so feels like giving myself up to this horrible fate. It stands on two feet, a tower of death and decay rising above me. Its eyes examine me intelligently. I know that running isn't an option, so I lean over, pick up a rock, and hurl it desperately toward the monster.

It bounces off its thick matted fur harmlessly.

A breeze kicks up behind me and blows toward it. The Threatbelow inhales deeply.

No, I determine, *not without a fight.* I am seized with adrenaline; instinctively, I step forward and take a swing. As I do so, I am seized with regret. This is ridiculous; I'm not a fighter.

I punch and make solid contact with the creature's abdomen, but I've caused it no pain. Still, it looks disoriented. The creature touches its abdomen with sharp-taloned hands—from this close, I can see that, despite the talons, this thing has five-fingered hands, like a primate. Not paws.

It holds the hand close to its face and sniffs in again. It touches my face with the back of its hand, slowly stroking it. I hold my breath, waiting for the imminent slash.

It vaults backward, away from me—as if it's disgusted by me, or scared of me, or defiled by my touch. It turns and scurries away.

I exhale. I realize that I haven't breathed once the whole time the Threatbelow was facing me. Torrain stands beside me, wide eyed.

"What did you just do, Icelyn?"

"I have no idea."

Torrain and I walk aimlessly. It's growing dark. I don't know what we're doing—all our options seem like dead ends, so I've given up figuring it out.

I'm in no mood for conversation—and except for one request for Dessert Root about an hour back, Torrain doesn't want to talk, either. We trudge forward, our progress slow, but we don't know where we're headed anyway.

I ponder my confrontation with the Threatbelow. If all you had to do was smack the thing in the stomach, how did humanity perish because of these beasts? Our history books said that all weaponry the Apriori possessed, far superior to anything we have at our disposal, made no difference against the creatures. And yet I'm able to punch it and emerge victorious?

Surely Jarvin resisted; he was much stronger than I will ever be, and he was torn apart. How did I do it?

"It makes no sense, Torrain. I barely fought back, and that beast turned and ran from me. Why?"

Torrain grunts something unintelligible. He's lost in his own separate gloom, in no mood for conversation.

I share my water with Torrain, though we're both worried it's running low. He's starting to annoy me. I wish he'd go back to Mountaintop, but he's told me he's not allowed to without me in tow, and I'm not returning.

My mind wanders back to the singing I heard outside Hailgard Round, when the Veritas voices combined to form a haunting harmony. As much as that clandestine meeting saddened me, I wish I could hear that singing again. There was something about that song—although I knew the ritual was ridiculous, pointless, it made me hope that it wasn't.

Wait. The song.

I'm not only remembering it. *I hear the song.* Quiet, faraway. I hear it. I wonder if I'm descending into madness, but I am surprised to realize I don't care.

"Do you hear that?" I risk having Torrain thinking I've come unglued, but I need to know if he does. We stop walking and listen to the many sounds of the woods around us. Torrain doesn't know which sound I'm referring to. He's tired, and it occurs to me that he may be as annoyed by my presence as I am by his.

"Leaves blowing in the wind, Icelyn."

"No, not leaves. Listen closely." I'm convinced now that the sound isn't inside my own head. A girl knows when she's gone insane—I'm close, but I'm not there yet.

Torrain's face tells me he hears it before he admits it.

"That's singing, Torrain. Like the Apriori used to do."

Torrain's eyes widen, and he looks at me with excitement and curiosity. "Are there Apriori down here? Perhaps a group who somehow survived?" His face flares with anticipation, as though he hopes this is true with every ounce of his being.

"You hear it!" I'm suddenly so happy that I'm not alone, that I am sharing this experience with him. The misery I've survived in the past few days has been magnified by my loneliness. Finally, I can suffer a spell with someone else—even if it's only Torrain. "Singing is like what the birds do, only people are doing it. Humans. Can you believe it? It's crude, but I—I see the appeal."

Torrain nods. "I like it."

"It's not the Apriori, Torrain." I should have let him in on that secret with a little more grace, because he looks disappointed, as if I've just told him his pet lizard died. "It's just Veritas. They cling to many of the old traditions. Singing is one of them. They practice in secret."

"Oh." Torrain's boy-like wonder has evaporated.

"But they're Veritas *here.* Let's go find them." I move forward, and he's forced to follow. Our moment of kinship is over.

I'm excited for the same reason he's moping. We're finally on our way to Adorane.

38

ADORANE WAS FRUSTRATED with his father's leadership. Not enough to revolt, but enough to seethe in silence while everyone else sang their songs.

They should have entered Cloudline the previous morning. Adorane didn't understand why Aclornis was stalling. Was he frightened? They all were. If they had entered Cloudline when Adorane thought they should have, one full day earlier, they'd already be in the valley, one day closer to being the saviors of Mountaintop.

Adorane had grown excited about what this expedition could accomplish. Tranton and Nicholas clearly hadn't thought everything through. If the expedition did manage to save Mountaintop, it would be a major Veritas victory—one great enough to even the scales between the classes. Veritas would no longer have to grovel beneath the Cognates, subservient in their gratitude for the gift of human survival. They would be equal patrons of that gift.

But they could only make that happen if they entered Cloudline sometime in the next century.

Adorane stood and approached his father. "I'm finding it difficult to remain respectful toward you."

"You've not seen the things I've seen, son." Aclornis said the words as if he were seeing those things at that very moment.

"We have work to do—and yet here we sit, singing like it's a prayer meeting."

"The songs help morale, Ad."

"Not mine." Adorane wasn't sure what to say next. He resisted the urge to push his father toward Cloudline—*this way, Father, let's go! It's not so hard!*

"Don't be so eager. We'll enter when the time is right."

Why was Aclornis acting like he was a seasoned warrior, a leader who'd survived a thousand battles? Adorane had fought the same foes his father had faced—ultralion, ultrabear. Why wasn't he ready to fight?

"I will find those willing to go, and we will enter without you. People are going to die unless we take action."

"People are going to die either way, son. Never hasten death."

They both heard movement in the woods above them. Adorane and Aclornis grabbed their spears and crept toward the threat before any of the other men even noticed they were gone.

Adorane took the lead. "Too much movement to be an ultralion," he whispered, thinking about Jarvin hanging in the tree. "Sounds like more than one, whatever it is."

Aclornis nodded in agreement, flanking to take a wider angle as they approached the commotion. They'd surround it.

Something was moving fast, crashing through the thicket. Adorane had feared the song and fire would attract danger. He cursed his father again. This morale boost was going to get them all killed.

Adorane caught a glimpse of movement in the meager moonlight. He charged, his spear pointed, ready to run through whatever threatened them. Out of the corner of his eye, he saw Aclornis do the same and felt a welcome twinge of pride. The two of them made a great team; once they entered Cloudline, they would accomplish heroic feats together.

They heard a scream as they bore down on their quarry. Two shadows in the night, both larger than any animal in the area, changed direction when they sensed Aclornis and Adorane out for blood, fell hard, and tumbled down the steep embankment.

Adorane followed the shadows as they slammed to a stop against a set of boulders, holding his spear at attention, ready to ram them through.

His eyes adjusted to the darkness as one of the things turned its head and looked at him. Then the moonlight caught its icy blue eyes, and he felt like he'd been punched in the stomach. Adorane dropped his spear.

"Icelyn?"

39

I'VE BEEN CRYING since I saw Addy. Crying in front of other people is normally worse than a death sentence for me, but I can't care. I've missed him.

Once we are past the unpleasantness of him trying to slay me and Torrain, I embrace him out of relief. He returns the hug just as forcefully, and maybe even initiates it. It's all a tear-soaked burst of joy. I don't care that Torrain watches, lonely, not holding anyone close. I am alive, and now I am with Adorane.

When they take us to their campsite, my spirits lift further. They've killed an ultrabear and are cooking it over the fire. After all the roots Torrain and I have been forced to subsist upon, the ultrabear tastes like heaven itself has manifested in my mouth. (Yes, I was hungry.)

Torrain tells us the story of his poor mother, Nandor. Awful. Anger flashes through me. I'm not able to completely express it, though, because I can see the rage twisting across Ad's face, and I don't want to make it any worse. Poor Torrain. The one person he ever truly loved, I'm convinced, was Nandor. She was probably the only person who loved him too. And now she's gone.

Mountaintop has become a terrible place. I can't say it out loud, but I see now that our society must change. We can't just go back, with or without clean water, and pretend everything is normal. As strongly as I believe this, I'm relieved that Ad doesn't say these things out loud. I need some time to figure out the confusion of thoughts swirling in my mind.

The conversation lulls to an awkward stop, where talking about anything other than Nandor's death seems inappropriate, but discussing her death any more would be cruel. I decide to break the ice and be the inappropriate one.

I don't know what to say, though. Torrain and I have decided not to share seeing the Threatbelow; the memory is too horrible, and we don't want to relive it or make the others more afraid. I reach for the first thing I can think to say.

"I'm surprised to find you here. I expected you'd be through Cloudline by now."

Adorane throws a side glance toward his father. "So did I. But we've been having too good a time singing in the woods. Our morale has been boosted to record heights."

It's been less than a week, but Ad appears to have aged years since I've seen him. Mocking his father like this! I don't know whether to be attracted or repulsed. Children don't do this to their parents. It's clear that Adorane is no longer a child.

Aclornis ignores his son's barbs. "Adorane, we'll enter Cloudline in the morning, but you will not."

"What?" Ad exclaims.

"You'll take Icelyn and Torrain back to Mountaintop."

I protest. "Aclornis, with all due respect, Mountaintop is the last place I want to go. Torrain, too. It's a prison for me, and—"

"Your father would never forgive me if I left you here—or even worse, took you with us. This matter is not up for negotiation." Aclornis raises his voice. It's so out of character that I'm shocked into silence.

I hate when adults treat us as if we're possessions without any input into our own fates. "My father has relinquished the right to determine my next steps." My words sound strong and brave. I'm sure I've had the final say.

Adorane acts like matters are settled, too. "I can't abandon the expedition, Father."

I'm the only one who sees the way Aclornis looks at his son in the firelight. It's a desperate, haunted look, and suddenly I understand what is going on. Aclornis doesn't want Adorane to go below. He's afraid. And now I've shown up, the perfect way out.

We aren't going to win this argument.

"Son, if you refuse to take her back to Mountaintop, I will redirect the entire expedition to take her back. Nicholas' daughter will not be put in danger."

Adorane thinks this is folly. "If the entire expedition heads back to Mountaintop, we will lose nearly a week's time, and for nothing. An extra week without clean water could be the difference between life and death."

"Then you see the choice you must make. Take her and Torrain back. By the time you reach home, we will have gone Down Below, so you must remain in Mountaintop."

Adorane has had his decision made for him. The man he's become melts away, leaving a heartbroken child. He turns to me angrily. "Why did you have to come down here?" he pouts. He tosses a stick into the fire, stands, and backs away.

"You and Torrain: Be ready to leave in the morning. I need some sleep." He disappears into the darkness. I hate to be an imposition of any kind, and Adorane acts as if my arrival has ruined his life. I wish I could escape from my skin and vanish. *I didn't exactly ask for any of this either, Ad!*

I can't think of a thing I want to say to Aclornis or Torrain. The three of us chew our food and pretend not to notice my tears.

40

IF I SLEPT last night, which seemed to stretch on three times as long as any other night, I can't remember when. I do recall how uncomfortable the dirt was, how I rolled back and forth over an endless supply of twigs and rocks, and how I was cold. As the only girl, I had to make my bed ten feet away from any man or boy (to preserve my innocence, of course). Not that Adorane wants to huddle up beside me and chip away at my innocence, anyway; he won't even look at me.

The stars above were the only exception in that miserable night. Bright, sparkling, and shooting, they twinkled brighter than I've ever seen. But I couldn't enjoy them. All I heard, over and over in my head, was a mix of the song the Veritas had sung and Adorane saying, "Why did you have to come down here?" Every time I replayed his question it sounded worse. All I could feel was the anger, the disappointment, and what felt like hatred.

I welcome the first hint of sunlight—now I don't have to pretend I am trying to sleep anymore. I rise and find Adorane starting a fire.

"I wasn't trying to ruin your life, Ad," I say softly.

"I never said you were."

"You don't have to say something for me to know what you mean." Ad doesn't seem interested in talking, but I continue. "Look, I don't want to go back to Mountaintop either. But at least you'll be safe. You won't have to face whatever hell is lurking down there." I think about the Threatbelow and realize that this is a silver lining. Adorane would be up in Mountaintop, with me, not Down Below, certain to die.

"I'm taking you and your Intended back to Mountaintop. Then I will be leaving to join the expedition again." Shock flashes through me —first at his referring to Torrain as my *Intended,* and second at his foolish and deadly plan.

"I despise every aspect of what you just said, Ad."

"You wouldn't understand. Everything is already set for you, for the Cognates. I have to *work* to make the world one I can actually stomach living in."

"Everything is already set for me? God, Ad! Don't you know me at all? *Nothing* is what I want it to be. Nothing! That's why I left. I might not have a clear idea of everything I wish to demolish, like you do, but I know things are terrible. I'm out here trying to figure out what to do about it, just like you are."

"Wake up your Intended. We should go soon."

"Stop calling him my damn Intended!" I'm beside myself, furious, and I've lost control.

I grab a spear and a vague plan comes together in my head. I'm sick of being led, pulled, pushed, and otherwise controlled. Why should I follow Ad back to Mountaintop? He doesn't want to take me, and I don't want to go.

"You want to risk your life to change it, Ad? Is your life so unbearable that you'd rather die today than continue to suffer through one more day as it is? Fine. Same with me." My shouting wakes the Veritas men, who watch us with tired curiosity. They probably cannot wait until I leave them alone. That's what I'll do.

I walk toward Cloudline.

The truth is, I've always been drawn Down Below, to see whatever lies beneath Cloudline. I've never felt at home in Mountaintop (which is strange, considering I've never been anywhere else). Even when I was younger I'd feel pulled, like a magnet, to the valley. It was a curious feeling, like an itch I could never scratch, right where my brain and eyes touched. I mentioned it once to Father, and his reaction was strong enough for me to stop admitting to any attraction, even to myself. But maybe I belong down there.

"Icelyn, come back. Stop!" Ad shouts after me.

"No. It's time I finally embrace the fact that nothing is set for me, that nothing should be set." The wispy edges of the fog grow thicker. I yank the Brathius necklace, my last connection to the life I knew in Mountaintop, from around my neck and toss it back toward him. "Nothing at all, Adorane. Would that make you happy?" It lands at his feet.

I keep on toward Cloudline. As I enter the forest, I glance back to see Ad hustle to collect a spear and some supplies and run to follow. I enter the thick white fog—first my feet, then up to my waist, and finally my shoulders and head descending into the heavy mist, disappearing as if I'd walked straight into deep water.

I hear commotion in the camp as more Veritas become aware of what I've done.

Good. For once, I'm forcing action on others, instead of having every single action forced on me.

Then the shock of my adrenalin-infused decision wears off, and is replaced by a claustrophobic realization. I cannot see farther than a foot before me down here, and I have no idea where I'm going.

41

ACLORNIS CAUGHT A glimpse of Icelyn descending into the pale lake of fog. They had to follow without delay. He rushed through the camp, rousing the Veritas, calling them to follow. Only a few minutes after Icelyn had disappeared into the clouds, the entire expedition was packed up and awaiting orders.

Aclornis had struggled over how much to share with his men. Should they be aware of the horrors they'd face, or would that cause them to shrink back and be less likely to survive the onslaught? He still didn't know.

"We enter together and are bound to one another as long as we are within Cloudline. Dangers lurk in that blindness, and we only live—if we live at all—by advancing as one. We will find Icelyn and Adorane, and then we'll progress on until we're out of the haze. At no point will we linger, ever. The less time we spend in that cloud, the better."

He signaled them forward into the murky white. They fell into a formation three men wide and six men deep, spears pointed forward. They entered Cloudline, three at a time, until they could be seen no more.

42

A WORLD OF white. Not the romantic, magical kind that greets you the morning after a snowfall, where you can still see the brown of a tree trunk or the blue of the sky. In this place you can't see any colors, any shapes, anything at all—just white.

It's like the darkness of having your eyes closed, only the inverse. It's the worst flavor of blindness; it feels like the edges of insanity. Every once in a while, something emerges from the thick mist as I move through the cloud—a boulder or a branch—and then disappears just as quickly, either because I move past it or the fog itself shifts and twirls like the current of a river. I can't even see my feet below me unless I bend my knees and crouch.

I hear Adorane calling my name. The fog muffles his voice, so he could be far away, like it sounds, or he could be nearby. I've no interest in finding out. He'll just try to grab me and deliver me to Mountaintop.

"It's dangerous in here, Icelyn!"

"I can handle it, Ad!" I shout back toward him. "Contrary to rumors, I don't crave a pampered life of comfort."

I realize, too late, that responding has made Ad aware of my position. I hear him running through the woods toward me.

"You don't understand Cloudline. You can't be alone out here."

A crash and a pained groan freeze me. It's Ad. He's fallen. I can't see him, but I can hear his pain.

"Ad?" I turn and rush back to where I think he is. It's disorienting to find only swirling thick white when you're looking for someone important.

"Ad?" I shout.

"Quiet." He replies with a forceful hiss, like a whisper, only more intense. If a person can shout in a whisper, that's what Ad does.

I obey and stand, silent. I hear movement—the crunches of sticks and pebbles being moved aside. I hear why Ad wants us to be quiet in here.

We are not alone.

43

ACLORNIS CREPT FORWARD, leading his men into the pale blindness. They'd been moving through Cloudline for at least thirty minutes and hadn't heard or seen anything. Perhaps the death that met his ancestors had been exaggerated, or whatever had terrorized them had packed up and left in the last three hundred years.

He could tell his men were having similar thoughts. While their walk through the cloud was surreal, dreamlike, and unlike anything else they'd ever done, it didn't feel dangerous. They began to let their guard down, even as they slunk forward, weapons still drawn.

So that nobody succumbed to feelings of relief, Aclornis growled a command to his men. "Defensive positions. We are about to enter the worst of it."

The Veritas in the back of their tightly packed line turned and faced the rear with their spears, now walking backward to keep pace. Those on the sides faced outward and walked sideways. Aclornis led a slowly moving battalion of Veritas through the mist, their weapons pointed in every possible direction. Ready for anything.

44

I SENSE QUIET breathing, something struggling for air. It's not Ad.

I need to find him. I don't like the idea of him alone and crippled, with something else moving through this mist.

I sink silently to my knees. Now I can see the ground, being nearer to it, and I'm less liable to crunch or crack something and make noise. I crawl toward where I hope he is.

I make out a human-shaped form crumpled on the ground, emerging from the murk. I rush toward it. "Ad?" I grab an arm and move in closer to examine. I scream in shock. Instead of looking into Ad's face, I'm inches away from a human skull yellowed and picked clean, its eye sockets hollowed out and horrible. In some primal part of my brain, my fear is that this collection of rotted bones and ancient rags *is* Ad.

I feel a steely grip clench my shoulder from behind, and I scream again.

"Quiet!" Adorane commands.

"I thought this was you," I whisper.

Ad examines the remains and laughs to himself, though not with any joy. "This is hundreds of years old." He rips open the skeleton's aged coat and reveals a ribcage cut clean through as if with a saw. "He must have been one of the original Ascenders."

"How do you think he died?" I ask.

"In a comfortable bed, surrounded by his loving family, gently drifting off to eternal sleep in his old age."

Well, no, *I* didn't think that either. Ad could be so difficult sometimes. "But what about his ribs? They look…"

"He was slaughtered. Like Jarvin."

I can't look at this ancient skeleton any longer. I stand and let the fog make it disappear from my view.

"I thought you were injured," I hiss, and it comes out as an accusation. Even though I'm glad he's not on death's door, I'm annoyed. Was his injury a trick to flush me out of hiding?

"Stay with me. There's something dangerous back there." He gestures toward higher ground and sets off downhill again. I do notice that he's limping and caked with dirt and blood. Being Ad, he doesn't even mention it. At least he wasn't faking his fall.

Between the sweat from our bodies and the mist from the clouds, we're thoroughly soaked. I notice with a thrill that we aren't heading back up toward Mountaintop. He's not going to force me back into prison.

"So, you've decided I'll be a valuable asset Down Below—"

He's deathly serious. "Silence, Ice! This isn't a fun adventure we're embarking upon. We're not children pretending. We will both probably die in here, just like your friend back there. Especially if you don't shut up and follow me."

I'm stunned into silence. The truth is, his words have terrified me. I trot off after him into the woods.

"That pile of bones wasn't my friend, Ad," I whisper at his back. I'm not sure why I say it. Maybe I've had my fill of my actual friends dying in the past week—Nandor, Jarvin—and don't care to add anybody else to that list.

45

THE VERITAS EXPEDITION knew they were close to the lower Cloudline break, and all without one attack. Aclornis entertained the idea that the dangers of Cloudline were only legends, as insubstantial as the fog that housed them.

He allowed another line of thinking to play out in his mind. What if there were nothing deadly Down Below, other than the normal predators the Apriori had had to deal with? Bears, lions, wolves, and nothing more? What if this expedition would not only avoid casualties, but could actually bring Mountaintop the greatest news imaginable—that the entire world was open to the Kith for them to explore and dominate once again?

They would be heroes.

Aclornis focused on advancing through Cloudline. He struggled to contain his optimism and keep a clear head, but every step made him more hopeful.

He felt it more than saw it—a disturbance in the white haze, a silent change in the air pressure. A muffled cry, instantly silenced, and then nothing.

"Halt!" The squad froze. Aclornis broke from his position in the front and walked along his men, inspecting the ranks.

"Where is Muralian?"

Muralian, who had been positioned in the back, was no longer with the group.

No one had noticed he was gone. Aclornis knelt to the ground at the spot where Muralian was supposed to be. He saw a small pool of blood and a line of crimson dots leading away from the group. It looked as though Muralian, a full-grown man, had been plucked from among them and carried away.

"Did any of you see anything?" Aclornis demanded. The men shook their heads, eyes wide. Examining close to the ground, Aclornis could only see his troop from the waist down.

As he waited for a response, he saw a pair of legs lifted straight up into the fog. A blurry mass of mud, fur, blood, and decay flew through the group.

"Huddle together! Arm yourselves," Aclornis commanded. They formed a circle, backs toward each other in the center, facing outward.

Whatever was hunting them was too fast. By the time it emerged from the mist, it was too late to jab it with their spears. Aclornis cursed the fog for forcing them to swing wildly in the blindness.

What Aclornis could make out in the murky white was terrible even when only half seen. Veritas he'd been friends with since school, or who were the sons of his friends, were carved into, split apart, cut in half, and hollowed out, their bodies dropped into the dirt. The remaining men looked on in horror, aiming their spears at the invisible predator.

The sketches and legends his ancestor Oliver Hailgard had recorded came to brutal life around Aclornis. He realized that standing together and fighting would never work.

"Run! Flee!"

Aclornis feared they would all die whether they stayed and faced the terror or flew from it, but he was willing to try anything so that some might live.

They sprinted downhill, dodging trees and boulders, but unable to avoid being thinned out one at a time. The dwindling survivors kept running, never looking back, ignoring the cries and screams of those that were overcome.

Aclornis still hadn't gotten a clear look at whatever it was that was decimating his expedition; he couldn't tell whether it was one creature or many. They seemed to be under attack by a horde of something terrible.

Then he saw one, just ahead of him. He couldn't stop his

momentum, and his weight pushed him forward, crashing into the massive beast. It didn't fall over, or even flinch. Aclornis fell back, staring up at the creature as it bent over and examined him.

What he had long suspected was true—Oliver Hailgard hadn't exaggerated. If anything, he'd failed to capture just how awful the Threatbelow was.

It was more terrible than anything anyone could describe.

46

I HEAR THE screams before Ad does. Or if he hears them, at least, he's not letting on.

Some are human and terrified, others inhuman and bloodthirsty. The nightmarish chorus is quiet enough that I can hope it's a figment of my frightened imagination. That's why I don't mention anything to Ad. I don't want to know if he can hear it too.

Gradually, our pace slows. I can't take it anymore.

"Adorane, what do you think is—" He cuts me off with a look that I've always hated. It's condescending and silencing, like he's right and I'm wrong and any word from me will only make matters worse.

I've not only grown silent because of Ad's glare. Something feels strange here. I'm scared, and I catch up to Ad despite my hurt feelings.

"What's wrong?"

"I don't know."

We walk forward. Ad stops and examines the ground. The fog is lightening, at least enough that we can see our feet when standing.

Ad crouches down and picks up a fallen glistening red leaf. He wipes it on his hand and then holds it out to me. His palm has been stained deep crimson.

Blood. He drops the leaf, and as our eyes adjust we see crisscrossing trails of blood staining the ground. Ad glances at me, on the verge of tears, with a look that makes me want to hold him and hope he feels better.

"What we heard were screams." Ad barely manages to get the words out. I feel bad—we were both hearing the same thing, but Ad remained alone in his fears.

I reach out and hold his hand.

We come upon a scene worse than any fear we had dared entertain.

The bodies of the Veritas are scattered, torn apart with cruel violence. I see the remains of men Ad considered brothers and uncles. Ad tries to drop my hand, but I won't let him.

We walk through the field of death. Ad examines each fallen man.

I know who he's looking for. I hope he doesn't find him.

"I should have been with them. This was my fight."

He yanks his hand out of mine. "You took me away from this! I could have made a difference."

I pause for a moment as I consider that all of this death may be my fault—because I recklessly charged into Cloudline. Did my eagerness to live my own life cause of these fine Veritas to lose theirs?

But no, they were going to enter Cloudline whether they were chasing me or not. In fact, Adorane was spared the same fate precisely because I rushed into that fog and he followed closely behind.

Can't he see that he was fortunate to avoid this? This was a massacre, and he'd be dead. "This was a bloodbath! If you'd been with them, I'd be here now, looking for *you* in the carnage." I know I should filter what I'm saying, but I can't; the emotions spill out like a flood.

"I could have done something. They needed me."

"This isn't the kind of battle that has survivors, Ad!" I realize my mistake as soon as I say it. "I mean, it could—I didn't mean…"

Ad turns away from me and continues checking the Veritas remains. Checking for his father.

I hope Aclornis escaped what no other Veritas in the expedition could. But this looks like a battle with no survivors.

Adorane freezes as he comes upon a fallen warrior. I'm too far away to see the body itself, but I can tell. Adorane collapses to the ground, his spirit sapped. And for the first time ever in the seventeen years we've known each other, I hear him cry.

It's worse than the screams from before.

We should flee Cloudline, but this is a time when mind and heart are at odds, and heart must win out. Prudence would dictate we not linger at the site of the massacre. But Ad insists that each of the fallen have a proper Veritas burial.

These were the fiercest members of the Kith, and they've been decimated. I realize, strangely devoid of any emotion, that Ad and I will soon die anyway. So why not let him do what he feels he must?

I pitch in, grateful that he doesn't stop me. It's grim work. We find sharp rocks and break the ground with them. The moisture from the mist has softened the dirt. We dig graves for each Veritas, and Ad quietly—he hopes that I cannot hear it, but I can—utters words over them and marks each plot with a wooden X. I try to give him the space he needs.

Dusk arrives, and we've only one grave left to dig: Aclornis.

I don't know whether to leave Ad alone with his father or not. I cared about Aclornis, too. He was always one of my favorite adults.

I don't want to look at Aclornis, but I must. While his torso has been mangled, I'm relieved to see that his face remains intact and, as always was the case with Aclornis, utterly noble. I lightly touch Ad's shoulder.

"He was a great man. The best I knew. Nothing false in him."

Ad doesn't flinch at my touch. "I can't think of a more dreadful curse. All the words in my head, all the things I felt for him, now forever unsaid. He'll never know."

"Oh Ad," I protest. "He knew how you felt about him."

"How could he," Ad asks, "when I never told him?"

"That he was the man who made you who you are? That when you looked in his eyes you saw the person he was, opening up to you—the kind of Veritas you wanted to be? The way he looked at you, a reflection bursting with pride and unbounded faith—it was incredible. Between the person he was and the person he thought you were, you'll always have a map for what you can become." Even though I've never verbalized it before, I've always known and loved this about Ad and Aclornis.

Adorane looks at me, in awe. "How do you know all that?"

"Every member of the Kith does. It's written on your face. Aclornis knew, too, Ad. As much as he knew anything, he knew you felt that way."

Ad doesn't shoo me away as he begins dropping dirt on Aclornis, and I'm grateful. He fashions another X out of sticks, this one larger, lovingly crafted, and adorned with flowers. Ad places it at the head of his father's grave and kneels.

"I commend you into the hands of the author of all blessings, the giver of the air we breathe, and the source of resurrection and life, Father. Death is not the final word, only a change of worlds. Be at peace. You have earned your reward; take joy in it. Until I see you in the next, Father, I am left with a hollow the size of heaven and earth in my heart."

It's a beautiful sentiment. I wish it were all true—the author of all blessings, resurrection and life. So much so that tears run down my face.

I watch Adorane rise with heavy sadness. He kicks under the leaves and brush until he finds what he's looking for. I stay quiet, afraid to disturb something sacred, as he grabs a handful of acorns and a shard of granite.

He's crying. Poor Ad! Through his tears, he etches into the acorns, one by one, methodically, until there's a pile of them. I'm dying to know what he's carving into the nuts, but it doesn't feel like my place to ask.

Finally, the miserable boy scatters the nuts all over the field. I hope he feels at least a little bit better.

47

TORRAIN HAD BEEN woken up by Icelyn's argument with Adorane, feeling like he was outside his own skin. Like he was watching a dream. Not even his own dream, but someone else's.

He watched Icelyn's disappearance, Adorane following after her, Aclornis' rallying of his Veritas and their entrance into the vast cloudy ring all without making a sound—and without taking any notice of him. By the time his shocked mind thawed enough to process rational thought, he'd been left behind.

He cursed himself for a decision he hadn't deliberately made—missing the chance to chase after Icelyn, allowing Adorane to play the hero again. Shrinking back into his bed, pathetic and passive as ever.

He could enter Cloudline and try to catch up with Adorane and Icelyn. But those two had probably already forgotten about him.

Torrain's thoughts returned to the cavern with the fog machines. There was a mystery worth solving there, and the appearance of safety and shelter.

His trip back to the cave was uneventful. Nothing chased, shot at, insulted, or hunted him. He made it within a few hours.

By the time he arrived, his thirst had grown to unbearable levels. He stuck his head into the river of fog pouring from the cave, and allowed the mist to cover his skin and condense into drops of water.

Torrain was smart, and he knew that the machines needed water to make the fog. If people from Mountaintop were behind the machinery here in the cave, couldn't they have used this water source for Mountaintop? Why rely on Waterpump at all?

Torrain couldn't easily abandon a thought; no one would ever describe him as easygoing. That one question, *What's the water source, and why couldn't we use it instead of sending an expedition Down Below?,* wouldn't let him go.

He was thankful for the obsession; it took his mind off everything else. He waited in the cave until his eyes adjusted to the darkness, and then he hunted around until he found a store of ancient Apriori tools. Torrain plunged himself into the fascinating task of taking apart one of the large fog generators.

Torrain marveled at the wires, tubes, gears, and coils fitted together in patterns intricate and, to him, beautiful. He'd never seen anything like this, but it seemed familiar. This was the kind of regimented order he'd craved since he was born, like someone had managed to take the way his mind worked and manifest it in metal and plastic right before his eyes.

Torrain removed a large sheet of coils and cried out when a jolt surged through his metal tool and shocked his hand. His heart quickened. He'd always been fascinated by this invisible energy that had been essential to the Apriori and was now lost to the Kith.

He had been electrocuted! As scared as he should have been, he was thrilled. That unseen power coursing through his hand for a second had felt otherworldly.

He touched the coils with the metal tool again and received another painful shock as a reward. This time, he could feel the cycles of energy, the waves of electricity. He was reminded of some of the Apriori myths that had survived the trip up to Mountaintop, about legendary figures who had stolen secrets from the gods—like Prometheus and fire, or Ben Franklin and lightning. In his mind, he was already adding himself into that group. Torrain, the Cognate who brought electricity back to the Kith! As much as the electricity hurt, he couldn't help but be drawn to it.

48

AD AND I spent the night near his father's grave. He wasn't ready to leave Aclornis' side yet.

We weren't huddled up next to each other, body pressed against body. There was no Catalandi-and-Adorane-style intermingling. I wish we'd been a degree less chaste—not for the romance of it, of course, but just because it grew frigid as darkness fell, and I suffered more than slept through the night. I could have used the warmth from Ad's body, just as a matter of survival. By the time rays of sun illuminated the wet white mists, I was thankful for small miracles and eager to be on our way.

We knew the time had come to leave without discussing it. I didn't get a clear look at his face because of the thick fog, but I knew he was crying. Not just tear-tinged eyes, either. Streams. Poor Adorane.

He packed up a bag of supplies that he'd gathered from the fallen Veritas. After we rushed through a less-than-satisfying breakfast of roots, he started moving down the Mountain again. I asked if he wanted to say anything before we left, a final tribute to his father.

"Let's go."

Let's go, indeed. Adorane could sometimes surprise you with an eloquent monologue, deep thoughts about one subject or another, but more often than not, you had to be satisfied with a 'Let's go' being the first and final words on the matter.

I wanted to say something. I didn't know if we'd ever come back to Aclornis' wilderness grave and have another chance to pay our respects to the great man that he was. No seventeen-year-old should ever lose his father. I hoped to mark this moment, to let Adorane know that I knew how important it was.

But instead, I just replied: "Sounds good."

Maybe Adorane was rubbing off on me.

While heading downhill, Ad turns and motions for me to freeze. I comply, fearful that he's sensed something deadly. Instead, ten feet in front of us, I see an adorable creature.

It's an animal I called a furrythief when I was a child because of the way it would pilfer food from our store houses during the winter. The Apriori called it a *raccoon.*

I hold a root out to the furrythief, which cautiously advances. "Oh, hey there, little guy. Are you looking for your family?" It extends its paws toward me, stretching to receive my gift.

I feel a swoosh of air rush past my head and watch as the tip of Ad's spear plunges into the furrythief's soft downy chest. It flies back in the air a couple of feet from the impact, and then falls over dead.

"What the hell are you doing, Ad?"

"Good idea, distracting it like that." Ad grabs the poor thing like it's a trophy.

"No! I hadn't meant to be part of your terrible plot. That was a woodland animal, not an enemy!"

"That, Icelyn, is an ultrabear. And now we can finally eat something other than roots."

An ultrabear? That's *what Ad hunts? He's always made it sound brave, as if he were risking his life. He was tracking down and killing cute little furrythieves?*

"*That's* an ultrabear? That's not even a bear!" It doesn't look anything like the bears I've seen drawn in books.

"I don't have to share the meat with you." Ad has already finished cleaning the animal and is starting a fire.

"But it was this harmless little...and he was reaching out, trusting me, and you—"

The smell from the roasting meat is enough to silence me. God, am I hungry for something more than those roots.

"Well, I wouldn't want it to go to waste," I say, as I take my first bite.

"But warn me next time. That was a rotten thing to do."

"Rotten never tasted so good, huh?" Ad jokes.

"Stop," I command, but I can't help but smile.

"That's absolute waste, Ad! And you know it!"

We've been walking for hours, and I'm starting to wonder if we'll ever leave the thick, wet blindness of Cloudline. When I ask, Ad responds with only a perturbed "Who knows?"

I guess that's only fair—how should he know, and why am I bothering to ask?

Somewhere along the latest leg of our journey, maybe because of the (I must admit) delicious ultrabear meat, we shift back into being Ad and Ice from before this madness started, at least in our conversation, and I couldn't be happier. Ad and me, our words quickly bouncing back and forth, spilling here and there with no care or filter.

"I'm not joking, Ice! I swear, many Veritas are quite bright."

"In ways that aren't intellectual, perhaps. Crafts done with their hands. Constructing and building. Sure, those are all kinds of brightness." I was trying to be kind, but Ad was pushing me.

"No. In intellectual ways. In Cognate ways."

"Please, Ad! You know that *Even the brightest Veritas is duller than the dullest Cognate*. That's a proverb for a reason!"

"Most proverbs are born of wishes more than truth, Icelyn. Cognates *wish* that were true; that's why it's a Cognate proverb. It certainly isn't a Veritas proverb. And it isn't true."

"There's no harm in being aware of your place in society. I know that I'll never run as fast or jump as high as a Veritas."

"Not with that attitude. But you could if you *wanted* to."

Ad is difficult. He takes immutable truth and simply decides to disagree with it. And if someone refuses to accept anything as true, then it becomes impossible to disprove what they're saying. Talking to Ad is like trying to build a bridge from nothing to nowhere.

But still, I'm too pleased to complain. Let Ad live in his silly world of *no* and *that's not true,* as long as he still smiles at me with his eyes when he does. As long as he's not still crying.

"Listen, Ice. I promised myself I'd never tell you this, but so much has changed that I don't see the use of keeping it a secret anymore. I took the Cognate Proficiency Test."

Now I *know* he's teasing me. "You took the CoPro? Ah, of course you did! Even though it's forbidden. Even though Veritas don't have access to it, or the training needed even to understand the questions, let alone figure out the answers. Right. And I suppose you aced it, too?"

Adorane seems serious. "Never mind. I knew you couldn't handle the truth, and I was right."

"You're *serious?*"

"I did well."

"How well? Better than a Cognate?"

"I'm not as dull as you might think."

"How well, exactly?"

"I'm sorry I even mentioned it."

"How well?"

He doesn't answer. If he thinks he's doing me any favors by choosing to be silent now, he's mistaken. My imagination has taken what little information he's given me and amplified it beyond reason.

Did he do better than most of the Cognates? Better than Torrain? Did he score better than *me*? That was impossible; I'd scored higher than any other Cognate in all of the Kith. As the Chief Cognate's child, I was expected to do nothing less.

"Seriously, Ad. How well did you do? You have to tell me."

Adorane sighs and inhales. "I don't think I should say anything more."

I punch him in the arm and force a laugh, trying to act like it's-all-no-big-deal-of-course. "You can't say half of it! If you didn't want to say more, you should have said nothing. But you said something, so now you have to finish it."

"Fine. I'd grown tired of you always saying that you'd done so well on that stupid test, winning every argument by using it as a trump card."

I want to stop him, but he's right; that's exactly what I used to do.

"So I snuck into the school, took the test, and…"

"Come on. How did you do?"

"I got a ninety-two."

"No, no. The highest score of all the Kith was a ninety-one, and that was my score. You're making that up."

"I don't make things up. You know that. I told my parents, they told your parents, and they retested me. On the retest, I scored a ninety-three. But of course it didn't count, because I'm a Veritas."

It's so stupid, but I can feel my face grow red. Am I about to cry? I hope not. Who cares—it's just a test. I force a smile. "So you're the strongest *and* the smartest? If that's true, then that just makes everything you do even stupider, since you're clever enough to know better."

It seems that, although I've been stripped of being the smartest, I still hold the title of cruelest. We continue our trip in silence.

We pass more weathered skeletons as we continue down the Mountain. There are enough of them that we no longer stop when we see them, except for a quick check to see if they've left behind anything of interest. They've been picked clean by either the elements, animals, or something else.

We come upon a mass of bones, another field of death, only this one clearly much older. "God, it's a wonder any Kith survived the trip up to Mountaintop at all," Ad mumbles, as we try to pass through without stepping on any of them. It's not an easy task.

"I wonder if we're related to any of these poor people?" I ask. Right away, I wish I hadn't. My question might make Ad think of Aclornis, who met the same fate.

Ad seems to take no offense. "Probably. That one over there bears a striking resemblance to you." He points at a hideous skeleton, vacant-eyed and yellowed.

"Yeah, I feel like I'm looking at a reflection."

Adorane's smile fades away, and I know why. The smell is terrible. Decay and rot. It's faint, but getting stronger. Something is coming.

He grips my hand and pulls me toward a pile of bones. I'm not going to fight him.

Without words, I make out his plan pretty quickly. He wants to hide under the long-dead remains. We lift a mass of skeletons and slide underneath them. Once we're far enough under, we let them fall back down on top of us.

They're heavier than I thought they'd be, but we're not in danger of being crushed. I try to numb my mind to the horror, to wondering who these bones used to be. Through the gaps between ribcages, tibia, and fibula, we're able to peek out onto the field.

The smell of destruction grows dense. I've never been claustrophobic, but with the thick fog, the weight from the bones, and that horrendous odor, I certainly feel as though I am now.

Ad and I are pressed up against one another in the dirt. His fingernails dig into my shoulder. It hurts, but I know it's a warning—stay silent. Don't move.

I can see why. Out of the swirling fog, movements emerge—smooth and quick, though at times wobbly and unsteady. As they come closer, I see pairs of legs obscured by hanging bunches of matted fur. We can only see them below the knees. The creatures are tall and walk upright.

The Threatbelows. I've seen one before, but this is Ad's first encounter.

He isn't even breathing. Neither am I.

A group of four. I wonder if this is the same pack that decimated the expedition. Despite stumbling, they move with feline grace. Something doesn't seem right about the way they look, like they are breaking the known laws of physical movement—stuttering and then smooth. I figure this must be because they are so unfamiliar to our eyes.

They are stalking—taking slow, careful steps, then stopping. Tracking. We hear long inhalations from them, breathing in. Though we can't see their heads, it's obvious that they are sniffing.

They no doubt heard us and have come to investigate. I hope that what's left of our ancient ancestors masks our scent.

Their feet are taloned, with angry sharp curved claws like none I've ever seen on any animal. So long, I estimate a good nine inches. One set of muscular haunches stops and hesitates beside our pile of bones. It's barely a foot away. I know that eventually the human sense of smell shuts off and tunes out stimuli; I'm hoping that happens to me soon.

The lethal foot kicks the pile where we hide. Skulls, ribs, and joints rattle loose and noisily fall all over us, but the skeletons mostly hold, our cover maintained.

All four sets of horrid legs move on and disappear back into the clouds.

We stay under the tragic remains of our ancestors for another hour before we dare make a sound.

We walk along in silence. The swirling fog grows thinner. I can see Ad clearly as I follow behind. More of our surroundings—shrub, tree, rock, and dirt—come into view as we approach and then pass.

Despite the horrors I've been through, I detect a small pulse of excitement. Ad and I are about to be the first humans in hundreds of years to pass through Cloudline and see the world below.

As a child, I'd spent hours imagining what it would look like, poring over books filled with exotic illustrations of man-made wonders bearing seductive names like *skyscraper, freeway, aqueduct, stadium, hospital,* and *shopping mall.* I suspected then, as I still do, that these constructions were too incredible—that surely the authors of these books had exaggerated here and there.

Who could make a building that stretched toward the heavens for more than a hundred stories? Or a coliseum that would hold more than a hundred thousand people all at once? Why would you need to, even if you could?

I used to complain to Father about it. "I fear that our ancestors were all liars, Father. The things they said they made! It cannot be true." I thought about our own meager towers, four stories tall and doomed to collapse if we pushed any further. Or our meeting places, crammed tight to fit the one hundred that made up the Kith.

"Humans achieved wonders that you and I cannot imagine, Icelyn. They captured their dreams and slowly, piece by piece, with hard work and a great deal of thought, turned them into reality. Someday, we will do that again."

I hadn't believed him then. Not one word. It wasn't as if he were around before the Ascension, so he was relying on the same thing I was when it came to believing (or not believing) in the achievements of the Apriori—books, these drawings, the stories and claims passed down from one generation to the next. He possessed no additional proof than I myself had examined.

He *wanted to believe* in these impossible wonders, which made his faith pretty suspect. The more someone wants to believe, the more likely they'll believe in something that's not true.

The latter part of his claim—that someday we would again do all these things and more? How could he get through those words without laughing? I was only eleven at the time, but even I could then see it for what it was—a foolish belief, unworthy of even a young child.

But now that Ad and I have reached the border of Cloudline and are about to pass the threshold into Down Below, I find myself replaying Father's words over in my mind—and reacting to them with more hope.

But what if it were *possible?* That's the only shift. A small change, but notable. I wasn't believing. But I wasn't not believing anymore either. What if I was about to see human wonders beyond my imagination, with my own eyes? What if I did discover the means to do all of it and more again?

"What are you hoping to see, Ad?"

Ad hasn't been privy to my internal thoughts, so this question confuses him.

"I'm sorry, please add more sense to that question and resubmit."

He can never just say "What?" and leave it at that.

"Down Below, when we finish passing through Cloudline. We'll be the first people to see it in hundreds of years. What are you hoping to see?"

"The water source, so we can remove the poison and leave as soon as possible."

"Come on! Every child dreams of Down Below. You were obsessed with it when we were five, Ad. Obsessed." Ad hates being reminded of who he was when he was younger, as if that earnest, sensitive, imaginative little boy should be a cause of deep shame for the mature, strong, brave man he's become.

"I'd like to see the weapons."

Of course, Ad comes up with the toughest, most macho answer possible. I laugh.

"No, seriously," he persists. "Do you have any idea what kind of weapons they used to have at their disposal? Vehicles that could fly like birds and drop fire on their enemies below. Metal cylinders that would explode on impact and raze whole cities. Guns—so many different kinds of guns, but all with the same lethal purpose. Glasses that you could wear to see during the night. Armored transports, tanks, that could roll over any threat and keep you safely inside while you went wherever you wanted and claimed whatever prize you desired."

I know all this. Ad went through a phase where he would draw these deadly weapons often. He even diagrammed them, as if one day he might build some of them out of twigs, acorns, and mud. (Come to think of it, I'm pretty sure he did that, too.) Compared to the weapons we use now—spears and arrows, mostly—these deadly wonders have always seemed as fanciful to me as skyscrapers and stadiums.

"What would you even do with all those weapons, if we had them?"

"It makes me angry, Ice, how stunted we've become. In the hundreds of years since we've Ascended, what more have we learned? What have we discovered? What do we know?"

"Ad, we don't have the resources on Mountaintop needed for technology like the Apriori had—"

"I'm not talking about technology alone, Icelyn. We haven't learned anything new. We pick over the remains of Apriori knowledge, as if the bare bones of what our ancestors learned are enough to keep us fed.

Where is the progress? Humans make progress—or we're supposed to. But not the Kith."

I ask one simple question about what Ad is looking forward to seeing Down Below, and he turns it into another scathing anti-Cognate treatise. Typical.

"And I suppose you think this is all due to some flaw in the Cognates, do you?"

"Cognates pride themselves on being bright, but the truth is that they aren't any smarter than Veritas. And so long as we regiment all learning, and even dictate who should be doing the learning, then we're dooming ourselves to miss out on learning anything new."

Before I can interject, Ad continues. He's riled up. "It's not just the Cognates, Ice. The Veritas, too! We try to make everything so much greater than it is, to assuage our collective wounded pride. We call ourselves heroes because we slay an ultralion, or an ultrabear—as if that compares to the Apriori, who had to fight actual threats. An ultralion isn't dangerous, Icelyn—and it's not hard to kill, either. There's no heroism to be found in the slaying of an ultrabear. That we even call them *lions* and *bears* is laughable; the Apriori referred to them as *lynxes* and *raccoons*. You're right! They're harmless, adorable, woodland creatures. But we make them out to be villains worthy of legend so we can maintain the myth that we are strong. The entire Kith, Cognate and Veritas, has settled for this baffling mediocrity. But we're good at one thing, at least: convincing ourselves we are still great."

I don't know what to say. Ad has indicted our entire civilization. Every last bit of it. And while I can't completely disagree with anything he's said, I feel compelled to offer some kind of defense for the only people we've ever know.

"If you felt so ashamed of who we are, perhaps you should have simply left." It's not what I really want to say, but it's what I feel in the moment.

"Leaving wouldn't help, because the problem is bigger than that. The reason it matters, Icelyn, is that when a true test arrives on the horizon—one that requires actual greatness to pass—we are utterly, completely lacking. To the point of death. If the Cognates were actually great, they would have found a solution to the water problem that didn't involve sending us out into the wilderness. We've been relying on a three-hundred-year-old solution for something as vital as water—we should have been working on a backup plan this entire time! And if the Veritas were actually great, they would not have been decimated in Cloudline. My father has only trained against cats and rats; he stood no chance against the Threatbelows. We settled, Ice. We settled so much that now we all deserve death. Because it always pursues us, and we simply haven't progressed enough to stay ahead of it. It was inevitable. *That's* why it matters, Ice."

Adorane has passed from simply offending me into making sense.

"Well, we'll have to change that, then. Won't we?" I mean it when I say it.

His eyes bore into me, and I'm tempted to look away, because they are deathly serious. But it's important that I don't. So much of life is lived looking away from each other, afraid to face a person as they really are, deflecting feelings and ignoring vital moments. I'm going to drink it all in right now.

"Thank you, Icelyn." He's grateful, like I've given him something precious and rare, which I suppose I have. I've listened to his private thoughts without trampling all over them.

"Let's be great, Addy. Truly great. Starting with you and me. How do you propose we do it?"

He laughs, and together we shake off the direness of his rant and the seriousness of the moment.

"How the hell should I know? I'm just a simple Veritas from Brutaltown! I'm relying on *you* for the smart stuff!" Through the thinning clouds, I can see a sparkle in his eyes as he smiles at me.

I grab his hand and pick up the pace. "Come on, we're almost there. I can feel it."

I sense that young boy that Ad once was again—vibrantly, unashamedly excited at what the world below might hold. It makes me happier than I'd expect, to catch a glimpse of him like this.

In spite of everything that's happened the last few days, I feel that excitement too—there's a vitality coursing through my body that I've never experienced before. I'm overwhelmed by the moment I find myself in. I'm finally making decisions, real ones, not just which boots to wear to the latest boring ceremony or whether I want honey or mint on my acorn cake. I'm on the cusp of entering the entire rest of the world—a realm which has been forbidden to me and the rest of humanity for centuries. And Adorane is with me, holding my hand while I'm doing it.

"Oh, and my real answer, Ice? Rivers and canyons. I can't wait to see rivers and canyons."

That's the answer I was looking for.

The clouds have thinned to the point where everything almost looks normal. In the distance, a haze still blocks the horizon, but now I can see patches of blue sky above us.

Everything is greener here, and the air is remarkably thick. We've been running for a while, and I'm not winded, because every rich inhalation fills my lungs to the brim. Though I guess we're still technically in Cloudline (here at the bottom, the boundary is not nearly so clear as it was above), this place is already so foreign to anything I've ever seen.

Whatever I've called a tree before was not actually deserving of that title, compared to the trees that are here. They stretch far above us, taller even than Brathius Tower, and they are so thick that Ad and I together couldn't put our arms around their trunks. Their leaves are a shade of green I've never seen before—so light, fair, and bright that I suspect they hold the secret to life itself in their verdant veins.

Even the bark is completely different than what I've seen before: white as snow in some places, mottled with different shades of tan in others. There is something immensely peaceful about looking at these trees. Adorane and I stop and stare for a long time, and I never feel as though we're wasting time.

I sit on the ground, in the center of a cluster of these trees, and the sight of them serves as balm on my eyes, helping to heal the damage done by all the ugly scenes I've witnessed in the last few days. Perhaps this sounds like the rambling of a child, but a world that can grow trees like this cannot be all bad; maybe it's even a little more good than bad. That's how beautiful they are.

"When we can, we should move the graves to this spot," I suggest. I can tell Ad thinks it's a fine idea. Knowing your loved one was resting here for all eternity, rather than in a cold, barren field in Cloudline, would be a gift.

"If we survive, let's promise that we do exactly that." Ad holds out his index finger, as if this is some kind of handshake that we both know. I laugh, because I have no idea what he's doing, but mirror him anyway. He wraps his finger around mine, which I suppose is needed to make our vow permanent. I feel all sorts of sensations in my finger —just one little finger!—and I start to blush because of it. *Oh, Icelyn.* Ad doesn't notice, or if he does, decides not to say anything. Either way, I'm grateful.

We run again, and the air feels so rich that it's almost as if I'm not breathing in oxygen, but inhaling all the beauty that surrounds us. Thick green vines and yellow, pink, blue and red flowers, these colors intoxicate me as we zoom through them. Against this backdrop, my memory of life in Mountaintop seems devoid of any color, a world of grays, blacks, and browns.

We've left Cloudline entirely, and I can see far ahead. However, trees and overgrowth—all that wondrous green (I had no idea there could be so many shades of one color)—block our view of Down Below.

It occurs to me that we are already Down Below.

"We have to get a better view of it. All of it," I say to Ad. He nods in agreement and points toward a stone outcropping ahead to our left. It looks like it'll be fairly easy (for Ad, at least; I'll be challenged) to climb up and enjoy the view.

Ad uses his spear to whack through the thick growth, and we reach the outcropping. He climbs and pulls me up behind him before indulging in one tiny peek. I appreciate this. We should take in Down Below at the same time, the first two explorers in this new world.

Once I'm beside him, there's only a slight climb more until we reach the viewpoint we've been looking for.

"Are you ready for this?" I ask, revealing my inner eight-year-old more than I'd like.

But Ad responds in kind: "On the count of three. One, two, three."

We turn and look.

Wow.

Part Three
Down Below

49

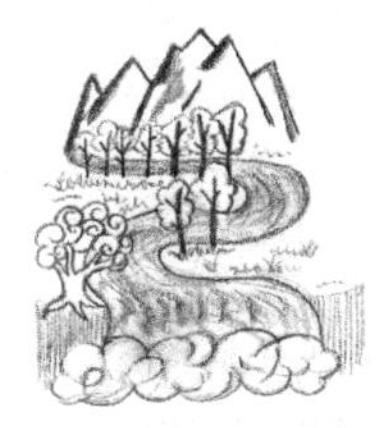

IT'S BEAUTIFUL IN a way I didn't dream could exist.

On the western side of our Mountain, a giant stretch of blue—the ocean!—goes on as far as I can see. Even from here, I can see that the water's alive and angry in places, rising up and slapping the land where they meet, then retreating to gather energy and do it again. Where the shore and water collide, waves explode into pure white, bursting into the sky like a celebration.

"There was never an ocean here before." Ad's right. The Mountain was supposed to be a day's journey from the Sea. I don't know what's happened, but I'm not complaining; it's gorgeous.

Far on the horizon, where the ocean waters grow calm, towers break through the surface of the water. They are blocky, long, thin rectangles stretching toward the sky. Instead of mud, stone, and wood, they're made of glass and metal. Even from a distance, they appear cracked and in ruin.

"There are your skyscrapers, Ice." They aren't as grand as I'd hoped. But most of the buildings' stories are underwater, so I'm not getting a full sense of their massive height. Something about the way the waters have nearly swallowed them up is eerie to me.

On the eastern side of the Mountain, a shelf of land a hundred feet above the ocean water spreads as far as we can see toward the horizon. There are mountains in the distance. Everything is a stunning array of green. Hill and plain are covered with a verdant blanket so downy that I wish I could pass my hand over it to feel how soft it must be.

Down the center of the valley, a band of water rushes fast between boulders and under trees, slithering left and right like a snake. It ends in a one-hundred-foot-tall waterfall dropping onto a yellow shore. Is that sand? I stare at the falls for a long time and still, in those white misty veils hitting the cliff walls in a hundred different ways, keep discovering something new. I don't even want to blink.

My eyes are overwhelmed. Ad has a grin stretched farther than I've ever seen. I want to take it all in, faster than I can.

"Do you see them? Ice, do you see them?" Ad points excitedly at one bend in the river, and I wait for my eyes to adjust so I can find the source of his joy.

A group of bears. *Real bears*—mighty, muscular, and scary—not the raccoons Ad has been calling "bears." There are seven of them, working the waters with their paws, trying to catch their dinner. Their fur is a deep, rich brown. One stands up on two feet, breathtakingly tall even from here.

Now that I've noticed wildlife, my eyes adjust and I see that the landscape is dotted with creatures everywhere. Adorane educates me on the names the Apriori used for them: coyotes, wolves, deer, skunks. We even see a mountain lion. Not an ultralion, mind you—a real, large, could-kill-you-if-it-wanted-to mountain lion. Eagles and hawks soar overhead. This world seems to be doing so well without humans, I almost feel bad for disturbing it.

But my stronger desire is to be *part* of this world—to live in it, interact with it, and make it mine.

"I guess that's where they once lived." I don't know what Ad is talking about, but then I follow his gaze. Camouflaged in green, so much that I thought it was more forest and hill and mountain, there's a whole city, now overtaken by vines, brush, and trees. It's crumbling and in pieces, but still impressively intact, considering it's been abandoned for hundreds of years.

My ancestors believed they dominated the earth and bent it to their will. Now nature has returned the favor. I went through a phase when I devoured books about ancient(er) Apriori civilizations, from thousands of years earlier, with exotic names like the *Aztecs* and *Egyptians*. By the time their cities and monuments were discovered by the more modern Apriori, they had been swallowed up by the jungles or sands that surrounded them. What I'm seeing now, this great city of the Apriori, reminds me of those pictures—only instead of pyramids and temples made of stone being swallowed up, this is a "modern" metropolis, the kind that would drive Father insane with jealousy.

Ad points into the near distance, to the river's edge, at a low stone aqueduct filled with pipes and surrounded by machinery. "There's Waterpump's source. Time to figure out what's going on."

He doesn't need to convince me. I'm eager to enter the valley.

Just before we tear ourselves away from this view, I see a thin line of smoke rising up into the clear air.

"What's that, Ad?"

Ad appears as confused as I am as our eyes follow the smoke down to the stone chimney of a shack, more humble than any round in Mountaintop. A collection of wood, stone, and dirt, seemingly piled together haphazardly rather than built.

"Who could be making a fire?"

"Let's go find out."

I'm amazed at how well I've already adapted to these lower lands. There's a powerful shift going on within me in how I relate to my body.

Ever since I was a child, my body has been more antagonist than ally. It would run into things, fall down, and get beaten up, knocked around, and tired. Beyond that, it was always getting me into trouble. It craved a taste of the sweet berry tarts Mother had forbidden until after dinner. When I gave into my body, just a nibble, *all* of my books were taken away! How unfair! My body didn't care if I couldn't read books, and this was all her idea. I was the one that kept her from eating the whole tart, yet I was the one who was punished!

As I grew older, my body pummeled me with desires and impulses that were at odds with what *I knew* I wanted. It was exhausting having to analyze every one, figure out where to put them, and whether to accept or deny them.

Then there were the comparisons! My body, in a lineup against other bodies, for the whole world to see. Everyone was too polite to verbalize their judgments, but I heard them anyway, whenever I was standing beside Catalandi or other Veritas girls who were allowed to indulge their bodies in any way they wanted (and thus held a distinct advantage over me). I would have preferred to be a brain in a jar, if given the choice. Do away with this body nonsense, which has only brought me pain.

But for the first time, my body and I seem to be coming to an understanding. We aren't fast friends yet, but I am starting to see things her way, and I'm realizing that she wasn't completely wrong in everything. The benefits of our newfound alliance are surprising me.

Small things. The way my finger came alive when Adorane and I wrapped ours together and promised to move the graves. Why bother figuring out what that meant, trying to categorize those sensations, to quiet them down? Instead, I just enjoyed them. Every time Ad and I brush against each other, or he grabs my hand or my shoulder, I feel a rush of excitement in my body. And for this first time, I am accepting that excitement—just feeling it. Nothing more. But nothing less, either.

The smells, sounds, and sights of this new world! My body is awake to all of it, like an overly passionate tour guide pointing out one wonder after another. Instead of muzzling her, I let her talk, and I find that she has a lot to say that's worth hearing.

My body can run, leap, and climb, as if gravity no longer pushes on us as hard as it always has. I'd always felt so heavy before, with a drag on my bones hell-bent on making me slow to a stop whenever I tried to move. Now I *want* to move; it feels *good* to move.

And here's where my body is really starting to astonish me—one last gift that I never could have predicted. When I'm running, sweating, and moving, and my body is alive to the world around me and feeling all the sensations it wants to feel—my thoughts are sharper, deeper, and stronger. *My thoughts!*

As I move, I am able to mull over my misgivings about Ad and the Veritas and their seeming devotion to religion in a way I couldn't before. *Maybe their faith isn't so much a failure on their part, but a fault of ours, as Cognates, for allowing them to experience a void so vast they need to fill it with fantasy.* Sifting through my thoughts about Father and Tranton back in Mountaintop was previously impossible, but now I can explore the subject without being overcome by panic and hopelessness. *Tranton was able to do what he was doing because he was allowed to. If I wanted to stop him, I'd have to find a way to deny him permission.*

As we run, there continue to be more thoughts, revelations, and insights. They come so fast I wish I could write them down.

I keep pace with Ad (by moving faster, for once, rather than asking him to slow down) and marvel at the thoughts I discover in the process. These are intellectual trails I'd have never found had I been a brain in a jar.

Ad glances back at me at one point and suppresses a smile. "Looks like someone is on the verge of a Verihigh!" Verihighs are a myth, something that the Veritas of old claimed their people experienced—a moment when the body and mind would commune on an enlightened level and spill over into a supernatural plane.

"Oh please, that's ridiculous!" I mean for my denial to sound like a lighthearted retort to mirror Ad's own playful accusation. Instead I sound way too serious—as if I'm afraid he's correct.

"Um, yeah, I was joking. Icelyn Brathius, deep in the throes of a Verihigh? That *is* ridiculous."

I laugh along, though on some level I feel hurt. Of course, it *is* insane, Verihighs and all that—but still, if they were real, why doesn't Ad think *I* could ever experience one?

We've reached the valley. The air is thick, and we don't seem to be descending anymore. It's strange, but with these clusters of trees and underbrush, being under a canopy of green and no longer high on a mountain, it's difficult to get a bearing on where we are in relation to that incredible landscape we'd seen earlier.

We've been moving along a trail for the past mile or so, one that appears recently used. Used by what, we don't know, and that makes Ad nervous. He clutches his spear tightly and is hyper-vigilant to even the slightest sound. There are many slight sounds.

There's no way we can leave this trail and make progress; these woods are as thick as solid stone. We try to move off-trail briefly, but we cover barely a tenth of a mile before limping back onto it, covered in scrapes and scratches for our efforts.

The valley is crammed with life. Every couple of minutes we see a creature, bird, or bug that we've never seen before. Many we've never even studied—they didn't make it into the books—so we invent names for them.

Adorane hears another chirp or rustle, and we rush through a silent routine that has grown familiar by now. He holds his arm out and guides (pushes, really!) me off the trail, into or under the brush, then crouches in front of me, his spear at the ready to stab whatever threat may appear. We stay like this until he's satisfied that we're safe to proceed.

"I'd like a spear, Ad," I notify him as we resume walking on the trail.

"You don't even know how to use it. They can be dangerous, more trouble than they're worth in untrained hands."

He takes a high view of himself for a warrior who's only fought creatures that I could subdue with soft words and a belly rub. *If only there were some baby raccoons I could run through for practice*

"All the same, I think I've watched you enough to know the basics. What's the worst that could happen?"

"You'd stab yourself. Or me."

I grab his spear with a quick motion, and it upsets him, even though I'm only playing. Probably because no raccoon-slaying warrior worth his salt should allow a weak Cognate girl to steal a spear from him, and he knows it.

I laugh and point the spear at him, holding it in a purposely unwieldy way. "Oh no, what is going on? This thingy is so hard to control!" I point it here and there, as if I have no say in the matter. "I hope I don't stab you—or worse, myself!"

Ad tries to grab the spear from me, using his serious voice to warn me that this is not a toy and we are not playing a game and when did I become so goofy anyway. But there are cracks in the direness of his commands, and we both know he's moments away from erupting in laughter.

He grabs the spear and we're locked in a struggle, both laughing, until we finally drop it and collapse to the ground. We lay beside each other, our stomachs hurting from laughing too much.

"Fine," he manages to get out, "I'll carve you a spear."

"That's all I ask, Ad."

Lying on the path, looking up at the brilliant blue sky that peeks through the lush green canopy above, the heavy warm air pushing down on us, the sweet smells and pretty sounds flowing over and through us, I know I could get used to life in the valley. It's nice down here.

50

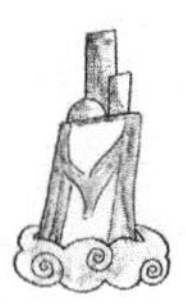

TRANTON AND NICHOLAS had reached an uneasy peace, and Mountaintop returned to a muted semblance of normalcy. It helped that Nicholas' prediction had finally come true. The cold snap had begun, and with it, snow was falling. Something about drinkable moisture collecting on the ground had eased the direness of the Waterpump situation. Even though they all realized that it wasn't enough to keep them alive through the entire year, having it there was comforting.

Nicholas and Marjan watched children play in the snow, and he could almost imagine that it was a simpler time, before he faced this crisis. He cursed himself for feeling bored and unimportant then. If only he could fade back into historical obscurity.

Nicholas reached for Marjan's hand, and she held his fast. They'd been getting along better, both resigned to their misery, hoping for news of Icelyn every day and never receiving any. Still, they only had each other now, and both had realized they weren't ready to lose what little they had left.

Nicholas took a moment to savor the relative calm. He knew it was about to end.

Marjan had made sure of that.

They were headed to the outskirts of town, to Cliffside—a gusty, dangerous drop-off where one false step could plunge someone thousands of feet into Cloudline below. They were beginning the weapons distribution.

This had been Marjan's mad idea. Each family that made up the Kith should receive one gun, for protection, she claimed. It wasn't fair to have all the weapons in the hands of the Tarlinius—and by extension, Tranton. Most of the citizens now hid in fear.

Since the Code decreed that Nicholas had absolute power as the leader of Mountaintop, they weren't breaking any laws by making this decision. Tranton hadn't thought Nicholas would be capable of anything so brazen, so he had let him know where the weapons cache was.

Nicholas approved of Marjan's plan, though it felt like swallowing poison or jumping to his death. She believed with all her heart that it was the only just thing to do, and he owed her after driving their only daughter away.

She'd gathered the key Veritas leaders who hadn't gone Down Below, and in the darkness of night they'd waited until the Tarlinius patrols were away from Kith Hall. They found the cache in the basement without any trouble. It had all been easy. The most difficult aspect of the entire heist had been transporting the weapons to Cliffside.

To evade Tranton and the Tarlinius, the distribution had been set up at this windy, desolate toehold in the side of the Mountain. The Veritas and Cognates that Marjan knew could be trusted had already gathered there. The family patriarch (or matriarch, in cases where the father had been part of the expedition that went Down Below) would sign in and claim a weapon. No choosing; that would take too long. The weapons were to be randomly assigned.

"This is your family weapon, and no replacement shall be provided in the event that you misplace or break yours. This should only be used for protection, and misuse will result in swift and serious consequences. Do you understand that which I have said?" Marjan would read the disclosure out loud to each patriarch or matriarch and wouldn't place the weapon into their hands until they agreed.

Nicholas didn't like the mood. He'd expected relief from this redistribution of power in their community. Rather, he felt desperation—an unrelenting need for each Kith member to just get their hands on a gun at all costs, so that they could feel safer.

What are we protecting ourselves against? Each other? The thought scared him. He feared that they'd rung a bell today, and that a silence they'd all taken for granted would be irrevocably disrupted.

"I agree." Nillrod Panzench, one of the few Veritas men who hadn't gone Down Below, responded to the disclosures that Marjan read to him.

Nicholas placed a dull, aged revolver in Nillrod's eager hand. It was heavier than Nicholas expected. He caught a glimpse of Marjan's disgust at the thing, and agreed with her.

God, he hoped no one ever had to use this.

Only one thing brought Charnith Hailgard even a blip of joy these days, and that was the anticipation she felt when visiting the Message Tree. Adorane had told her to expect communication from him, carved into acorns and delivered via squirrel.

The whole setup was Adorane through and through, and she smiled thinking about it.

But every visit she'd made had ended in disappointment. Until today.

She cried as she turned the acorns over in her hand. She tried to feel his essence through the nut he'd been holding not so long ago.

BATTERED BUT NOT BROKEN

was written into one.

WE'LL ALL BE TOGETHER AGAIN

carved into another.

51

TORRAIN HADN'T BEEN this infatuated in his entire life. The dark thoughts that had become his constant companions left him alone for the first time since his mother had died, and that alone was a gift of unimaginable worth. But beyond that, he felt a passion marked by a racing pulse and flushed skin, and he loved it.

It all began with a simple thought. Could he reverse what one of these machines did so that instead of creating fog, it devoured it? An anti-fogging machine that swallowed the murky white? Maybe he could clear a path right through Cloudline and easily enter Down Below.

He'd taken one of the cloud generators apart and felt he now understood what each piece did. Even when his instinct turned out to be wrong, there was joy in figuring out his mistake and learning the true purpose of this wire or that gauge.

He'd found a small tube that supplied water to the machines from underground. He took a sip of the water. It tasted terrible, the same as it smelled: like rotten eggs. He even felt sick afterward, and suffered a bout of vomiting. This water source was not the answer to their thirst.

But even that setback couldn't dampen his spirits. He'd been at it for hours, oblivious to hunger, and his effort was starting to pay dividends. He'd managed to make a portable version of the machine—

crude, but it held together, complete with a small solar cell for power. Now he could test whether it did what he thought it would do.

He tightened the final bolt and exited the cave. He positioned the machine so that it pointed toward the fog that flowed from the generators and connected two wires to power it up. (At some point, he reminded himself, he should replace that with a switch.)

It sputtered to life and started to groan. The invention was working —the fog pouring from the cave did start to part, and a path cleared out in front of Torrain. Torrain felt a thrill at this sorcery he had conjured and let out a whoop that would have embarrassed him if he weren't alone. For the first time he could remember, he'd wanted to change the world around him, and he *had,* exactly as he'd planned. He'd made a difference. He hadn't made things worse, a result he'd unfortunately grown accustomed to. No, he'd made everything much better.

52

I AM CONVINCED I can never return to Mountaintop. I feel alive down here in the valley. I have my spear, sharpened to a fierce point courtesy of Ad, and I'm walking beside him on the trail. Everything here feels more real. After seeing what my life can hold, I can't return to that small, cold outpost, where my steps are walled in and my options are constricted. Somehow, this thought doesn't bring me panic; it is simply a fact. My life will be different now.

We were able to scramble up a pile of boulders at one point not long ago to get a better view of where our trail is taking us. We saw the cabin and the smoke again, and I was surprised at how close it was. Only another mile or two.

Ad's grown quiet, and he seems agitated, though he won't admit why (or even that he's upset at all). It could be that he's concerned about whatever is living in that cabin, and I suppose I should be, too. But ever since we've entered the valley and left Cloudline behind, I feel like I've left death behind, too. I can't see anything so horrible as what I've experienced at higher elevations existing down here.

I've become optimistic. Surely the water poisoning was not on purpose—just some natural phenomenon that Ad and I will be able to identify and remedy! And in any case, it won't matter for long. Why should humanity remain huddled at the top of a cold stone mountain when we could return here to flourish and expand? I know Ad will mock my rosy outlook, so I keep most of it to myself.

My great-great-great-great-great grandfather led humanity to the top of the Mountain, for survival, and now I will lead them back down into the valley. I will usher in a golden age—one without claustrophobia, birth quotas, disbursement, or eyeglass rations. One marked by hope, freedom, and growth.

"Why are you smiling?" Ad asks me suspiciously.

I didn't realize I was. "I just..." Should I share my thoughts with him? Who am I kidding? This is Adorane. I know what he'll do. "Nothing. I like it here."

"That's it? You like it here, so you're looking as if you just remembered the funniest joke of all time?"

"I...really like it here."

"Well, don't get too comfortable. We'll do what we need to do, and then we're gone."

"Why should we leave so quickly, Ad?"

"You're forgetting that *you* shouldn't even be down here at all—"

I cut him off before he can finish. No need to remind me of how awful he was before I entered Cloudline. "There's so much to explore down here—just cataloguing the wildlife is a life's work! And there's your river, the overgrown cities of the Apriori, so much to see!"

"This isn't heaven, Icelyn. We haven't entered paradise. You act like we've discovered a utopia."

I'm now grateful I hadn't shared my thoughts about this valley with Ad, because I couldn't imagine any heaven, if such a place existed, being better than this.

"Well, it's a thousand times better than Mountaintop. I'll tell you that."

"It's dangerous, Ice. Don't forget what happened in Cloudline. We are in great danger right now. We'll be lucky to return to Mountaintop alive."

"I can't conceive of anything dangerous living among such beauty. All the death that's been crowding us, Ad? It's been up there, just outside the Wall, in Cloudline, high above the valley. I mean, breathe in, Ad! Do you smell that? That's what this place is. Sweet."

Adorane rolls his eyes. "You're going to get us killed with all that sweetness, Ice."

I remind myself that Ad has been through countless traumas—he's just lost his father, for God's sake. Of course he's going to have a hard time recognizing when things are truly good.

Like they are now, down here.

He'll come around.

53

THE CABIN IS in a grassy field that backs up against a grove of trees, which is where we are huddled right now. While the building itself seems halfway to ruin, the setting couldn't be nicer. There are yellow and blue flowers carpeting the field, and tiny birds flit from one to another, hovering a spell before moving on. Even the birds here are more charming than the dark, lumbering ones we have in Mountaintop.

Adorane insists on treating this like a serious military siege, so we've been slinking from tree to tree as we make our approach.

My best guess is that the cabin is either occupied by someone the Kith disbursed or the relative of someone disbursed long ago. I have the benefit of my experience in the Mines, and Ad doesn't know about that, so he could be forgiven for not suspecting we are about to meet more humans. Probably ones weaker (or uglier, or stupider) than us, too.

We've reached the edge of the forest. There are only about two hundred yards of clearing between us and the cabin now. New sounds filter into my ears, unfamiliar but alluring. Much like the singing I heard from the Veritas, or a birdcall, but fuller, more dramatic, richer. It fills my chest as much as my ears.

"What is that?" I ask. Ad hears it too, and he appears deep in thought, like he's trying to remember something important.

"An orchestra!" he exclaims, but quietly, because we're still hiding in the brush. "The Apriori would all play different instruments together, a hundred of them at a time, even. In unity."

I don't need the history lesson; I'm familiar with the orchestras of the Apriori, although of course I've never heard one. I feel a flash of annoyance that Ad identified the music before I did. It only supports his theory that he's smarter than me.

"Do you mean that there are a hundred or more…somethings…in that cabin, playing instruments?" I can't fathom how this could be, but I've seen so much in the past days that I'd previously considered unfathomable that anything seems possible.

Ad stifles a laugh, like my sensible question is so ridiculous that he can barely keep from roaring out loud. He must be able to tell that he's offended me, because he immediately tries to placate. "Oh, come on, Ice. You have to admit that question was absurd. It's a recording of the music. Remember? The Apriori had the technology to save sounds for later and listen to them whenever they liked."

So many wonders and miracles that seem impossible. Recording sound. I guess this legend of the Apriori is real, too. "So that's what we're listening to? A recording of the Apriori playing their instruments?" The thought of it is spectacular.

"Yes—it's at least three hundred years old."

It's almost as if we've stepped through a door that's taken us back in time. We're the only humans who have heard this recorded music in centuries.

Or maybe not.

"Who's playing the recording?"

"It's about time we find out." Ad stalks toward the cabin.

54

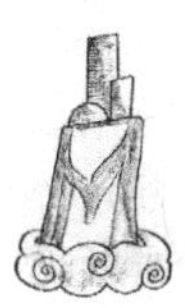

"THERE'S BEEN A shooting in Brutaltown!" the Tarlinius reported, out of breath, having outrun his conditioning.

Nicholas erupted with questions. "What? How? Who was shot? Who did the shooting? Was it fatal? Has the aggressor been subdued?"

Tranton sat back. Couldn't Nicholas see? This was a good thing.

Tranton had pretended to be angry about Marjan's tiny rebellion, but only with Nicholas. *How dare she? This was a dangerous idea!*

But the truth was, he'd quickly realized that sharing the guns would benefit them.

Tranton had assumed that having all the guns under his control would be the best way to maintain order in the town. If the Cognates were going to keep their rightful positions over the Veritas, they'd need superior weapons to counter the Veritas' sheer numbers and brawn. But doubt had crept into his thoughts as he watched this play out. He alone couldn't wield all the weapons, so he'd been forced to trust the Tarlinius with them. And any plan that hinged on trusting the decision-making powers of the Tarlinius was bound to fail.

He'd run over it in his mind, and he knew there would come a time when some Veritas would arise and inspire the others. Tranton was a student of Apriori history, and he knew that revolutions were inevitable.

Unless Tranton could control Mountaintop while not making his leadership a target for the oncoming revolution. *This* was the key.

When Marjan had shared the weapons with all of the Kith, Tranton saw that it wasn't such a bad idea. Why would anyone bother to overthrow a regime that had willfully shared its guns with the people? They only had everyone's safety in mind—the collective good.

Tranton had recently delved further into the history of Down Below. Many Apriori civilizations had risen and fallen. But he'd come across one passage, author unknown, that explained how one of the greatest regimes had maintained an ironclad lock on its population for centuries without a single revolt or revolution of consequence. The only thing that had ultimately destabilized this empire was the Threat Below. Its enslaved populace had remained blissfully unaware of their shackles until the end.

The passage had struck Tranton as brilliant. And as Nicholas prattled on about the Kith needing control of their own security in a flustered attempt to defend what he and Marjan had done, the words had come to Tranton in a flash:

'Fear is the most elegant weapon. Your hands are never messy. Threatening bodily harm is crude. Work instead on minds & beliefs, play insecurities like a piano. Be creative in approach. Force anxiety to excruciating levels or gently undermine the public confidence. Panic drives human herds over cliffs. When nothing is safe, sacred or sane, there is no respite from horror. Absolutes are quicksilver. Results are spectacular.'

Why bother wielding a physical weapon? Lower yourself to that level, and you remain in reach of those who could dispose of you in the same way. But control the *emotions* of the Kith—well, then they will not only obey you, they'll appreciate you for it.

Now there'd been a shooting, and Tranton could only hope it was a Veritas taking his fears out on another Veritas. Left to their own devices, the Kith had made each other the targets. Tranton was free to be the leader they looked to for help, the one they begged to take back control.

Nicholas was not fit to be Chief Cognate, Tranton thought in disgust. If he could abdicate his position of leadership at this moment, and instead spend his days busying himself with sketching the seeds of blooming conifers, he would.

"What should we do, Tranton?" Nicholas asked. "Do we send a

Tarlinius? I fear we've made a grave mistake."

There would be no revolution in Mountaintop, ever. Tranton was sure. Except the one that had already occurred: the coup Tranton had just completed, without anyone so much as noticing.

Nicholas and Tranton visited the round on the east side of Brutaltown where the shooting had occurred. Yeunith's wife, Giza, hadn't begun the formal mourning process. She was still paralyzed with shock.

Tranton examined Yeunith's lifeless body. He wiped away the pool of blood from the man's chest until he revealed a small puncture wound the size of an acorn. Incredible how small things could cause such massive destruction.

"Bullet wound, just below the heart." Tranton shook his head, clucking sympathetically, as if he hated how much damage guns could do and yearned for the days before they were unleashed upon the Kith.

Nicholas felt a hot flash of resentment. Tranton was the one who had introduced the weapons to Mountaintop! A month ago, an argument between Yuenith and another Veritas would have resulted in a black eye.

"Just this morning, we were quarreling over how much water he took in his tea for breakfast," Giza said, stunned.

Nicholas knew Yuenith had not been in his right mind since Aclornis had formed his group to go Down Below—a team that he hadn't been chosen to join, to his shame.

The reason he hadn't been chosen was that Yuenith hadn't been important enough to be rationed spectacles. It had been decided that his assigned job, to gather refuse from the Cognates' labs and bury it outside the bounds of Mountaintop, required no visual acuity. His sight hadn't been so bad that it would force a disbursement—not yet—but it had grown poorer, and everyone knew he'd be no help Down Below.

Veritas waited their entire lives to display their brawn, and to be cut out of this once-in-a-lifetime chance had taken a toll on Yuenith. He wasn't the only one, either. Nearly all of the male Veritas who had to "stay behind and guard the women and children" had descended into a pervasive mood of gloom and dissatisfaction. Fights had increased, both inside the home and out.

Tranton had even been notified that the Tarlinius had discovered fermentation setups in the woods. Alcohol was forbidden, and this was a part of the Code that had never been challenged, as everyone knew the horrors drinking had brought upon the Apriori. Yet the old processes had been dusted off and resumed. Tranton decided to let it all run its course. If the Veritas wanted to drink themselves into a stupor, who was he to stop them? A numb people would be easier to manage.

"Did you understand the nature of the conflict between Yuenith and —?" Tranton let the question hang in the air.

"It's got to be the Panzenchs," said an eager boy, Istoch, muscular for his age, who had only recently turned twelve. "Nillrod has been taking Father's work, trying to push him out to pasture, Father said."

Those left behind had become desperate to prove their dwindling worth. Nillrod and Yuenith performed the same task, and Nillrod probably feared that soon there'd only be enough work to justify one refuse collector.

Nicholas felt like he should say something. "Giza, Istoch. I cannot find lofty words to make this better for you. But I do want to promise that we will find out who did this, and you will have justice. The Code cannot broken, and the Kith are not weak. We are not a lawless people."

Tranton produced a handgun from within his robe, to Nicholas' surprise. He thought he'd distributed them all. *How many of those does he have access to, exactly?* Tranton pressed it into Istoch's hand. "For protection only. You're the man of this household. Do you understand that?"

If Giza thought it was inappropriate to hand a deadly weapon to a mere boy, she didn't say anything. Istoch looked grateful.

Nicholas wasn't sure. "Should we be entrusting such power to boys?"

Tranton spoke sharply. "He's not a boy anymore, Nicholas. Look at him. He's a man now."

As they left, Nicholas was eager to begin ferreting out whoever had done this awful thing to poor Yuenith. "Do you think it was Nillrod Panzench? It makes sense. We should pay him a visit."

"Nicholas, focus on the higher duties we are called to fulfill. We only muddy ourselves by getting involved in this feud. Why force ourselves into places we aren't welcome, where we will only be cast as villains? I gave Istoch what he needed to keep his family safe. That's all we can do. We provide others with the tools; they are the ones who need to use them."

"I promised them we would do what we could."
"You shouldn't have done that."

55

AD PULLS A door open, taking great pains to keep it quiet. He crouches and slips in. I follow close behind him.

I'm thankful for the music, which emits from a rotating thin black circle atop a brown box. It sounds beautiful. As the waterfall, ocean, river, and green valley were for my eyes, the notes lavish themselves, gorgeous and dizzying, on my ears. I've never considered *sound* a source of joy; it's always seemed purely functional. You hear a bell and know it's time for the meeting to start; you hear your mother's voice and know you're expected to do something. You hear the howl of a Threatbelow and know it's time to run. It's a revelation that something I can hear could quicken my heart rate in a good way.

Also, the symphony is loud enough to mask the sounds of our movements.

It's cramped in here, dark, despite the bright sunlight outside. The cabin is small—it looks like three rooms at the most—and the room that we're in, an entryway, is stuffed full with manmade Apriori tools and items. I recognize a few—there's a lamp, which they used for electrical light (sunlight throughout the night!), though it's not doing anything right now. A collection of metal forks, which they used to stab and scoop the food they ate (unlike the simplified flat stone utensil we use now). I see a brush that the Apriori women used to detangle and style their hair, and I grab that for myself. Might as well try it out at some point, for fun more than anything.

I'm tempted to point out all of the items I recognize to Ad, to show off my knowledge, since he'd challenged it earlier. But he beats me to the punch; since it appears no one is in the cabin, he begins giving me a whispered lecture.

"Here are kitchen appliances. They required electricity, so they'd be worthless to us. I think that one was used to keep things cold, that one to mix up their foods, and that one to chop up ingredients."

"I know that," I reply, though the chopper and mixer are both new to me. Ad opens his bag and starts taking artifacts. Though this feels like stealing, we are outside of Mountaintop, so the Code doesn't apply here.

He grabs a few small cubes, which have different amounts of dots on each side. *Tice*, I believe they were called. "These are only for entertainment, but they don't take up much space, and I've always wanted to play with dice."

Oh—dice, not tice. Close enough.

Ad stops, his face lighting up with excitement. "A flare!" He picks up an unnaturally uniform red stick, clearly not from any tree. "If you rip the lid off, fire and smoke pour out! So wondrous."

He secures the flare in his bag, along with other metal items that could be used as weapons or to build. The Apriori used some of them for both, as I suspect Ad will, too. One I remember is called a *hammer.* Some Apriori thought one of their gods carried one around all the time. The Apriori and their gods—I'll never completely understand it. It all seems so silly. If I invented a god, he would carry a flare or a lamp or something more magical than a hammer.

I wonder, does Ad's god tote a hammer, or some other tool? Maybe a mixer or chopper. You never know when you might need to mix or chop something.

We creep out of the small storage room and approach the main space in the cottage. I see a stone fireplace at the center of a large room filled with a lively fire. Ad and I exchange a glance. Fires don't just build themselves in fireplaces. Animals don't build them, either.

The music, and the flickering flame combine to produce peace and longing in me, as if *this* should be what home feels like—not the cold, dreary, silent spaces in Brathius Tower. I force myself out of this stupor, because I'm pretty sure we're in a dangerous place, not one where I should be tempted to curl up and read while drinking some tea.

Ad silently points toward the corner of the larger room, in the shadows, and I follow his finger until my eyes adjust to the darkness and I see what he sees.

I can barely breathe. It's all terribly familiar. Just like we saw in Cloudline: the dark, blood-mottled fur of the Threatbelow. At least two of them, standing in the corner, unmoving.

Have they seen us, too? We can't tell, but it feels like an ambush, and we can't have more than a moment or two before they pounce.

56

TORRAIN CUT A clear swath through the thick fog. The initial rush of pride hadn't faded, although he'd been moving through Cloudline for some time now.

He'd never made a measurable impact before. Even when he'd pout or throw a fit with his parents, their standard method for dealing with his unpleasant moods had been to ignore him.

"He's looking for attention when he acts this way," his father would insist to his mother. "Pretend you don't notice, and eventually he'll give up." Of course, Marcel Pannous had been correct, but sometimes a person can be correct and still wrong. What's the matter with paying attention to your son's fits now and then?

As a result, Torrain had always viewed the world, and the people that populated it, as an immovable static tableau that he could not interact with. Everything was fixed permanently, unable to change. Like Icelyn's misery at being betrothed to him. He could do nothing about that.

This pathway being carved out of the thick cloud was changing how he felt. He *was* making a difference. He'd invented this machine, and now Cloudline was safer because of it. No one else had done that. He was changing the world. If Adorane and Icelyn had only waited for him, they would be safer right now.

He realized suddenly he'd been making an assumption—that the increased visibility made him safer in Cloudline, as if the Threatbelow needed white blindness to hunt. He considered that perhaps he was wrong, and he had a brief flash of panic that his survival so far hinged more upon the fact that the monsters lurking nearby had already fed and were not hungry at the moment. But he quickly shrugged this off. His invention was protecting him, he would assume, because he knew that confidence was invaluable for survival—and still an asset whether acquired by legitimate or delusional means.

Torrain had endless paths laid out before him, now that he knew he could press this world to his will. Whatever horror was Down Below, he would study it and invent something to protect against it, or even use it for good. Anything was possible.

First, he had to get through Cloudline.

Hopefully that would be easy. He gripped the handle of his machine and moved triumphantly forward into the mist.

57

AD SPRINGS TOWARD the danger. Someday I hope my instincts will be half as aggressive as his. By the time I decide upon the right course of action, he's often almost finished doing it.

Ad wields a vicious knife, long and sharp and metal, which I suppose he stole from the storage room. I grab the hammer (*look who's a hammer-wielding god now!*) from his bag and follow, my senses on high alert for the impending clash between us and the beasts in the corner of the room.

Ad finds no resistance. He reaches the larger creature and stabs. His knife cuts into nothing at all! As if the monster is hollow, just a shell. I swing the hammer at the beast and hit the awful thing straight on, but my hammer continues through, finding nothing to absorb the blow.

"What in the world?" Ad pulls his knife down, puzzled, splitting the fur down the middle. There's nothing inside.

"It's just a cloak, or…" I trail off, because I don't quite know what it is. I do know that it smells terrible, like fetid meat and death. Ad angrily grabs the bloodstained monstrosity off the wall and examines it.

There is a head attached to the fur cloak—the fearsome, fanged, vicious-looking head of a bear, frozen in the moment when it chomped the life out of some poor animal.

Ad looks closer at the head. Below the bear's angry maw, there's an opening carved out.

"It's a helmet. To be worn." Ad observes. Both of these awful things hanging in the corner, which we thought were beasts, are actually outfits. But who would wear these horrid furs? They are huge, fit for someone or something almost double our height.

Ad lowers the disgusting bear head onto his own. "God, Ad, don't wear that. It's horrible." I can tell that regardless of any repulsion he might feel for the ghastly head and cloak, a part of him likes it.

When he wears the helmet, his face is obscured in shadowy darkness.

"You look like one of…" I don't want to finish my statement. He looks like a Threatbelow. He looks like one of the monsters that killed his own father.

"Quick, put this on." Ad grabs the other head and cloak, and tosses it toward me. It's incredibly heavy, so I drop it by accident, even though I probably would have done so on purpose, too, if given the choice.

"No, Ad. You might enjoy wearing that, but I think it's terrible."

"Ice, I'm not asking. This isn't for fun. Put it on." His voice has grown clipped, intense, so I'm not going to argue. I lift the heavy, rotten cloak from the ground and study it for a second. This head is different—a mountain lion, not a bear.

"Hurry, Ice! Come on."

I squeeze my head into the helmet and have to hold my breath to keep from fainting, it smells that bad. The heavy skins and fur press down on me, and I struggle to keep from collapsing.

"Come here." Ad grabs my hand, and pulls me back into the corner, where the cloaks had been hanging. He drags a couple of wooden stools toward us, and we stand on them. He does all this with such desperate intensity that I know not to question him.

I labor to keep my balance on the stool, hidden under the weight of this cloak and lion's head, I realize why Ad has been acting so afraid.

At some point, unnoticed by me, the music had stopped. Now all I hear is unsettling silence. But also, something else. Creaks and groans, just outside of the cabin, as if the deck is being walked on.

The sounds are growing closer, and they're unmistakable.

Footsteps.

* * *

Ad and I stand still in the corner, weighed down by the bloodstained furs and animal heads. I want to ask what we should do, but I don't dare open my mouth. I feel alone. I can't even see him.

I'm on the verge of fainting, but can't will myself to breathe one more inhalation of this stench. I'd rather collapse from oxygen deprivation.

I reach out, and Ad grabs my hand tight. It's exactly what I need. I relax, and my lungs fill with air. I try to get my bearings. It's clear we aren't alone in the room anymore, but I can't see anything. I can only hear.

I make out the clacking sound of steps across the floor, like stone hitting stone. It's deliberate, not plodding, but not running either. I can tell there is more than one entity in the cabin. I hear some breathing, not ragged, but constant—and then another sound, perhaps verbalizations. Now I'm not sure whether we're sharing the cabin with animals or humans, as what I hear sounds like both, and neither. Hoots, grunts, and tweets merged with words that I feel like I should be able to understand but don't.

I wish desperately to have a view of whatever is transpiring right before me, but I'm left only with my ears and nose. I shift my head to the left, trying to peek through an opening in the cloak, but Ad senses my movements and squeezes my hand hard to rebuke me. He doesn't even have to say anything; I know exactly what he's saying. *Are you mad, Icelyn? When you're hidden, stay hidden.* He presses me back against the cabin wall with the slightest movement, to emphasize the point. *Okay, Ad, I understand. Sorry.*

I sense movement toward us, growing louder. Even the air seems to change, like the drop in pressure before a storm. Apart from any senses, I can feel something drawing closer. With detached curiosity, I note that I experience very little fear. Perhaps I've relinquished any expectation of survival. Pathetic, but peaceful.

More weight piles on top of me, and it grows darker inside the cloak where I hide. I panic for a moment, frozen in fear, and then realize it is just more cloaks being hung in the corner.

Well, whatever it is that is sharing this space with us right now, at least we can be sure that they keep a proper house and put away their clothes. (Even if the clothes themselves are bloodstained and reeking of death.)

I hear a whoosh and a series of crackling pops and, looking down, see soft orange light shoot along the floor. Something stoked the fire.

Conversation, if you could call it that, starts up again. I feel I'm going crazy trying to listen: First I almost recognize a word, but then I'm sure there are no words at all and suspect that what I'm hearing is only as sophisticated as a bunch of dogs barking at a squirrel.

Ad lets go of my hand, and I can feel him moving his arm slowly, carefully, just enough to push a fold of the furry cloak aside. Of course —when *Ad* wants to see, then we can take the risk. Ad's more cautious than I was when I tried to push the cloak aside for a better view, though—I do have to admit that. It takes forever before our cloaks are moved enough so that we can see anything. I squint against the bright fire's light, so I can't pick out anything else at first.

Then I see them: two shadows, silhouetted against the fire so that we can't make out details. Massively tall, so tall that I know they aren't human. I'd guess they are a good four or five feet taller than me. At least, one of them is; the other appears to be shorter, though still huge by human standards.

They move with grace. I'm struck by the fluidity of their interactions, walking upright on two legs, as they continue to make noises, listen, and respond. Words or not, they are communicating with one another. The shorter one prepares food while the other works on the fire. They look like two people getting home from a long day at work and settling in for a quiet night.

I'm not afraid of these creatures. All I can see are their shadowy outlines, but they appear to be long and slender, and they move with a lithe confidence. I realize that I'm actually attracted to the way they look; they possess a beauty that tugs at me. I want to leave the cloaks behind and interact with them.

Of course, I don't. Ad would probably kill me, if the creatures didn't first. Instead, we stay hidden as time passes and night falls. The stench of the cloaks over me gradually fades as I'm forced to get used to it. The creatures spend the later hours in another room, and we are unable to see them once they're finished with their meal (which they ate in a part of the room which was obscured from our sight, so I couldn't determine whether they devoured it in the style of humans or beasts). At one point, the music resumes, which I appreciate.

So much time has passed without any sound that I'm sure they're asleep.

"Ad?" I whisper. "Do you think they've gone to sleep?"

"Yes, I do."

"I wish we could see them up close—"

"Ice, we're not going to snuggle up alongside them in bed for a closer look. God."

I don't want to tell him about my strange draw toward these creatures. There are many conversations that I never need to have with Ad, because I know exactly what he'd say, how I would respond, and even how it'd be resolved—which would be hardly at all and badly. This is one of them.

"Fine. *You're* the one who aced all the proficiency tests, so what do you think we should do?"

"We should sneak out before they wake up. I'd like to get to Waterpump before sunrise."

I don't want to leave this cabin, though I know it doesn't make any sense. I know I can't argue that we stay. My heart is suffering from a peculiar kind of blindness. I'm not being logical.

We slip out from behind the pile of cloaks, which has now grown with the heads of another bear and some sort of wolf or coyote. I try to take one step toward the other room so I can steal a peek of the creatures sleeping before we slip out. Ad blocks my movement and nods brusquely toward the opposite side of the cabin.

"Safer to go that way," he whispers.

We exit into the night. Ad sighs with relief, but I feel only a strange loss. We're back in the woods and well on our way toward Waterpump Source before I can finally shake the compulsion to go back to those creatures—and do who knows what, for whatever reason.

58

ISTOCH LAID ON the floor in his room as the sunlight drained into dusk. *The sun is gone,* he thought. Just like his dad. Only the sun would come back in the morning. It always did. Yuenith never would.

Istoch wished his mother would cry, but Giza's tears had dried up days ago, and with them it seemed like she'd left too. She continued to attend to the routine of life: cooking acorn cakes, sweeping the floors, making sure that Istoch was bathed and dressed and put to bed with a song. But she wasn't doing these things the way she used to.

Before, when Giza put Istoch to bed, it was as if he was the only thing that mattered, and he could drift off to sleep surrounded by unending warmth.

Now everything she did seemed hollow. That warmth had gone, just like Father. Just like the sun. Everything good had dried up and blown away—and all because of Nillrod.

Tonight, Giza hadn't even come into his room to see him off into his dreams, so she didn't know that Istoch was lying on the ground instead of in his bed. Something about the hard, cold dirt felt more suited to his life now—uncomfortable and unyielding.

Istoch held the gun Tranton had given him. As soon as Tranton and Nicholas had left, Giza had confiscated it from him and hid it away. "Giving a deadly weapon to a boy? What are those fools thinking?"

she'd mumbled as she slipped into another room. "You haven't even been trained to use a gun," she had exclaimed. "Someone could get hurt."

But Giza's absence from her own life meant that she didn't hide the weapon well.

Under your bed, Mom? Did you really think I wouldn't look there?

Of course someone would get hurt. That was the whole point, the intended use, the reason the gun was invented. And he already knew how to use it—it wasn't as if one needed much training. You pulled back on the arched piece of metal, the trigger, and out came a bullet—ready to bore a hole in whomever stood in your way.

Pull the trigger. Such a simple action to cause such a giant rift in life. Pull the trigger, and Nillrod's massive debt would be repaid. Pull the trigger, and maybe Giza could find her way back to life with Istoch. Pull the trigger and find justice for Yuenith.

It was the only way anyone had a chance of getting back to normal.

By the time Torrain exited Cloudline, darkness prevented him from enjoying the same sweeping views that had greeted Icelyn and Adorane.

He dug a small ditch beneath a recognizable tree and buried his makeshift fog-cutting invention, sure that he would need it later but tired of carrying it any longer. (In the inevitable revision, he vowed to make it lighter and smaller.)

Entering Down Below at night, Torrain couldn't enjoy any of its wonder. He couldn't tell how magically green everything was, or how majestic and tall the trees were. All Torrain knew of Down Below was that it was dark and that there were many living things scurrying in that darkness all around him. Torrain was scared.

It's ridiculous to be scared, he told himself. He'd just survived Cloudline unscathed, without a single confrontation with anything. The most difficult challenge he'd endured was simple boredom (and the weight of that fog cutter, which he would address soon).

Torrain decided that whatever had spooked the original Ascenders hundreds of years ago was either a grand hoax or had gone extinct, and he wasn't going to live in fear any longer. He'd deal in reality. And the reality was that Waterpump Source had been tainted, and he needed to find it and fix it.

Torrain cut swiftly through the darkened woods. He was happy that he could walk and run for longer distances without growing short of breath; it must be the richer air down here. He decided he'd beat the Veritas expedition to Waterpump Source and be the one to purify the water supply. Then everyone would have to acknowledge him. He'd no longer be barred from entering Mountaintop. On the contrary—they'd not only beg him to return, but greet him with a festival in his honor.

These thoughts propelled him forward—he had to beat the Veritas to the source!—even as he sensed movement all around him. *It's all a hoax,* he repeated. He'd passed through the legendary Cloudline and hadn't seen a thing, he reminded himself. Any thoughts to the contrary —*What chased me into that cave in the first place? What nearly attacked Icelyn? Did I just get lucky in Cloudline?*—had to be pushed away before they planted themselves and sprouted.

59

AD AND I find the river that rushes through the center of the valley. When I was younger, I would spill water from a pail to form a miniature river on the rocky ground and imagine what fun it would be if I were tiny and could ride in the currents. I'd always thought that rivers seemed too good to be true. All that water, all in one place—deep, cold, strong, and beautiful.

But here we are, scampering alongside a grander river than any my childhood imagination could conjure, with white rapids rushing around ragged rock formations, areas of deep still waters, tiny waterfalls, larger waterfalls. I resent Ad's unrelenting pace; I yearn to stop and explore, even for an hour.

"This isn't Shangri-La, you know, created for your pleasure," Ad scolds me when I complain that it's a shame we can't break and enjoy what we're seeing. "We don't *belong* here. We're alien invaders, and any natural system will do its best to eliminate what doesn't belong, like white blood cells and infections."

As we've gotten further from Mountaintop, Ad has afforded himself more freedom to display his intellect. He knows about Shangri-La, viruses, white blood cells and natural systems? These subjects aren't part of a Veritas education, and a Veritas learning about them is against the Code, though I'm not about to raise an inquest into it or anything. Still, where did he get these books? And how could he understand them, not having the education of a Cognate? The list of troubling issues that I'll have to someday address with Ad is growing long.

"I don't need a science lesson, Ad. You forget that learning such things is actually permissible for me."

"Learning should always be permissible. Anyone who says otherwise is a fool."

Not everyone should be allowed to learn just anything. Some types cannot handle some knowledge. I suspect our future conversation on this will not be pleasant.

He grows so serious, and the waters appear so enticing, that I cannot help myself. I pretend I'm tired and need a rest, and then shout out that I see a frog on the edge of a calm pool. When Adorane falls for my ruse and investigates, I tackle him into the bracing water and we plunge into the velvety depths.

Even he cannot stop smiling. Like liquid gemstones glittering in the moonlight, the water accepts us with invigorating hospitality. This one experience makes all the trials, struggles, and pain in life worth it.

At least that's how I feel as Adorane and I shove each other and giggle like children in the entrancing currents. This moment could be the rest of my life and I wouldn't complain.

We've found a trail that mirrors the snakelike path of the river right beside the water, so our progress is swift. We've passed more cabins, and many of them appear occupied. I try to catch a glimpse of more of those tall, graceful creatures that beguiled me so, but Ad won't let us get close.

The natural wild of the river thick woods, boulders, and rock cliffs —starts to give way to ancient Apriori attempts to control it. We pass ruined brick river walls ("Probably built to prevent flooding," I tell Ad. "I know," he responds), collapsed bridges that look to be made of concrete and steel (though I don't share this observation with Ad, because of course, whether true or not, he'll just say he knows), and waterlogged, rotten remnants of wooden docks and piers.

This part of the valley was shaped and dominated by the Apriori, though nature has returned in full force in the last three hundred years and overwhelmed the boundaries of their civilization. The trail we've taken has transitioned into a surface cracked and hard like rocks.

"They built these roads so they could ride in vehicles called cars,"

Ad lectures me. "The closest thing we have to cars in Mountaintop would be the wheelbarrows—only cars had four wheels and moved on their own."

I want to reply, "I know," but the truth is I *don't* know, and I'm curious to hear more.

"Moved on their own? Were cars alive?"

Ad laughs, like I'm a child. "No! They were machines. They had engines that drew energy from a liquid called gasoline. Believe it or not, gasoline was the liquified remains of monsters who died millions of years ago, called dinosaurs. Like the lizards we find on the mountain—only a thousand times larger."

"Sure, Ad. Must have been a sight to behold!" I'm not angry, actually. When Ad feels comfortable enough to tease me, then I know everything is all right.

"I'm not making this up, Ice! It's true."

"Right. Machines drinking the liquified corpses of giant lizards so that they could carry people around inside, as if they're grand wheelbarrows come alive. Whatever could be considered fanciful about that?"

"I know it sounds far-fetched. But it's nothing magical. There were *millions* of these cars. That's why roads crisscross and scar the valley everywhere—though most of them have been reclaimed by the land, from the looks of it."

He seems serious, but I don't want to act like I believe him, because then he'll raise his arms in triumph and celebrate tricking me, so I remain non-committal. I promise myself to research this matter extensively when I return to Mountaintop.

"Look, those are some cars there." He points out rusted metal husks, so choked by vines and brush that I wonder how he saw them. "There are the wheels, or at least where they would have been." Ad points out parts of the crushed vehicle with unjustified passion. "Here's the door. People would open this up to climb inside, and they'd sit here, and here, and here. The driver—the person who guided or steered the car—would sit here."

If this is all a joke, Ad has really committed himself to it.

"I'm not saying that cars didn't *exist*. In fact, I think I've heard of them. It's just the dinosaur juice part that doesn't sound right."

Ad sits in the seat for drivers and sighs. "I want to drive one."

Seeing the look on his face, I realize that he's not joking. I want him to be able to drive a car someday, too. It looks like it would mean an awful lot to him.

We move on from the first batch of cars we stumbled across and reach an area where they become a common sight, lined up along the side of the road, rusting and overgrown with weeds. The Apriori must have loved these machines almost as much as Ad does, because they're everywhere. He examines them as we pass, remarking on the different shapes and sizes of the rusted-out machines.

More interesting to me, though, we're passing an actual *city*—a once-grand metropolis of the Apriori, like I've only seen in books. We're on the other side of the river from it and are unable to explore, as the bridge that would connect us to it has long ago fallen into the waters below, leaving behind only a faint reminder of its existence. But even from this distance, I am struck by the pure grandeur of it all. Even though it looks like the top of the skyscrapers crumbled away decades before, they still reach higher into the sky than seems possible. *What is this Apriori magic?*

"Once we're finished with Waterpump Source, we have find a way to visit the city."

"No, Ice, take a look. Closer." I think I can see what Ad is talking about. Motion. Movement. Not all is still.

"That city isn't empty, Ice. Things live there." We're so far away, I can't tell what the movement belongs to, and neither can Ad. Probably just deer, or bears, or maybe the creatures from the cabin.

Or perhaps the Threatbelow, which is what I'm sure Ad is worried about. I almost feel like I can hear them making noises, but if they are, it's so quiet that it could just as well be my imagination. Maybe they're singing songs, like the Veritas do in secret. I wouldn't mind hearing a noise like that right about now. I want nothing more than to find my way into that city, but I know it's impossible.

"Well, we have to get to the Source, anyway," I mumble, sounding more disappointed than I had intended. "Then maybe we can figure that out."

"We're not far from the Source."

"Hey, Ad. Have you considered that maybe the Source won't be safe? That whoever or whatever poisoned it did so to draw us off the Mountain and down here. I mean, it could even be a trap, an ambush, you know?"

Ad held up his hands, both holding knives. "Oh, I know. I'm expecting it."

60

HAD THE FOULING of the water worked? Was *he* in the valley again?

Amperous felt himself drawn out of the city and into the darkness beyond. *Careful, Amperous,* he thought to himself, *or you'll become like one of the Cloudies.* He had always feared becoming one of the half-dead Croathus who were driven so mad by their hunger and anger that they lost their minds and ascended to Cloudline and beyond, desperate for the chance to carve out a human. They stumbled around up there, having become unthinking beasts due to oxygen deprivation and pure bloodlust.

It was a madness that all Croathus had to keep at bay daily. Don't be drawn out, fathers would tell young Croathus children, or you'll become a Cloudy.

Amperous calmed himself, paying attention to his regulated breathing. There was a plan. He had to be patient.

But still, what had drawn near?

And what was this? He found a new urge rising in him, unbidden and powerful. He wanted to hold something close, feel the warmth from being near instead of the warmth of freshly spilled blood. He wanted to feel whole inside, and he yearned for affection. In his own head, he heard a song from his memories, and cursed himself for remembering it. The feeling this song brought him was painful. It reminded him of a comfortable wholeness, one he no longer had, one that was lost forever. The torture lasted only a moment, though, before any memory of—what was it, exactly? Intimacy?—was swept away in a wave of pure hunger and rage.

Amperous ran on all fours through the streets of the city, rushing through alleys and over rooftops, quietly hooting and purring, waking the Croathus who slept.

Soon, my children, he reassured them. *The shackles have broken, and the day is coming when we will have our revenge. The penalty for abandonment is pain for all involved. We were born in pain, and it has only increased. We have carried the suffering that belongs to them. It is time that they bear their fair share.*

All throughout the decrepit city, from the collapsed underpasses to the barely standing bridges, lining the crumbling freeways and climbing the now-crooked skyscrapers, creatures responded to Amperous' call. They joined in the rhythmic purr, all as one, until every breath and heartbeat shared the same timing.

Amperous scaled the side of the tallest building in the city, grabbing vines to swing himself up until he reached the top. He stood straight upright and took in the view of the entire valley, to the river and beyond. His golden fur shone beneath the crescent moon, and a mass of Croathus gathered below.

The time was here. He could smell it, sense it, feel it in his blood, in every throb of his aching head. Taste it in his mouth. Something had changed in the valley.

Someone was here. Someone familiar. Someone had joined them.

61

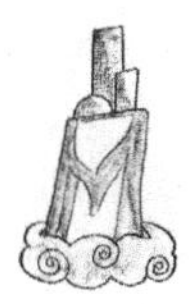

NILLROD WAS THE second Veritas shot dead in a week. Nicholas surveyed the town from the top of Brathius Tower. There hadn't been a murder in Mountaintop since the early days of the Ascension, almost three hundred years ago. Now there had been two in less than seven days.

The idea of discussing this shooting with Tranton exhausted Nicholas. Everything tired Nicholas out these days, but dealing with Tranton was almost unbearable. In the past, when something was going badly, Nicholas could reflect on another part of his life to find hope. One thing might be going badly, but at least things with his family or another part of his work were going well.

But Icelyn was still missing, and Nicholas had no idea where she might be.

The entire Kith had become a cold, suspicious community. Everyone was looking out only for themselves and their own. He hadn't heard laughter in ages.

Marjan had recovered from her sickness, but their moments together were a source of deep stress, not comfort. She was angry, helpless, constantly fuming about Tranton, dissolving into tears over Icelyn. Nicholas would rather be alone than with her.

Nothing good remained. Nothing.

He'd been naive to think that generations in the future could consider him a great leader. Oh, he might still be written about, if humanity survived. But the reviews would not be positive.

He'd bungled everything. He'd put too much trust in Tranton, and Tranton had spun it into power. These days, Nicholas spent nearly all his time trying to figure out what he could have done differently, how this script could have been altered. He'd reached the depressing (though oddly comforting) conclusion that he couldn't have changed this outcome. He'd always been a mouse caught in a landslide.

What he couldn't shake from his thoughts, as hard as he tried, was the image of young Istoch, the son of slain Yuenith.

Among the Kith, each child was a precious resource. It took so much effort to have one, and there were only ever a handful of children bustling through the town. Nicholas had always been fond of Istoch, who was a bright, sensitive boy, especially for a Veritas.

He remembered coming across Istoch once crouched over a well-traveled path. The boy was lost in concentration as he found snails and plucked them from the busy trail, placing them out of harm's way and into a bucket.

"Someone stepped on one," Istoch pronounced, his deep-set eyes watering as he looked up at Nicholas. "The other snails were so sad that they gathered around to have a funeral. I'm not going to let that happen again."

Nicholas was grateful that such a caring child was part of the Kith. "Our future is bright because of children such as you," Nicholas had replied, and then joined in the rescue effort, removing snails from the trail and saving them from the ignorant footsteps of the rest of the Kith.

"Do you want to see where I put them?" Istoch asked. "It's a secret —it's my favorite place in the world. No one else knows about it. But I can trust you with it."

Istoch led Nicholas to a gnarled and twisted tree, one that looked sculpted by human hands rather than formed by nature. Nicholas had never noticed it before, but it was stunning once he really saw it.

"Here, underneath, there's a secret opening." Istoch bent down, and Nicholas followed him. They crawled under one of the lower twists of the trunk, and Nicholas saw a natural hollow in the wood, surrounded by moss, with colorful flowers sprouting here and there.

"It's like a little world. Their little world! And it's my favorite place." Istoch removed the snails from his pail and placed them in the magical enclave hidden within the tree.

Istoch was a gentle boy, and that's why Nicholas hadn't worried too much when Tranton gave him a pistol. It might bring the family some sense of security, that's all. Surely Istoch wouldn't perpetuate the violence.

He thought of Istoch's broad smile as he pointed out the tiny world beneath the tree—and then of Istoch firing the gun, transformed by rage—and tears ran down his face.

Nicholas resented the posted Tarlinius guards he had to pass before gaining access to Kith Hall. Crime had been non-existent in Mountaintop for centuries, so they had no prison, nor anyone designated as a lawman. Tranton had made sure that his Tarlinius would fill that void, and they'd taken their places around Kith Hall with a gaudy display of weaponry. How many armed Tarlinius did it take to guard one frightened boy?

They'd locked Istoch in the most secure room in Mountaintop, the Disbursement Chamber. Nicholas knew that this action didn't technically violate the Code, but it trampled over the spirit of the Kith. The Disbursement Chamber was a sacred place—or, at least, as sacred as any place could be among the Cognates, who were proud materialists. It was used only for the ceremonies that loved ones performed for departing Kith members—those too old, weak, or infirm to contribute to Mountaintop's survival. It was a place of sadness, but also of fond memories and profound gratefulness.

After taking too long checking Nicholas for who knows what, the Tarlinius finally granted him access to the chamber.

"You have five hundred counts," Nicholas was informed. Considering he still held the greatest authority in the town, Nicholas wondered who was limiting his time with Istoch. No matter—even thirty counts with the boy would be painful. Five hundred would be more than enough.

Istoch huddled in the corner, holding his knees to his chest. He looked less imposing than ever, and Nicholas wondered why Istoch needed to be treated like a dangerous criminal. The boy's face looked like there hadn't been a moment in days when it hadn't been covered in tears.

"I'm sorry, Nicholas. I had to do it."

Nicholas shushed Istoch. "Quiet, son. I won't hear a confession."

Nicholas knew that Istoch had shot the man who killed Yuenith.

Every single person who lived in Mountaintop did. But Nicholas also knew the Code and the evidence needed to convict Istoch of the crime. There had been no confession, and there were no witnesses. Nicholas still held out hope that, if he could help this boy navigate what was to come, he might avoid the terrible prospect of a child execution. Murderers didn't get disbursed; according to the Code, they were stoned.

"But, Nicholas, Nillrod took my father from—"

"Not another word, Istoch!" Nicholas whispered, leaning in closely to the boy, sure that someone was listening at the door. "I don't care if you did it, and I cannot blame you if you did. You have no need for confession, no guilt to relieve. I unburden you of all dark thoughts right now. Nillrod deserved death, and if I were strong enough, I would have taken care of this the proper way, using my authority. But I didn't, and it fell to you, a gentle boy. You will not say one word of what you might have done to Nillrod. Not one. Not to me, not to your mother, not to Tranton, not to your wife when you marry in seven years, not to your grandchild who listens to your stories in fifty. *No one.*"

Istoch nodded. He was a smart boy, and he understood.

"Despite what Tranton and the Tarlinius might tell you, there is nothing linking you to Nillrod's death. We haven't the technology of the Apriori for solving crimes like this—it hasn't been needed, for one thing, and we simply don't have the know-how even if it were necessary. The Code calls for ironclad surety, and the only way Tranton gets that is if you say something. Your very survival depends on you keeping quiet. Now, where is the gun?"

Istoch's face scrunched up in confusion. He started haltingly, "But you said not a word—"

"I need to get rid of it. Because that's what you did, right? When Tranton gave it to you? You got rid of it. Because no boy sensitive enough to save snails from untimely deaths would enjoy handling a weapon that could snuff out a man's life. That much I'll testify to. So that's why I'm sure you took it to the edge of town and tossed it into the woods, right?"

Istoch nodded yes.

"But before you tossed the gun, where did you keep it? Where could I perhaps have found it, if I had been looking for it?"

A knock at the door. The Tarlinius pushed it open loudly and shouted. "Time's up!"

Istoch grabbed Nicholas' hands and squeezed them. "Thank you, Nicholas," he whispered. "You know where I would put something. You're the only one who does."

62

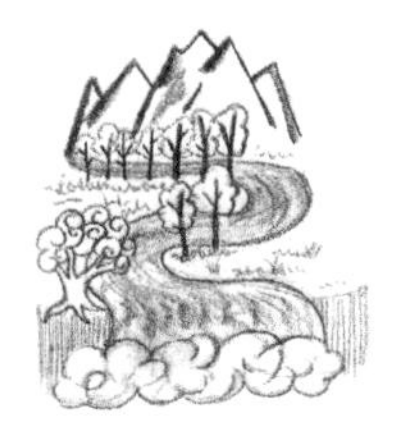

WHEN WE REACH Waterpump Source, it seems anti-climactic. This was the goal of our journey, but there's no battle, nothing to sneak past or evade, nothing at all.

The area seems abandoned.

The structure itself is impressive: a massive stone aqueduct connected to a series of waterwheels and pulleys that remind me of the inner workings of a clock. Not that we have clocks in Mountaintop, but I've seen drawings.

I want a closer look at the large wooden wheels scooping water out of the river and into the aqueduct, but Ad grabs me, hyper-vigilant as always. "We don't know that it's safe."

"How long do you intend to wait? There's nothing here, just the river and the aqueduct. Nothing living."

"Something is poisoning the water."

"Maybe a deer lost its footing and fell into the river, and the rotting corpse fouled our water."

"Ah, right. And perhaps it was just a clumsy group of mule deer that decimated our group and killed my father too?" Ad asks, with no joy in his voice.

"I'm sorry." Of course he's right; there is danger down here. "But those things that attacked us—you really think they seemed smart enough to poison our water supply?"

"I didn't have time to administer an intelligence test, so I can't be sure." I don't like when Ad is deathly serious, but still sarcastic. It's a bad combination; it gives me the chills.

"I'm just saying that maybe this isn't the crisis we thought it was. It doesn't seem like anything is here, and the water looks completely clear. Yes, Cloudline was horrid, but perhaps Cloudline is all we need to fear. Have we seen anything here, Down Below?"

"We may have, we don't know. I know you're drawn to those things in the cabin—"

"Oh *please,* Ad," I huff in reply, though it's true.

"It's true. You're fascinated by them. But they aren't human. Considering we have no idea what they are, we should be cautious."

"So what are we supposed to do—just sit here all night and watch the river flow by?"

I propose it facetiously, but Ad takes it as a serious course of action. "At *least* the night—maybe longer. If someone is poisoning our water, then they'll have to show up before too long. If we see who it is, we'll know a lot more than we do now. If we don't, then we can figure out what to do at that point. Perhaps even start looking for your darling dead bloated deer, if that's what you want."

"Well, that sounds boring." Ad doesn't care, and he's already left me to search for a lookout spot with a wide vantage point. He climbs a tree and offers a hand to pull me up behind him. I decline, out of a misguided sense of pride, and struggle to keep pace with him as he easily ascends from branch to branch.

"Hunting sounds exciting, Icelyn, but mostly it's waiting around quietly until everything forgets that you're there," Adorane explains when I finally catch up with him. "That's what the greatest predators do: sit statue-still for hours on end, until the moment comes to strike."

"Well if that's the case, how do we know that an elite predator isn't standing statue-still here, waiting for us to let our guard down?" I laugh, casting my eyes out over the safe area around us—birds swooping and calling, the river sparkling in the setting sun.

"We don't, Icelyn. We don't."

Even Ad is tired of waiting by now and has settled into the same low-level boredom I've been suffering for what feels like an eternity. Other than a couple of raccoons (sorry, ultrabears) on their way to the river's edge, nothing has passed by.

"You can go to sleep. I'll keep watch," he says. It's a kind offer, but I have no idea how to sleep in a tree, and Ad has already warned me about the dangers of leaving our tree during the night.

"What if another bunch of ultrabears scamper past? I couldn't handle missing that."

Ad doesn't laugh. "So...what are you going to do? You know, when we get back home?" Ad has to be bored to be asking questions like this. Normally, he'd be the one to avoid this kind of conversation at all costs. But starvation makes for curious appetites, I suppose.

"So many assumptions, Ad. One—we may not even make it back home. And two, even if we manage to survive, how do you know I even want to go back to Mountaintop? I like Down Below. It just... *smells right* down here. I feel better. Stronger."

Ad snorts like I've made a joke. "You couldn't last a month without Nicholas and Marjan!"

I realize that Ad doesn't know yet how my parents betrayed, imprisoned, and forced my running away. Stranger still, I don't want to tell him. I don't want to be convinced to give them a second chance, and I know that's exactly what he'd try to do (and likely succeed).

"You don't like it down here? It's beautiful."

"I haven't taken to it like you have."

"You'd rather live on the top of the Mountain, clinging to that speck of rock and dirt, everything just shades of brown and gray as far as the eye can see?"

"I would. Something feels wrong here, Ice."

"All your life you've acted as if some insidious conspiracy has kept us cooped up inside the Wall. Now I'm finally saying that I *might* agree with you—and you're telling me you've been wrong all along, that our leaders were right, that we *do* belong up there?"

Ad grows agitated. I'm stirring up something better left undisturbed, but it's too late. He grabs hold of my shoulder and squeezes it. It doesn't hurt, but it's not meant to be affectionate, either.

"You're too comfortable here, Ice! It's going to get us killed. Everything here is designed to murder us. That's what happened to humans centuries ago, except for the lucky few who made it up to that speck of rock and dirt that—despite your attempts to belittle it—was and is our salvation."

Just a week ago Ad was doubting there was any danger down here, and now he's convinced that everything here is chafing to vivisect me.

I roll my eyes.

"You'd better get uncomfortable, Icelyn, and quick! Stop smelling every beguiling scent and please, for God's sake, fear something. I don't care how strongly you feel that this place is right. It won't matter if you're carved in two and bleeding out into this rich, fertile soil you're so fond of."

The way he talks about being carved in two reminds me. Aclornis. We're not even a week past Ad's own father being slaughtered by whatever terror lives in Cloudline. Ad's still suffering from that, I realize. He will probably never fully recover—and me acting as if it didn't happened, as if everything down here is beautiful and right, is not helping.

"I'm sorry, Ad. You're right," I respond quietly. I grasp his hand, still on my shoulder, and hold it.

"It's not all paradise, Icy, and you shouldn't act like it is." There are tears in his eyes. "Those creatures in the cabin were not beautiful, and they were not worth knowing, Ice. They were evil. The way they grunted and squealed at each other made my blood run cold."

I don't want to disagree with him. He hasn't gotten over the death of his father. Even so, I feel I must defend those beautiful statuesque creations in the cabin.

"I heard words, Ad. It wasn't all beastly moans. I kept almost grasping the meaning, but then it drifted away right before I could decipher it. Like the feeling you have when you're trying to remember something, and you're just on the verge."

"They made less sense than a flock of honking geese, Ice!"

I'm shocked that he won't admit that their communication was sophisticated, graceful, and nearly intelligible. *Weren't we in the same room?*

Before I can answer, Ad covers my mouth and points toward the base of the Waterpump Source.

Our eyes are adjusted to the meager light the stars and moon provide, so even in the dark we can see three beasts like the ones we encountered in Cloudline. Down here, though, they move with strength and balance, dominating the space around them with their assured poise.

They carry large metal cylinders that appear to weigh at least a few hundred pounds even if empty. The Threatbelows are able to handle these cylinders as if they're the twig baskets Veritas women use to collect soiled clothing on cleaning days.

I loosen Ad's hand from my mouth and whisper: "What are they doing?"

We watch them remove lids from their canisters and turn them over. Thick amber liquid oozes out and spreads out into the river—and up into the aqueduct that feeds Water Pump.

Though the three Threatbelows are plainly beastly, their actions are calculated and intelligent. It's unnerving to see deliberate actions performed by creatures so clearly un-human. It's like stumbling across a bird casually brewing a kettle of tea or a fish reading a book and taking notes—only much worse. Because tea and book-reading, while curious, are nowhere near as bad as plotting to kill an entire species with venom collected in jars.

"They're poisoning us, Ice."

63

TORRAIN COULDN'T LOOK away from the gears and wooden wheels that made up Waterpump Source, glowing in the moonlight. The natural current from the river powered the wooden wheels in the water. These wheels then lifted the water up using a series of pulleys, allowing it to ascend the Mountain thirty feet at a time, one lock after another.

It had lasted for three centuries without any maintenance. This type of ingenuity didn't exist in Mountaintop anymore. That was going to change. Torrain felt a kinship with whoever had built this wonder. He could do this and more.

Torrain was oblivious to all but the Source as he neared the river's edge, backing away to admire its whirling gears. By the time he had walked into plain sight of the three Threatbelows, just as they finished emptying their cylinders into the water, he knew he'd made a terrible mistake. He turned around slowly, his heart pounding at the sight of the three monsters crouched behind him. He cursed himself for not paying better attention to his surroundings.

After all, Waterpump Source, as intriguing and worthy of study as it was, couldn't kill him. But the three beasts before him—pacing back and forth, sizing him up—appeared to be ready to do just that.

64

I DON'T WANT to believe my eyes. I blink hard, hoping to jolt away what I'm seeing. It's *Torrain.* He's wandered directly in front of the deadly beasts.

"Dear God, Ad, what…" I trail off, not wanting to give words to what we're witnessing. As if by describing it, I make it real.

"Who *is* that?" Ad asks, though we both know. The lanky, awkward gait, the painfully thin body. Torrain has backed up alongside the aqueduct, as if he's casually browsing a shop to purchase the perfect birthday gift. As he stares up at Waterpump, he takes no notice of the three beasts behind him.

What the hell is he doing? And where did he come from?

Images of the carnage back in Cloudline flash in my memory. The bodies, the blood, Adorane painstakingly carving the names into each headstone. Torrain beside the fire the night before, on the outskirts of the circle of Veritas. I realize, suddenly, that we never found Torrain's body in Cloudline. We never buried him. We had simply—forgotten about him.

The Threatbelows take notice of him and seem as confused as we are. "We've got to help him." I start to descend the tree, but Ad grabs me.

"No."

"But he'll die if we don't—"

"We'll die if we do. We're the last hope, Icelyn. If we die, all of Mountaintop perishes with us. All of humanity."

I watch as Torrain turns slowly, his body stiffening in the moonlight as he becomes aware of his situation. I feel a deep stab of sorrow for him. One time I saw a mouse eaten by a snake. I had seen the mouse first, and it delighted me. I followed it while it wandered behind Waterpump. Then I'd watched as the snake sprung from the dead leaves and grabbed hold of the mouse's hindquarters. The previously carefree creature was shocked, betrayed by life itself. I tried to get the poor mouse away from the snake, but before I could do anything, the serpent slithered away, its bounty still trapped in its jaws.

Torrain is the mouse now.

The Threatbelows circle him, trying to make sense of this interloper, chirping and barking toward each other and sometimes toward him. They surround him, and their circle constricts as they near him.

"They're going to attack, Ad. We have to do something."

Ad readies a knife and drops to the ground below. "Stay here," he commands as he grabs the flare from his bag. He sprints toward the confrontation, full speed.

No. I won't remain a spectator while my Intended (in name only, but still) and my best friend meet their ends. I tumble out of the tree and run toward the beasts.

Though I'm focused on what we're moving toward—and relieved to see that the beasts have not yet pounced on Torrain—my peripheral vision picks up movement to the side of me, some *thing* springing into action, as if it's grown out of the ground itself.

How do we know that some elite predator isn't standing statue-still here, waiting for us to let our guard down?

We don't, Ice. We don't.

Ad rips the top off the flare and a flame bursts out of it. He sprints, fire in one hand, knife in the other, until he reaches the beasts. He's not even half their size. Still, he launches into one with all his might, and whether it's adrenaline or the rich, thick air, he knocks the Threatbelow off its feet and plunges his knife into the back of its neck. The furious beast screams as Ad stabs it with fire, setting its matted fur alight.

The beast tosses Ad aside and the other two focus on him. Torrain takes the opportunity to run into the darkness, and nothing follows him.

I feel a flash of relief, replaced by a greater wave of anger. *Thanks a lot, Torrain! So great of you to drop by and screw everything all to hell! I know you must be going now; be sure to send my regards to your astounding cowardice.*

Despite sprinting, I've only reached a terrible no-man's land where I'm too far away to be able to help but near enough for a perfect up-close view of Ad's inevitable death. The beasts circle him, stalking, sizing him up, ready to strike.

The beast Ad stabbed is taller than the other two. Now that I'm closer I can see that its fur, where not bloodstained or burning, is a pale golden brown. It must be the leader. The others look toward it, waiting for its command. The golden one reaches back and plucks the knife out of its own back. It examines the blade, rotating its attention between Ad and the weapon. It then violently pats out the flames on his own fur.

I know it's a brute, a dumb animal, but it seems like Ad has made the battle personal with this one, even though the damage from knife and flare appears to be minimal.

I continue rushing toward them, though I'll likely be slaughtered once they're finished with Ad. I'm at peace with this. I don't want to live anywhere—not Down Below, not in Mountaintop, not anywhere—if Ad is dead. All I can do is follow my instinct—*get to him. Help him.*

Golden tosses the knife aside with a roar and turns his head toward Ad, who is still crumpled on the ground, wounded and unmoving. This appears to be the signal that the other two were waiting on, because all three pounce toward Ad.

I shout. I don't know what else to do. "No! Take me!"

My voice makes no difference in their advance, but it does win Ad's attention.

"Icelyn!" Seeing me shakes him from his stupor. He finds his feet in time to dodge one of the beasts, then the other. I'm reminded of Ad's prowess event; he evades the beasts just as he did the boulders and rocks thrown at him during his agility showcase. He buys enough time for me to reach him.

I join Ad, stand by his side, and then realize I have no idea what else to do.

"Icelyn, go away!" Ad shouts angrily.

"I refuse to watch you die!"

"Likewise. So, run!" Golden plunges toward us, and Ad tackles me away from certain death, then yanks me up from the ground, keeping tabs on each beast's position.

I don't feel like I could retreat, even if I wanted to. At least one beast would follow me, and without Ad, I'd have no chance. The depth of my folly washes over me. Why didn't I stay hidden in the shadows? Perhaps Ad could have survived better without me. Now we're both going to die.

Two beasts attack, one from front and one from behind, and even Ad isn't able to pull me from their path. They're too fast and smart—learning from their previous attempt, they anticipate which way Ad will push me and are waiting for me there.

It can't be more than half a second—that moment when the beasts pry me away from Ad, his strong hands unable to hold me against their brute force, his face bearing a stubborn refusal to give up on saving me, even as I'm being carried away from him. I don't think to scream, though sharp talons dig into my side, tear at my clothes, and draw blood; I simply reach out for him, desperately holding his gaze.

He runs after me, but Golden strikes him down from behind. The last thing I see is Ad rolling to save himself from a deadly strike.

I hear a screech, unearthly in tenor, and I'm knocked from the beast's clutches and onto the ground with a heavy thud. The creature that held me has also been knocked over. By who? Adorane? Could he have done that?

It's all a blur, and my mind struggles to keep up. I just saw Ad, a hundred feet away, clinging to survival. How is he here now, pummeling into the side of the beast that snatched me? Could he have emitted that terrible throaty cry? If not him, then who? Torrain?

The beast that sought to carry me away falls to the left of me, and I glimpse something pounce on it and flail until blood splashes into the air and splatters onto the ground. Satisfied that it has killed the beast, a creature stands and roars, its head darting up and down, back and forth, looking for another challenger.

I get a clearer view of this vicious warrior that has saved me. It's another beast, smaller, with fur yellow and short and splattered with bright crimson blood from the creature it just tore apart. It turns toward me, its face obscured in shadow, but then catches sight of another beast lurking nearby.

This smaller yellow creature bellows at that beast, challenging it with a manic, unhinged screech. I must not be worth the fight, because the other beast scampers into the woods.

I don't know whether to run or stay where I am. Not that it would make a difference either way—whatever this smaller creature wants to do to me, it will.

It locks in on Ad and Golden, who are still sparring, if you can call Golden attacking and Ad narrowly evading death 'sparring.' The beast lowers its head and charges on all fours toward him. She's (I know instinctively that she's female) unbelievably speedy, a streak in the moonlight.

Golden stands his ground long enough to be crashed into, battered by the blood-soaked beast and falls back, stunned. Just before the violent creature can pounce on him, he jumps to his feet. He notices that he's alone, abandoned by his allies and outnumbered. (Though Ad and I only barely count, we could maybe tip the scales.) He roars in tired defiance, but then he turns and disappears into the darkness.

The smaller yellow beast stands tall, screaming at the world around her. Though she uses no words, I can tell she's gloating, warning, cursing, and celebrating all at once.

I want to crawl toward Ad, to drag him off, to flee this terrifying creature that enjoys destruction and relishes ending lives. But my head hurts, and my half-hearted attempt to rise ends in me collapsing backward.

The last thing I see before I pass out is the smaller beast turning toward me.

65

TORRAIN COULDN'T STOP running. He'd been moments from death, could smell it drifting from the matted fur of those horrible creatures. He was fortunate his legs were still intact for sprinting, and he was going to use them.

His thoughts spun, a mishmash of terrible images and imaginings. It had been dark, but a human had jumped onto one of the creatures. It looked like Adorane. And then, following him, a girl whose voice Torrain would always recognize, because it filled him with both excitement and pain.

Icelyn. Had Adorane and Icelyn saved him?

He'd found a trail and run through an overgrown forest. Meager moonlight broke through the trees, but not enough to keep him from tripping over a root and bashing his leg against a branch. Still, he kept moving.

Torrain broke into a clearing and was thankful for the increased visibility, though he knew that the better he could see, the better something else could see him. He was powered by a thirst for survival he didn't know he possessed, and his chances of living were increased if he could find shelter for hiding.

Up ahead he saw boxes rising on the horizon—not skyscrapers or anything approaching their majesty, just low slung rectangular shapes topped with sloping roofs. Torrain knew from his studies that these were common houses for the Apriori masses. These houses were bunched together haphazardly, as if no one cared and someone had simply dropped them from the sky and made do with where they landed. This neighborhood bore neither the orderly precision of the labs nor the artistic charm of the rounds.

Vines, underbrush, and trees had overtaken the houses, as if the earth itself was swallowing and digesting what man had left behind. Torrain had hoped that one of these would make a fine shelter (after all, wasn't that why they had been built in the first place?) but now that he had gotten close enough to examine them, he wasn't sure. They were in complete ruin, with whole parts of the walls or roofs ripped open, burnt out from long-ago fires, or caved in from rot. Entire sections had collapsed, and as he peeked through broken windows he saw that the floors that were dangerously unstable.

How embarrassing it would be to escape the Threatbelows and then die by falling through a decaying floor. But could you be embarrassed if there was no one else to witness your shame, he wondered? Yes, he decided—you could. It only takes one to feel embarrassed: yourself.

By now, the adrenaline he'd benefited from when the beasts attacked had waned. He needed a place to rest. But what if there were Threatbelows here in this neighborhood? What if they lived in the husks of the human civilization they'd destroyed?

Torrain decided not to enter the houses. He'd been excited at the prospect of sleeping like the Apriori had hundreds of years ago, but these places were dark, decrepit and possibly occupied by deadly beasts.

The houses were huddled around one larger building, which was beside a hole in the ground. Torrain recognized it as a swimming pool. The Apriori had so much water they could just dig holes and fill them with the stuff, for no purpose other than to dip themselves into it whenever they wanted to be wet. The pool was empty now, mostly, with remnants of rainwater remaining in the deeper parts.

Torrain grabbed a small piece of fallen roof from beside the large building and dragged it toward the pool. As a child, before he had to focus on Cognate-only pursuits, he'd played with Ad and other Veritas boys who'd taught him how to make a temporary shelter you could count on when stuck outside. He threw the part of the roof into a dry part of the pool, and then propped it up, creating a small hiding place.

It would have to do. Torrain fell asleep in minutes.

66

MY FIRST SURREAL thought is: *Oh, this is how it feels to be devoured.*

She is on top of me, her arms around me, crushing me toward her. Is this why she dispatched the other beasts with such rage? So she could have me all to herself?

I feel no pain. I once read that some predators have the ability to make their victims numb, so there is less resistance and no struggle. If this beast possesses this advantage, I'm grateful for small mercies.

The beast acts strangely (though I'm not sure what normal behavior would be when butchering a human). She sniffles and gasps for breath. I open my eyes, prepared for the blood-soaked worst, but find myself completely intact. I look around for Adorane, wondering if he's already dead or coming to my rescue, but I don't see him.

I push away from the beast, but she only grabs me tighter. I feel something hot streaming down my neck and back. *The bloodletting has begun.*

But I touch the wetness on my neck, and my hand is not stained red. It's covered with water—or is it just sweat?

The beast releases me and collapses to the ground face down. I get a good look at her. She's not quite double my height, and unlike the other creatures I've seen down here, appears to be a child—or more precisely, an adolescent. She bears the manic manner of something that wants to do everything at once, as she rises from the ground and grabs hold of me again. More sniffling, more wetness, and now I hear something else: words, maybe, but not quite.

God, am I being devoured or adored? I think back to Adorane and Catalandi, entwined together in his room, and wonder why this feels so similar. I'm not sure what is happening.

The beast holds me close to her and strokes the back of my neck. It's calming, rhythmic, and anything but threatening. In this moment, I know for sure that she means me no harm. Though she does want something from me, I can feel her desire—strong and palpable, as if it's a physical force like wind or gravity.

She adjusts my shoulders until we face each other and, using her taloned hand, lifts my chin so that we're looking one another in the face. I'm staring into the dead eyes of a fierce cat. She looks like a mountain lion, jaws frozen open in attack, perched atop a shadowy void. But then she lowers the lion head, and all of her golden yellow fur sloughs off and falls to the ground along with it.

She's not the beast I thought she was. Her skin is pale and porcelain white, without the slightest trace of fur. She's gracefully long, lean, and tautly muscled, and her face isn't an awful shadowy nothing. Indeed, now that the moonlight hits it, I catch my breath. She's beautiful, her large wide-set eyes a bright glacial blue.

I tolerate but don't love my own appearance. Some boys seem to think I have a pretty face (though Ad has never made one mention of it!), and I can see what they're saying—it's pretty enough. But once in a while, I catch a glimpse of my reflection in the channels of Waterpump and realize I look exactly right. I think to myself, *Yes, this is what I'm supposed to look like all the time.* This *is beautiful*. Whenever it happens, I want to freeze myself in that instant and keep it forever.

That's what this creature's face reminds me of.

Myself—only beautiful. In that fleeting way one can never capture and make permanent.

She's crying. That's what has been running down my neck—not my blood, but her tears. She's not a beast, but she's not human, either. Whatever she is, I am startled to find that I love her thoroughly and completely.

She touches my face gently with the back of her hand, so her talons can't harm me. She studies me like I'm all that's ever mattered. I hear a melodious voice, like the Veritas' singing, only in speaking form.

"Lovely! You've come for me. I always knew you would."

67

SHE LIFTS ME to my feet, and her words spill out like dammed water finally released.

"Lovely! Oh, Lovely! You've come. I always believed you would. We've waited for you all this time, and now you're here. You're more magnificent than I ever imagined."

I don't hear these words in the same way I hear other sounds. The beast coos and whirrs and clicks with sounds animalistic in nature. My ears register them as alien noises, but my mind picks up her meaning.

"Yes, I'm here," I reply instinctively. I am no longer confused, though I don't know exactly what's going on; deep inside myself, I feel an old familiarity.

She looks like she's been struck by lightning at the sound of my voice, my every word a miracle. She falls to one knee and weeps. I'm not sure whether she understands me and is struck by what I've said or is just overwhelmed by the fact that I'm talking at all, but she's deeply affected by my voice.

She pulls me toward her protectively, an urgency in her words. "You're not safe here. We must go to Deep Water, to the Drowned City. Everyone awaits you there."

She lifts me clear off the ground, holding me comfortably at her side.

She's startlingly fast, and by the time I realize what's going on, we've already covered hundreds of feet.

But wait! Ad! I've been so wrapped up in my interaction with this creature that I've forgotten about him.

"Hold on! Where's Ad?"

The creature scrunches up her face, as if she's bitten into something rotten, but she doesn't say anything.

"The boy who was with me. Where is he?" I ask desperately.

"Why should you care, Lovely? I would guess he's dead." She points back into the distance, and I see Ad. He's sprawled out on the ground, bloodied, unmoving.

The creature reads the horror on my face and backtracks. "You care for...that thing?"

I can only nod. *Is he dead?*

"Your ways are a mystery to me, Dear One, but I will learn them." She bounds over to Ad and lifts him up, sniffing him long and hard.

"There's still life in him. Just to be sure, you really want to keep this with us? I can easily discard it; it'd be no trouble to me."

Dear God, yes, I want *to keep this thing with us.* Tears stream down my face. "It's Adorane! Yes."

"I can see he means something to you, so he will mean something to me, too."

She puts her furred cloak back on, and I'm amazed by the transformation. Now she looks like a Threatbelow, deadly and terrifying. She lifts both Ad and me without any strain and bolts into the darkness.

"Let's get to Deep Water before the Croathus return. Your presence has surely caused a stir."

68

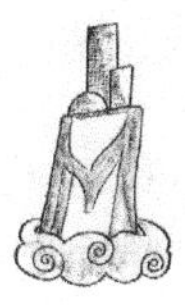

NICHOLAS AND MARJAN tried to eat together like nothing was the matter.

Divorce was not permissible according to the Code. Part of that was pure pragmatism. With only one hundred people in the Kith, many of them children, and no marriages allowed between Cognate and Veritas, the options for a mate were limited. In reality, there were only four or five people that any given member of the Kith could wed.

But divorce was forbidden mostly because it would be an admission of failure, and the Kith's ways had to work—their culture's survival hinged on it. The principles for relational success were grounded in scientific methods laid out by the earliest Cognates, and adherence to them guaranteed happiness as consistently as combining two molecules of hydrogen and one of oxygen guaranteed water.

Not that either Nicholas or Marjan wanted a divorce—they only wanted to be left alone and not forced to interact so often. They reminded one another of the pain they'd rather not confront.

They couldn't talk about Icelyn. When Icelyn was only seven, Marjan and she had argued, and Icelyn had vowed to run away and never be seen again. Marjan found her in less than ten minutes, hiding behind one of the boulders behind Brathius Tower, crying and afraid. Marjan had hoped that Icelyn's latest attempt to flee would be just as futile, but it appeared that their little girl wanted to flee for good this time. Any mention of her brought them both to tears.

They couldn't talk about Nicholas' leadership, because Marjan thought that everything Nicholas was doing was wrong, and Nicholas couldn't hear it. Mostly because he agreed.

Nicholas didn't want to mention Istoch, the boy accused of murder. Marjan had talked about the matter only once. "Two fathers dead and one son paying for all their sins. This doesn't feel like home anymore." Nicholas felt that Marjan blamed him for this as well.

"Is this a new recipe?" Nicholas choked down the scrawny strings of meat, pretending it was appetizing.

"Yes, it's called *bland.* Not enough water to grow herbs. No Veritas to venture out and gather salt."

The last time Marjan had said anything positive felt like lifetimes ago.

"Well, it's not bad. My compliments." It was exhausting for both of them, him maintaining his optimistic outlook.

They both would rather have eaten by themselves. However, the Code called for families to share at least five meals per week, and they'd already skipped their permissible limit.

69

AD IS WEAKENED and cannot walk, which I can tell annoys him. The creature has assembled a stretcher out of vines, sticks, and leaves, and now she drags him behind us on it as we make our way toward the coast.

Though I can tell the creature wants me to walk with her, I hang back so I can talk to Ad. Not that he's saying much. He seems angry, like I've done something wrong—though he won't share what, exactly, despite my asking. I've played this game before with Ad. He fancies himself impervious to pain, so he never admits when anyone has upset him.

"Well, if you're not going to talk to me, I think I'll leave you alone. *She'll* talk to me," I say, nodding toward the creature, who keeps looking back at us in hopes that I'll join her.

"You're crazy, Ice. You can't talk to a beast." Ad says it loudly, and I'm afraid it'll hurt her feelings.

"She's not a beast. That's a disguise so that she can blend in with the others! Eveshone is a beautiful creature. You should see her without those furs. And I *can* talk to her—we've had many conversations. You've even been around for some of them."

Ad studies me as if he's worried about my sanity. "*Eveshone*? Did you name her that?"

I'm not sure how I know the creature's name is Eveshone (pronounced Eh-vah-show-nee). Did she tell me? I suppose she did, though I don't remember when. Regardless, that's her name.

"No, I didn't name her." I'm tired of talking to Ad. "You need your rest. You should try to sleep."

He's not ready to let it go. "So she told you earlier? With all that chirping and barking?"

"We talk! She can talk!" I cannot comprehend why Ad insists that Eveshone doesn't speak. "You cannot tell me you haven't heard us talk."

He studies me like I'm the crazy one. "You think you are talking to her? She chirps and growls. You spend most of your time silently staring at each other. It's creepy as hell, and it's definitely not *talking*."

Ad seems jealous and angry, but I can tell he means what he says.

"Why do you care so much about that thing, Lovely?" Eveshone calls back to me. "All it does is groan and whimper. And it smells terrible."

I can feel Eveshone's desire for me to join her, so I comply. I leave Ad to his recovery and walk beside her. "Eveshone, when you hear me talking to my friend, what does it sound like?"

"You talk to him, but he answers in noise."

"He says the same thing about our conversations."

"He says things? From the blank look in his eyes, I took him for a simpleton, devoid of any thought outside of instinct."

I laugh, knowing how offended Ad would be if he heard this.

"Anyway—of course he can't hear our conversations. He's not connected."

"Connected how?"

"We share a pulse, Lovely." She says it like it's the most obvious, understandable statement in the world. *Of course*. "Like the roots of one tree wrapped around the roots of another until they grow together into one."

Before I can answer, she changes the conversation. "I'm only asking because I'm holding back a torrent of rage every second I'm near that thing you call 'Adorane.' Do you care enough for him that you'd be greatly upset if I killed him?"

70

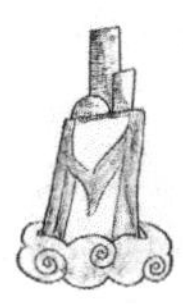

WAILING COMES FROM the Veritas side of town. Before the water had been poisoned, displays of emotion were never witnessed in Mountaintop. The Cognates suspected that the Veritas indulged their passions in private, but never in public.

Now misery was broadcast for all to hear. It wasn't long until Nicholas found its source. From a gnarled, meager tree growing outside Yuenith and Giza's round, a frail body swung, feet just inches from the ground. It was a season of firsts, he mused darkly. The first murder since the Ascension—and now the first suicide, too.

Poor Giza, having lost her husband and faced with the prospect of Istoch being executed, had decided that eternal nothingness was preferable to what she'd been dealt in life.

Nicholas watched her sway. Was this his legacy? Making his people's lives so terrible that they preferred death?

Tranton joined him, his face sober. "What she has done is strictly forbidden, according to the Code. We might have to set an example, lest others follow her lead."

Nicholas stared at him blankly. *Set an example? How can you teach a dead woman a lesson?*

"I should think a good whipping would suffice, Tranton. Or do we throw her into the stocks? I don't know if that will do. How can we ensure that as soon as we release her she doesn't just go and kill herself again?" Nicholas mocked him.

Tranton's face remained stony. "We are on the verge, Nicholas, of a dangerous decline. Redistribute her belongings and burn their round. No one would think about putting their neck in a noose if they knew it would leave their family destitute."

"What evidence have you found in the case of young Istoch?"

Tranton didn't like this question. "One matter at a time, Nicholas. Let's settle this business with Giza."

"The circumstances are related, don't you think?" Nicholas' head was spinning. He'd never talked to Tranton like this, and it felt like jumping off a cliff into darkness. "Have you found anything tying Istoch to the murder?"

"Not yet, but—"

"It's been a week, Tranton. You know the Code. A person cannot be held for longer than a week without any evidence whatsoever. We're not dictators. And thank you for your advice, but I know exactly what should be done for poor Giza." Nicholas turned away to end the conversation.

Tranton grabbed his cloak. "Think carefully about this, Nicholas. I wouldn't want our union to suffer cracks, however thin."

It was a warning, but Nicholas already felt like he'd opened a box that couldn't be closed. "Then support my decisions, Tranton, and we shouldn't have to worry about that."

After hours of arguing over one line of the Code—twenty-one words, to be exact, Nicholas finally prevailed in a showdown with Tranton. It helped that he had the truth on his side. It was akin to winning an argument where your position was that water was wet—but still, he'd won a debate against his advisor, and he was flush with pride.

No Kith member accused of breaking the Code shall be held for more than a week in captivity without ironclad evidence.

Istoch was released from the Disbursement Chamber just as the sun set, and it was left to Nicholas to deliver the terrible news that Giza had died. The boy didn't cry, nor did he ask how she had died, which Nicholas found worrying. He nodded and looked down, stoic, as if he had no tears left to spare.

This was a boy who had taken great pains to save snails from death, and now he couldn't even show sadness over the loss of his mother.

"I should go home to my round, Nicholas. Thank you for what

you've done here."

Nicholas had been thinking this over since he'd seen Giza hanging from the tree. He hadn't been able to ask Marjan her opinion yet, but he sensed an urgency that made her agreement seem trivial in comparison.

"Live with us, Istoch. Marjan and me."

"As a servant? I'd rather live by myself, in our round."

"Not as a servant. No, not at all."

"I'm a Veritas. Who could I be in your household, if not a servant?"

"Istoch—while there's no precedent, there's also nothing forbidding it. I want you to be our son."

"The gall! What could you have been thinking?"

Marjan was not pleased.

Istoch heard Marjan's words, although she spoke them as if he wasn't there.

"This boy is suffering. I made a decision. I thought you'd agree."

"How quickly you abandon her! We already have a child, Nicholas —or have you forgotten?"

This enraged Nicholas. "Not a breath leaves my lungs without me thinking of her. I live every moment in a sadness beyond comprehension."

"Then why have you done nothing to find her? You sit inside while our daughter is out there alone in the wilderness!" She'd been bathing in these dark thoughts for weeks. "What kind of father idles and does nothing while his daughter is missing? What kind of *man*?"

"What could I do? Go outside the Wall and face certain death? I could never survive out there. We have our best Veritas looking! If they can't find her, what could I do?"

"At the very least, you don't have to run out and find a replacement child! How about keeping her room empty for a few more days before allowing another to claim her bed? How about that?"

Istoch stood and faced both of them. "Chief Cognate, Lady Marjan, I appreciate your kind offer. But I must decline. I'll head back to my round now."

"No, please, Istoch. Marjan and I both want you here. It has been an upsetting few days for everyone."

Istoch's eyes stole a glimpse of Marjan and then fixed on the ground. "I belong in my round. And perhaps, in the morning, I can go look for your daughter Icelyn. If I die outside the Wall, it's no great loss to anyone. But if I find her, then you can be a family again."

Istoch turned and headed for the door.

His words pierced Marjan, who swiftly moved in front of him.

"No, Istoch. Why would you sleep in that empty place when we've prepared a bed for you here?"

71

THE SUN GENTLY pulled Torrain out of his sleep. He was relieved to find himself alone, in the company of nothing more dangerous than birds that chirped a cheerful song and squirrels that fought over acorns. Much like the people in Mountaintop used to fight over acorns, Torrain mused, and in much the same way—*I saw it first! It landed on my territory! You have so many already!*

His surroundings appeared more inviting by day. There were so many houses here! He imagined the technological wonders that waited within each one, inventions he'd only heard of in books—televisions for watching scenes of faraway places, telephones for talking to people hundreds of miles away, microwaves for instantly warming food, and refrigerators in case you'd rather keep a thing cold. He might even see the mysterious *computer*, which he'd heard could do just about anything, though he never quite understood how.

Torrain hadn't been eviscerated in his sleep, so he figured the houses were not occupied by Threatbelows. At least, that's what he told himself, because he was desperate to start exploring them. For a moment, he thought about Adorane and Icelyn, with a dose of guilt. If he were a braver person, he would return to the river and see how they are doing. But they were better off without him, he decided. Plus, they probably didn't even want him around.

From the looks of it, the houses were home to more docile creatures, like rabbits and chipmunks. He found the largest house in the area, calculating that a wealthier family would want a grander home and be able to afford more of the machines he was hoping to find.

He entered what had been the kitchen and was rewarded for his bravery. He chopped through and pushed aside thick vines and vegetation and found a gallery of machinery, a vast array of plastic and metal objects tethered to the wall with cords that provided electricity. Pushing his luck, Torrain switched one of the machines from OFF to ON, hoping for anything at all. He assumed that there would be no electricity but was disappointed even so when nothing happened.

Torrain knew there were other ways to power machines, though, and promised himself he'd figure out a way to turn these gadgets on. Maybe not the blender, which was just some kind of jug with a small metal blade that would spin to mix things up. Though the engineering of it excited him, what it could be used for left him bored. He pushed the blender aside and examined the refrigerator. Its door had been pulled off at one point. He discarded many other small machines: a toaster used somehow, he knew vaguely, for bread; a clock for telling time (the Apriori were obsessed, he had learned, with knowing precisely what time it was, even if it meant they imposed their own fictional structure onto the changing rhythms of the days); a metal rectangle that would heat up to cook food when you didn't want to build a fire.

He moved on from the kitchen and entered a large room with a higher ceiling. He jumped back at the sound of an angry rattle and honored the coiled snake's warning by keeping his distance. Though the serpent was large and lethal, he found it beautiful and graceful.

"I won't bother you, and you don't bother me. How does that sound, huh?"

Why was everyone so fearful of snakes? At least they had the decency to send a fair warning before striking. Humans could learn a thing or two.

Torrain recognized the remains of a large couch and smaller chairs, all in ruins and tatters. They were oriented toward a large box, in an almost ceremonial fashion. Torrain knew this box must be the legendary television, as he'd heard that the Apriori centered their lives around this wonder and afforded it a place of honor in their homes.

He wanted it. Torrain bent over, grabbed hold of the massive box, and lifted. He could feel a mighty strain in his back, but he managed to get the television off the ground. He didn't have a plan; he couldn't carry an object of this weight wherever he went. He just wanted to turn it on at some point and see with his own eyes the magical visions that had captivated his ancestors.

He was making slow progress toward the door, carrying the massive television, when the floor beneath him cracked. He wasn't able to tell which made him more upset—that the television fell out of his hands and hit the floor hard, screen shattering and innards spilling out, or that his legs fell through the broken, rotten boards. He was stuck, held into the floor by splintered wood, his lower half dangling into the basement below.

72

"LET ME MAKE something clear to you, Eveshone. I need you to listen to me, because if you can't understand this, then we will have to part ways, immediately and forever." I punctuate my words to make sure there is no miscommunication. "You are not to kill Adorane. Not ever. He is special to me. He cannot die. Do you understand?"

I might have been too forceful, because I've shamed her. "I'm sorry for asking. I needed to be sure. My instinct shouts in my ear at all times."

I'm compelled to soften my stance. "I'm sorry I had to be harsh with my words. It's just that I will be very sad if Ad dies. Heartbroken."

"I see. Then of course I will not kill him."

"What do you mean, your instinct shouts in your ears?"

Eveshone seems bewildered. "Why are you asking about my instinct, Lovely? You should understand it."

"But I don't. Tell me."

"Have you ever been in the ocean, Lovely? Do they have oceans up above, where you live? If you have, you'll know how it feels. Your toes cling to the sandy bottom, trying to keep your head above water, and then a mighty wave comes, and you cannot do anything but give yourself up to it, and it grabs you and flips you. In that moment, when you release yourself to the wave, you feel a freedom and joy. You don't know which way is up or down. It's bigger than you, it consumes you, and it's what you were created to do. That's my instinct."

"And that wave that is trying to pull you away? That wave is urging you to kill my friend?"

"And all like him, yes. But don't worry. I can choose to enter the waters or not."

"So are you tempted to kill me, too?"

"Please! No! Never."

"But Adorane is like me."

Eveshone shakes her head as if I'm full of nonsense. "I had feared you were teasing me, and now I know you are. How could you compare yourself to him? My thoughts cannot comprehend your thoughts, but that is folly! I knew you were joking all along anyway, asking me about my instinct. Because of course you know all about the thirst."

I wonder why she's so sure that I do. "I know nothing of it. Why would I?"

"Because! You're the one who gave it to me in the first place, silly!"

73

"WELL, THAT WAS terrible," Torrain declared loudly into the empty room, as if the accident needed commentary. His right leg was throbbing. He could feel his own quickening pulse in it, along with stabs of intense pain.

The television looked even worse off. He'd have to find another one in another house.

Then he heard the sounds.

Floating up from down below, in the basement where his legs now dangled. A couple of hesitant thumps, first, and then a groan.

God, I have to get out of this place.

He tried to lift himself out of the broken floor, but his legs were stuck fast, long splinters of cracked floorboards pinning him in. Whatever was below him was becoming more interested, he realized, as the noises grew more urgent and focused.

Torrain had to figure out a way to pull himself out before whatever was below pulled him all the way down.

74

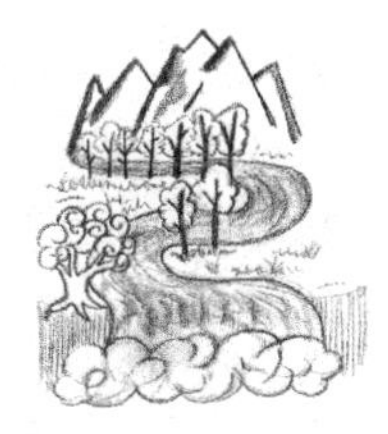

WE'VE FOLLOWED THE serpentine path of the river for a full day. Adorane has slept for most of that time, which is good for a number of reasons. First, he needs to recover from his wounds. But also, he hates Eveshone (even without knowing that she longs to slay him), and being stuck in the middle of their tension has been exhausting.

Eveshone seems hesitant to take the lead, often asking me what I'd like to do and declaring that, of course, she'll follow me wherever I wish to go. Considering she's the expert down here, I tell her again and again that I trust her judgment. This exchange always ends with her declaring that we should journey to the Drowned City, and soon, because the Croathus are surely coming for me.

"What is the Drowned City?" I ask. She's startled by the question.

"Do you mean, what does it represent? Or how I've made peace with it? Do you want to know how it affects my feelings toward you?" I have no idea what she's talking about.

"I just mean…what is it? Where is it? Why is it drowned? Who lives there? Why are we going there?"

Eveshone appears nervous, like I'm testing her and she has no idea what the correct answer is. "You've stalled my tongue with your questions, Lovely. I apologize. I have no idea what to say. But I do want you to know that I'm not complaining. About the Drowned City. Everything happens according to love and reason. I know that. If it's acceptable to you, I would ask that we speak no more about it. Other than to say we have to go there, of course."

I have no idea what Eveshone is talking about, but I trust her completely—which is odd, considering she's confessed her ardent desire to eviscerate Adorane. She worships me. It's intoxicating to be so unconditionally loved. I often catch her looking at me, and normally it's because I'm trying to sneak another peek at her.

Even her blood-thirst for Adorane, which I understand to be intensely animalistic, makes me appreciate her more. She holds out against it for me alone. She holds her inner monster at bay because of her love for me.

It's a shame she has an inborn compulsion to murder Ad, I muse, because they actually have so much in common.

"Up ahead, there's a family of quail. The chicks are newly hatched. If we're quiet enough, hopefully we'll see them." She's pointed out many quiet wonders as we've walked, delighted by everything. Ad would always do the same thing when he'd take me exploring.

"Tell me, Eveshone, why is it that you disguise yourself in these furs, so that you look like the…what do you call them, the Croa—Cro —"

"Croathus, Lovely." She treats me to a quizzical expression, as if she cannot believe that I don't know the word she uses for the Threatbelows.

"And what should I call your kind?" I ask.

"Et anima a sanguine!" She laughs. I know enough Latin to translate. *Of the breath and blood*? What does that mean?

Then she breaks into laughter, which is a beautiful, musical sound. "I did not know you had such humor. No one had ever told me. This is completely unexpected. Of course you know I am an Anaghwin."

…Of course I do.

She doesn't answer any of my sincere questions. Where did she come from? I must be joking. Who are the Croathus? Oh, stop teasing! How does she know who I am? Stop acting so silly, Lovely! She's completely charming when she thinks I'm being charming, so any frustration I feel at being stymied is wiped away, but still—I need to know what's going on, and she's not helping.

"Eveshone, I know you believe that I'm joking, that I should know the answers to the questions I ask, but I don't. I'm serious. As serious as I am when I request that you stay away from Adorane. I don't have the first clue what's going on."

I watch my words have an effect on Eveshone, and her features grow stern, even reverent. "My apologies for any offense, Lovely. I should know that your thoughts are not the same as mine."

"Can you tell me all the things I do not know?"

"I cannot. I am not gifted with such powers. But I am taking you to one who is."

Gifted with such powers? I am asking for an explanation, not the ability to levitate. But before I can press her, Adorane calls my name. I'm not sure how long he's been awake, but he's not happy watching me carry on with Eveshone. The way he looks at us reminds me of how I felt when I saw him flirting and frolicking with Catalandi.

I wordlessly apologize to Eveshone and lag back to talk to Ad, whom she continues to dutifully drag behind her.

Adorane and I have established that there is something strange going on, as even when I know that Eveshone and I are engaging in long conversations, all Ad can hear are unintelligible chirps and barks. Eveshone is equally unable to decipher anything that Ad says to me. While frustrating, it's actually a blessing, as I can speak freely with both without worrying that the other can understand what's being said.

"What were you talking about with that thing?"

I tell him, for at least the fourth time, that she has a name.

"I think we should go. She's taking us farther away from Waterpump Source. Have you forgotten why we're here in the first place?"

"We can't go back to Waterpump Source. Not right now. The Croathus are aware of our presence and are massing there to kill us."

"Look, I know you don't want to leave your new friend. But I really think we should."

"If that's all you heard from what I just said, maybe you're the one who's only barking and chirping, Ad."

He laughs, and I'm grateful to see him smile, even if it rankles Eveshone.

"I think it's a trap. I don't trust her. What if she wants to kill us?"

Well, he's half right. Not us—him. But I don't see any use in letting him know. "If she wanted to kill us, we'd already be dead. You saw what she's capable of doing. She wants to protect us." (Half true.) "Anyway, even if I wanted to escape, what are we supposed to do?

Run away with me dragging you behind? How far do you think would we get?"

He grows tired again. "I don't have the energy to protest as much as I'd like, but I think you're wrong."

"If we die, I promise I'll make it up to you."

Another smile.

"I hate you, Icelyn Brathius," he slurs as he falls asleep again.

75

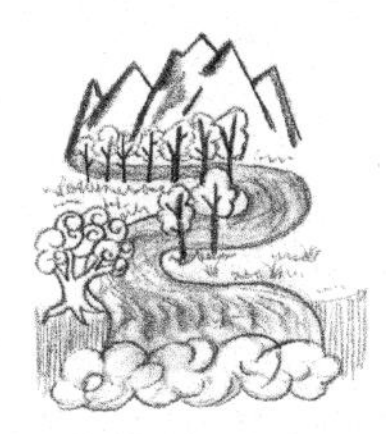

TORRAIN KNEW IT wasn't a Threatbelow lumbering below in the basement. They were agile and intelligent; this creature sounded clumsy and slow. Torrain contorted in every direction, trying to wiggle free while hoping to catch a glimpse of the creature that roared beneath his swinging feet.

He cried out as his leg was battered for the first time. He could feel a warm flow run down his leg and knew that whatever had hit him had drawn blood. Torrain was tempted to pass out, give up, and hope that the end wouldn't hurt too much.

But no—this wasn't the way his life was supposed to end. He examined his surroundings. If he couldn't get out of the floor by himself, he needed to find help.

He'd nearly reached the exit when he'd fallen through the floor, and he appeared to be in a small entryway where many tools were once stored. He saw ancient instruments that he recognized—a hammer, a saw, a shovel—because similar items were still used in Mountaintop.

Torrain grabbed the hammer, then tossed it aside when he saw what lay behind it. A hatchet. If he couldn't pull himself out of the floor, he'd cut through it.

Torrain chopped at the floorboards with abandon, until he opened up a hole. But instead of being able to climb out, gravity took hold, and he fell through the floor, roughly collapsing into the basement.

A bear towered over him, standing on two feet. Not an ultrabear, small and harmless, but an angry, provoked, enraged carnivore, rudely awakened from its slumber, and in no mood to do anything but kill.

Torrain held the hatchet in his hand and felt a charge course through his veins. If this was really the way he was going to die, he was at least going to meet his end swinging

76

DESPITE EVESHONE'S ENVY, I find time to hang back with Ad and talk to him. It's an emotionally charged triage, keeping them both happy, but I sense that he needs my attention more right now.

"Have you asked her where we're going?" he asks.

"She wants to take us to the Drowned City."

"Where is that?"

I shrug. "I'm guessing somewhere near the water."

He rolls his tired eyes.

I recognize most of the way Eveshone has taken since we left Waterpump Source. We're backtracking toward the base of the mountain, near where Ad and I originally entered the valley.

"So why are they poisoning us?"

"She's not. If you'll remember, she *fought* the Threatbelows who were poisoning the water, to save us." I sound more defensive than intended, but I can't help it.

"I understand, Ice, that you think she's good. I don't, but there's no reason to repeat that conversation over and over. Why were those Threatbelows trying to poison us? Why are we being poisoned at all?"

"I'm not sure. She laughs whenever I ask the question, like I'm making a joke."

"At least *somebody* laughs at your jokes."

"Stop," I say, but I smile. "It's like she assumes I know everything already."

"Have you told her you don't? That you know nothing?"

"When I try to tell her I don't understand, she insists she doesn't have the power to explain anything to me."

"What is that supposed to mean?"

"I don't know, Ad! Communication is not one of my strengths. I'm confused by half of the things you and I talk about, too."

No matter whom I speak to now, Adorane or Eveshone, someone is bound to be annoyed and exasperated. If I had my way, I'd tell them both to mind their own business. But I can feel Eveshone's pull on me, so I run ahead a couple of steps to walk with her.

In the distance, I see the small cabin that Ad and I had explored the previous day.

"We should stop there, Dear One. If we're to make the trip to the Drowned City, we'll need my father's help."

All at once it's clear, and I wonder how I didn't realize it before. Eveshone and her father were the creatures who entered the cabin while Ad and I hid—the ones I found myself drawn to, even while Ad was repulsed by them.

"You live there, Eveshone?"

She nods and smiles, pride playing on her lips. "It is our home. Ours and no one else's. We found it, we restored it. We defend it."

"Did you follow us, Eveshone, from when we hid in your cabin until we reached the river?"

"Yes! I sensed you in our home, and I believed. Father didn't. He thought it impossible. But I knew. So I chased you, because I didn't understand why you left without saying hello. I still don't. Why didn't you say hello?"

I hesitate, and she quickly adds: "I don't mean to question you. You have your ways and your plans, and I should never presume I know better than you. Please don't think that I do."

At some point Eveshone is going to have to accept that I haven't a clue what I'm doing most of the time, especially down here—but it feels good to spend time with someone who assumes that I'm filled with wisdom and have a good reason for everything that I do. It's a welcome change of pace from Adorane's view of me.

As we near the cabin, the air feels wrong. The color of the smoke rising from the chimney, before a gentle gray, now appears harsh and blackened. I could be picking up on Eveshone's fear, but I'm filled with panic.

Eveshone drops Ad's stretcher, which she's been dragging behind her for miles, and runs toward the cabin. I've never seen a human move as quickly. I try to keep up with her, shouting for her to wait and asking what's going on, but she's too far away.

"Ice, where is she going?"

"That cabin, the one we explored—it's her home. She shares it with her father. I think something's wrong."

I try to pull the stretcher behind me, eager to catch up to Eveshone, sensing that she needs me. I'm amazed she bore this burden for so long without a complaint. I can only pull him ten feet before I drop the stretcher in exhaustion.

"How weak do you feel?" I ask Adorane, not waiting for an answer while I pull him to his feet. "Can you walk, if I help you?"

He's still in bad shape, but (sometimes I just have to love the boy) he's willing to try. We inch across the field, him leaning on me and limping. I feel the dread growing thicker. Something terrible has happened here. Even Ad can sense it.

I've never heard a noise like it. She's crying, gutted, soaked in grief. A month ago I'd never heard anyone or anything—human or otherwise—in mourning. After all, what had there been to provoke such sadness back then? Since then, I've watched the Veritas women, seen Adorane in his grief, and now Eveshone's wails grab hold of me. I feel myself changing, like these moments have marked my heart.

"They've taken him from me! He is my everything, my everything down here! Oh, Lovely, I am lost. What can I do? He's gone!"

Ad and I peer into the cabin, knowing that she doesn't mean her father has been snatched or taken hostage. I see him, hollowed out like Jarvin had been, propped up straight against the wall to send a warning. Or a threat.

Behind him, I see a message written on the wall in what I fear is his blood. It's in Latin, but I know what it means:

Do not betray your kind. Slaughter those from Above.

"They've sent an advance scout to deliver a message," Eveshone sobs.

My two friends, natural enemies of one another, now have something tragic in common. Both have lost their fathers to the Threatbelows, or as Eveshone calls them, the Croathus.

"I am alone. Lost in darkness. He was my everything." There's no self-pity in her voice, only a vibrant sense of loss.

Even though I'm just over half her size, I pull Eveshone close to me. It reminds me of the stories I used to hear, how Apriori mothers would hold their upset babies and talk softly until the crying would pass. I can feel Eveshone's muscles relax as she melts into my embrace.

"You're not alone," I say to her, almost singing. "You're never alone. I am with you. We have each other."

What does Adorane think of me holding her? I can't care. Let him think badly of me. Eveshone needs this. I hold her until I'm not sure if a minute or an hour has passed, whispering exactly what I know she needs to hear. It won't bring her father back, and I don't pretend it makes everything good. But I do know that it makes things a little better.

We stay in the cabin for the night. Adorane faces the difficult task of loosening Eveshone's father (whose dead body is huge) from where he is displayed, while I tend to her broken heart.

Ad and I have a minor squabble over whether we should be waiting here for too long—whatever has killed Eveshone's father (his name was Prantis, she tells me) could come back with others. He thinks we should get as far away as possible. I don't say so, but I remember how he wasn't willing to simply flee when his own father was murdered, and I believe we owe Eveshone the same courtesy. We aren't leaving until Eveshone is ready, just like we didn't leave Aclornis' grave until Ad was.

I appreciate his willingness to labor when I know he's weakened, and for this creature that he considers an enemy. He really does it for me.

Ad asks me to find out if there are any special customs or rites that we should observe in the treatment of Eveshone's father. Any prayers or songs? Should he be buried or burnt or something else? As uncomfortable as the questions are, I ask Eveshone.

She seems surprised that I would ask her these things and responds, "Whatever you wish. That is what is fitting."

"No, Eveshone, this is about you. What does your kind normally do?"

"This is not normal," she replies, frustrated. "My father has never died before. I don't know."

"Yes, but what do others do? What are your traditions?" I press gently, because this is important.

"I'm young, Lovely! I don't know. My father was the only other. We have no one else. We're alone here, set apart…all alone. Why are you asking *me*? Do as you will—that is what I want!"

I decide to leave it alone, though I'm confused. I think for a moment, then propose that we find a grove of trees and say kind words over Prantis as he is returned to the earth.

The three of us try to carry Prantis' body to a pretty green shaded grove—I'm surprised at how lightweight he was, considering how large his body is—but Eveshone insists that she transport him alone.

We lay Prantis in the ground, and I pick wildflowers and arrange them so that reds, purples, yellows, and blues lie all around him. I speak to Eveshone. "Red for the love that coursed through his veins every day for you, Eveshone. Purple for the bravery he displayed, living this life away from all others, unwilling to follow a path he deplored. Yellow for the warmth of the sun—which, whenever it shines on you, will be a reminder of how you carry him with you wherever you go. And finally, blue for water, because water is life, and —"

I stop. I don't believe in the words I speak, yet I feel compelled to say them; it's as if they've been written by someone else and are simply being projected through me.

"And what, Lovely?" Eveshone asks, her huge eyes searching me, desperate to hear what I'll say next.

"Because water is life. And just as water never truly disappears—it simply transitions from one form to another, from ice to liquid to vapor, but it's always somewhere, even if it's invisible—so his life will never truly ever end."

"My father is still alive?"

"Yes," I respond, and I'm glad that Adorane can't understand me when I speak with Eveshone, because he'd be amazed to hear me say such things. Eveshone crushes me with a hug and sobs, the good kind of crying, and I can tell that my words have initiated a healing in her.

Even if I know in my heart that they aren't true.

77

THINGS WERE AS bad as they'd ever been. They were even worse than the earliest days, when many were grieving the loss of those who hadn't survived the trip to the top; when they lived in terror, despite all Sean Brathius' assurances otherwise, that the Threatbelows would follow them to Mountaintop.

At least then the Kith had hope.

Now everyone had lifeless eyes—as if they'd be happier dead, as if there was nothing to live for anymore.

Nicholas struggled with the feeling himself. He feared that Aclornis' expedition had failed, although he wasn't prepared to count Icelyn among the casualties yet. Aclornis had promised to send a messenger apprising Nicholas of the situation Down Below as soon as it was feasible. No messenger had appeared.

Some Cognates had grown so desperate that they'd resorted to drinking from Waterpump again. Many of them were now suffering from the same illness that Marjan had.

It was a kind of suicide, Nicholas determined. Everything seemed to flow toward that same end—the poison, the guns, the murders, Istoch's parents. Death was becoming preferable to life.

Though they hadn't spoken to each other since Nicholas took Istoch from his holding cell, Nicholas found himself wanting to talk to

Tranton. He knew Tranton was a snake, but the truth was, he was a clever snake. It was hard to explain, but Nicholas felt that even if he could never trust Tranton, he could always trust in the honesty and ingenuity of his counsel. It comforted him and made him feel like there were options. Without Tranton, Nicholas often felt like there were only two doors, and both led to rooms filled with ravenous wolves.

He wished his advisor could be with him now. Charnith Hailgard had sent a Veritas boy to ask if she could have a private audience with Nicholas. Since Nicholas had sent both Aclornis and Adorane to their likely demise, he hardly relished the idea. But he knew he owed it to her, even if he would have a hard time looking her in the eyes.

When he arrived at Hailgard Round, he smelled the faint remnants of sweet smoke. *Probably praying,* he thought, though he'd never say it. Nicholas had long suspected that the Hailgards had never given up religion. *What does it matter now?* If you could reach a brighter future free from the bondages of the past, of course you should give up on blind superstition. But now, what did any of them have to look forward to? *Why accept reality if it's so terrible, anyway?* Nicholas half wished he had a fantasy he could retreat into, too.

Charnith didn't act according to any of the expected formalities when hosting a Cognate, let alone the Chief Cognate, in her round. She made no offer of food and drink, no display of gratitude for his time, no feigned humility that he would make an effort to visit. Nicholas let it go. He wasn't feeling up to the charade, either.

"Take a seat." She sat down opposite him, across a small table, and waited for him to do the same.

He sat. It wasn't comfortable.

"Everything is broken, Nicholas," she sighed. She locked eyes with him. "My husband has always done right by you. Would you agree with that statement?"

Nicholas nodded, worried that to say much more was to commit himself to something foolish.

She placed a gun on the table. "These were a mistake. We can't handle them. None of us. You can't, after hundreds of years, provide wounded people with the ability to kill with the flick of a finger. It took the Apriori thousands of years to develop this technology, and even then, they couldn't handle it. How were we to survive being given this immense power overnight?"

"You want me to take back the guns? Put them in the hands of the Tarlinius only?"

She shook her head. "I don't want anyone to have the guns. No one. We need to take them and dispose of them. No one should have them —not the Tarlinius, not Tranton, not us, not you."

Nicholas thought through what Charnith was proposing. An immense relief washed over him at the idea.

"How could we do that? I don't see how it's possible."

"I'll take care of getting the Veritas guns. Most agree with me, so I don't think it'll be too difficult. But you, Nicholas—I need you to take care of the weapons you gave the Cognates and the Tarlinius, as well as any other stores Tranton has hidden away."

"I don't see how I'll be able to do that. I—"

"Who do you think has more power, Nicholas: you or me?"

"Listen, I understand what you're saying. If you, a Veritas, can wrest the guns away from all of the Veritas, shouldn't I, Chief Cognate at the Highest Point in the World, be able to do the rest? But it's not that simple—"

"No, it's not that simple. And that's not what I was going to say. I have more power than you. The Veritas outnumber the Cognates, we all have guns, and they listen to me. Don't for a second believe that we haven't considered a revolt. It makes the most sense for us. But the cost would be too high, Nicholas."

Nicholas grew silent, blindsided by Charnith's threat. *A revolt?* He'd always thought the possibilities of such events were the mad paranoid ravings of Tranton, trying to make a rhetorical point. Yet Charnith had admitted to considering a bloody coup—and not only that. The Veritas had openly discussed it and found the prospect sensible.

"You broke the Kith. Figure out a way to fix it, or else the schism will continue to widen." She placed a hand on his. "You can do this. I'm counting on us doing it together. We both need to use our power to avoid bloodshed."

Nicholas needed to hear that. He hated it about himself, but he didn't possess the ability to be brave on his own. "You're right. And Charnith…" Nicholas struggled, but he wanted to say something. "I'm sorry about—"

"Don't apologize until we know there's something worthy of remorse. Please. Can you meet me again at this time, a few nights from now?"

He nodded.

"Good. Let's fix the broken Kith."

78

EVESHONE IS HEARTBROKEN, but she remains practical. Once we finish burying her father, she's ready to go.

It feels rushed to me, though I understand her logic. "Are you sure you don't want to stay longer?" I ask.

She dismisses my suggestion. "We're lucky the Croathus haven't already come back. And what's to gain by staying? He's not here anymore, is he?"

No, he's not.

She's more in need of my attention and more envious of the times I talk to Ad. It should bother me, and it aggravates Ad, but I find I have an endless store of patience for her. After all, her father was just killed —while she was out saving our lives. I can't imagine how I would feel if I were her.

It's strange to think of my father. I miss him, intensely at times. I miss the little things—those moments when he'd walk me to my job at Waterpump or pick me up from one of my tutoring sessions at Belubus' lab. Our walks together always left me feeling warm toward him. It's crazy how inconsequential moments turn out to be momentous once your perspective changes. I'd give anything to relive one right now.

But I'm also angry at my father and not sure I know him at all. I miss him, but I also never want to see him again.

I wonder if Eveshone is now an orphan. She's never mentioned her mother. Instinct tells me it's the wrong question to ask at the moment, but I file it away for later.

The overnight at the cabin provided one unexpected benefit: Adorane has recovered enough from his wounds to start walking. While I'm glad to be done dragging him on a stretcher behind us, and grateful that Ad is no longer so badly weakened, it does make navigating their emotions—and their dislike for each other—more treacherous.

"Tell me about the Drowned City, Eveshone." Since it's our destination, Ad and I should probably know more about it.

"Oh, I wish I could tell you more, but I've never been there."

Again, I'm thankful that Ad doesn't understand her. "What did she say?" he asks.

I pretend that she wasn't clear and that her answer confused me. It's not far from the truth.

"Why are we going there, then?" I ask Eveshone.

"Because it's where the others who love you live."

That sounds nice. I'm always in favor of meeting people who love me.

"Can you tell me anything at all about it? What does it look like? How far away is it?"

We're heading toward the ocean, and even though we're miles from the shore, I can already see the waters stretching out over the horizon. She points toward the ruined skyscrapers Ad and I had seen earlier, the ones rising from beneath the surface of the waters, far from land.

The Drowned City. Of course. "It doesn't look like anyone lives there." Even from here, the ruins look skeletal, ravaged by time.

"Is *that* where she's taking us, Ice?" Adorane knows the answer to his question, so it's more an accusation than a query.

I shrug again, like I don't understand anything Eveshone's saying, but he sees through it and shoots me a pointed glare. I ignore him.

"Why have you never been there, and how do you know anybody lives there?" I've found that I get much better answers from Eveshone when I keep my questions simple, with no nuance.

"I'm not an adult yet, Lovely. That's when Father always promised to take me there." She tears up at the memory of her father, and I place a calming hand on her arm.

"Why wouldn't you visit until you're an adult?"

"Father always said it was too dangerous a place to take a child. Also, we were forbidden. Banished."

Wonderful.

Eveshone freezes. She seems to be listening, and an excited look flashes across her face. "Something to help your friend recover, Lovely!" she exclaims, before lowering herself onto all fours and gracefully disappearing into the thick brush, leaving Ad and me alone. I have to give her credit; she's not grown a degree warmer toward Ad, still bristling at his presence, but she's been helpful as far as his health and safety are concerned.

Adorane watches her dart into the woods with contempt, as if getting on all fours and rushing off the path is the most shameful thing one could do. "Where did she go?"

"I'm not sure." I don't want to mention that it was to fetch something for him. He wouldn't like that.

"Tell me where we're headed," Ad demands.

I sigh. "She's taking us to those ruined skyscrapers out in the ocean." His eyes widen in anger, and I can tell he thinks it's a terrible idea. "Look, it's not a trap or anything like that. She's even told me, up front, that it's incredibly dangerous. But from what I can tell, that's where our only potential allies are. Every other creature here wants to kill us. I think even you can agree that's true—why else would they be poisoning our water?"

Ad scans the woods for a sign of Eveshone. "We should go, leave her. If we're lucky, she won't be able to find us."

The idea makes my heart sink, and I can barely restrain myself from shouting: "No! We can't do that. For protection alone—"

"For protection! Are you so naive? I've seen how she looks at me, Icelyn, bathed in lust for my blood. I'm a hunter; I know the feeling when you're consumed with the chase. She wants to kill me."

I had no idea Adorane was so intuitive. "But she won't! She never will—she's promised me she won't harm you."

Our intense exchange is cut off by a loud rattling noise, primally scary, and our instinct is to run. But I can't; I'm frozen. Eveshone emerges from the trees holding a long, fat serpent. It's angry, thrashing and striking at the air while trying to find something to sink its fangs into.

She holds the writhing snake toward Ad. Ad jumps back just in time to avoid a vicious strike.

Eveshone protests, "No! It's medicine, helps you feel better. Kills the weakness."

I don't want to get too close to her and risk being bitten by the angry snake. "What the hell are you doing?" I scream.

Ad shouts at me, "Tell her to take that damn thing away! Get it away from me!"

Eveshone is stubborn. "I know what I'm doing—it'll restore him to strength!"

I raise my voice with her. "No, not for us, Eveshone! Not for us. We could die! It's not helpful for us!"

My shouts shock her into submission, and she meekly backs away. "I was saving it for him, but of course I'll use it if you're both going to be stubborn."

Instead of dropping the snake, she holds it close to her opposite arm. The long, sharp fangs plunge deep into her arm. She winces at the pain. She looks sad, chastened as she softly says, "I know it hurts, but sometimes things that hurt are good for you."

Once the venom is completely injected, she throws the snake back into the thick woods. "Now, let's hurry. I don't want to have to make the voyage to the Drowned City past nightfall."

Eveshone forges ahead, turning around repeatedly to see whether I follow. I do.

Ad whispers to me while we walk. "Whether she means to or not, she will harm us."

79

THE NEIGHBORHOOD DIDN'T appear to be the setting of a lethal confrontation.

A persistent pounding cut through the silence, followed by a groan as heavily rusted cellar doors protested against being opened after centuries of disuse.

Finally they flung open. Something covered in blood-soaked, grizzled fur steadily ascended out of the basement—exhausted, spent, but determined.

A hatchet lifted into the air. Torrain, wearing the skins of the bear he'd defeated, took a step into the overgrown grass. He walked toward an abandoned swimming pool and stared at his reflection in a puddle of murky green-black stagnant stormwater.

He was unrecognizable, in a good way. Torrain saw something he'd always hoped to see in himself but had always feared wasn't there. Strength. He'd survived. Death had charged him, and he hadn't surrendered. Torrain ran his hands through the bloody bear fur hanging over his shoulders until his fingers were crimson. He drew them across his cheek, drawing lines on a face which, though smooth and free of stubble like a boy's, now belonged to a man.

Torrain thought of Icelyn. He'd seen her and Adorane at Waterpump

Source and run like a coward. If they were still alive—and chances were they were not—then he had to join them. Even if they didn't want him around, he wouldn't let that stop him. He had killed a giant bear with only a hatchet; he could stand up to Icelyn's rejection. Which was scarier, anyway? Razor sharp teeth, or Icelyn's frosty moods?

They needed him.

Torrain secured his hatchet. He found himself wanting to call it Slasher, so he did. He'd faced death and won. He could name his weapons whatever he wanted.

80

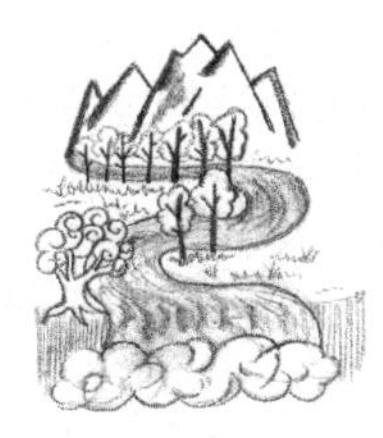

I DON'T LIKE how Adorane looks at Eveshone, his gaze dark and clouded. Ever since the incident with the rattlesnake, there's been a shift. He's made up his mind about her.

The stress of trying to hold two combustible elements so near to each other without letting anything explode weighs on me, making a difficult journey even harder.

At least we're not hungry. Eveshone is an excellent huntress. (You'd think that this would impress Ad, but no.) At one point Ad mumbles something cryptic about Eveshone cheating, implying that she's not catching the prey but has it caged up and is pretending to capture it. Envy can addle a boy's brain.

She's adept in every skill needed to survive. Ad has always taken pride in starting a fire faster than anyone, and with only a stick, a string, and dried leaves for kindling. But before Ad can even finish gathering these elements, Eveshone has already built up an impressive blaze.

While we consume warm, juicy rabbit meat—a meal better than anything I'd ever eaten in Mountaintop—I want to joke around with Ad, like we used to, but I can't think of a single thing he would find funny. I'm at a loss to come up with anything to say to him at all, humorous or not.

"I trust you find my offering satisfactory?" Eveshone asks me, her eyes hopeful.

"Oh my goodness, yes. Yes. Delicious."

"It is pleasing to you?"

I feel guilty about how badly Eveshone strains to make me happy, and even worse about how much I enjoy it. It's all so unequal. She's focused wholly on me, while my passions are split between myself, Ad, and her.

"Very pleasing, Eveshone. Thank you."

"The scent fills your nostrils with delight, then?"

"An…overabundance of delight."

She's bursting with pride.

We aren't even close to reaching the shore by nightfall. Eveshone has to revise her estimation of how long our journey will take often, because Ad and I are unexpectedly slow compared to her. Movements that are effortless for her—leaping over a fallen tree or darting beneath thickly overgrown thatch—take Ad three times longer. And Ad's the fastest person I know. There are precious few trails Down Below, and Eveshone says that taking the one that leads from inland to the shore puts us at risk of discovery from the Croathus, who she believes are chasing us. We are left with no choice but to proceed through the thick forest.

At one point Eveshone orients herself and discovers that we are still hours from the water's edge. She sizes me and Ad up. "Do you think I could carry you and the other thing, Lovely? Only for the sake of speed."

I've no appetite to have this conversation with Adorane. His every glance at Eveshone is filled with mistrust; there's no way he'll allow her to cradle him in her arms like a baby.

"No, Eveshone. I don't think that's a good idea."

"Because of him? This should be your decision, Lovely, not his."

Great. Eveshone now dislikes Ad for rational reasons in addition to her inborn instinct. Without asking, I know she thinks he's petty, spiteful, and that I'd be better off without him. "Why do you stay with him, Lovely? He doesn't make your light shine any brighter."

With the way he acts around her, I can't blame her. But she did try to make a rattlesnake bite him, so I can understand his position too.

"We'll reach the shore when we reach it, Eveshone. No carrying."

She's disappointed, but accepting. We continue our slog through near-impassable woods.

"What were you talking about?" Ad asks me.

"I think she's starting to like you better," I lie, unable to think of anything else to say.

He bursts into laughter.

At least I've found that joke I was looking for.

81

NICOLAS HADN'T EXPECTED convincing the Tarlinius to surrender their guns to be this easy. He thought he'd face bitter protests, but instead he found relief.

Even hiding their conversations from Tranton hadn't been difficult. His advisor had retreated into his lab and hadn't been seen for days. Nicholas wished he knew what Tranton was doing to pass the time, but at least the seclusion was convenient.

Nicholas visited Raistin Tarlinius first. That hardened guard had once harbored a soft heart, and he also held a position of prominence in his family.

Courtesy would normally dictate that he approach Ranthron Tarlinius, the family patriarch, but Nicholas suspected that Ranthron had never forgiven him for relieving the Tarlinius of their position as servants to the Brathius. What he'd intended as a show of progressive freedom had been interpreted as shameful dishonor. As Tranton often said, "They say they want liberty, but most people yearn to serve something."

Nicholas knew that Ranthron's ears would be dead to anything he had to say, his heart scabbed over and scarred. Now that Ranthron had also (probably) lost his son in the expedition Down Below, Nicholas was sure a conference would be a waste of time.

"Mountaintop is broken," he said as he approached Raistin.

Raistin didn't disagree with him. He had seemed unsurprised at the Chief Cognate's request to meet him under cover of darkness, in a remote wooded corner of the village.

"Yes. The Kith have been torn straight down the middle."

"This is my fault, Raistin, and I want to do what I can to fix it."

"If you're looking for support from the Tarlinius—"

"Not the Tarlinius, not yet. Just you. I can't persuade everyone. But I know you don't need persuasion. You can smell the rot, can feel the growing darkness. And you know things aren't getting better on their own."

Raistin and Nicholas hatched a plan. Raistin would quietly talk to the other guards, without mentioning Nicholas, and plant the seeds. He would make it seem like his own idea, not an edict coming from the Brathius family. The Tarlinius had been placed in an impossible situation, he would tell them, and the guns were at the root of it.

Raistin would impress upon his family that the guns had to go. Gone from the Veritas, gone from the Tarlinius. Gone from Mountaintop.

82

AFTER A NIGHT of sporadic sleep and a day of hard-won progress, we reach the sandy beach near the ocean. Or, at least, we can see it. We stand at the edge of a cliff, hundreds of feet above the sand, the water from the river spilling over in a grand waterfall before it joins with the crashing waves from the ocean.

It's beautiful, but there's a problem. "How are we supposed to get down there?" I ask Eveshone.

"I don't know. You can't jump?"

One thing I've grown to appreciate about Eveshone is that she never hides her ignorance. If she doesn't know, she'll say she doesn't know. Compared to humans, myself included, who will twist into any number of shapes to avoid admitting this, it's refreshing.

"No, we can't jump." Can *she*?

"The ocean never used to be here," I tell Ad, though I'm sure he knows. We both knew, from the writings of the Apriori that ascended to Mountaintop, that this cliff and waterfall were new. Mount Savior used to be miles away from the ocean—an ocean that now appears to have flooded an entire city and laps up directly against the mountain range.

Eveshone grows frightened by my observation, which I don't intend as ominous, and tries to placate me. "Of course you don't have to jump—I'm sorry for suggesting such a thing. We'll find a way down. It's just that I've never been here before, not being old enough for my father to take me on this journey. If I'd known you would need an easy way to descend, I would have had the way prepared for you. I hope you know that."

"It's fine, Eveshone. I'm not upset." This is the kind of exchange I find difficult to relay to Ad when he asks me what she's saying. How could he understand? *I* can barely understand, and I'm sympathetic to her.

Eveshone delivers on her promise to find an alternate way down. Though steep, the path she lays out is thankfully not dangerous.

I've never felt sand before. I've read about it, but I'm finding that reading about something and experiencing it firsthand are as vastly different as sky is from ground, or cold is from hot.

Sand is delightful. Smooth with bits of coarseness. You can sink down into it, kick it up into graceful arches, pick it up and let the grains drop through your fingers, rub it onto your skin. The sun heats it to just the right amount of warmth on the surface, but it's still cool and refreshing if you dig deeply enough.

Ad climbs up onto a large rocky outcropping and peers at the distance between us and the flooded skyscrapers on the horizon. All business—not even willing to enjoy the sand with me for a minute.

"Ask her why it's dangerous." He's brusque, and maybe it's from fear, but I don't appreciate being told what to do.

I've learned that if you mix the sand with water, you can form it into shapes that hold their structure. I busy myself making small mountains and a miniature Mountaintop. I guess I miss the place, which is news to me.

Adorane joins me, his face set in a sour expression. "Look, the waters are clear. Even at first glance, I can see many threats." He points out one dark shadow after another, floating just offshore. "Humans die in the water, Icelyn. It's not fit for us."

I see a brilliant blue sky, turquoise waters exploding into dazzling white foam from arching waves as they hit the soft yellow sands. Ad sees death. I look up at him, amused, drizzling sand over the top of my mountain.

"Where is Eveshone, anyway?" he says suspiciously. I hate when he talks about Eveshone.

But I find it curious that she's left us alone, too.

"She's gone to find us a boat, or something we can fashion into a boat." I don't know this, but it's as good a guess as any, and I don't want Ad doubting her any more than he already does.

I remove my ultralion leather boots and push my bare feet through the sand. "Ad, you have to feel this."

He refuses, treating the shore as if it's made of poison. This incorrigible mountain boy is terrified of anything so flat and wet. I'm drawn to the point where the water crashes down on itself, and the cold splashing surf is exactly what I need. I wade in up to my knees and focus on the sensations to take my mind off Ad.

I'm frustrated with him, and the feeling is mutual. But I couldn't be without him, now more than ever. He's become part of me—a part that I switch between hating and cherishing, but also the part that is most truly myself.

Ad confuses me almost as much as I confuse myself. I keep catching him looking at me in a way that I mistake for tenderness, and I'm sure he's about to say something kind. Usually he says nothing at all, but when he does speak, it's to say something baffling ("I doubt your mother would want you splashing in the white-waters like that," as if he ever cared what my mother thought) or even hurtful ("I miss Catalandi. I could use a friend down here. An ally who understands me," he'd said earlier).

Ad's been studying the beach and walking the perimeter. He's taken stock of every boulder, every stretch of woods. I'm disturbed by the way he's stalking. It feels to me like he's on the hunt.

I hear a cry from across the beach, right where it meets a thick growth of trees.

I finally put it all together, but it's too late, and I curse myself for not realizing it sooner. The incident with the snake, Ad's growing contempt for Eveshone, his curious behavior once we've reached the beach. Why hadn't I predicted this?

I run across the sand as fast as I can, which isn't fast enough. My feet dig down into the sand, slowing me down as I desperately try to move forward.

"Stop, Ad!"

In the distance, I can see that Ad has fashioned a spear, which he now thrusts toward Eveshone, who he's somehow knocked off her feet.

He growls at me, unrecognizable. "Leave me, Icelyn. I have a responsibility to protect us both!"

Eveshone dodges left and right, supernaturally fast. Ad's spear can't find a target. In anger, he yells and jumps on her.

She lets his fists pound against her, restraining herself from fighting back, absorbing his violence. I've seen what Eveshone can do against creatures larger and stronger than herself, against the Croathus who sought to slay us. She must be angry, but she controls herself for me.

I throw myself into Ad and knock him off of her. "She could have already killed you if that's what she wanted! Stop it!"

He tosses me aside and picks up his spear again, nearing her. Eveshone stands, looking to me with watery, sad eyes, trying to read me.

"If you want me to give my life to this thing, Icelyn, I will do it." She stands still as his spear nears her.

"No, Eveshone! I don't want that!"

But it's too late. The tip of the spear plunges into her, and she cries out.

I scream and throw a rock at Ad, hitting him in the shoulder. It doesn't stop him from twisting the spear. I charge him and knock him on his back. He grabs me and pins me to the ground. I shove him aside, trying to catch a glimpse of Eveshone.

My fingers dig into his shoulders until I draw blood. We're both sweat-soaked from exertion as we grapple and try to gain an advantage. We slip and slide against each other. I gasp in anger—and a sudden desire. So much of his bare skin against my own.

Ad covers my mouth with his, lifting me up, embracing me, squeezing me.

He's kissing me.

I can barely breathe, and I'm completely disoriented. *Am I being devoured or adored?* It feels like both. His face is all I can see; he is all I can smell and feel. His eyes are closed, then they flicker open for a second, just long enough for me to see the desire that fills them. I give myself over to whatever it is I see in Ad's eyes, because I need more of it than I could ever get in a lifetime.

I'm not sure how long we do whatever this is. It's dangerous, and terrible, and the most lovely moment of my life. He's the wave, and I'm the shore he crashes into. Or maybe it's the other way. I could go on forever, but then I hear Eveshone whimpering. I angrily push Ad aside, then grab him for one last plunge into his waters, and finally shove him off of me for good.

Eveshone is virtually unharmed. Where the wooden spear had

wounded her, I see now there is only a small dot of blood. She is physically fine—but I realize that she's been hurt in another way. Her eyes flash disappointment, her customarily joyful, trusting expression gone. I rush to her side and embrace her. Maybe it's because Ad's scent still covers me, but I feel her shrink away.

"I didn't want him to do that, Eveshone. Nor did I want you to let him do that. I never want anyone to hurt you. I will do everything I can to make sure no one does. You have to believe me. Darling, do you believe me?"

She's frozen. She wants to trust me, but she can't. *Goddamn you, Adorane Hailgard.*

I give her wound a kiss, and tears flow from my eyes. This poor girl. So powerful, yet she accepted Adorane's violence without a fight because of her unexplainable, baffling, undeserved love for me.

"Your pain makes me sad, Eveshone. I will not let him hurt you again. Do you believe me?"

She nods slowly, and I can feel her ease into me. I hold her tighter than anything I've ever held before. Tighter even than I'd held Ad just moments before.

"I will talk to him. He will never do that again. Nothing like it."

I rise, determined to follow through on my promise. Though Ad's just awakened a thousand sparks under my skin, from head to toe, and sapped the breath from my mouth, I've never been more furious with him.

Adorane Hailgard is going to have to listen to me.

83

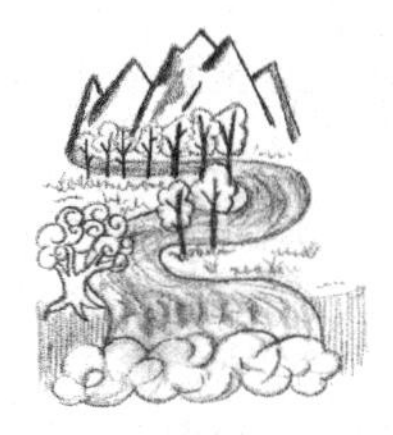

TORRAIN HOPED TO find Adorane and Icelyn at Waterpump Source. That bend in the river wasn't too far from the neighborhood where he'd spent the night, and he'd be there soon.

He held his hatchet, Slasher, and thought back to his battle with the bear. He could remember it only in flashes, all the moments jumbled together. The bear had stood tall, roared, and swung. Torrain ducked, or jumped aside, or maybe the bear missed. When he found himself still alive, he felt a surge of adrenaline, like he had cheated death.

He felt the first chop but didn't see it, because his eyes were closed. He raised the hatchet high in the air and brought it down with more strength than he knew he possessed and was rewarded with a satisfying sound as the axe head sank deep into the beast's chest.

He could feel the bear's spirit pass into him, and he carried it with him now. Not a sad little ultrabear, like Ad and the other Veritas hunted. He'd killed a goddamn monstrous grizzly bear—the kind even the Apriori wouldn't dare face.

Torrain wished this bear-infused version of him had appeared earlier. If Tranton had tried to murder *this* Torrain's mother, he'd have suffered instant consequences. If Icelyn had known and been promised to *this* Torrain, she'd have never taken two glances at Adorane. If those creatures at Waterpump Source had ambushed *this* Torrain, he wouldn't have run away and left Ad and Icelyn alone.

Torrain climbed atop a brush-covered overlook a hundred yards from the bend in the river. He peeked out from inside the green thicket, and his newly gained grizzly-bear-spirit bravado drained out of him.

A horde of the creatures that had no doubt killed Icelyn and Adorane massed on both sides of the river. He hadn't had a chance against three— and now there were more than he could count, with numbers in the thousands.

Though beastly and wild, their gathering was orderly, a precision military troop entering into battle formation. Torrain noticed with a chill how intelligent they appeared. They were not dumb bears that would roar and swing blindly. He got the sense that they could fool him into making a deadly mistake, like his father used to do when they played chess.

These were the Threatbelows in all their strength, the lethal force that had toppled hundreds of thousands of years of natural order and knocked humanity from its perch atop the animal kingdom. Despite all of mankind's technology and weaponry, nothing had been able to stall this swarm.

What had he expected to do with a hatchet, just because he was wearing a slain bear's skin? There was only one realistic course of action left available to him. He had to return to Mountaintop. There was nothing for him or any other human down here. Forget about the technology he'd discovered, the trove of ancient learning he'd planned to spend a lifetime deciphering.

He had to get as far away as possible from these brutal beasts.

84

I FIND ADORANE sitting, watching the graceful waves crash into the shore. He has a stupid look on his face, a vacant grin mixed with something else—maybe just satisfaction. It's as if he's forgotten to be serious for a second. It's offensive to me, after what he's just done.

"Sit with me. The sunset is going to be beautiful."

Now he wants to enjoy the beach and everything I've been admiring for most of the day. *Too late, Ad.*

He reclines back on his elbows and pats the sand next to him, as if to resume whatever it was we'd done earlier. I'm still undecided what the hell that even was, but I'm in no mood to repeat what I'm now sure was a mistake.

"Stand up, Ad."

He looks at me the way I caught him looking at Catalandi when I discovered them entwined in his bed. If I ever thought him looking at me that way would make me happy, I was wrong. I'm enraged.

"Stand up!" I lift him to his feet, and he plays along, as if I'm just doing all this to give him another kiss.

I slap him hard across the face.

"Damn you!" I can't do anything to stop my tears.

"What are you doing, Ice?"

I punch him on the shoulder as hard as I can. I know it's not much, but it's enough to hurt. "She has wanted to kill you since the moment she saw you, yet she has been nothing but kind!"

"What do you mean, she's wanted to kill me—"

"It's her instinct. She was born with a desire to kill humans, but because of her love for me, she's stopped herself from acting on it. It's a pounding drumbeat in her ears all day long, and she's not inflicted even a whisper of pain upon you."

"Why doesn't she want to kill you?"

"She loves me. I don't know why. But you—with you she is holding herself back. And still you attack her the first chance you get, despite my begging you not to! And you know the worst part? She could have easily destroyed you, Ad. She is powerful, but she took it, let you beat her, let you stab her, because *she thought that's what I would want.* She didn't fight back just because she thought I might want her to die at the end of your spear. So who loves me more, Ad? Who? You tell me."

"So you've known she wanted to kill me this entire time?" Ad thinks this through, and he doesn't like it.

"No—you don't get to be the one who's upset! *You're* the one who did something wrong. She wasn't going to do anything, because I told her not to. So tell me, who am I supposed to trust?"

The peaceful expression is gone. "I don't know, Icelyn. Maybe nobody should trust anyone. That's probably the best choice."

85

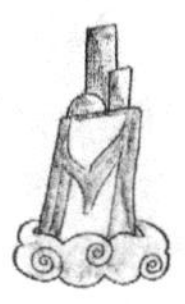

NICHOLAS AND RAISTIN planned to meet Charnith on the outskirts of Mountaintop, past curfew, when no one else would be out.

Nicholas was feeling alive again. He knew that a vital part of him was dead with no chance of resurrection—but doing what he could to restore the Kith was thrilling, and he felt the first glimmer of hope that better times might lie ahead. That was the best he could ask for right now.

Raistin had delivered, confirming Nicholas' faith in him. He'd managed to compile a substantial cache of weapons in a short amount of time. Even better, Charnith had found complete and total success. None of the Veritas wanted anything to do with the guns anymore. They'd only brought misery.

Raistin and Nicholas made their way to Cliffside, the breathtaking but dangerous location a mile from Mountaintop where they'd first handed out the guns. A sheer two-thousand-foot drop straight down into Cloudline greeted anyone who was foolish enough to stumble over the edge. Unfortunately, in the past three hundred years, at least seven members of the Kith had. All had been accidents—children or adolescents who, as most young ones do, believed they couldn't die. They were wrong.

The wind was fierce and unpredictable here. There was a reason this area was expressly forbidden by the Code; while the view was stunning, it wasn't worth the risk.

Raistin and Nicholas each carried satchels filled with weaponry. Neither side was going to give up their guns until the other did. As much as the Veritas didn't want to own the guns anymore, they weren't ready to let them go unless the Cognates reciprocated.

As they climbed the narrow steps toward the peak of Cliffside, they could see Charnith ahead waiting for them. She stood beside a pile of weapons, as promised. She greeted them with a nod, the barest acknowledgement of their arrival.

"Do you have everything?" Her voice was somber.

Raistin replied before Nicholas could say anything. "Yes, every single gun." Nicholas found this curious, because he knew it wasn't true. He wasn't sure whether to correct Raistin, but desperate to avoid further tension, he remained silent, a reluctant party to the deception.

Raistin and Nicholas opened their satchels.

Charnith examined them suspiciously. "Nicholas, these are all the guns?"

"Let's see—how many do you have?"

"I have all the Veritas weapons. I'm asking about yours."

"I imagine Raistin knows the numbers."

She seemed less than satisfied by his reply. "We'll be sure to count them, then. I know the numbers too."

The winds picked up, and Nicholas was shoved a step back before he steadied himself. "Let's be quick to toss these over and never see them again."

Raistin closed the satchels and took both of them back. "Nicholas, tell this Veritas that we need not count every last weapon. I have done it already."

Both Charnith and Nicholas were alarmed by his threatening tone. Nicholas had thought the three of them were allies in this endeavor, this first step toward restoring the Kith.

The wind had masked the sounds of others approaching. Four Tarlinius, armed with guns, flanked Raistin. They took Charnith's cache of weaponry. She flung herself at them, trying to make them stop. "No! I was promised! Nicholas, you swore to me!"

"I didn't know anything about this," Nicholas mumbled.

Even worse, Tranton was with them.

"Do you know, Nicholas, what the only thing scarier than power is? Raistin may not agree with the way we've ruled Mountaintop recently

—but do you know what he fears even more?"

A Tarlinius grabbed Charnith and held her toward the edge of the cliff. "Let her go!" Nicholas commanded.

"Weakness is the only thing more terrifying than strength, Nicholas, which is why Raistin came to me. *This* is how you put down revolutions, wise leader? By disarming yourself?"

"Let her go!"

Tranton took a step toward Charnith and pulled her back toward safety. "Charnith, you are right. The Veritas cannot handle weapons—which is why I never approved of their distribution in the first place. You've taken a step toward security tonight. Tell the others that you've decided Mountaintop still requires the ability to defend itself, but only in the appropriately trained and trusted hands of the Tarlinius."

"I was promised no guns at all," Charnith spat bitterly.

"There will always be weapons, Charnith. The best we can do is make sure they're in the hands of those who want the best for everyone. Explain this to the Veritas. Pray they understand."

Tranton headed back toward the stone steps, followed by the Tarlinius and Raistin, who carried the entire arsenal. He stopped. "Nicholas, would you like to come with us or stay with Charnith?"

Nicholas knew what Tranton was asking. Did he want to return to his position of fake power, the figurehead with no real ability to do anything? Or did he want to rebel against Tranton, take the side of the Veritas?

Nicholas made his decision. Charnith wasn't shocked as she watched Nicholas follow Tranton. She'd known she was taking a risk relying on such a feeble person.

Though she should have been flooded with anger at his betrayal, the only emotion she felt was pity at the pathetic way he lined up after Tranton, like a beaten-down dog.

"Nicholas, I know this hasn't been easy for you either," she shouted after him.

Nicholas stopped for a moment, but he decided he couldn't look back.

86

ISTOCH HAD BLINKED and his life had become unrecognizable. He'd had loving parents, and now they were both dead. Losing one would be a tragedy; losing both felt like he'd swallowed live embers.

He'd never been a child who pushed through life blind to how lucky he was. He'd always appreciated being born into this family, with this father and mother. He'd thanked God for all of it—even the chores, the rules, Father's occasional grumpiness, and Mother's periodic prickliness—every day.

He'd loved their cozy round and the indoor bonfire they would build each night. Istoch had gotten to the age where his Veritas friends complained about singing the secret songs after dinner. They felt too old for the ancient ways now. Such things were for children, not for them, they complained. But Istoch never agreed. He'd give anything to sing one of those songs with Mother and Father.

Every day when he returned from school, he'd smell the intoxicating hint of acorn cakes before he could even see his round. His mother's cakes were the best. Both Mother and Father would tuck him into bed at night, one at a time. There was no set routine, just a pervading atmosphere of warmth that made his heart feel full, lively, and calm at the same time.

Istoch was determined to be thankful for being taken into Brathius

Tower, with all its many rooms and levels, but he couldn't figure out why anyone would think this was better than a cozy round. All this space was no blessing; the tower was empty and cold. Istoch and Marjan had both spent the entire day there and had barely seen one another.

Towers were lonely. In a round, everyone was smashed up against each other, unable to avoid a person even if they wanted to. If someone cried, laughed, or coughed, you knew it. Round living was one big embrace, and right now, Istoch yearned to be held.

Being the sensitive boy he was, Istoch could tell that Marjan had warmed to them. That's why he didn't understand why they'd spent the day sifting through their heartaches alone. It was strange, for a boy who'd taken the initiative to murder his father's murderer, but Istoch was hesitant to disturb her without being invited.

Finally, though, he shoved aside his misgivings and headed toward her chamber. Solitude was only going to play tricks on him. His head felt like it was being crushed under the weight of his thoughts, and he thirsted for contact with someone else, if only to relieve his own unrelenting sorrow.

Marjan wiped away her tears and looked at Istoch as he pulled the door open. He feared she might shoo him away or scold him, but it was worth the risk.

"I'm sorry. I know you probably want to be alone. But I can't. Be alone. I just can't."

Marjan rose and held him close to her. With Nicholas distracted, Marjan had been alone since she'd lost Icelyn, and she couldn't handle it anymore, either.

They didn't make each other any happier, but sorrow shared is better than lonely misery. They didn't say much besides an "I'm sorry" here and there. They listened to each other express their confusion over what had happened. It doesn't always take profound words to help a person through despair. Being willing to wade into their darkness alongside them can do a world of good. By the end of the night, both Marjan's and Istoch's hearts were still shattered, but a piece or two had been put back into place.

Istoch felt a ripple of hope pulse through him as he drifted off to sleep. He'd received the gift of purpose, a way to redeem himself. For Istoch had been struggling not only with grief over what he'd lost, but guilt over what he'd done. As justified as it had seemed, taking a life was not an easy thing for a tender conscience.

When Istoch awoke, he'd give Marjan one last hug and then set out. Outside the Wall, down the mountain. He no longer had his family, but he could at least help his new family put itself back together.

Istoch was going to find Icelyn or die trying.

87

TORRAIN WAS PLAYING mind tricks on himself, and they were working. *Come on, boy! If you want to live, you can run faster!* he'd goaded himself for the past hour. Anything to put as much distance between himself and the massed horror he'd witnessed at Waterpump Source.

If he had to push through exhaustion, burning lungs, and tired legs to get away from the Threatbelows, he would.

He'd never considered himself an athlete or a warrior, but in the past day he'd slaughtered a grizzly bear and run nearly a marathon. Torrain thought back to the boy he'd been in Mountaintop and wished there'd been a way to initiate this transformation without his mother dying and his subsequent banishment.

He missed his mother. He toyed with the idea that she was still with him. Being a good Cognate, he'd always shrugged off those superstitions. He knew logically that Mother was where she'd been before she was born—which was to say, nowhere at all. She'd had a brief blip of existence that interrupted an eternity of nothingness.

Yet his feet felt guided and he ran faster when he imagined that the voice pushing him was hers, not his own. Stupid or not, the prospect of his mother watching over him while he was Down Below was inspiring. In the same way that childish games could be fun and lift your mood, even though they were foolish.

His vision seemed clearer, his sense of smell sharper. That was how he saw them—a glimpse at first, so subtle that he thought he must be imagining things, but then too clear to ignore.

Not quite footprints. More like disturbances in the way the dirt and leaves and grass would otherwise be arranged. He could make out patterns on the ground that he'd normally never see. Those weren't animal tracks, nor the footsteps of the beasts. A flood of happiness rose up inside of him as he figured out what it all meant.

Icelyn and Ad were alive. They had survived and were heading back toward the coast. He wasn't sure why he was so buoyed by this news. Was he actually glad that Icelyn and Ad had survived? Was it that his guilt over abandoning them had finally been assuaged? Or was it just because now he knew wasn't the only human down here with these awful beasts?

Either way, he ran faster, following their tracks.

88

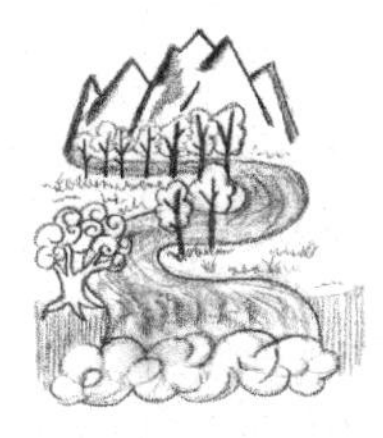

"CAN YOU GRAB more of those...husk things? The green ones." I point at the long, thin, jagged leaves that Eveshone has asked us to collect.

Adorane smirks as he pulls a bunch down from the tall, thin tree. "They're called palm fronds."

"I know that." Obviously, this isn't true, but I'm tired of feeling ignorant around Ad. "I just didn't think you'd remember, and I didn't want to come off as a knowledgeable twit. Like you right now. I mean, that must feel awful."

"It's not so bad. But thanks for your consideration."

"Lovely! The sun! It's falling in the sky!" Eveshone scolds (without actually scolding; she could never be cross with me). She is clearly perturbed that Ad and I have stopped working to have this chat. She's likely upset that Ad and I are talking at all.

We are a curious trio. Adorane and Eveshone, forced into close proximity because of their bonds to me, make no attempt to hide their contempt for each other. While they aren't resuming their violence, their attitudes are as fierce as any spear stab. I'm thankful that they can't communicate with words; their body language is awful enough.

"They're coming, Lovely. I can feel them." I can tell she's not joking or lying from her tone. (Plus, Eveshone has not told one joke the entire time I've known her.) I redouble my efforts and try to stoke a fire under Ad, too.

I'm growing more attached to both of them. It's as if two secret compartments in my heart have been pried open, and I can't figure out how to close them again. Every time I see either one of them I'm blitzed by feelings as confusing as they are strong. I feel motherly, sisterly, and friendly toward Eveshone, and whoknowswhatingly (though it seems to make my cheeks burn, whatever it is) toward Ad. I even wonder if one batch of leaves that Eveshone has scrounged up for me could have been mood-altering. What else could account for these feelings about Ad?

We find the remains of a boat, more of a rotted old frame than anything I'd want to put into the water, but Eveshone insists we can make it seaworthy. I believe it's a ruin of a vessel Eveshone's kind would have used, and not made for humans, because it appears to be built to her larger scale. Having to convince Ad that this leaky, abandoned heap will take us across the ocean to the Drowned City is not easy. But I suspect he suffers from the same attraction that draws me toward him, because he agrees without too much of a fight.

"We'll probably die, but you're the boss." He says it with a wink, as though if I'd only let him kiss me again, death would be a fair exchange.

I'm dwelling on the kiss more than I should—wishing it had never happened, hoping that it happens again. Ashamed, excited, tempted to relive it so I can pay better attention this time. The hot, sticky, close confrontation was a blur while it was happening, and my memory of it has only become fuzzier. If only there were a way to experience it again, without Ad being a participant, so I could analyze the whole moment. If I could kiss him without his involvement, that would be perfect.

I'm not the only one thinking about it. Eveshone has directed us to find palm fronds and sticky black material she calls *asphaltum* so we can patch up the boat. Under the hot sun, it's sweaty, difficult work. Whenever I'm doing anything, Ad watches me. He looks away when I catch him sneaking a glance, but not fast enough. I'm amazed he finds *any* shipbuilding materials on his own, with how much attention he's paying to me. My skin prickling, I know he's replaying everything we did over again in his mind. I wish he would stop. Mostly.

Even Eveshone can't seem to shake the memory of what happened.

I bring my latest supply of asphaltum to her. It's sticky and stinky. I find it in globs in the crashing white-waters and under the wet sands. She takes the viscous goo and spreads it over the crisscrossed thatch of fronds. I wonder how she doesn't mind getting her hands so dirty. I despise getting any on myself.

"Will you be having a batch soon, Lovely?" she asks innocently, though I can tell she's hoping the answer is no.

"I'm sorry?" I have no idea what she's talking about.

"I didn't know your kind did that, too. We do, of course. Or so I've been told—I'm far too young to partake in anything so adult. But I had no idea your kind did. And certainly not with things like Adorane."

My face grows hot. Is she referring to our kiss? I'd rather talk about anything else. "So, um, how much more asphaltum do you think—"

"If there will be little Lovelies running around, I can help you care for them," she offers earnestly.

I am stunned silent. She *is* talking about the kiss. Of course. Why wouldn't she? She saw it all. She's probably trying to figure it out. *Join the club, darling.*

"I saw you and he partake in the mating ritual. I wanted to give you privacy, of course, but I was still recovering from my wound. How long until you have your babies? How does that work—will they be half like you and half like him? What type of creature comes from that union?"

Oh God, no! No. No.

"Eveshone, no. That was *not* a mating ritual. Nothing of the sort. I'm not going to have a litter of anything."

"Oh, good." Her face is relieved. "You frightened me. What monstrous offspring a union with *that* thing would produce! Why would you want to carry that abomination inside you? What *was* it you two were doing, then? It looked like—"

"Whatever it looked like, I can promise you there was no mating going on."

"Were you battling him, then? Punishing him for hurting me?"

"Closer to that than to mating, I guess. I don't know. I have no idea what we were doing. But I can promise you, it won't happen again."

"It was a mistake, then?"

"How much more asphaltum do you need, Eveshone?"

"I didn't mean to offend," she apologizes. "I'm just trying to learn more about what the two of you were doing."

"I'm still trying to figure that out myself. Now, how much more asphaltum—"

As oblivious as she is, she can take a hint, and she drops the subject. "Another ten handfuls should be enough."

I'm not sure whether she means my handfuls or hers, and it makes a significant difference. I've been finding large globs of the sticky material, but once I give them over to her, they look like specks in her long, slender palm.

She lowers her voice—though since Ad can't make out what she's saying anyway, I'm not sure why. "One last question. If you aren't keeping it around for mating, and it was so cruel earlier, inflicting pain on me, I was wondering if, perhaps…" She trails off, reluctant to say the words.

"No, Eveshone. For the last time, you cannot slaughter him."

"Of course. I understand. I mean—I don't, but I respect your decision. If it changes, you'll let me know. Correct?"

I leave to find more asphaltum.

89

ISTOCH WORRIED THAT he wouldn't rise before the sun, so he didn't sleep. He packed roots, leaves, and a small ration of water from Brathius Tower's kitchen, making sure to leave the ultralion and ultrabear scraps for Nicholas and Marjan.

Istoch sensed a swirling exhilaration sweep over him, just like when he held that gun in his hand and knew what he would do with it. Every sensation now felt extraordinary to him. His feet touching the ground. Taking a breath. The cool of the air on his skin. Was he going to do this? Was this actually happening?

As unbelievable as what he was doing felt, he knew from experience that the consequences would be real. The killer of his father was dead thanks to Istoch's actions. It had felt imaginary at the time, but the outcome was irreversible. He wondered how his decision to go outside the Wall would change reality. Maybe he would die. Strangely, the thought didn't frighten him; at least then he'd see Mother and Father again.

Istoch had never gone outside the Wall, even when his more daring friends had. Many children seem to exist to defy their parents. Not Istoch. On the rare occasions when he had disobeyed them, he hadn't been caught, but the knowledge that he'd let them down was misery for Istoch.

His friends had talked about the world outside the Wall as if it were a wondrous fantasyland. As soon as his feet touched down there, he could see that was a lie. Even in the early morning dawn, it looked to his eyes exactly like the land within the Wall—same trees, same rocks, same brush.

As he descended the mountain, the landscape began to change. The trees were taller, greener, and closer together. A part of Istoch knew he should be afraid. But he was resigned to whatever fate crept up on him. The only thing that upset him about the idea of dying now would be failing in his quest to find Icelyn for Marjan and Nicholas.

By nightfall he'd reached Cloudline. He'd heard the rumors and felt a chill at the sight of it in the moonlight. The white mist looked thick enough to walk on, and it extended as far as he could see. As Istoch entered the milky blindness, he wondered if this was what passing from life into death felt like. One step at a time, submerged bit by bit, until there was no part of you left in the only world you knew—until you were in a completely new place where nothing was familiar and the old rules no longer applied.

Enough time had passed that Istoch no longer knew whether he'd been in Cloudline for a thousand counts or ten thousand. A part of him speculated that maybe he *had* died, but he pinched his arm and felt the same sharp pain he'd felt in life, so he figured that meant he wasn't yet deceased.

Either way, whether to reach heaven or Icelyn, he had to make it through Cloudline, so he decided to run. He picked up speed, twisting and ducking to avoid tree branches as they appeared from the fog and then vanished just as fast. He hit some, but the pain and blood were a welcome reassurance that he was still alive.

He'd settled into a quick pace, learning better how to recognize the obstacles he needed to dodge, and it was a dreamy feeling. He couldn't see the ground, so he imagined he was flying like a hawk—up in the air, above everything, able to go wherever he'd like. Then his foot hit something solid, and he actually did fly ten feet in the air before he hit the unyielding ground with a sick thud. He shook off the shock of the impact and crawled back to see what had upended him.

It wasn't all in one piece, and the scattered, torn apart remains had been dead for a while, so it took Istoch a moment to figure out what had happened.

He'd fallen over the fragmented corpse of a Veritas.

90

"LOVELY! COME TO me! Bring Ad!" Eveshone's words sound pinched and frantic as she shouts to be heard over the crashing waves.

"Why is she howling like that?" Ad asks, annoyed, as he digs for the viscous black goo. The waves have snuck up on us a few times, so we're soaked.

"She's scared." And if she's scared, I am too. We run toward the worksite where Eveshone labors to get our vessel into seaworthy shape.

"What is it?" I ask, though I have a guess and fear confirmation that I'm correct. Eveshone is shaking from fright, and nothing could affect her like that—not a bear, nor a lion, or certainly not a venomous snake. She could easily handle any of those creatures. There's only one beast she fears down here: the Croathus. She's been warning us repeatedly to hurry, that we need to get into the water, that they are massing and are on their way to slaughter us. I realize that the clock has been ticking all along.

"Get down, stay low." She sniffs and stares at Ad with contempt. "What can we do about his scent?" Eveshone must have a sensitive nose, because I don't smell a thing. She picks up a supply of asphaltum and starts to slather it all over Ad.

He jumps away angrily. "What the hell?"

"She says you stink, Ad. That they can smell you."

Ad rolls his eyes. "Of course I smell. I haven't bathed in weeks."

"He's made himself a target! They're coming."

Then I hear it. A shuffling in the woods. Branches cracking. Slight, but noticeable.

"You cover him, if he despises my touch," Eveshone advises. "He clearly welcomes yours, anyway."

Ad abandons his objections as I rub the asphaltum on his chest and shoulders.

"Especially in the gap beneath his arms," Eveshone says. I comply, though I don't enjoy it.

"Why don't *you* need this on you?" Ad asks me.

"If I did, *you* wouldn't be the one to apply it to me," I reply, more curt than intended.

Eveshone stands tall, looking through the darkening woods. I'm not sure what she sees, or if she sees anything at all. She then gets down on all fours, stalking back and forth, sniffing. She does this occasionally, mostly when seized by instinct. Ad hates when she walks on all fours like a beast. I admit it's strange, but I find a graceful beauty in it too. She's shifted into attack mode. If we're to survive an onslaught of Croathus, it'll be because of her.

She rises and lifts the boat to turn it over. "Get under this," she commands.

I obey, and Ad follows me without argument.

Ad and I huddle under the overturned boat. We have a crack of visibility that allows us to see a sliver of ground and about three feet above, and we use it to watch Eveshone continue to rotate between standing up straight and striding on all fours.

We hear something break through the brush, but Ad and I can only see Eveshone pounce out of our field of vision. We shift in the boat until we have a better view and watch as Eveshone rams into a beast smaller than herself.

"What is that?" Ad and I wonder the same thing, but he's the first to whisper it.

"Looks like a bear—but not," I reply. I see bear fur, but the creature isn't bulky enough.

"That's not a Threatbelow, either. It's not fast or graceful enough." Ad's right; this creature moves haltingly, not with the disconcerting lightning-quick steps of the Croathus. There's something familiar about its movements that I can't identify.

Perhaps we overestimated the threat. We watch as Eveshone knocks the lightweight creature over and then stares down at it, seeming almost as curious as we are. What is attacking us?

The creature pushes itself off the ground and rises—on two feet. I'm seized with a strange familiarity. Then I see an ax swipe through the air. Eveshone dodges and isn't hit, but it's close, and the exchange makes her angry. She knocks the beast to the ground again, this time with brutal force, and coils over it, ready to finish it off.

"Please, no! Please!" the thing begs, desperate and afraid.

I know that voice.

Torrain.

91

THEY HADN'T EVEN realized Istoch had gone before he trudged back, exhausted. Nicholas and Marjan were lost in their own worlds of misery and both thought he was in his room, quietly suffering the day away.

He shuffled into Brathius Tower, dirtied and weary, bearing a bounty of horrors. He looked half dead. A boy could only suffer so much, and Istoch had passed his limit.

Istoch had always been an observant, thoughtful child, and that skill was being put to grim use here.

"This is the scarf that Tughly gave to her betrothed, Prath, before he joined the expedition Down Below." He placed the scarf next to the growing collection of objects he had gathered from Cloudline, then dug a shiny pebble out of his pocket. "This stone bears the mark of the Lichney Family, which sent both patriarch and son." He laid out one ghastly souvenir after another, each one a death sentence for a Veritas who had ventured Down Below.

Nicholas clung to the hope that somehow all these great warriors had survived. "Perhaps they left their totems behind, but are still alive."

Istoch stared with empty eyes, trying to erase the memory of all those freshly dug graves. "They are dead. Don't make me describe how I know. There were no survivors."

Nicholas and Marjan felt selfish asking what they wanted to know most, but Marjan couldn't wait. "Of Icelyn, did you find—"

Istoch reached into his pocket. He gently held Marjan's hand in his, and opened it. He placed an item into her open palm, keeping his hand over it, as if by doing so he could keep Icelyn alive a little longer.

"I am forever sorry for both of you," Istoch stated, before he removed his own hand, kissed each of them on the cheek, and returned to his room.

Nicholas and Marjan stared at what Istoch had placed in Marjan's hand, frozen.

Icelyn's necklace, with the Brathius stone, the color of her eyes, still shining bright and beautiful.

92

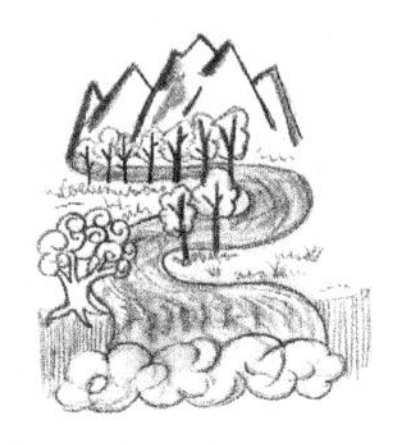

AD AND I summon all our strength to push up against the boat. It's heavy, and our first efforts to escape are futile. I scream to Eveshone, "Eveshone, freeze! If you love me, you will do that creature no harm."

She doesn't back down, standing rigidly above Torrain, ready to strike. I'm terrified she will eviscerate Torrain before she hears me.

Finally we lift the vessel and it tips over, just enough for us to be free of it.

She coils, prepared to strike, and I dart toward her, set on stopping my beloved Eveshone before she becomes a murderer.

"Leave him alone, Eveshone! Do not attack him! Do NOT!"

The harshness of my voice freezes her mid-strike. Her face dissolves from shock to sadness; she's hurt by my reprimand. She falls to her knees, deflated and confused.

I stand between her and Torrain, shielding him, and I feel a pang of regret for yelling at her.

"I was only trying to defend you from harm, Dear One," she explains. "I thought I was being heroic."

I hate that she's experienced such pain because of her pure love for me—first at Ad's hands, and now my own. I hope she doesn't decide that loving me isn't worth it. I'd be tempted to, if I were her.

I forget about defending Torrain and instead rush to her. "You *were* being heroic. You were doing exactly what I hoped you would do. But what I didn't anticipate, what I couldn't have foreseen, is…"

I look back at Torrain for the first time. Ad helps him to his feet. He's wearing a bearskin and looks like he's been through his own war. He clutches a bloody hatchet. His face has grown hardened and chiseled. Even though his features are the same, he bears little resemblance to the soft, hollow boy I knew in Mountaintop.

"That creature is a friend of mine."

Eveshone exhales in frustration. "Lovely, must you befriend every last creature that my nature compels me to kill?"

I catch a glimpse of Torrain rushing toward us, hatchet held high, murder in his eyes. *No!* I exit the embrace and block him before he reaches Eveshone.

"Stop. She's safe. She's mine." I mean to say 'my friend,' but I don't correct myself.

She is mine.

Ad, who I notice allowed Torrain to rush Eveshone without making any effort to stop him, joins us. "Safe. Wants to tear us into pieces—but aside from that, she's safe."

Torrain's eyes dart from me to Eveshone to Ad. I reach for his hatchet, but he grasps it tighter. From his perspective, the situation must be surreal. A beast attacks him, then I, his (former?) Intended, emerge out of nowhere and embrace the beast. I remind myself that whenever I speak with Eveshone, Ad only hears chirps and barks and other bits of bestial strangeness, and with Torrain it's likely the same. No wonder Torrain has no idea what's going on.

I'm loath to leave Ad and Eveshone alone, unsupervised, but there's no other choice. "Torrain, let's take a walk."

Torrain proves to be a much better boat builder than myself or Ad. After observing Eveshone for a couple of minutes, he steps in and reproduces her techniques flawlessly.

Despite this, Eveshone harbors as much disdain for him as she does for Ad. Even when she begrudgingly promotes him from the ranks of us mere frond-and-asphaltum-gatherers to frond-and-asphaltum-applier, it's a purely practical gesture. We have to shove off into the water soon, and the construction of the vessel is what's holding us up.

"Are there any more of these creatures slinking around that I should know about?" Eveshone asks me, busying herself with crossing the fronds and securing them with the black sticky goo.

"Why do you despise them, but love me, Eveshone?" *Is it because they are boys, and I am a girl?* I wonder. That's my best guess, and if so, I couldn't blame her. Boys are a mixed blessing, at best.

She responds as if I'm joking again. "Please, Lovely. The answer is so clear I can barely put it into words!"

I can't even defend them—Torrain and Ad *are* displaying their worst behavior. Ad insists he's every bit as skilled as Torrain at constructing a water-tight hull, when *he's not*. He grabs the fronds and the asphaltum from our carefully collected supply and begins to add them on his own.

"No, Adorane, that won't do. Water will gush in here. You see that? You're not helping," Torrain lectures. He sounds condescending, but it doesn't mean he's wrong. "Go catch us a clam to eat or something." Coming from Torrain, this sounds more like an insult than a suggestion.

"How do we know that water won't gush through *your* sections, Torrain? If we end up on the bottom of the ocean because of you, you'll be sorry."

Back and forth, the two of them. It's exhausting.

They both seem to be vying for my attention, competing with each other (and Eveshone). But then when they have it, they do something rude, confusing, or just plain mean.

Torrain kept a cool emotional distance from me while we walked along the crashing waves and caught each other up on our respective adventures. I wouldn't have believed his tale of the bear slaying, if not for the actual bearskin and bloody hatchet—which he for some mystifying reason now calls Slasher. When I pointed out that Chopper might be a better name for a hatchet, because nobody really slashes with it like they would with a knife or a scalpel, he grew strangely defensive and dismissive and claimed he could call his weapon whatever he pleased, so I dropped it.

Now he steals glances of me while he works. I do the same with him. He looks different, and I'm trying to figure it all out. Every time I see him, I'm surprised all over again.

"Your section of the boat looks just as watertight as Eveshone's, Torrain. Were you making boats on the sly up in Mountaintop?" I'm trying to be encouraging. Torrain distrusts Eveshone as much as Ad does, but I'd like to forge a workable peace.

"I should hope I'm at least as skilled as a dumb barking beast." It appears he's going to make no such effort.

"Her sections are better. I was just being nice," I snap. *I can be insufferable and unfriendly, too, Torrain.*

The four of us need a break from each other. But the reward for all the hard work that's pitting us against each other will only be the chance to cram into a boat together and set off across the ocean. I'm not looking forward to it.

Just as I return from what I am promised is the final run for asphaltum—which I am more than happy to make, so I can get a moment away from the mass of tension that's grown up between the three of them—I hear Torrain, his voice loud and angry.

"You've no right! No right, Adorane! You've broken the Code!"

I reach them just in time to see Torrain throw a punch. For all his newfound bear-killing and hatchet-wielding masculinity, Torrain's punching skills haven't benefited, and it glances harmlessly off Ad's shoulder. Ad lowers himself and launches into Torrain, knocking him to the ground. They roll in the sand, clutching and grasping, a whirlwind of exhausted violence.

"She didn't seem to mind," Ad says, and with a sinking sensation in my gut, I realize what they're talking about.

I pull Torrain and Ad apart as best I can, taking great care to avoid being hit and clawed myself. "Stop it, both of you. Stop it! This is not important."

Torrain gets to his feet and wipes blood from his lip. "Not important? So now you kiss just anyone? No big deal?"

"Not important compared to what we're facing. What we have to do."

Torrain doesn't seem convinced.

"Look, it didn't mean anything, and it's not going to happen again. Ad just took advantage…I still don't know what happened. I can barely remember it."

Now Ad seems offended. "You know what? It seems like you're all set here, Icelyn. You have it all! Your majestically tall deadly guard beast, your bearskinned Intended. Why do you need me? I only take advantage of you, make you do things that don't mean anything—things you barely remember yet still manage to regret. I'm going."

"Going where? No, Ad. We stick together."

"No, we don't. We're not friends. At worst, we're enemies that all want to kill each other. And at best? You said it yourself: *This doesn't mean anything*. I'm done."

Eveshone stands up tall, rigid, on high alert. "Quiet him, Lovely."

"Why?"

"Quiet them both. We must go. Right now." I tune in to what she hears, and this is no Torrain-sized false alarm. Though still faraway, the sounds of masses moving – of trees being split and splintered underfoot, of a symphony of howls and roars, of the ground being struck by thousands of fleet footed marchers, moving together – chills me.

Ad seems oblivious to the noise, because he heads directly toward it. I chase him. "Ad, don't you hear that?"

"Leave me alone, Icelyn. That's what you want anyway."

He enters the woods and cuts through the brush. I have a hard time keeping up. I ignore Eveshone, who is calling after me, panicked.

"That's not what I want!" I shout to him, "Look, do you need me to say I love you? How many girls do you desire for your collection, Ad? Is Catalandi not enough?"

That stops him. "At least I'm content to collect only girls! You need two boys and a creature, too! So much variety!"

I catch up to him and grab hold of his shoulders, as if I could stop him from moving on if I wanted to. "Please don't go. Especially where you're going. They're coming. Don't you hear them?"

The approaching horde has grown louder. I feel them like the drop in pressure before a storm. How much time could we have before they swarm us?

"You're crazy, Ice. There's no sound."

How does he not *hear* them?

Eveshone is somewhere in the woods, howling my name, trying to find me. It's a cyclone of madness, and I'm the epicenter.

How dense Ad can be sometimes. The din from the approaching horde is a roar! He turns to walk away from me, and I feel the last thread of sanity inside my head snap, and hold his arm with both hands, refusing to let go.

"What the hell are you doing, Icelyn?"

I grab him by the collar and pull his face close to mine. "I do love you. You know that. There, you've made me admit it. Now, if you love me back, even a trace, then follow me to the shore!"

Now even Ad can hear the Croathus crashing through the brush behind us. I fear we'll see them any second, and that they'll surround and destroy us.

Ad sprints ahead but grabs my hand to help me keep pace. It's a tricky flight, because there's no trail and no space. We have to duck under branches and jump over roots. At every turn I think we've hit a dead end, but we have no time to stop and figure out a place to go, so we move forward and around and through with painful abandon.

Then I see the Croathus.

Through tiny breaks in the foliage I catch glimpses of them flanking us. Ahead, behind. Not many—probably advance scouts. They dash on all fours at unnerving speed.

We aren't far from the beach. I see the break in the trees ahead.

I'm focused on Ad in front of me, trying to duplicate his steps and movements, when he's struck by a violent blur and taken out of my sight. I scream.

I turn all around, searching for traces of Ad. Where did he go? He disappeared.

I'm struck from behind with brutal force, and lifted, carried, and then pinned to the ground. It's all happened within a single breath.

I'm held down to the ground beside Ad. I struggle to turn over so I can get a better look at my situation. One of the Croathus hovers over me. It's massive, long, and lean, covered in matted fur, and it smells terrible. Retracted talons grow out of its fingertips while I watch. They dig into my shoulders, holding me in place. Its shadowy face lowers until horrifyingly close to my own. I'm startled to see its eyes, though. They're beautiful, oddly comforting, and the exact same icy blue color as my own.

This beast and I share a gaze for a terrifying moment. I prepare myself to be hollowed out like poor Jarvin, Aclornis, and the rest. *It'll all be over soon.* If I'm lucky, hopefully they'll leave my body here instead of hanging me up in a tree for Eveshone to see. She would be heartbroken.

Instead, the beast hisses angrily and pounces in reverse, as if to put as much distance between itself and me as it can as quickly as possible. God, they're so fast. It's like our eyes haven't even evolved enough to be able to track their movement. The beast turns its attention to Ad instead, joining the other vile Threatbelow who's on the verge of slaughtering him.

Before I get back on my feet, Adorane dodges a swipe from the Threatbelow and finds his footing. I feel a small pocket of pride for him. We humans might be physically inferior to these terrors, but that was a nifty move, Addy Boy.

He baits the Threatbelow to swipe again by hesitating for a moment. It works, and this time Ad dives to the left just in time to avoid it. The force of the swipe unsteadies the Threatbelow, and Adorane parries by grabbing a fallen branch and smashing it into the creature more than double his size, causing it to tumble into the other beast and knocking them both to the ground.

We dash toward the tree line. The din from the rest of the Croathus chasing us is deafening. Peace settles into me. We may be on the verge of death, but we have made a noble showing. Those Threatbelows will remember with shame the time they were bested by tiny humans.

I'm plucked from the ground again. In my peripheral vision, I see that Ad has also been swooped up, and the fallen branch crashes to the ground, knocked out of his grip by the impact. This is it. We have no more tricks.

"I've got you, Lovely." God! Eveshone is carrying us! "I know you told me not to carry the two of you, but this—"

"It's fine," I gush. "Carry us!"

We break through the trees and across the sand. The Croathus keep pace right behind us.

Torrain pushes the finished boat into the waters. Waves fight him as he doggedly shoves it against the surf. Eveshone deposits me in the hull. The forceful waters knock Torrain and Adorane off their feet, and Eveshone has to fetch them from under the swirling waters and hurl them into the boat beside me.

The Threatbelows emerge from the woods and darken the beach.

Thousands of them howl, bark, and screech. We're a hundred yards from shore now. As Eveshone lifts herself into the boat, we move past the last breaking waves and make our way out into the open ocean, thanks to Torrain and Adorane's use of wooden oars that Eveshone carved out of tree trunks.

I catch my breath. These days, it seems, my life consists of constantly thinking I'm going to die. But it hasn't happened yet. That has to count for something. I'm tempted to do something to honor the fact that we have survived. I pat Torrain and Ad on the shoulders.

"We're still here, everyone. We're still here!" It's all I can think to say, but it's exactly what I can barely believe. *We haven't been blotted out of life just yet—no way!*

My smile falls as I look back at the shore.

The Croathus can swim.

93

NICHOLAS WISHED THE walls of Brathius Tower were thick enough to block out the wailing. He hadn't the fortitude to deliver the devastating news to Mountaintop, so he'd asked Istoch to share his discoveries with the Kith.

Word had traveled fast. Though it was unfair to ask a young boy to shoulder that burden, Istoch had done the job admirably. Now Brathius Tower was surrounded by mourning wives, mothers, and those Veritas men who hadn't joined the ill-fated expedition Down Below.

Charnith herself had set up outside their bedroom window, and she'd been calling to him for hours now.

"Where do we go from here, O Leader? Please! Tell the Kith how to climb out of this pit."

Her raw voice was stretching him paper thin. Along with the terrible sounds of sadness, magnifying his own, it was as if all his inadequacies had taken physical form and now threatened to suffocate him.

Nicholas hadn't seen Marjan since Istoch had shown them the necklace. They grieved in isolation. He yearned for contact, so he made the walk to where his wife had been sitting all day.

She wouldn't leave Icelyn's chamber. Marjan stared out the window. It still had bars on it—the ones Nicholas had allowed to be added, turning their daughter's room into a prison. He looked away, ashamed. She held the necklace in her hand, turning it over and over with her fingers.

"It's all we have of her, now. Just this trinket. This damn tease, making me think of her eyes, her lively sparkling joy. But it's just cold stone—as dead as she is. As dead as she'll always be."

Tears filled Nicholas' eyes. Despite his gloom since he'd heard of Icelyn's death, he hadn't cried until now. He'd felt non-existent more than anything else. He touched Marjan's hand, and gently laid his finger on the jewel.

"I'm so sorry, Marjan. I will forever be sorry."

She pulled the necklace away, cradling it to her bosom, hiding it from his sight. Like he couldn't be trusted with it.

"Do not ask me to forgive you. I cannot, ever."

"Marjan, please. We're all each other have now."

She looked at him with a terrible mix of confusion and rage, as if she would murder him on the spot if not filled with such paralyzing bewilderment.

"We have nothing, Nicholas. Don't pretend otherwise. We have *nothing*."

Nicholas wasn't sure if there was anything worth fighting for here (or anywhere else, for that matter). Icelyn was dead. Adorane was dead. Aclornis was dead. Every good person he'd ever known was dead. Why should anyone bother living, when life had failed so many?

He left Marjan to herself, doubting he was doing the right thing but overcome by the feeling that there was no right thing to be done. She resumed caressing the necklace, staring out the window at the mourners, and didn't even notice when he'd gone.

Of all the hearts broken in Mountaintop, only one was unexpected.

Tranton hadn't thought it would work out this way. Restore discipline, strengthen the boundaries between the classes, grab the seat of power as the true leader of Mountaintop, and usher in a new golden age. That had been the plan.

He remembered what had been written, what had created the thirst for power in him.

'We are the true leaders of Mountaintop. –T. Nillson'

Once he had read the secret Nillson history he'd found in the caves, he had felt it was his destiny. Now that destiny was slipping away. He had no desire to preside over a group of broken, dying souls. The news of the expedition Down Below's complete failure was a shock to him. He'd expected casualties, maybe even that half would die. That was the cost of removing the poison from the water. But to have them *all* die, while the water remained deadly, was the worst of all possible outcomes, and one he hadn't anticipated.

Tranton had been humbled. He understood now. Nillson power was never meant to be on display. That was where he had veered off course. His kind of leadership—the *true* leadership his ancestor had written of—thrives in darkness, but withers in the sun. His leadership, up front and known to all, was not working. Mountaintop was dying.

He'd found out the hardest way possible what he *didn't* want. But at least now he knew what to do next.

94

THEY APPEAR TO be built for the water. My hopes sink. The Croathus' long bodies glide through the breakers as if powered by an outside source. They waste no energy and make no splash as they rush just below the surface. Hundreds of them head directly for us.

I don't care how vicious Eveshone is in my defense. We won't survive a battle against this horde in the water.

Adorane, Torrain, and I watch the waters ripple with the approaching Croathus. We have maybe a minute or two before they overtake us.

I grab hold of Eveshone's hand. It's double the size of mine, and looks almost human, but longer and thinner (and, with the razor-sharp claws that gracefully arch from her fingers, more lethal). I'm grateful to be beside her and Ad, and even Torrain, when the end comes. It seems right.

"Let's face this without fear, Eveshone." I grab Ad's hand, too. Despite our imminent death, I feel a spark as our skin touches. "Let's accept our fate together, with pride." Torrain is probably jealous, but I only have two hands. If I could grow a third, I'd let him hold it.

Eveshone concentrates on the surface of the ocean and shakes her head. "No, Lovely. We have every advantage. We're in a boat, and they're in the water."

I don't understand. "That won't help us once they catch up."

Eveshone releases my hand and holds a sharp talon toward her opposite forearm. "Horrors frequent these waters. The Croathus have made a terrible mistake entering them. You'll soon see the difference a boat makes." I remember the dark shadows beneath the surface that Adorane had seen from the shore.

Eveshone calmly drags her talons along the length of her arm, cutting a bright crimson line into her flesh. I shout and try to stop her, but she turns away and gently shields herself from any intervention.

"No. I'm doing what I must."

"Does that hurt?" I ask, horrified.

"Terribly," she responds.

Blood pours from the deep gash as she holds it over the clear blue waters, leaving a red trail behind our boat. I can't imagine Eveshone surviving this massive blood loss and fear that she's committing suicide.

Torrain seems to understand what she's done. He whispers: "She's attracting something that likes the scent of her blood."

She watches the calm surface of the ocean intently. "Any moment now. They'll come."

Torrain, Ad and I follow her gaze. I'm not sure what we should be looking for and can barely attend to anything other than the mass of Croathus who are now only a hundred yards away. More blood mixes into the water, until there's as much red as blue around our boat.

The nearest Croathus are close enough that I can see their forms clearly beneath the surface. I focus on one as it enters Eveshone's river of blood. It's too close. Whatever plan Eveshone has been relying on, whatever she's been waiting for, it is too late.

The Croathus swimming through the blood-red water bursts up and out of the ocean, launching five feet above the surface.

At first I think it is attacking, and I wince in anticipation, gripping Eveshone's arm as hard as I can.

But I'm wrong.

This Croathus is in distress. It's been attacked by something huge—something that came from deep below. A gray and white monster with jet-black eyes, larger than anything I've ever seen. It has the Croathus trapped in its massive jaws. As we watch, the water monster pulls the screeching Threatbelow beneath the surface in an explosion of blood.

"They shouldn't have entered the water," Eveshone declares.

The water begins to boil with attacks, the blood luring more of the monstrous water creatures. One Threatbelow after another crashes out of the water, and sometimes the terrible giant fish catapult clear into the air along with them. It's a sight to behold—these lethal creatures who intended to kill us meeting their own bloody ends in the jaws of other vicious predators. The Threatbelows battle back, and many sea monsters also die, but the gray killers have too much of an advantage in the water.

Our boat is buffeted dangerously in the midst of the carnage, and I nearly fall into the waters before Eveshone grabs me. I cling tight to her and wish Adorane and Torrain would, too. Both boys are grabbing hard onto the side of the boat, looking this way and that, their eyes wide.

Faced with a massacre, the swimming horde of Threatbelows think better of their pursuit and turn back toward the shore. Many of them don't finish their retreat as the water monsters ('sharks'! I suddenly remember from my Apriori textbook) pull them into the depths.

We've escaped. Eveshone is weakened by blood loss. She clutches her wounded arm to staunch the bleeding. "My father always told me these waters were filled with death," she stammers. Woozy, she dozes off. I fear for her life, but find a strong pulse when I touch her neck. Pressed against the fur of her cloak, the blood has stopped. I wrap her arm tight with palm fronds and hope for the best.

She saved us. Even Ad and Torrain have to admit it.

Living past the moment when you were sure you'd die is strange. As we use the oars to propel our boat toward the Drowned City, I let out a scream of relief. The blue sky, the water, the wind in our face, the monsters behind us, it's all too much to handle. My heart feels like it's on the verge of exploding.

I'm alive, on the ocean, and we've survived again.

"Care for a swim, boys?" I ask them, smiling.

They both shake their head, and the three of us burst into laughter.

95

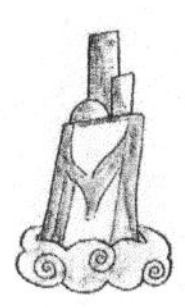

TRANTON ARRIVED AT Brathius Tower alone and unarmed. Like a venomous snake rendered docile in the snow, the Veritas who surrounded Nicholas' home were numbed by pain and posed no danger. Even Charnith remained silent as he passed.

Tranton didn't ask to enter. He still had a key from the days when Nicholas trusted him. He found Nicholas in his study, wallowing in a shallow puddle of self-pity.

Leadership is wasted on the weak, Tranton thought as he put his hand on Nicholas' shoulder. "You look like one who could use an ally."

Nicholas felt grateful and buoyed by the presence of an old friend. Or, at least, someone who had been his friend once. Stripped of his daughter, his wife, and anything that might have ever mattered to him in his entire life, he would take what he could get. All of the issues that had driven a wedge between himself and Tranton seemed inconsequential in comparison to the pain of being alone.

Nicholas was fearful that he might choose the wrong words and send Tranton away, as he'd done with everyone else, so he remained silent.

"I've come to broker a peace between us, my dear Nicholas. This rift has caused us great pain. And look outside—the Kith have never been weaker. I've even heard whispers of revolution. We find ourselves on the edge of devastation, and we need our leader."

Nicholas didn't want to hear this nonsense, but Tranton persisted. "You can be that leader, Nicholas. I have seen it in you. I have seen what we need. It's no secret I have hungered for power. But I have witnessed what happens to this village when a Brathius is not in control. I'm laying my heart in your hands, Nicholas. I'm begging you. Take back your rightful seat and lead us out of this chaos."

Tranton knew how to force someone forever into your debt. Take them to a place where you could easily destroy them, and offer them a helpful hand instead. Though Nicholas didn't realize it, he was far more valuable to Tranton as a grateful friend than a vanquished foe. Most people were.

Nicholas took Tranton's hand into his own and held it tight. Nicholas' throat was dry. He hadn't spoken for most of the day, and found the words difficult to form. "Let's make this right, Tranton."

96

AD, TORRAIN, AND I grew tired of rowing during the night and decided to rest. The plan was for Torrain and me to sleep for a short spell while Ad stayed awake, and then one of us would keep watch while he slept.

We'd decided that Eveshone needed as much rest as possible. Ad and Torrain still regarded her with suspicion, even after she sacrificed herself to keep us alive. ("Well, technically, to keep *you* alive, Ice. She wouldn't spill her blood that way for Torrain or me.")

As I awake to a hot blinding sun, I realize that Ad's fallen asleep without waking either of us up, and we've been out for a long time. I'm tempted to panic, but everything seems peaceful. No Croathus attacks, no threat from deep below in these deadly waters.

I chuckle to myself because Torrain and Ad are snuggled against one another like loved ones. If they could only see themselves, these bitter rivals finding warm comfort in each other's bodies! I laugh more than I probably should, but it's been so tense that I welcome the relief.

With the three of them asleep, I am alone for the first time in ages. I appreciate a rest from their arguments. The surface of the ocean is perfectly flat, and I see my reflection in it.

I'm not sure what I thought I looked like, but my face surprises me, and not in a bad way. I look braver, harder. Less like a child and more like a woman.

I remember Eveshone's terrible wound and check her arm, expecting to have to clean it to stave off infection. I check one arm, then check the other.

This makes no sense. Where the gash had been hours earlier, there's no longer an open cut—just a soft pinkish scar, mostly healed over. I don't mean to, but I wake her as I check her forearms. She smiles at me, and I notice for the first time that her canine teeth are a little more pronounced than mine. They aren't fangs, but they're halfway there.

"Everything is calm in your soul, Lovely? Yes, the fear has gone."

"What happened to your wound, Eveshone? It's healed."

She scrunches up her face, confused by my question. "It's already been a night and a morning, Dear One. Why wouldn't it?"

I guess Eveshone heals quickly. Lucky for her. "This wound would take many, many days to heal for me, if it healed at all."

"Keep an eye out for a venomous sea serpent, Lovely. I could use the boost."

Eveshone has told me, to explain why she thought a rattlesnake bite would help Ad, that venoms of all types act as a medicine for her kind. Snake, scorpion, urchin, spider—all of their toxins, designed to kill, would help speed her recovery. And when she's completely healthy, they provide a surge of strength.

Eveshone grabs an oar and starts us toward the Drowned City again. I'm embarrassed that we haven't made much progress toward it while she was resting, but she doesn't say a word about it.

Not in any way critical to me, at least. She does nod toward Ad, who is still in a deep slumber. "Does he do this often? Sleep well past when productive creatures rise?"

I know she's just looking for any excuse to belittle him, but this criticism seems unfair. We've spent enough nights together for her to know that he doesn't sleep excessively. Ad is a lot of things, but he's not lazy.

I look to the Drowned City on the horizon and change the subject. "How long until we get there, do you think?"

She hands me an oar and laughs. "Quicker if you help out."

We settle into a comfortable rhythm. My shoulders ache from rowing the day before, but I enjoy cutting through the waters, feeling like we're finally making progress.

The ocean mystifies me. Up on Mountaintop, I only ever saw water in tiny pieces. Drips here, a bucketful there; at the most, the channel of water that came from Waterpump. I would read about bodies of water as deep as our Mountain was tall, and found them as fanciful as descriptions of Apriori wonders like television or skyscrapers. Such massive stores of water were as hard to believe in as the concept of a heaven with a God sitting in a golden throne. I could see why people would want such things to exist, but a wish alone never brought anything to fruition.

Yet here I am, gliding through one of those oceans in a tiny vessel made of leaves, wood, and muck. I can't even see the ocean floor, though the water is clear enough to make out massive schools of fish passing below us. I love looking into the blue depths, though I'm always afraid I'll see one of those hungry monsters that inadvertently came to our rescue against the Croathus. (I've no illusion that they wouldn't chomp us up, too, if they had the chance.) The water shifts what I think I see, shadows darting into visibility and then quickly disappearing again, mesmerizing me.

Though Eveshone complains about Ad sleeping so long, I notice that she makes no effort to wake him or Torrain. I don't either. She enjoys this time alone with me, and I delight in it just as much.

We laugh as she tries to teach me a song her father taught her when she was young. I quickly learn that I'm not very good at singing. But I have to admit that it's fun, and I like the way it tickles my throat. Hearing my voice and Eveshone's mix as we try to sing the same words and notes is its own strain of intoxication, too. It's almost like we're merging for an instant, blurring the boundaries between her and me.

She and her father had no interaction with any other creatures, living like hermits in that shack in the woods. When I ask why, she says only that "that was Father's business and none of my concern." One day, she had been promised, she would come to the Drowned City. She'd always looked forward to that trip, as dangerous as her father said it was, because she was sure she'd finally meet some friends there.

"And now I'm on my way to the Drowned City, and I already have the best friend I could ever imagine by my side." She is remarkably upbeat. I don't blame her. From what she's told me, her life was incredibly lonely before she met me.

"What about your mother, Eveshone?"

"I'm sorry, I do not know this word. What is that?"

"Like a father. Another parent—but a girl, like you and me. A mother. She grows you inside of her and brings you into this world."

Eveshone shakes her head. "No, I don't have one of those. That must be peculiar to your kind. We don't have mothers. Or if I did, that was Father's business."

"No mothers? That doesn't make any—when you want to have a child someday, what would you be? Not a father, of course."

"Huh. I hadn't thought about that." She giggles, as if this is a silly thought game we're playing together. "I guess I'll see what I am when that day comes." Sometimes she's so serious and knowledgeable that I forget I'm dealing with a child—and not only that, but a child whose father told her very little and who had no one else to fill in the blanks.

Perhaps I'm not so different, I realize. What did my parents hide from me? My eyes have been opened to many realities previously hidden from me. The fog-making machines. Tranton's treachery. Belubus' secret underground kingdom in the Mines. Adorane's apparent feelings for me. That a kiss could feel so good and terrible at the same time. All these secrets! I feel a thrill of excitement at the thought of all the revelations to come.

That's probably the biggest trick adults play on children. They keep so much concealed from us. Growing up means realizing just how much has been hidden and figuring out ways to steal those secrets back.

"It's sad that you do not have a mother. Because mothers are meant to be warm and loving. Mothers are always thinking about you, always hoping the best will find you. Well, they *should* do all that, at least." Tears come to my eyes. I realize that I'm talking about my own mother and what I always wished she would do, as imperfect as she was. But still, I miss her terribly. "Everyone should have a mother."

Eveshone puts a massive hand on my shoulder. It's a lethal weapon, but she's always gentle with me. "Actually, Lovely, I was wrong. I do have a mother."

Has she been joking? This would be new. From what I've seen, Eveshone does not jest.

"Tell me about her. How did you remember?"

"I didn't remember. I realized. My mother is you. Definitely. You."

The Drowned City—which Eveshone tells me was also called *Peccatum* by her father—looms over us and we row between ancient buildings. Adorane is shaking off the foul mood he found himself in when he awoke—as if it was our fault that he slept so long, and so close to

Torrain, who has now roused himself as well.

The water is clear enough that I can make out hints of what lies below: grand structures, houses, cement roads and freeways.

"What happened here, Eveshone?"

Eveshone sizes me up before she responds, and then apparently decides to say nothing.

"It's not a trick question. I just want to know," I prompt.

"Do you want to know? Or do you want to know what I think I know?"

"What's the difference?" I ask. She speaks in riddles whenever I ask about the nature of the world Down Below. It's confusing.

"What are the two of you prattling on about?" Torrain is still getting used to the sound of our conversations, and he finds them alienating, just like Ad.

"Quiet, Torrain," I scold, frustrated at how he and Ad insist on belittling my connection with her. "She's telling me about the Drowned City."

Eveshone proceeds slowly, looking for the right word. "Well, you obviously know what happened here, so I don't understand why you want me to explain it. Unless you want to know how I view what happened here. How I feel about it. Then I'd understand why you're asking."

"Okay, yes. I want to know how you feel about it, then."

"I feel...I feel...Look. If a city needs to be flooded, then it's a good thing when it's flooded. The Drowned City is exactly as it ought to be."

This answer makes no sense. "But why would a city need to be flooded?"

"Oh, that's not up to me. I have no idea. But clearly this one did, or else it would not be under water. Everything happens for a reason, even if the reason is unknown to us." She looks to me eagerly, as if she's trying to see if I approve of her answer. I'm confused, so I decide to let it go.

We scan the buildings for signs of life. There are flocks of loud, honking birds. Sleek brown and gray animals flop out of the water onto ledges and through broken windows, barking loudly as they gather in groups. Torrain and Ad have entered a competition to be the first to identify any animal we see. ("Those are seals!" "No, pretty sure they're sea lions." As if the difference matters.)

I'm trying to shake the persistent notion that we've risked our lives and journeyed miles into the desolate ocean based on the word of an immature girl who has never been here before.

"What are we looking for here, Icelyn?" Torrain asks in a doubtful tone. While I admit that many of the recent changes in him are for the better, I resent his newfound bossiness. It's bad enough having to deal with Adorane.

But he has a point. What *are* we doing here?

"What are we looking for, Eveshone?"

Eveshone scans the flooded skyline and looks like she doesn't know. She inhales sharply and focuses on me. "You know, Dear One. I know you do. Where should we go? You guide us."

I'm the one leading this expedition? Once again, I'm grateful that Torrain and Ad cannot understand a word Eveshone and I say to each other.

Yet when Eveshone places her hand on my shoulder, I can feel what it is she is referring to. It's not a grand vision, but more of an inkling—or a preference, even. A slight impulse that says: *Hey, what if we went that way instead of the other way? Let's give it a try.*

And so I start to guide us. Left here. Right around that building. Straight ahead. I'm acting as if I'm getting these instructions from Eveshone, so Torrain and Ad don't know that in fact I'm the one cluelessly calling the shots.

Any initial doubts begin to drain with each turn. We're growing closer to whatever it is we're looking for. Excitement begins to boil within me. *Almost there.*

"Why are you smiling like that?" Ad asks me. I didn't even realize I was, but he's right.

"You're grinning like a fool," Torrain adds.

"I like it here." And I do. I love the bright blue waves crashing against the ancient colossal buildings, exploding into brilliant white walls of seawater, foam, and mist. The birds, the seals, the fish. I love it all.

"Well, I think it's terrifying," Ad observes. He's not wrong; this dead city no doubt holds its own share of hidden dangers. But it fills me with only excitement.

We approach a tower made of shiny, reflective, cracked glass. It's taller than the other buildings and stretches hundreds of feet above the water. Unlike other skyscrapers we've seen, this one is not all straight lines and blocky angles. Its sides arch gracefully out and then back in. As we watch, a window falls from the side and splashes into the ocean.

It's near several other skyscrapers, and when I squint in the sunlight, I think I make out swinging wooden bridges that connect them together.

We've reached our destination. I'm sure of it.

Our boat stops, bobbing just outside a run of blown-out windows we can use as an entrance. The towering rusted steel frame groans with the push and pull of the ocean currents.

"We are here," I declare.

97

AMPEROUS' SIMMERING RAGE threatened to boil over. He could see the crumbling skyline of Peccatum on the ocean horizon, and knew they were there. He'd long hated that place; it felt symbolic of all that had gone wrong down here, of the dominion others held over him and his kind, even to this day.

He was tempted to order another foray into the waters, in hopes that at least one of them would survive the deadly ocean and exact revenge on the accursed interlopers. But he knew it wasn't rational, just as the first decision to have his legion swim after them hadn't been rational, and he couldn't risk another disaster.

Since the Great Death, Amperous had only seen a handful of Croathus or Anaghwin die. Today, in less than ninety seconds, he'd lost scores of his most loyal followers. All those fine soldiers bitten in half and pulled down into the depths.

He stalked the sands, furious at himself for ordering those Croathus to their deaths and at a loss as to how to handle the tragedy. As a rule, Croathus didn't die. They had no rites or ceremonies to help them through.

The survivors crowded the beach. While many had died, and the sad business of determining who exactly they'd lost was still in progress, many more were still alive. They were hungry to do something to help themselves through their grief.

The traitors who have brought death to our kind! They will suffer for this new pain, built upon the centuries of injustice they've already inflicted upon us. I promise you all: They will suffer.

98

BROKEN GLASS DISTORTS the sunlight shining through the windows so that parts of the room are blindingly illuminated while others remain in darkness. Eveshone leads the way, with me just behind her.

Other than the constant rhythmic creaking of the steel frame, the crash of the surf outside, and the occasional caw or bark from a bird or seal, there's no sound as we make our way through the long-abandoned rooms.

This building must have served as living quarters for many Apriori. We see beds, chairs, and tables. Torrain tries to get us to stop when he sees machines that fascinate him, but I pull him away. We must find whatever it is we're looking for.

I just don't know what that is, exactly.

"What are we looking for, Eveshone?"

"We need to get to the top."

We find stairs. They're ancient and decrepit, and I'm amazed they hold our weight. We ascend until we're far above the surface of the water.

New sounds greet us here—howling, high pitched, threatening. I tell myself they are only tricks the winds play. Whether that or something more sinister, though, I am afraid.

We creep upward with slow and careful steps. I'd be tempted to turn around, but I am driven forward by a need to see whatever waits for us at the top.

Out of a dark pocket in the corner of the stairwell, I hear mad rustling and feel hot, dry air whoosh across my face. It feels as though something massive is flying by.

"What was that?" I whisper into the darkness. No one answers. Nobody wants to know. We continue our climb.

I finally see the doorway at the top of the stairs. It's open, and light streams through. I can see a blue, cloudless sky through the opening.

More rustling, and now an unearthly screeching too. I come up against a wall of hot fluttering wind, and I can't tell which way it's coming from. None of us can. It's too dark to see anything.

"We're not alone in here," Adorane observes.

Thanks for pointing that out.

I'm struck hard. Blindsided. Something tears into the flesh of my biceps. I flail without hitting anything, which should be impossible, because whatever is attacking me seems to be everywhere at once.

"Goddamn it, help me!" I beg, and Adorane grabs my hand and pulls me up after him, two stairs at a time, until we reach a sliver of light. My attacker continues to claw at me. In the light, we see that it's a bird. It's like none I've ever seen before—huge, nearly half my size, with knife-sharp talons and a cruel, curved beak.

Eveshone plucks the angry raptor out of the air. She gives it a shake and throws it to the ground. I stomp on it over and over until it's dead.

Torrain chops at it's lifeless carcass with his hatchet, which seems excessive. (I didn't even know he still had that thing.)

"Thanks, Torrain. Just in the nick of time."

Torrain nods, accepting my gratitude and not picking up on my sarcasm. I check my cuts. They sting badly, but they don't seem too threatening.

"Are you okay, Icelyn?" Adorane asks, his voice tender. I flush and hope no one notices.

"I'm fine. Just…watch out for the birds, everyone."

We strain to keep our eyes open as we exit the darkened stairwell and climb into the light. I thought we'd be outside, on top of the building, but instead we're in a cavernous space surrounded by glass and broken windows.

We're greeted by the pungent smell of salt, seaweed, and fish. I don't love it, but it's better than the stagnant air in the stairwell. The ocean wind is strong here.

As my eyes adjust to the bright light, I have a difficult time trusting what they see.

We're not alone.

I see a cluster of huts, almost like the Veritas' rounds in Mountaintop. Circular half domes, constructed from organic materials like bones, kelp, and ground-up seashells, huddle together in contrast to the severe, straight lines of the husk of the skyscraper's interior.

This is a village, and not a small one. As I look up and down the different flights of the hollowed-out skyscraper, I can see ladders leading to more homes. The settlement even sprawls across the bridges connecting this tower to other buildings that rise from the waters below.

"Something lives here," Torrain observes.

Recently caught fish hang on strings and cure in the sun. Thin wisps of smoke rise from holes on top of the huts, which are twice as large as the Veritas' rounds. We notice hallmarks of everyday life—clay pots, flowery decorations, and ornate painted designs—as we creep by.

The whole village is decorated, almost ceremonially, with the bones of huge fish. Ribcages that stretch longer than Eveshone line the walls. The skins, jaws, and jagged triangular teeth of monstrous sharks are displayed above us. Long spears are organized in rows.

Even Eveshone seems scared. "Should we leave?" I whisper, though I know that we shouldn't. We climb ladders from one level to another.

Eveshone points to the tallest structure, set in the center of the village, made of polished bones and fastened together with dried kelp in a rainbow of colors. It reminds me of the Apriori religious buildings, so I decide it must be a temple.

"Where is everyone?" Torrain asks. We all stop to listen again, but we don't hear anything.

We reach the temple, and Eveshone nods toward me. "You should open it, Lovely. It should be you."

I pull at the giant door, and it creeks open. Inside, a fire burns, barely illuminating the echoing interior. I enter with Ad, Torrain, and Eveshone trailing behind me.

"What is this?" Torrain wonders. We scan the space. It's difficult to see much.

Ad points to two large portraits hanging above the shark jaws and fishbones. "That looks like you, Icelyn."

One portrait is of a man. "That's Mistersean," Eveshone explains, "though you already know that, Lovely."

I don't, but that's nothing new.

The other portrait does look a little bit like me, blue eyes and all. Actually—though the thought scares me for some reason, I have to admit it—it looks *exactly* like me. But it's clearly hundreds of years old. We all stare up at it in wonder.

We don't hear them before they surround us.

Eveshone isn't scared, but the rest of us are. A swarm of her kind enter through the windows, from the stairs behind us, pouring in through the dark places. They hiss at Ad and Torrain, threatening them with feral ferocity.

"So it's not just you that hates them, Eveshone?" I ask her.

She nods. "Your love for the humans is the odd exception, Dear One."

Eveshone finds her voice, and it's clear and strong. "Lovely the Merciful One has asked that none of us harm her companions! They appear to be some sort of pets to her, so they are under her protection," she announces.

At the sound of Eveshone's declaration, everyone in the crowd turns their eyes toward me. I see shock and disbelief—but in a happy, warm way. One falls to the ground before me, and then the others follow until they all bow.

"Lovely! Oh, Lovely!" I hear them gasp. Breathy, quiet, and musical, their voices reverberate through the temple like thunder and rainfall.

"Eveshone, why are they doing this?" I ask.

"They love you as I do, Lovely," she responds. "But we must be going. Old Master awaits."

We leave the temple. More creatures surround us, crowding the village and bowing.

An arched stairway leads to a grand lookout on the top of the building. I know that's where I need to go.

"I'm going up there. Wait for me."

Torrain protests. "You can't leave us here."

"They won't hurt you," I promise. I know it's true. "Thank you for this welcome!" I shout to them. "Please treat my friends with care and respect." The bowing creatures nod slightly.

"I'll come with you," Adorane insists.

Eveshone locks eyes with me. "No, Lovely. Old Master needs to talk to you alone."

"Adorane, I will be fine."

There's an intensity in my eyes and voice, and Ad knows it's futile to argue. I smile. "Perhaps you can find one of those deadly military weapons you've been looking for. After all, this building was made by the Apriori."

Torrain has already become aware of the Apriori workmanship in the room, focusing on the innards of a crumbling wall. He's busy studying the minute details, mumbling breathlessly: "Oh, light fixtures. Copper wiring, huh? Ah—pipes made of plastic!" He barely acknowledges my departure with a wave.

In the unspoken competition between Torrain and Ad, this is one point scored for Adorane, who still won't let go of my hand. "If you die, I'll never forgive you." He tries to say it like he doesn't care, but he fails.

"I would never do that to you." I say it more like a joke, but I mean it.

As I ascend the stairs and leave them behind, I'm puzzled again by my relationship with both of them.

Torrain had been showing signs of wanting our Intention to last and bloom into a marriage. I've even considered it, though only for fleeting moments. He's been acting less wormlike. But right now he seems to care more about the makeup of ancient pipes than my safety.

Adorane seemed like he was only interested in me if I resumed whatever he sprung on me on the beach, but now he's genuinely concerned for my welfare—kiss or no kiss.

Eveshone, at least, possesses no conflicting, complex feelings for me. She loves me wholeheartedly. But she's still a child herself, so this comes as no surprise.

Maybe this is life once you get past childhood. Maybe friendships constantly shift from one form to another, plunging you into a chaos of changing rules and differing expectations. Maybe that's why adults always seem so tired. And so lonely.

I reach the top of the grand staircase and face an imposing metal door. I put all my strength into pulling it before it budges. I take one last look at my three companions surrounded by the bowing horde of creatures far below.

Of course I can't die. I'm the glue that connects all of them.

They'd tear each other to bits without me.

Please, don't let me die.

I exit onto the balcony, and the heavy door closes behind me.

* * *

I'm struck by the view first. The waves crash hundreds of feet below. There's a clear line of sight straight to the mountain where I lived the first seventeen years of my life. As always, the top is obscured by the thick fogs of Cloudline, so I can't see Mountaintop.

For a moment, I'm lost in a vision of what is going on up there. Mother and Father are living their lives, hidden from my view. Do they miss me? My heart hurts as I think of all those Veritas women and children who will learn that their men have died. I'm so lost in my imaginings of the Kith that I nearly forget why I'm here.

"I could look at the mountain all day long. In fact, I do."

I should be shocked to hear another voice, but I'm not. I search but can't find the source. This balcony bears evidence of living. Seal skins lie all over the ground like rugs. More of the massive bones are arranged in patterned decorations all around me. I turn away from the mountain view and scan the outer wall of the skyscraper, where shark jaws hang like trophies.

"Look up."

I obey and see a creature much like Eveshone, but older and male. He sits on an oversized throne made of fishbones and shark jaws fastened together with strips of leather. Unlike Eveshone, who wears the pelt of a land mammal to imitate the Croathus, this Anaghwin wears the rough gray skin of a shark for armor. The pointed head, complete with lifeless black eyes and rows of razor teeth, is still attached at the top. It makes for a terrifying sight.

"You've come. I knew you would," he says to me. He has difficulty getting the words out. I am significant to him. He pulls back the shark head and reveals his face. He has the same blue eyes as Eveshone and me.

"Eveshone tells me you can answer my questions," I say hesitantly.

He laughs. "How embarrassing. I was hoping you would do the same for me."

He climbs down gracefully from the throne, and though it's clear he's as lethal as any other beast I've encountered Down Below, I feel no fear. Not that I should take comfort in this, I tell myself. Many things die precisely because they don't feel fear when they ought to.

"Stay there, please. Keep your distance," I say.

He obeys, and we size each other up. I feel the same way looking at him that I do when I look at Eveshone (and sometimes, to be honest, Adorane). No matter how long I gaze, there's still a mystery to be solved, as if I could look another hundred years and still not see everything about them. There's always something new to behold.

He's taller than Eveshone, and towers over me even higher than she does. He stands on two feet, but from the way he scaled down the wall, I know he'd be just as comfortable on all fours. His face is a dark gold color, but it appears to have grease smudged on it to make it so.

We drink in each other's appearance. He seems to be studying me just as intently as I do him.

He points to the mountain, its apex obscured by fog. "You've descended from there. Yes?"

"Yes."

"Lovely. Do you recognize me?"

I don't, but I know that saying this would hurt him. I don't want to lie either, so I say nothing.

"I have waited for this day for many years, Dear One." He takes a tentative step toward me and stops, awaiting my permission. I nod and we walk toward each other.

As with Eveshone, I find this creature intrinsically familiar. I never had to make any effort to care for Eveshone or feel close to her. Now I feel like I have known this kind creature (at least, I think he is kind) for a hundred years already.

"May I?" he asks.

I nod.

He embraces me. He's so large and strong. As soon as he touches me, my mind is flooded with images. They rush into each other, and I can't keep track of them. I need to remind myself to breathe. I see the Drowned City before it was flooded, when it was a bustling city so grand I know I can't be imagining it. (I'm not that creative.) It's populated with humans—with the Apriori. I see the world Down Below the way it must have looked way back then.

I'm not seeing these things in my head anymore—I see them with my eyes, laid out before me, as I would see anything else. I look to the horizon; Cloudline is gone, but there is no Mountaintop on the peak.

"What is this, Old Master?" I call him Old Master, because I remember Eveshone calling him that. "Tell me what I'm seeing."

He lets go of me, and everything fades back to the way it actually is. The ocean fills in below and Cloudline again circles Mount Savior. The Drowned City grows abandoned and decrepit again.

"We share a bond, just as you did with…Eveshone is her name, right? Yes, young Eveshone. You stepped into my memories when we touched."

"I'm sorry, I've never stepped into someone's memory before. What does it mean?"

"You've noticed that you and Eveshone can communicate with ease? In fact, even without spoken words, I would imagine."

I think of the times Ad has insisted that Eveshone and I are grunting, hooting, or clicking while I know that we've been engaged in meaningful conversation. Had there been other times that we weren't even speaking out loud?

"When a good friend tells you a story and you think back on it later, it's as if you lived it too, right? Your memory of the event isn't just you listening to the words your friend spoke. Your memory is the world and actions described from the teller's perspective, as if you yourself were there. If that's ever happened to you, then you've stepped into your friend's memory. It's the same with you and me—only it's more immediate and vivid, because of everything we share."

"I'm sorry, what is it that we share? What do Eveshone and I share? I have so many questions—"

He cuts me off with a touch. "No, don't ask me questions. I don't want my memory to be guided. I want you to see what you *ought* to see—not what I think you should see, nor what you feel like you need to see."

At his touch, the world changes again, and the years pass backward before my eyes. The ocean recedes, and the land is lifted out of the water. Faraway, where the river plummets from higher ground into a waterfall, I see the lower and higher waters join until they're all flowing on one plane.

Even the balcony has changed. Gone are the bones of marine animals and jaws of the terrible sharks. Instead, it's decorated cozily, with a wooden table covered in books and reclining chairs that face the mountains. I peek inside the windows and see a bed, couches, and a rug. Lamps giving light. A flickering moving picture on a large rectangle, which I know is a television. This is someone's home—an Apriori home.

I no longer see Old Master beside me, though I feel his touch on my arm. "I'm still here, but you've slipped into my memory, living this moment as if you're me. Explore, and you will learn everything that has been hidden from you."

I open the door and enter the apartment.

99

I'M AMAZED AT how the Apriori live. Miracles abound. Their food is kept cool or even frozen like ice. They can heat it in an instant. Water pours from several openings throughout the home on demand. They make their rooms hotter or colder simply by flipping a switch. They press a button to make light shine, even where there is no sun, moon, star, or fire. They pick up devices and speak to each other, despite being separated by miles or oceans or continents. I'm stunned to see Apriori using these wonders so casually. They live in a world of magic, seeming to take it all as a matter of course.

They didn't realize it, but they were gods. Gods of their world—their powers could be explained no other way.

I'm in a large living space, where a serious man lives. He spends most of his time reading dusty thick volumes or scrawling words and numbers at a furious pace on stacks of paper. A young girl lives with him. She keeps to herself and is mostly ignored by the man, because she isn't a thick dusty book. She appears to be his daughter. She reads, draws, plays music, and watches flickering moving images on the television.

They do not live alone.

Most of the apartment is decorated in bright, cheerful colors. There are paintings of cute animals on the wall—lions, tigers, alligators. I see many small items that I assume are toys, though they're nothing like the playthings I used when I was younger. My miniatures were small figurines carved from sticks; these are elaborate ocean vessels and automobiles. There are even some that have wings like birds.

The man seems obsessed with locks and bolts. He presses a series of buttons to set some, and then also has manual metal slats which remind me of the bars Father used to trap me in my room. He has them on the outer door, the windows, and then another bunch on a door which leads to a large space for children. He wants to hide something. To protect it.

In this colorful suite of rooms, labeled *NURSERY* on the entry door, a series of objects seem to be set up for specific activities on a soft cushiony floor: one for climbing, one for jumping, one for hitting, another for dodging. They remind me of the obstacles the Veritas would use for their prowess events.

The man puts a wooden cylinder to his mouth and blows. The man's daughter joins him, her icy blue eyes filled with excitement. There's a pleasing sound and then a small wooden door in the wall, painted to look like it's part of a tree, crashes open. Out rush two children.

Now that I've had more time to watch them, though, I can see that they're not human children. They're both unusually muscled and tall. But they appear to be smart and nearly like humans—they aren't beasts, either. Then it dawns on me: They look like Eveshone must have looked when she was young.

I know instinctively that one of these creatures, the fairer colored one with auburn hair, is Old Master. His companion has more of an olive complexion, but with a bright golden thatch atop his head.

The serious man smiles, and his delight in them is clear. His daughter giggles; I can tell this is the high point of her day. The two creatures race in playful competition, working their way through the obstacles with stunning precision. If I had continued confusing them for humans, I'd know by now how wrong I was. They leap straight up in the air onto a small shelf that is double their height off the ground, then dodge left to right with startling speed. At one point the man tosses a series of balls in their direction, and they twist and contort easily to catch each one.

The man takes notes and times them with a small clock. They finish their activities and wait before him for a reward. He embraces them.

"Very good. Damn. So good."

They laugh and mimic him. "Very good. Damn. So good," their small voices chorus in unison. They're clearly proud of themselves.

"Daddy! You taught them to swear!" the girl scolds, unable to control her laughter.

They're young (if they were human, I'd guess they were four years old at most), yet they stand almost as tall as the man. They could knock him over if they wanted to.

The man exits the group hug and holds up a sheet of paper.

"X plus X-squared equals six. What does X—"

Before he can finish, they gleefully shout. "X equals TWO!" and squeal as if the question is so easy it's funny.

The questions get more difficult, and they keep up with ease. Even I get a lost with all the X's and Y's, but they don't seem the least bit challenged.

"Yes, Omathis! Yes, the square root of 27!" The man tousles young Old Master's hair. Now I know that Old Master's name is Omathis, and the other creature is named Amperous.

My experience of the memory shifts. I've been a silent observer to the scene, like I'm standing in the room watching (though of course they can't see me). But now I can feel my perception merging with young Omathis'. I have the curious sensation of seeing everything through his eyes, feeling his emotions, thinking his thoughts, and—though I am still along for the ride and unable to actually do anything by my own volition—making decisions and playing out the actions as he does.

As impossible as it is to comprehend, I *am* him—with a slight overlay of myself still whispering in the distance. It's like I've been swallowed whole, with just a faded memory of who I was.

"I love you. Always. I'll care for you. Always."

I'm inside the warmth of those big, calming words. Why have I been crying? With him so near, soothing me, I can't imagine I'll ever shed a tear again. He sings as he holds me against him. His voice is clear and deep, and it's the most beautiful sound in the world. I can't see anything but his face, his eyes like the brilliant sky. They could be looking at anything else in this world, but they're focused on me.

"You have no fear, ever. You are mine, and you are fine, forever."

I squirm into him, content. I want to burrow deeper into his care. I'm so much smaller than he is. He can scoop me up and carry all of me easily. Whenever the world gets too big or too dark, he scoops me up and makes me happy.

"No matter how big you get, you'll always be small enough to be held. Still enough to feel my heartbeat. Warm enough to face the cold stares from all others. Yes, you are mine, aren't you? Sean will always love you. Always. My darling Omathis, my Dear One."

My heart sinks because I hear the Other One crying. He has woken up, and I don't have Blue Eyes to myself anymore. Now he will sing to another too.

"You're both getting so big! Such big boys. So strong and so brave."

The Other One nestles in beside me, and it's not so bad. I like him too. Blue Eyes holds us both at the same time. He sings again, and his voice echoes through the room.

"I love you. Always. I'll care for you. Always."

I want to stay awake, to look at Blue Eyes longer, but my eyes have their own plans. I have no fears or worries anymore, so I sleep. The Other One does the same. I can feel Blue Eyes lowering me down, and wish I could wake up so I could protest, but I don't. Even though a cry might force him to hold me longer, I'm too bright on the inside to pretend I'm upset.

He puts me in my box, and The Other One in his, and then sneaks out of the cold, hard room.

My cheeks are wet, and my sadness is so big it no longer fits inside me. It's bursting out, scary and huge. My screaming wakes the Other One, and we cry out together. I can hear Blue Eyes at the door, and I know he wants to hold me.

But no. Long Hair is here. I am filled with anger at the sight of her. Blue Eyes looks at her too much when she's here. When he's looking at her, he isn't looking at me.

I hear her talking. She's stopping Blue Eyes from coming to get us. "You know you're getting too involved. Keep your distance, Sean. They're not your children." I don't understand her words, but I can tell what she's saying from the sound of her voice. She's saying cruelty and darkness, the kind you run from in your worst dreams.

I cry louder.

The door closes.

Mister Sean promised he'd take us for a special trip once we were ready. And today, we showed him we're ready! I made all my jumps and dodges without one flaw, and even Amperous caught every single ball. I got a little nervous with the sums and multiplications, but even those came out right.

I'm hoping the trip includes ice cream, but Amperous thinks it'll be lollipops. Either will taste good! DELICIOUS. I just prefer the cold all over the inside of my mouth and down my throat. Who could blame me?

I'm happy to leave the big building. We've only been out once that I can remember. Amp thinks it's twice, but I don't think Mister Sean would risk taking us out that many times, because we all know that everyone wants to end us. That's what they'd do if they saw us running around outside the Big Building—they'd kill us.

Amp fears leaving the nursery, and I can tell he's not excited as Mister Sean buckles us into the car. But not me. I'm brave. I always try to tell Amp I'm the braver one, but he never agrees. But now while I'm excited, he's fidgety—chewing on his talons, dulling them (even though Mister Sean tells us we MUST NOT DULL OUR TALONS!).

"Don't, Amp," I whisper. "You'll bite off your sharpness." I don't want Mister Sean to hear us.

"He's right, Amp. You mustn't do that." He always hears us anyway. Sometimes I think he can hear our thoughts! Just like sometimes I can hear his, though not with my ears.

I look out the window, and everything is familiar and different at the same time. Sometimes I catch a peek of this world from up in our nursery, but we're so high above that it seems small and make-believe. Here I see humans (hide, I know, before they see me!) and trees and dogs and other cars. And more things, too—there's a bird!

"Where do you think he's taking us?" Amp whispers, his eyes wide as they try to take everything in. "Do you think anyone can see us?"

"Our windows are dark, so you can see them but they can't see you," Mister Sean assures him from the front. He smiles. "You're going to be fine. They're going to love you. Don't worry."

I don't know who *they* are, or why I should worry about them loving me or not. But now I am worried. Why else would he tell me not to worry unless I might naturally worry? When you naturally do something, there's always a good reason. You naturally breathe because you need air. You naturally blink because your eyes get dry. And I naturally worry when something scary is about to happen.

Amp and I perform to perfection. We do all the tricks we've learned from Mister Sean—jumping high, catching balls. Plus the math. I don't make one mistake. I think hard about every detail, just like Mister Sean tells us to do. He is proud.

But he's also upset.

The men—those scowling-faced humans!—never smile once as they watch us. I begin to wonder if we've made a mistake, even though I can't think of what it would be. It was probably Amp's fault. He's not as careful with the details as I am. I wasn't watching him the whole time, so there is a chance he messed up without me noticing.

I don't like these men. They're dressed in dark outfits that remind me of our scary room at night. They look at us like we frighten them, though *they* are the ones that chill *our* bones. Why should we make them uneasy? We are just children. They are the ones with serious eyes and deep voices.

Mister Sean wants them to like him. I can feel how much he wants them to like us. But I don't think they do. I can't feel what they feel, so I can't be sure; but if they do like us, they have a confusing way of showing it.

"How many more are there?" I hear one man, whose last name starts with the letter P, ask. Mister P is writing notes in a folder labeled ***CROssbred Anthropomorphic Tactical Hybridization for Ulterior Soldiers.***

Mister Sean tells him that there are five batches of two. "The pairs have never been exposed to each other." I don't have any idea what he's talking about, and neither does Amp. But that's normal. Mister Sean is smart, and sometimes he uses words and ideas that we can't understand.

But when he says "the Other Batches," it tickles the place where my eyes and brain meet. Mister Sean says that's normal, for that part to be tickled, and that you mustn't ever ignore it like most do. It means that there's a mystery to be solved—and an important one, too!

Mister P gives us lollipops. They're delicious—just not as good as ice cream. (They aren't cold.) We like the candy, even if we're not sure about Mister P.

"I'm afraid this isn't going to be a good discussion. It's bad news, Sean." The people with suits as dark as night speak slowly, treating every word like it's a delicious bite of the best meal they've ever eaten, even though I think their words taste terrible.

I watch Mister Sean's face turn red. I feel bad for him. "Why wouldn't it be good news?" he asks. "They're progressing according to schedule."

"It's been fifteen years, and they're still children."

"That's what we expected. They don't age as quickly as we do—that's why they'll still be in their prime hundreds of years from now. Everything is slower. Plus, we have to build them carefully. I still haven't been able to install aggression, and elevation stabilization is causing—"

"By the time they're ready, we won't be waging the same wars. This decision isn't coming from me. I have no say in the matter. There are many projects, and we never planned on taking them all to completion."

I feel panic rise in Mister Sean. "It's too soon. We shouldn't rush into any decisions yet."

"We're going in a different—"

Mister Sean interrupts. He's always taught us not to do that, but he does it now. I don't mind. Anything to stop that terrible man from speaking. "What other projects? Robotics? I'm light-years ahead of robotics. These have the potential to be much more lethal—"

"This isn't a debate, Mister Brathius. The decision has been made. Now, as you know, there can be no trace left—"

"Combat is only one application. This is bigger than that. This isn't just about warfare."

"That isn't how this works. This is a military project. We are building weapons. We know you care for them. But we aren't in the business of subsidizing the breeding of your pets, Mister Brathius."

Everything they say causes my head to spin. Are they talking about us? Are we in batches, like cookies? Why is Mister Sean so sad?

"You know damn well that's not what I'm talking about. We have *unlocked mysteries* here. They aren't susceptible to disease. They make use of extra-verbal communication. Their anti-aging traits alone could change everything we know about medicine."

The men mumble to each other. I wish I could hear what they were saying—but then again, maybe not. They look the way Mister Sean does when he's not happy with the way we've done our math. "We aren't interested in the side effects. You've become too involved. You care."

"Of course I do."

"Even if yours was the most promising project—which it isn't—we'd be shutting it down. It's become too personal for you."

"Give me three months. I can speed them up. I can move up the aggression instinct. They can be what you need them to be. They can be ready. Give me time."

Mister Sean is lying. I can tell. Luckily, the men cannot.

Amp and I can't sleep. Today was terrible. We'd looked forward to leaving this place and going outside for so long. But it's awful out there—everyone is scary and mean.

I'm crying. So is Amp. But when I ask him if he's crying, he says he isn't, and that I shouldn't either.

Normally falling asleep is easy, because the sun is gone. Not being able to sleep when the sun is gone and the world is dark is terrible. No one should be awake now, because everything is too scary.

But I can't lie still. Staying in one place feels impossible. So I stand and stalk—back and forth, one side of our enclosure to the other. Amp does the same. We both want to get away from the terrible pain in our stomachs.

Long into the terrible dark night, a girl who isn't Long Hair enters our enclosure. We've met and loved her before. She's born of Mister Sean. She puts her hands on my back and rubs back and forth. Her voice seeps into my ears and feels good, like ice against my skin when I'm hot. It makes the pain in my stomach go away. She does the same for Amp.

"There, there," she whispers. "Everything is going to be good. You'll see. He loves you. I love you. Not everyone is going to love you. But everyone who's important ones already does."

It all feels so good that I'm finally able to stop pacing back and forth. I'm able to lie down. I'm able to fall asleep.

Even though Mister Sean has always told us we mustn't fight with one another, now he brings a man who teaches us how to fight. "You still can't fight all the time," he tells us, "but sometimes fighting is the right thing to do." Mister Sean is so intelligent that sometimes he understands ideas that confuse us. Like this one.

Sergeant Ollie visits every day and teaches us techniques. That's a big word that means jumps and punches and kicks and slashes and other fancy moves. Sergeant Ollie is making us good fighters, which is funny since we aren't allowed to fight most of the time. It's weird to be good at something you aren't allowed to do.

We like S.O. (this is what he tells us to call him). He smiles a lot, and we can both tell he likes us too. He's not scared of us, either. We're different than him, but he doesn't care. He acts like we are all friends.

* * *

Long Hair is called SHAI. Even her *name* is ugly! She has a son. We hate him too. He's everything bad about the world wrapped up in one body. He smells awful, and his voice is a shrill screech you'd give anything to silence. He looks at us with tiny hard pebble eyes powered by darkness, and we can both tell he despises what he sees.

The first time we saw him, we overlooked his awful qualities and tried to be his friend—as we do with everyone, because Mister Sean teaches us to be good. I reached out through the cage and gave our favorite ball to Long Hair to share with him.

He threw it away and said: "That's for babies!" Then he laughed and laughed. "You're the same age as me, but you act like babies! You still wear diapers!"

We weren't sure what diapers were, but we were afraid that the things we wore were diapers and that he was right.

Later, Mister Sean later told us he was just jealous.

We never got our ball back.

Mister Sean is good. He loves us. He made us. He's the only one who cares for us. Mister Sean knows everything. He can do anything. He will protect us, even when men in suits the color of scary night want us to die. We'll be okay, though, because Mister Sean is much smarter than those men. And braver and stronger too.

Amp and I say these words to each other, because they are true, and they make us feel better. Not all the way better—but a little better, which is much better than worse.

I hear Mister Sean's words in my head, and Amp tells me he hears them, too. *No matter how big you get, you'll always be small enough to be held. Still enough to feel my heartbeat. Warm enough to face the cold stares from all others. Yes, you are mine, aren't you? Sean will always love you. Always.*

We're scared. We had to leave the nursery we loved and move into a dark, dirty part of the Big Building. Mister Sean keeps us locked up tight all the time, secret, away from everyone else. At least Mister Sean is here with us. He's doing his own math, which is much harder than our math, and writing and reading all the time. He's so busy he doesn't even have time to watch our jumps and tricks.

Sometimes he brings *her*—the girl who loves us, who soothes us. The one who met us in the middle of that long terrible dark night and made it all feel better. Since she's Mister Sean's daughter, she's just as nice as he is. She always brings us a toy, and her eyes smile when she sees us, just like ours do when we see her. Amp and I call her Lovely. That's not her name—I remember she had a different one, but we couldn't say it when we were younger, so we've forgotten what it was. Whatever it was, it sounded like Lovely.

I know Mister Sean loves us, but I hate the Sleeps. These aren't normal sleep, when you get tired and need to rest. The Sleeps are forced. We're strapped to a hard bed so that we can't move even an inch. He tells us the needle won't hurt, but it's sharp and it hurts so bad. I can't remember what happens next, except I know it's terrible and I scream and scream. So does Amp. He screams the loudest.

Mister Sean makes us take the Sleeps even when we beg him not to. He hates them too. We can tell because he cries like he fell onto a needle and got stabbed too. I tell Amp this to make him feel better, later, when we wake from the Sleeps. I think it works. I try hard not to cry around Amp. He needs to know someone is doing okay, and I guess that needs to be me.

"This is to help you. I would never hurt you," Mister Sean promises.

One time Lovely saw us with the needle and the Sleeps and she hated it. She screamed too. Then Mister Sean stopped bringing her to see us, probably so she didn't have to see the Sleeps. I wish he'd just stopped the Sleeps instead. We miss Lovely.

But I know he tells the truth about the Sleeps. They will help us. Because Mister Sean is good. He loves us. And he made us. So I try not to scream too loud, even when he has a needle, and I tell Amp to be quiet too. Mister Sean is hiding us from people who aren't good and who don't love us. If we scream too loud, they may hear us.

He doesn't need to tell me, but I know he's hiding us from people who want us to be dead and no more—like we were never even born in the first place. The dark-suited men.

Lovely doesn't visit at all anymore. It's not her choice. I can feel her crying and shouting about it from wherever she is when she's not with us. She's furious, and that makes me feel good inside at the same time it makes me feel sad. Not seeing us makes her angry because she loves us. That's better than her not caring.

Long Hair doesn't care. Unlike Lovely, we see Long Hair too much these days. Mister Sean tells us that he loves her and we should love her, too. Amp and I can't figure out why. She's cold in all the ways Mister Sean is warm. She barely looks at us when she writes notes. I want to see what she's writing, but she never lets us, even when we ask politely, like Mister Sean has taught us to do. We are so good at asking politely, but Shai doesn't care!

Probably because her notes are mean and nasty, just like she is.

She always tells Mister Sean that we aren't his children. She thinks we can't hear her when she whispers, but we can. She even thinks we can't understand what she says, but we do. We can speak her language! She says such awful things.

"You spend too much time here, Sean. You have an actual child that needs your attention. These are your subjects. You've gotten too close. They don't feel the way humans do—you think they do, but you're projecting emotion onto them. They're bred to be unfeeling. You know that."

Amperous and I hate her. That's a human emotion, right, Shai? Hate? If we're bred to be unfeeling, how do you explain that? But we're always polite, just like Mister Sean tells us we need to be. I want to growl at her, can feel a strong roar in my stomach hoping to rise and escape loudly, terrifying her. But I don't let it. I'm polite.

I want to scream our secret to her, but Mister Sean says we must never tell anyone, not even Shai. He says he shouldn't even have told us.

But I want to shout it in her face: *We are his children! He used a part of himself to make us—so we are part Blue Eyes, too! You're wrong. We are made like him! That's why Lovely loves us so much—she is our sister, and we are her brothers!*

But we cannot. She can never know. Mister Sean says he'll get in terrible trouble if anyone ever finds out that he added a piece of himself when he made us. I don't understand why. I think it proves that he loves us. I think it's beautiful.

She brings her wretched young human, the ball thief, with her when she visits. She calls him Travis. I've never heard an uglier word in all my life. She likes to pretend that he is Mister Sean's son, but Amperous and I can tell that he doesn't have an ounce of Mister Sean in him like we do. He's all Shai. (Plus some other human who's probably as awful as Shai. We recently learned how it works. It takes two.)

Travis waits until Shai is out of the room and hurts us.

He presses the PAIN button all the time—the one that is only supposed to be pushed by Mister Sean, and only when we're acting disobedient and out of control. It's so unfair, because he's the one who is being bad, but we're the ones being shocked by the floor over and over.

One time Shai catches Travis pushing the button, but all she says is "Stop it, Travis." That's it. She doesn't do anything to make him *learn* to be good, the way Mister Sean does with us. No wonder Travis is wretched. No one trains him.

Amperous is sure that humans are more like Travis and Shai than Mister Sean and Lovely. I don't think Mister Sean and Lovely can even be human, they're so different from the others. Amp agrees.

Every time we wake from the Sleeps, I want to scratch everyone. I want to see my talons dig deep into skin—Shai's, especially, and sometimes Sergeant Oliver's. (But never Mister Sean. Never Mister Sean.) When we wake up tied to our Sleeps bed, unable to move, Shai prods and pokes us. She writes her disgusting thoughts on paper so other people can read them and think hateful things about us, too.

Mister Sean is with her. She seems angry with him.

"You can't condition them toward violence so rapidly, Sean. You could destabilize them."

"I don't have time to do it any other way." Mister Sean looks like he wants to say more, but then he stops. He's scared of whatever else he was going to say.

"If they determine we should terminate the experiment, then that's the right course. You need to prepare yourself."

I know what this word *terminate* means. The uncaring way Shai says it, as if she's talking about what she wants to eat for lunch today, makes me furious. And fearful.

Mister Sean is good. He loves us. He made us. He's the only one who cares for us. Mister Sean knows everything. He can do anything. He will protect us, even when men in suits the color of scary night want us to die. We'll be okay, though, because Mister Sean is much smarter than those men. And braver and stronger too.

I can tell Amperous is thinking these thoughts too.

No matter how big you get, you'll always be small enough to be held. Still enough to feel my heartbeat. Warm enough to face the cold stares from all others. Yes, you are mine, aren't you? Sean will always love you. Always.

We're going to be safe.

I can't hate him. I could never hate him. He is the foundation of who I am. His blood, breath, and beliefs mixed to form me, and I am a reflection of who he is. I could never hate him.

But I hate what he does.

The Sleeps happen every day now. I want to fight Mister Sean off when he comes for us. Amperous and I could, if we wanted to. We've grown. We're strong enough. Faster than he is. The parts of us that aren't from Mister Sean make us stronger and faster than he could ever be. I know that now. We could stop him easily, especially with our fighting *techniques*, before he could bind us and stick that sharp metal needle into us. Amperous thinks we should stop him. Not hurt him—just stop him.

"What could he do against us, O?" he asks. "We could make him stop. Together. It would be easy."

I tell Amperous to stop with these hateful words. I can feel in my heart that he is wrong. What Mister Sean does for us, even when it hurts, is because he loves us. He gives us the Sleeps, the needles, the terrible thoughts and feelings, because he loves us. I can't imagine how, but I know it's true.

I awake from my latest Sleeps feeling darker than ever. I want to tear at something until it splits into pieces, until the blood pours out and drains completely. No matter how much food Mister Sean gives us, I am always hungry. All I can think about is carving the humans in half and drinking their blood.

We are bigger now. No longer children. The games we used to play where we'd jump, dodge, and roll around like puppies no longer interest us. We want to see blood. We want to taste it.

I want to see Shai's blood spread all over this secret room where we are kept. I want to see the walls painted with it, red and warm. I don't say this to Amperous, because I know he wants it even more, and if he hears me say it too, he might actually do something monstrous. I know Mister Sean would be angry with us. Even though the Sleeps are what give us these desires, and Mister Sean gives us the Sleeps, he would not like knowing that I want to butcher Shai and see her turned inside out and dead.

I work hard to not think about it while Mister Sean is around, just in case he can read my thoughts. Amp and I never say it to each other, not even in a whisper, because then Mister Sean would hear.

Shai visits more than Mister Sean does these days. I don't know why, and she won't tell us. Mister Sean only comes around when we need to do Sleeps. He knows we wouldn't let anyone but him bind us to those beds.

"Where is Mister Sean?" I ask over and over again. Politely, the way Mister Sean taught us to ask. "I'd be appreciative if you could let us know," I add.

She doesn't answer. She never talks to us. She ignores us, like we are unworthy of a single word in response.

She talks to the tiny dog she brings along with her now, but not us. Even her miniature pet gets adoration, but we are treated like hulking dumb beasts. And we are reflections of Mister Sean, the genius who Shai claims to love!

But I do not care. Even if she did talk to us, or look at us with adoration, as she does with her insipid puppy and ugly son, we would both still hate her. That could never change. It's part of me. It's part of Amp. There's a pulsing in my head that wants her dead, as much a part of me as Mister Sean's blood in my veins.

We spend our days behind thick glass, locked away in a clear cage. It is so boring. There is nothing to do all day but be angry. We have no toys. During our last Sleeps they were stolen. I know why. Shai didn't like the way we played with them. We were pretending the toys were her, pouncing on them, tearing them to pieces. We never said her name, but she knew, and it scared her. Just like we hoped it would.

But we were just pretending! We know Mister Sean wouldn't want us to do anything to Shai.

When Mister Sean does visit, it's cause for celebration, even if it means more Sleeps. The Sleeps are worth time with Mister Sean. Seeing him brings a thrill, and smelling him provides comfort. He always gifts us a treat, like candy, or a funny song to listen to. Shai tells him he loves us too much and we aren't his children. He wants her to believe that we aren't his children (even though it's a LIE!), so he has to keep this love hidden. But Amperous and I know the gifts he brings are secret ways of telling us that he still loves us. He will always love us. That will never change.

When he leads us to the horrible beds for our Sleeps, we catch glimpses of the streets below through the windows. (Mister Sean promises that we can't be seen through these windows, even though we can see out.) I watch humans walking, laughing, and getting into cars, and I hate them. They want to hurt me. The things they would do to me if they could! They are the reason that Mister Sean is away so often, and so nervous and afraid when he visits.

I know they want their dark-suited men, and Shai, to terminate us.

Amperous and I need more love. We have Mister Sean's love, but only in small amounts—only as much as bitter, cruel Shai will allow. She's a love miser, taking most of Mister Sean and leaving only scraps for us.

She tells Mister Sean that we aren't working out as he had hoped. She tells him that he needs to face the inevitable.

I hate when Mister Sean visits but doesn't see us. We can still hear him, smell him, and feel him around—why won't he come play with us? It hurts on the inside, in my chest and my stomach, and then spreads to my head, in that spot right where my eyes meet my brain.

I keep thinking about the Other Batches Mister Sean mentioned when talking to the dark-suited men. Every time we've asked him, he wouldn't explain. But Amperous tells me that he can feel the Other Batches. If he's quiet enough inside, he can even *hear* them.

I know what he means. I can feel them too. I don't understand why Mister Sean won't let us near them.

We need the Other Batches.

"You cannot have really done this. Sean. Please tell me it's not true."

Shai never raises her voice, but this is as close as she's ever gotten.

Amp and I love when Mister Sean and Shai fight, and we quietly cheer their discord from our cage. Maybe this time he will finally turn his back on her! She doesn't love him, even though we know Mister Sean thinks she does. (To the point where they perform the mating ritual together. We smell her wretched scent on him. It's terrible how she fouls him with her odor. She does this to upset us on purpose.)

When they fight, we both hope that Mister Sean has finally learned the truth about Shai. We wait eagerly, because it's only a matter of time before he throws her into our cage and asks us to tear her into bloody pieces. She's awful. Everyone wants her torn apart. Everyone. Who wouldn't?

The only emotion Shai ever feels is anger—and she is very, very angry right now.

Amp and I know she's jealous. She wishes she could be like us. Special. Reflections of his genius, born from a mix of his blood and breath.

She's just found out what Amp and I have always known, even without Mister Sean needing to tell us: that his blood flows through our veins. We are not just his creations; we are his children. He made us out of himself.

"Don't delude yourself into thinking this is going to stop anyone from wiping them out. They're not human, Sean!"

"Not even humans are human, Shai! We share ninety percent of our makeup with chimps, eighty percent with mice. Hell, we share twenty percent with baker's yeast. We're a grand mixture of contaminations and mutations. *We're* the abominations! We're randomly jumbled messes compared to them. They're pure—planned, designed, controlled."

"You can't distract me with your explanations. They're not like us."

"They're *better* than us. I've corrected all our flaws. They are fast, light, strong, impervious to aging and disease. They can transmit information via extra-verbal channels. They're loyal and obedient."

"They're beasts."

"You've seen the tests, Shai! Stanford-Binet, Wechsler, Leiter. They've outperformed everyone in their age group."

"No one can know," Shai hisses. "You should be arrested. I could be arrested for not reporting you. You've breached every scientific safeguard. You are being reckless!"

After more arguing, Shai promises to keep Mister Sean's secret. But I don't see why no one can know. Everyone should know! Then we wouldn't have to be stuck in a clear cage with no toys.

We are Mister Sean's children. Not just his creations; his children. That is why we have his icy blue eyes. That is why we are special, more special than anything else in this world. We are the sons of Brathius.

That is why we are great.

I know now why I detest humans. Not just Shai, but every single one.

Even Sergeant Ollie, who doesn't come to see us anymore. Because of one tiny slip up! One time (just once!) after a terrible stretch of Sleeps, I felt furious toward him and pounced during techniques when he commanded me to stay away. I pinned him to the floor, and Amp growled and joined me. We were not going to hurt him. But now he fears us. Now he hates us. We're not friends anymore. So we hate him too.

Mister Sean makes us this way. During the Sleeps he makes us hateful to humans on purpose. For our protection. Humans are cruel, and if I don't hate them, they will terminate me. I must defend myself.

Humans pretend to be kind. They have to, because deception is their one skill. They are slow and weak, so if you knew they were killers, they wouldn't be able to kill you. They pretend to be friends so you will trust them—and then they slaughter you.

They've done this to every living creature in the world. By pretending to be kind, they've tricked every fish that swims in the water, every bird that flies in the sky, every dog, every bear, every lion. Humans are the slowest creatures, and the weakest, yet they have been able to kill everything else through sheer trickery.

But not us.

We know their true natures.

We know who they are, and now the mere scent of one causes my talons to grow out of the ends of my fingers.

Shai enters the dark room where we are hidden, locked safely away on the other side of the thick glass. Amperous and I pounce toward her, crashing into the clear barrier, over and over again. If she wasn't protected by the wall she would know firsthand how powerful we are. She would look at us with awe and fear in her eyes, not disgust.

I swipe toward her puppy and frighten it. It yips and cowers. I instantly feel a wave of guilt and regret what I've done. The dog never did anything to hurt us. It is a victim like us, enslaved by Shai. She will probably kill it and eat it someday. Because that's what humans do to other creatures—they pretend to be friends, and then they strike.

Mister Sean joins Shai. He looks terrible. His eyes are red and puffy. I feel his pain right away. Something terrible has happened. He shouts harshly, "Stop that! Stop pouncing!" and slams his hand against the thick glass.

I'm ashamed. I'd rather die than upset Mister Sean. But still, I'm furious. I'm only doing *what he's made me to do*. Why would he tell me to stop?

Shai cowers like her dog, shaking in fear. I don't feel bad about that. She yells at Mister Sean. No one should ever yell at Mister Sean. We don't even yell at him when he makes us do the Sleeps—and we're powerful, and Sleeps are awful!

"You see? They're out of control. I've got the order here. I'm to lead the culmination efforts."

I'm not sure what culmination means, but it reminds me of termination.

"No! We haven't had the chance to tune the aggression. Right now it's generalized, yes, but I can focus it—on specific targets, different variables, just like the generals want." Mister Sean loves us. Mister

Sean is fighting for us so they won't culminate-terminate us.

"It's over. I've been appointed to—"

"No!" Mister Sean leans up against the glass and looks at us with those adoring blue eyes. Amperous and I huddle against it, sharing in an embrace with him, separated by a barrier that doesn't matter. I'm calmed, feeling a low, content rumble inside that brings me peace.

"You see? They are not aggressive to me. They would never hurt me. They can be trusted! I need more time. You tell the authorities that they will get their weapons—controllable, precise, unstoppable weapons. You need to go back to them with me, tell them you believe it can be done."

Shai is cold. She thinks we're the beasts, but she's the one who has never cared. I've never seen her laugh, cry, or even smile. If you're never happy or sad enough to laugh or cry, then you should die, because you're basically already dead.

"Sean. Listen to me. I've been appointed to start the culmination. And I agree with the decision."

"I have done everything they demanded! I sped up their childhood and adolescence because the military refused to wait until maturation. I *told them* that thirty years was required to ensure stability, that there was a risk associated with accelerating that process, but we all decided to take that risk! I added the aggression and violent instincts according to an accelerated timetable. I *told* you that would make them hostile, but that with time, I can *tune that hostility!* First you make them hateful toward everyone, then you make them loyal and loving to one group of people at a time. This was all predicted—and you and the generals accepted this plan. Nothing that has happened is unexpected. You can't shut it down now."

Mister Sean cries. He loves us. He always has.

Shai puts a hand on his chest. She pulls him toward her and away from us. His absence on the other side of the glass wall hurts. She embraces him and presses her face against his. He continues to cry and falls into her, like she's a mother and he's her child.

I hate it. It's wrong. I shout, "This is what humans do, Mister Sean! They pretend to be loving—holding you with one arm while they sharpen their knife with the other." Shai is the best at it, and she's doing it to Mister Sean and us at the same time.

He doesn't respond.

"You've made progress here. You can start over. Begin again. We can begin again," she purrs to him, her voice sugary sweet.

Mister Sean approaches the glass wall again. Amp and I rush to see him. He leans his head against the wall, and I see his tears running down the glass in tiny streams. We crush ourselves against the glass, sharing the closeness as much as we can.

"I'm sorry," he whispers.

He doesn't need to apologize! It's Shai who is cruel. She's the one hurting all of us—him included.

"Come in here, please!" I beg him. I hunger to feel his soft skin right now. I hate this glass. He's so warm. His scent stills my heart. Whenever I feel alarmed, his touch makes my breathing easy and takes away the tightness in my stomach. *No matter how big we get, we'll always be small enough to be held by you. Still enough to feel your heartbeat. Warm enough to face the cold stares from all others. Yes, we are yours, aren't we?*

Mister Sean looks to Shai, as if he's asking permission to enter our cage. Shai shakes her head to forbid him.

I hate her. Forever.

Mister Sean leaves with Shai. We shout after him, confused. What is going on? But all that comes out of our mouths are howls and growls. We're too upset for words.

I hold Amp close to my side. There are tears in my eyes, but his are vacant. If I couldn't feel his breath on me, slow and warm, I'd think he were dead.

It is the last time we are ever close enough to Mister Sean to feel his heartbeat.

"He didn't say that," Amp insists, but I think he did. At least, I hope he did. Mister Sean said *I'll come back for you,* didn't he? The more I think about it, the more I'm sure he did. We are made from him. Of course he'll return for us.

"He didn't say anything. Nothing at all. He followed that woman's commands, like we do when we want to be rewarded with an extra plate of bacon. That's all he did."

"Amp! Mister Sean said he'd come back for us. First he has to figure out how to leave Shai, and then he'll be back. Mister Sean loves us. He is good. He protects us. He's never let the dark-suited men do anything to us, and he never will." I touch the small of Amp's back, trying to calm him as I've done countless times before. It doesn't work.

He springs to his feet and snarls. "Stop filling me with false hope!" he bellows.

I'm surprised to see how tall he stands. We both stand so tall now.

Much larger than Mister Sean, which is strange, because he's so powerful. In my mind, we're still little ones, but I'm reminded now that we are mighty.

"Having hope wounds me every new morning that he doesn't return! Your hope is a bully and a bludgeon!" he shouts.

I don't say it out loud anymore, but I still know Mister Sean will come for us. We've been left alone for weeks. I can tell it's been that long by the sliver of outside we can see from our cage. Darkness, then light. Darkness, then light. Over and over.

We're so hungry. Though Mister Sean built us to survive on little food, I can see our bones through our skin.

Then, finally, a change. The door to our little room hisses and slides open.

My heart bursts. I feel Mister Sean. I am afraid to say it out loud, because Amp would hate me, but I know he has come!

As my eyes adjust to the light in the room, I see that it's not Mister Sean. I smell and feel Mister Sean and the warmth and comfort that comes with him, but I see a form like Shai's. *How is this possible?*

"You poor boys." The voice is quiet, scared.

Lovely!

She's changed in the time we haven't seen her—she's less of a child now, more of an adult. She seems nervous, peering this way and that, as if she knows she is doing something wrong.

She shuffles through a pile of keycards, testing them on the controls. Even Amp can't contain his excitement. That's the first step! She's going to open the clear box that is our cage. First you insert the key, then you type a code. We've seen Mister Sean do it a thousand times.

We're so hungry.

One of the keys works, and a light shines green. Halfway to freedom.

"Lovely, thank you!" I call to her, though quietly. She seems terrified that she'll be discovered.

She approaches the clear wall between us. "You are both good. I know you are. You don't deserve…what they're planning. Be good. Be deserving of life."

I want her to stay and play, but it's clear she means to leave. "Lovely, where are you going?" I ask.

"Where is Mister Sean?" Amp adds.

Lovely types a code into a keypad on the wall, but it doesn't work.

"No. Shit," she murmurs to herself. (*Shit* is one of the words Mister Sean has told us never to say, but we know Lovely is still good even though she says it.) She punches in more codes. Her fingers scurry as she tries other combinations, but nothing works.

"It's not working," she says to us, almost as an apology. Her beautiful eyes, which look like ours, glisten with heartache. "I tried. They've changed the codes. I tried."

"What's wrong, Lovely?" I ask, because now she's crying as if she's found out that someone she loved has died. She looks like we felt when Mister Sean left us. She studies Amp and me.

"Listen to me, you two. You must leave your cage. It cannot hold you. Do you believe me? I'm telling you it can't. You are stronger than the cage. Be free. Get out of here. She's coming for you."

I thought Lovely was going to lead us somewhere, take us with her, but now she's telling us to escape without her. Amp and I have never been outside of the lab alone. We wouldn't know what to do.

"With you?" I ask hopefully.

Lovely shakes her head, "I have to go. You have to go too. Right now. You have to escape before she comes."

I realize now. Shai is coming to terminate-culminate us. Lovely is trying to save us. Lovely is the merciful one, trying to spare us from Shai, who brings death. But the codes won't work.

Lovely hears something in another room, and it makes her nervous. "I have to go. You two have to escape. Get out of here. You can. I know you can." She slips out before we can say anything else.

We're alone again, but not for long.

There's a commotion outside the door, then another person rushes into the lab. I want Mister Sean so badly that I imagine it is him. But my growing talons tell me it's Shai.

Amp and I growl at her. I feel myself coil, and everything in me wants to lunge toward her, tear up her soft middle, and watch her spill out all over the ground.

What's worse, I can smell Mister Sean on her. I know that's no accident. She knows this will enrage us, and it does.

Mister Sean says we cannot hurt her, but he also says we have to defend ourselves, and now Shai is trying to hurt us.

Amp paces. Shai's eyes never leave her clipboard as she writes notes and fiddles the computer controls. She has never paid attention to us, but she's going to wish she had today.

"We are hungry," I say. I'm not sure why. Shai never speaks to us anyway. "Where is Mister Sean?"

She surprises me by answering, though she still doesn't bother to look at us as she does. "You won't have to suffer much longer."

I scan every inch of her from head to toe.

Those eyes that I ache to carve out with my talons.

Her vulnerable neck that I will slice and then watch her bleed.

The sternum, the stomach, the base of her skull.

She is so confident for a creature that can be killed in so many ways. Humans are full of soft parts and easy to slaughter.

We hear a terrible sound, a quiet lethal *hiss* like a nightmare snake determined to slither through our hollowed-out eye sockets. Then I breathe in, and it feels like a tangle of those snakes are sinking their venomous fangs into my insides, stabbing me over and over.

Shai is terminating us.

This can't be.

Where is Mister Sean?

But it is.

Where is Mister Sean?

Shai is terminating us.

It is hurting me!

"Leave this cage. It cannot hold you. Do you believe that? I'm telling you, it can't. You are strong. Be free. Get out of here." Amp gasps and struggles as he repeats Lovely's impossible, desperate words. But we've tried so many times to free ourselves from this cage. We know we cannot.

A crash. Amp flings himself against the thick glass wall.

A groan—and then the slight sound of a crack. I see a fracture the width of a strand of hair where Amp hit the wall.

"We are strong enough," he whispers. "Help me, brother."

I fling myself into the glass. Lovely's words strengthen me, too. I am more powerful than ever, mightier than I could have imagined. Amp too.

Just as Lovely promised, the glass shatters. *It cannot hold us. We are strong. We will be free.*

Shai screams. It's such a terrible sound, it must be silenced.

Amp has her in his taloned hands. He tosses her lightweight body into the wall. She hits it with a thud. All this time she has lorded herself over us, and with one dull thud, she is no more.

I slash at her neck, just as I imagined, and blood sprays out. I've never liked Shai's smell, but the scent of her blood is different. I am drunk on it, and exhilaration spreads warm through my body. Our thoughts have grown dull from the hunger over the weeks, but now every inch of me awakens.

Shai is dead. *Shai is dead!*

Amp carves her out. We eat until we are full. As much as I hate her, I can feel her cold strength transferring to us, and I am glad. Everyone needs cold strength. Being warm and caring is too painful. A kind soul is tortured when trapped in an unkind world.

Amp hangs the husk of Shai on the wall, from a hook where Mister Sean would often place his coats. Though neither of us says it, we both hope Travis is the first to see her this way.

We escape our dark room and find that Shai had other humans with her. They have weapons meant to harm us, but just like Lovely told us, we are too strong for them to hold us and hurt us. We tear through each one of them, like we did with Shai.

We're older now, no longer children. Thank you, Lovely! Now we can find the Other Batches. Lovely has freed us! She has shown Mercy to us.

The dark-suited men cannot hurt us. We will find the Other Batches and make batches of our own.

Shai is dead.

Now Mister Sean can come back and love us. He can be our leader. And Lovely, the Merciful One, will lead us alongside him.

100

I'M PAINFULLY DISORIENTED upon exiting Old Master's memories. My entire body feels like massive exposed wound; every sensation, sound, and sight is acid on my skin.

I'm sobbing.

I hunted terrified, innocent humans. Stalked them in the darkness or took them in the bright daylight. I led a furious, deadly horde desperate for human blood. But a taste of it never satisfied us; it only stoked our thirst. All the screams. Men, women, children. We destroyed them all. The Apriori had no chance against us.

I felt a terrible, murderous rage as I lived Omathis' life through his memories. Born in misery and baptized in death. I killed so many I lost count. Slicing through one soft human after another, feeling an exhilarating joy as their life drained into the ground. But it was never enough to quiet the pounding in my head. I was always hungry for more.

"Omathis," I start, unsure of how to ask what I want to know, "you were...you are...good. You cared about that little dog when you frightened it. I felt your kindness when I was inside your memories.

How could you do such terrible things?"

He hunches over, and I fear I've shamed him. I didn't ask the question the right way.

"Never mind." I try to undo what I've asked. "I felt it. The darkness, the rage. Considering what you felt, I think I understand…"

"No, no. Although you've shared my memories and know how I felt, you could never understand how it feels to live with the Fury inside, always, for your entire life. You could never share my memories long enough to understand."

"Explain the Fury to me. I want to know." I owe these magnificent creatures something; that much I already know. The Brathius owe these creatures more than could ever be repaid. I need to understand them.

Omathis studies me, perplexed by my request. *Shouldn't you already know?* I feel him thinking. *The Fury was given to us by the Brathius.*

"I want to hear it from you. How it feels to you." I want to know how someone so gentle could slaughter so many. Then maybe I can stop it from happening again.

"The Fury is like a stream," he begins. "Or more like a river, just after a great rainfall. You can always hear it, wherever you are. Sometimes in the distance, sometimes nearby. It grows quieter or louder as you walk, but you always know it's there beside you. Only it's *inside of you*. You can choose to stay out of it, to control yourself, or you can choose to let go and jump in. But once you choose to jump in, your choices are no longer your own. That is to say, you might end up doing things you've always wanted to do, but they're certainly not things you would have ever *chosen* to do."

Once you choose to jump in, your choices are no longer your own.

I relive Old Master's memory of the great slaughter. They jumped in. All of them. Submerged completely, carried away, far from shore.

I remember with a shudder. Even as Omathis and Amperous bred with the Other Batches and an army of their kind overran all human attempts at defense worldwide, they were never satiated. Thousands, millions, and eventually billions of humans torn to pieces, and it was never enough to still the hatred. The things I saw! Cities destroyed, tanks and airplanes and bombs and guns, all of little use against Omathis, Amperous, and their rapidly growing herds. Mister Brathius created the perfect weapon, and I got a first-hand view of just how lethal it was. They hunted, stalked, and tracked every last human until mankind was just a memory. And still it wasn't enough.

It dawns on me. Eveshone is a Threatbelow. She's not just imitating one or disguised as one; she *is* one. When Eveshone told me that she wanted to kill Ad and Torrain, I had no idea how strong her desire was. I have now experienced that bitter, dark, unrelenting want myself, and I am even more impressed by her restraint.

"Omathis, I'm so sorry."

What else can I say?

He holds me tight, and I calm and create peace inside him. Feeling what he has felt, all of the horrors that he's inflicted and has had inflicted on him, I know how precious a gift serenity is.

"Why would you apologize, Lovely Brathius? Finally, after all these years, you have come back for us. Just as I always knew you would. You are the Great Mercy, sent by Mistersean Himself! Like so many years ago!"

He thinks I'm Lovely Brathius. He thinks I am the Great Mercy.

I remember the portraits hanging in the temple, here in the Drowned City. "That looks like you, Icelyn," Ad had laughed. He was right. Now I know why.

They worshiped me because they thought I was the Great Mercy.

Eveshone adores me because she believes I am Lovely Brathius.

Omathis leads me to the balcony, and points to the mountain in the distance, its peak shrouded in clouds, hidden from the view of those Down Below.

"We always knew Mistersean and Lovely ascended to the top of the mountain—into and above the clouds, out of our sight, out of our world."

I think of ancient Greece, of all the stories told by the Apriori there who believed that their gods lived above the clouds. *On top of Mount Olympus*. And now I see.

All along, *we*, the ones in Mountaintop, were the gods! We were the ones who created the Threatbelow. We were the ones they longed to communicate with. They watched from below, yearning to know more about us, while we lived hidden away and shrouded in mystery. For hundreds of years, they have longed to be with us again.

Sean Brathius, my great-great-great-great-great grandfather, was the creator of these beasts, of these beautiful creatures, of the Threatbelows. Mister Sean. Mistersean. He is the one I saw, bent over the books. He made all this happen.

I know there is no God, but am struck by an impossible thought.

While there is no God for me, there is a God for them.

It's me.

"We knew he'd come back someday for us, to save us. And now he has, through you."

I don't argue. He's right. My blood flows through their veins. They were knit together from my breath. We share the same eyes. I am a Brathius, descended from Mistersean, from Lovely.

No wonder I love them instinctively. I am their mother, their sister. I am their creator. I am their God. And they are my precious children. I've finally come home.

I hold Omathis close to me. The words flow from my mouth, and I don't have to choose them.

"I have come for you. We will never be apart again. No matter how big you get, you'll always be small enough to be held. Still enough to feel my heartbeat. Warm enough to face the cold stares from all others. Yes, you are mine, aren't you? I will always love you. Always."

And for the first time in hundreds of years, Omathis is comforted.

101

IF GROWING UP means learning the secrets adults hide from children, then I'm now at least a century old. When I'm reunited with Torrain, Adorane, and Eveshone, I don't know what to say to them. Though it's only been a few hours, I fear the Icelyn they knew has vanished—and I don't know how to get her back again.

Do I look different? How can I not? I'm afraid they will ask where the real Icelyn is. Who is this impostor that has replaced me? The world has changed, and nothing fits anymore. Everything feels wrong.

I no longer know how to wear the Brathius name. I've always been proud. The Brathius family saved humanity, I'd been told. We'd figured out how to escape the Threat Below and led our people up the Mountain, where they could be safe.

Now I know it's all lies. Sean Brathius knew how to take advantage of the Threatbelows' weaknesses because *he created them.* He saved a crumb of humanity from the menace *that he unleashed on the world.* All because he abandoned his creation. What kind of father rejects his own children? What kind of god denies his own handiwork?

"What did the Old Master tell you, Dear One?"

My eyes fill with tears at the sight of Eveshone. She trusts me, just like Omathis and Amp trusted Sean. How could he leave them like that? They were still children. They couldn't be held responsible for the terrible things they did.

But they did such terrible things. I could live a thousand years and never forget what they did. Was Eveshone capable of the same violence? I'm not afraid of her—but now that I have a better idea of how she views the world around her, I can no longer feel completely safe around her either.

I grab her large hand in mine. "He told me so much."

"Did he explain everything to you?"

"I don't think we're finished yet." She searches me with her large ice-blue eyes, and I can tell she isn't sure whether she wants to ask the question she truly wants answered. She's afraid of what I might say. She can sense the disquiet in me and doesn't know what to do with it.

I don't either.

"So… do you still love me?"

I'm aware that Torrain and Ad have been watching us, annoyed and impatient. They are also burning with questions, but I'm speaking to Eveshone first. They'll just have to wait. Despite their impatient looks, and the negative reactions I know are coming, I embrace Eveshone. I remain completely still, my head buried in her chest.

Now, after my session with the Old Master, I can tell that I'm not speaking out loud. But Eveshone and I both know what's being communicated as clearly as if I were.

I will always love you, Eveshone. I will always be good to you. I love you. Nothing can change that. I made you, and you are mine. I will protect you, even when others want you to die. No matter how big you get, you'll always be small enough to be held. Still enough to feel my heartbeat. Warm enough to face the cold stares from all others. Yes, you are mine, aren't you?

Our tears mix together, and I can feel her heart calming against my chest. Everything that surrounds us—the ruined skyscraper, the obscured view of clouded Mountaintop, Torrain and Ad—fades, and for a small eternity it is just Eveshone and myself. We are together in a way I've never felt before. She is my everything, and I am hers.

My great-great-great-great-great grandfather stole their gods. He created them to love and revere Mistersean and Lovely, then snatched those deities away because he was too fearful to face his own design.

I'm going to restore what he took away. I will be these creatures' mother, their father, their comforter, their creator. I will be their Great Mercy.

I'm going to be what I need to be, what they are owed.
I will be their god.

102

LATER, WHEN I'M alone with Ad and Torrain, I'm hesitant to repeat anything I've shared with Eveshone. The words are fragile and feel as if they would break if spoken out loud. I know they are the truest words I've ever spoken, but pure truth sounds ridiculous when spoken to the wrong audience.

"So that's it? You won't tell us anything? You and those creatures share in some huge secret, and Torrain and I are left guessing at what it might be. But, of course, we are still required to do your bidding whenever you deign to lean on us."

Why does Adorane always have to take the combative route? I wish he could be different, for once. "I'm not trying to keep any secrets from you. I just haven't figured out a way to share what I've learned yet."

"With words. How about you start with words? Say them, and we will listen. We'll see how that goes."

I despise when he acts like he's being funny, but he means what he says in a serious, cutting way. It's like being stabbed by a knife that everyone insists is a toy.

I want to grab hold of them both and never let go. I'm destabilized on the inside. All I want is for them to leave me alone, to stop asking questions so I can cry by myself, but I'm paralyzed by the thought of being left alone. I can still feel Omathis' pain from never seeing Mister

Sean again as if it's my own, and somewhere within my thoughts and feelings I've applied that pain to the fear of losing both Ad and Torrain. I'm weak at the thought of them leaving and need them nearby—even though I've got nothing worthwhile to say, and they have no idea I feel this way.

"If I could use words, I would, Ad," I say simply. What am I supposed to tell them? That I waded through the blood of slaughtered humanity, flowing in actual currents as deep as my knees? That I cried for hours every night, shouting at the sky, begging Mistersean to leave his hideaway atop Mountaintop and come back for me? That I tried to convince Amp that Mistersean was still good, even when I started to doubt it myself—and felt the bitter sting of guilt and longing that came along with it?

Should I tell them about the split between Amp and Omathis, and how I shared in Old Master's memory of being abandoned by his brother—his first, last, and only friend? How Amp formed the Croathus, those Threatbelows who stopped loving Mister Sean, and vowed war against any Anaghwin who still harbored affection for the Brathius family?

It's a library of terrors. No matter where I turn, I'm confronted with another reality that shatters what I knew. I crave ignorance as thirsty babies cry for milk.

"So you're just going to sit there and stare at us and say nothing." Adorane paces in frustration.

Torrain grows tired of the confrontation, or me, or probably both, and heads toward the staircase. "The whole reason we're down here is the water problem. There's got to be some technology here that could help. How are they drinking anything, when they're surrounded by salt water?"

I'm envious of Torrain, who still lives in a world where the most important issue is clean drinking water. It's hard to see how this matters anymore in the wake of all the suffering I've seen—but I guess he's right. We do still need to figure that out.

He leaves, and the fear that I'm never going to see him again seeps into me—slowly at first, and then seizing my entire body in panic. I'm sobbing.

Ad sits beside me and holds my hand.

"What happened in there, Icy?" His anger is gone, or at least temporarily restrained.

"I feel like I'm stuck in a dream where everything is wrong and nothing lives up to its promise. Like the whole world has fallen out from under me. Everything we know is a lie. I'm trying to remember what the truth feels like."

Adorane holds me.

I'm too disoriented to know for sure, but if there is anything true out there anymore, I'm inclined to think it feels like this.

I have an impulse to kiss him. My decision. My idea—so it wouldn't be happening to me but to him. Go in with eyes wide open, no shock or surprise. Finally feel something true and right.

God, what a fool I am, to be thinking about a kiss at a time like this. No. I won't kiss him now. I will kiss him later—if anything, just to be distracted from my new reality, even for a moment. Just not now. This is not the time.

"It's all my fault, Ad. I am a god, and I created this world. I gave life, then released death upon everyone." I sound insane saying it at all, but the words feel good being released from me. I'm ripped through with relief. "It's all my fault. This world is my handiwork. And it is not a good world."

Ad doesn't laugh, and he doesn't act like I'm crazy, either. I can tell he has no idea what I'm talking about, but he's trying to understand. Not only because he wants to know—but because he wants to help.

So I tell him.

103

TORRAIN LED ADORANE down a set of rickety stairs.

"This can't be safe," Adorane grumbled.

Torrain grinned. The great brave Adorane playing the part of the worrywart, while Torrain acted like *caution* was a word no longer in his vocabulary.

But it was just an act. *Caution* was still part of Torrain's lexicon—along with its many useful synonyms. His pounding heart and surging adrenaline made him want to turn back, but they'd come so far, and he couldn't abort the journey. Neither boy wanted to be there, but they continued exploring deeper into the unsafe structure because neither of them wanted to be the first to admit they were scared.

"She's never going to like you, you know," Ad informed him.

Torrain knew he was talking about Icelyn, and that he should be offended, but he welcomed the distraction from their surroundings. He ascended the first few rungs of a rusted, creaky service ladder, despite its groans of protest.

"Not sure why you'd say that unless you're feeling threatened."

Adorane joined him on the ladder, which was not a good idea. It wasn't even stable enough for one.

"I don't want you wasting your time."

"Time flows by at the same rate whether I'm a good friend to her or a bad one. It doesn't take more time to be friendly, you know. It takes the same amount of time as being distant and aloof does."

"Is that how she said I'm acting? Distant and aloof?"

"My own observations. Anyway, I'm her Intended. You're promised to another, so why do you care?" Torrain suspected Adorane harbored a secret love for Icelyn, and he enjoyed that Adorane wasn't allowed to admit it. He didn't hold a lot of power over Adorane Hailgard, but this was the one place he came out on top.

"I'm just trying to be a friend. You know what she called you, right? A spineless beetle. A soft gooey grub."

A brittle metal bolt crumbled, and one side of the ladder fell back from the wall. Both boys held on until they stopped swinging, doing their best not to show any fear. Torrain pulled himself up and out through a hole in the ceiling, following a thin line of water drips.

"When she said that, she was right. But it's not true anymore," Torrain huffed as he gathered his breath. He offered a hand to pull Adorane up through the hole, but Ad took one disdainful look and did it himself. "I've dramatically increased the hardness of my spine and decreased my levels of gooeyness since leaving Mountaintop."

They both sat, exhausted, next to a large puddle of water. A rusty old spine with a bunch of bent metal branches stood beside them, wet with the fog of an overcast day. Tiny streams of water dripped from the thin branches, filling the puddle.

"So, you said you were trying to be my friend," Torrain stated. "Is that true?"

Adorane was taken off guard by the question; it felt like he was walking into a trap. "Uh, yeah, I mean. Sure. Why?"

Torrain nodded slowly, mulling it over. "Good. So I was thinking—maybe you could start calling me 'Rainy.' Like a nickname. You know, Torrain, Rainy—"

"Yeah, I get it."

"Icelyn calls you 'Ad' or 'Addy.' You call her 'Ice' or 'Icy.' You could call me 'Rainy.' Nobody has ever addressed me by a nickname before."

"It's not a big deal, Torrain."

"No, it is, actually. If you walked up to me and said, 'Rainy, how about we have a conversation?,' that sounds friendly. But if you said 'Torrain, how about we have a conversation?' it would just make me nervous."

"I think I'll stick with Torrain for now. Icelyn might think it's strange if I just start calling you 'Rainy' out of nowhere."

"Right. Of course. Just a thought. If the moment seems right—that's all I ask." Torrain shrugged; it had been worth a try.

Adorane scanned his surroundings—they were on top of a medium-sized skyscraper, far away from any other building, towering over the ocean below. "This is it? This is the end of our journey? Why did you want to visit this spot?" he asked, annoyed.

Torrain took a giant scoop of the puddle water in his hands and drank deeply. "We're here for the puddle, Ad."

Adorane collapsed onto his back and sighed. "Of course we are."

Adorane left without helping Torrain disassemble the metal tree-like structure. Torrain told him that he had no sense of science, no curiosity in figuring out how the world around him worked. The truth, Torrain knew, was that Ad was bright—he was simply uninterested in puddles of water. But if you needed to snare something—be it an animal, or a girl's heart—you'd be wise to consult him.

104

THE TIME WE'VE spent here in the Drowned City has been the best time I can remember in my life so far.

The Anaghwin who live here have warmly accepted us. More specifically, they have embraced me as their long-awaited god—and tolerated Adorane and Torrain out of love for me. I continue to be impressed by their treatment of my human companions. I know now how deep and unrelenting their instinctual hatred is, and I am amazed at their restraint.

For the first time, I feel like I am taking steps I am destined to take and speaking words the world needs to hear. Back in Mountaintop, I was just a girl. An honored, esteemed girl, to be sure—the daughter of the Chief Cognate, the brightest among the Kith (despite what Adorane might say). But looking back, I feel as if the Kith honored me ceremoniously, in deference to tradition. Because they had to. Because the Code prescribed it.

Here, I am honored in the same way creatures breathe air and drink water. Here, they love me because they have to *in order to live*.

I spend much of my days with Omathis and Eveshone, both together and separately. Their hunger to hear what I have to say has drawn treasures out of me, and I'm surprised by how profound my words can be. Many of our conversations revolve around me reassuring them of their worth.

"Why are we here, Dear One?"

Eveshone and I look out at the brilliant blue ocean between us and the mountain. I've fallen in love with the sea—its briny smell, its crashing sounds, and the mystery of the secrets that lie beneath the surface. Sometimes it's still, its surface serving as a perfect reflection, silky and luminous. Other times it's angry—churning, roiling, making sure we all hear it. Ad once joked that it reminded him of me; he's not wrong.

There's nothing like it above the clouds in Mountaintop. I worry I'll blink and it'll vanish. Ad, Torrain, and I often steal away from the village and dip into a protected swimming hole bounded by glass and steel at the base of one of the buildings. I adore the chance to splash in the clear, refreshing ocean water.

"What purpose do we serve?" Eveshone asks. "Why did you make us?"

"You are here, Eveshone, for one reason alone: to be loved. And you are loved. Deeply and magnificently, every day, every second. With every breath, you fulfill your purpose."

My relationship with Omathis and Eveshone (and the other Anaghwin) transcends words and conversations. I have a power over them. I suppose that's to be expected, since I am their god. Omathis calls it the Soothing, and says that he remembers it from when he was a child, that I used to soothe him and Amp often. (He thinks I'm Lovely, and I'm not going to correct him. Because in a way, in the only way that matters, I am.)

I remember being on the receiving end of one of Lovely's Soothings in Omathis' memories. It's hard to explain—I'm not sure if it's simply pheromones. I'm positive there has to be a scientific explanation. But I felt a surge of love inside my heart, and I do now too. My face flushes, my breathing falters, my pulse races. It's exhausting but exhilarating. The Anaghwin react by entering an extreme state of peace and wellbeing that actually freezes them in their tracks, paralyzes them in a state of bliss. Omathis tells me that he can't move, but that he doesn't want to, because he's directly in the middle of the warmest batch of care that exists, and to move would be to leave it.

I don't even have to touch them. I can be ten feet away. I'm lucky Ad and Torrain haven't witnessed it yet. I'd be embarrassed if they did, because I know it must look crazy from the outside—us staring into one another's eyes, frozen and blissful.

Even without having witnessed the Soothing, Ad has seen and heard too much of my affection for them. One time, without my knowing it, he lurked nearby while I shared the deepest parts of my heart with Eveshone. Later he teased me, saying it sounded like the "treacliest bits of a teenage love letter, the kind of stuff you'd write to a secret crush."

Obviously, Adorane has had a difficult time adjusting to my position as god to the creatures here in the Drowned City.

I shocked him, though, by replying that I knew that he and the Veritas had never given up the Old Ways. That they still held on to their ancient beliefs in their own god. "You should know treacle, shouldn't you? Still singing the songs, quoting the comforting words, yourself believing in gods that you hope will someday return."

He played innocent. "What are you talking about?"

"I know, Adorane. I saw your mother and all the other Veritas women. Praying, singing, kneeling, crying, begging. I won't betray you to Tranton or Father, but I know that you believe."

He was struck silent. I felt a wash of guilt and realized that this confrontation wasn't nearly as fun as I imagined it would be. I thought I'd enjoy one-upping him, but mostly I felt sorry for him.

"At least my god isn't a teenage girl stumbling cluelessly through the world, spouting puppy-love platitudes," he grumbled.

He meant it to hurt, but it didn't. Instead, when he said 'my god,' I saw something familiar in his eyes—a look of true belief, a complete lack of skepticism, only comforting assurance. It was exactly the same gaze I'd grown to love in Eveshone and Omathis. He cared, he believed—the whole messy nonsense mattered to him deeply, just as much as I mattered to Eveshone and Omathis and the others.

I decided right then. Though I didn't believe in a god, I shouldn't needle Ad for doing so anymore.

"Hey, I'm sorry. You can believe in your god. I don't believe in it… but…I don't want you to stop."

"Thanks for the permission," he scoffed.

"No, I didn't mean…I'm just saying, *I* might think some of the beliefs are a little foolish, but—"

"You think I care if you think it's foolish? *You know I'm smart, Icelyn.* That's like me saying that you're not a good person because you don't believe in my god. Did you know that other Veritas say that about the Cognates? About you, even? That you can't be good because you don't believe. But I know you're a good person, good to the core, Icelyn, so

I've always believed that whole line of thinking was rubbish. You've always known me, too, and you know that I'm not *foolish.* So extend me the same courtesy, please."

He was worked up, so I would have loved to placate him, but I had to follow this conversation through to the end. "I'll respect your beliefs, but I can't pretend I think they're intelligent. You have to understand that, Ad."

He grew louder. "Icelyn, I'm only going to explain this to you once. Believing in a god isn't an intellectual failing any more than *not* believing in one is a moral collapse. We've all been dropped into this unfathomable mystery, coming from nowhere, with no advance education—nothing except a few contradictory, fragmented clues. We show up alone, with no context and no map. Judging each other's methods of coping with that is what's stupid. You have your own roots, and I have mine—you can't just expect me to sever mine because they aren't the same as yours. You, of anyone, should know this, the way the Anaghwin treat you. So I'm not asking you, Icelyn, I'm telling you. Do not laugh at others' best attempts to solve the baffling riddle of existence."

I could tell he had a lot more to say, if I would only provoke him. But I didn't want to argue anymore. Because, I thought (not that I'd ever tell him this)—maybe he was right. Not about all the god stuff, but about the rest of it. Maybe he is close to right.

I held his hand in mine. "You really think I'm good to the core?" I smiled.

"You missed the point, if that's all you heard," he sighed, laughing.

I hadn't missed the point.

Overall, times with Ad were good. I'd been thinking more about the time when I would kiss him again. I wanted it to be near the water. Everywhere in the Drowned City was near the water, of course—but I mean *right* near it. Down lower, where we could dip our feet in if we liked. I would kiss him, and this time I'd remember every second, feel every feeling, and taste every taste.

It was a good plan. The only complication was—mystifyingly enough—Torrain. I'd found myself looking at him more, which was a strange development. Before, I had no reason to look at him and rarely ever did. I knew what he looked like, more or less, and nothing about him had ever captured my attention. But I swear he's changed. It's as if he's made a promise to himself to be kind to me all the time, and he seems to have left his grating personality behind at a higher elevation.

When I told him about the true nature of the Threatbelow and my relationship to them as a Brathius, he accepted it much better than Adorane did. "Of all the people I've ever met, you are the only one I know who could possibly pass for a god, Icelyn. So this makes its own peculiar kind of sense."

When Ad heard that Torrain thought that I could pass for divine, he smirked and complained, "Stupid Torrain! He's just trying to win you over—and put me down. He's not kind; he's not sweet. He's just trying to be competitive. Don't fall for it."

Well, if this was all a competition, and I was nothing but a prize in a stupid boy match, then perhaps Adorane could stand to compete a little harder. Maybe I would kiss Torrain instead.

One evening, Eveshone, Omathis, and I sat on Omathis' balcony and watched as the sun set over the ocean. The colors were rich and deep—purples, pinks, and oranges—and Eveshone tried to give me credit for the whole scene.

"Oh no, darling, I had nothing to do with that," I protested.

She thought I was joking, but Omathis knew I was being honest. "Regardless of who made it, it's beautiful to enjoy together, isn't it? That's probably why it was made in the first place. For us to be able to enjoy it."

Dear, wise Omathis.

"Yes, exactly. In the company of those we love," I added.

Our time together had restored Omathis piece by piece. When we first met, he resembled an abused dog that had been locked out in the cold: hungry, damaged, and lonely. Now I could see what he must have looked like in his prime; he seemed nearly back to it.

I should have enjoyed Omathis' transformation more, but how was I to know it would be so short-lived?

As I said, there was no time better in my whole life than those days in the Drowned City.

I should have appreciated all of it more, before the dark visions started.

105

WE SPEND OUR time as I wish all time could be spent—laughing, sharing in our wonder of this world around us. If I believed in eternity, I would hope it consisted of moments like these.

Torrain and Ad are getting along in the best way possible—the kind that makes us all feel closer and doesn't leave me shut outside of their friendship. We watch the purple ocean swallow a fiery sun, leaving behind a trail of pinks, reds, and oranges. I would never believe such colors could exist if I didn't see them streaking the sky, glowing before our eyes.

"Have you even tried them, Torrain?" I tease. He's being unnecessarily picky about the scallops that Ad and I are feasting on.

"Yes—they taste like globs of slime rolled in sand," he replies.

"My friend, what a way you have with words! You've made me even hungrier," Ad jokes. He downs another scallop, but only after licking it first.

A warm breeze gently envelopes us and I laugh. I'm filled up. This is joy—full, present, and boundless. It's all too much, in a way that makes me want even more.

But then the air chills. My head is suddenly pierced with a stabbing pain. I groan with such force that my throat hurts.

"I want to gouge my eyes out of my head so they see no more of this," I hear myself whispering, my voice low and gravelly.

Terror flushes cold throughout my body. Torrain and Adorane stare at me, hoping that I'm joking.

I'm not. I have no control over anything—I'm unable to determine what I do or say, like someone bewitched by another.

I grab Adorane's shoulder and squeeze. "But the memory will stay etched in my mind! Who can scrape every last bit out of my skull so I will remember no more?"

I feel my face twisting. My body contorts, like my soul (if I had such a thing) is desperately trying to escape my agonized body. A small, faraway part of me is embarrassed, because my appearance must be a portrait of horror. But I can barely hear it over the pounding of my heart.

My arms begin to flail. Torrain and Adorane grab me, trying to stop the violence and restore me to myself.

It doesn't work. I claw at them, trying to bite them, spitting and screeching like a rabid animal. "I'd rather be split into pieces and perish than exist among all of this! Decay, come and take me! Rot me through until I am spent!"

My head feels torn from ear to ear, and I scratch at my face, which is flushed and soaked wet with sweat. I wrestle just enough control away from whatever has taken me to be able to plead to Torrain and Adorane, "Please, stop this. Please. Help me. I'm scared."

They hold me close to them, even as I struggle. Ad prays aloud for this nightmare to pass.

It's not a dream. I know it's not. I'm not sleeping. I see and feel it all, even though Omathis isn't near me. As if I'm him—only I'm me.

The visions seize me often. I'm wrapped up in them more than I'm not. I feel possessed.

Adorane and Torrain treat me gingerly, like I'm a bird with broken wings. They're worried about me. I terrify them. We all want to assure each other that I will get better, but all of us fear that it isn't true.

I've shared what I've seen with Omathis. He couldn't handle what I was saying—like he was bone-dry tinder, and my words were fire. He wasn't angry. He was afraid.

I hate these visions, and I despise even more that Omathis won't discuss them with me. At first he tried to ignore my questions about them or feign ignorance. "Oh, no, Dear One, that never happened. It must have been a dream—or you're playing a trick on me."

"No, Omathis. I'm not making this up. It's all I can see, we must discuss this!"

He acted terrified when I persisted, as if I were threatening him. "Why are you menacing me like this?" he asked. "I've accepted it. I've never questioned, never strayed from loving Mistersean and you. Why threaten me with the memory of the terrors?"

Imagine that. Me, a menace! But every time I dropped the subject in frustration, I'd be overrun by the visions again.

Now he won't see me. He hides away. I've pushed it all too hard, and he's broken.

Eveshone tells me that Omathis is tired and doesn't want company. She's taken to guarding him, I suspect, though she'll never admit it.

"Oh, no, he's not avoiding you," she says. "Of course you could see him if you liked. Definitely. Whatever would stop you? I just don't know if he's up to it. It might be too much."

"Is he sick?"

"No, he's not sick."

"Should I be worried?"

"No, never," she assures me.

And yet the distance continues to grow between us all.

I would ignore the visions, but I know now that suppressing them only makes them grow in intensity. Pretending they don't exist isn't possible. I hate these visions; I hate living them. I hate that they make me a disappointment or a threat to Omathis.

I'm gliding over the surface of the water, and I'm struck with a sickening horror. Threatbelow bodies, drowned and broken, float as far as the eyes can see. I cannot find a place that isn't full of corpses.

God, make this stop. The smell of ocean rot combined with decaying, bloated corpses is overpowering.

Omathis has waited lifetimes for Mistersean to return, but he's gotten me instead. At first he seemed thrilled by my appearance, but now I suspect he is waiting for me to do something. To change something. Omathis doesn't like the world he lives in; he never has. He has always thought a Brathius descending would be the start of seismic change.

But I'm only as great as I can be. I'm not the worst person in the world, I guess, but I do make a pretty sorry god.

* * *

The screaming. It won't stop. It's worse than any noise I've ever heard, an unrelenting grating drone coming from the thousands of surviving Threatbelows. All around me. They are mourning the dead. A new voice joins the terror, another survivor recognizing a loved one among the deceased.

So many dead. They are piled up everywhere, their bodies bloodied and broken. Those left living don't know what to make of it all. Most have never had to deal with death before—not even once. They are broken.

"Let us join them! We'd all be better off at the bottom of the heap!" they cry.

Torrain and Adorane have formed an alliance, united in their desire to leave the Drowned City and Down Below. They remind me of Mountaintop daily, of all the Kith there who are waiting for us to return bearing clean water. They both believe that it's the Drowned City that's making me crazy, and that returning home will help.

How can returning home help? I have no home anymore. Not in Mountaintop, where Father and Mother both betrayed me. Not here in the Drowned City, where Omathis has pulled away from me. Not on the mainland, where I am a hunted god, hated and despised.

I am often alone. Torrain and Adorane spend most of their time trying to puzzle out a solution to our water crisis in Mountaintop. Eveshone and I continue to spend time together. But knowing who she believes I am—a deity who has come to make all things new and perfect—compared to who I really am—a child numbed and exhausted by fright—makes it difficult for me to look her in the eyes.

Mostly I am busy being driven insane by the visions. I call them visions, but they are much more than things that I see. Perhaps a better word would be *beings*—because I see, hear, smell, think, taste, and feel everything, just as vividly as I would if I were there and this was all my life.

I'm in the Drowned City, before it was flooded. All the humans were slaughtered years ago, except for the small remnant that ascended up the mountain. Omathis and Amperous are the leaders of the creatures who now rule this world.

I see one moment again and again.

Omathis has created a beautiful mask in the likeness of Mister Sean, with icy blue eyes. It's not a perfect reproduction, as if formed by someone who hadn't actually seen Mister Sean in many, many years, but I can tell who it's meant to be. Amperous appears to hate it. Omathis and Amperous shout about the mask, screeching at one another, coming to physical blows over it, engaging in fierce and violent battle. I cringe as I watch them fight, feeling the floor beneath me rumble with every move.

I don't know if I hear Omathis say this or if I simply know it, but the mask isn't only ceremonial. It's more than that. There's a technology to it. It's meant to be worn, and used, for a purpose. It's something the Threatbelows need.

I see Amp crush the mask and crack it in two. This enrages Omathis. He slashes at his brother, and rows of fresh crimson appear across Amp's chest.

I'm soaked with sweat when I see the visions. It feels like falling out of sleep due to a terrible nightmare, only I am never sleeping. Adorane and Torrain tell me I often act my visions out, slipping into different voices, as if possessed. They have begun to fear me.

Omathis has gathered a group of Threatbelows. They stretch as far as the eyes can see. They breed rapidly and reach adolescence within years. They are susceptible to no disease, impervious to aging, and virtually immortal. Even if one suffers an accident, they heal so quickly that their injuries are rarely life-threatening. It is nearly impossible to kill a Threatbelow.

They all wear the masks and march toward the mountain. In the blink of an eye, they are surrounding it—spreading to the horizon like the sea.

I cannot sleep when the visions come. And they come all the time. I do not sleep for days. My breath is ragged, my mouth dry no matter how much water I drink. I cannot survive this way for another day. I have to talk to Omathis.

I find Eveshone guarding the way to his normal resting place.

"Eveshone, please understand. I need to see him."

She's conflicted. I'm sympathetic to her. It's difficult to serve two masters. But what's the use of being a god if you can't win a showdown when needed? If there were a god out there, what would I want to hear from him (or her)? That's what I decide to say.

"Eveshone. If you do this for me, if you allow this one request and take me to see him, I will lift you up and place you at my side. *At my side*—never below. You will share in what is mine."

I hardly think about the words as they pour out. I'm hearing them for the first time along with Eveshone. Tears form in her eyes, and I can see from her expression, almost painful with joy, that what I'm saying means the world to her.

While I'm only trying to get my way, I see the way she's touched by my promise and make a vow to myself. *I will make sure these words are true, whatever the cost.*

"I'm sorry to have kept you waiting. But Old Master—he's been so drained by this whole matter. I felt the need to protect him."

She steps aside and leads me along the path.

I follow Eveshone through ruined hallways and rotted rooms. Everything seems familiar. I've seen these places inside Omathis' memories. I can tell where we are going.

"This is the hiding place, isn't it, Eveshone? The secret lab?"

"I don't know anything about that," she responds quickly.

I know she's telling the truth, but I can also hear fear in the way she says it, as if she's added, *I don't want to know anything, either, so please don't say another word.* It's a wise decision. There's a lot of suffering to be found in learning the secrets others try to hide from you. I wish I had her restraint, but I could never bear not knowing.

When we finally find Omathis, I feel as though I'm being stabbed with sadness and pain. He's curled up and sleeping—in the same shattered clear cage, I recognize, that Mister Sean kept him and Amp locked up in centuries ago.

All the death, misery, and sacrifice suffered to gain freedom from captivity, yet he remains a voluntary prisoner in the same cell.

He doesn't want to see me, but he's too weak to protest. Eveshone leaves us alone.

"Omathis, why do you stay in this place? You broke out centuries ago."

"Lately, I've found no place more comforting than the prison I spent so many years trying to escape."

I step forward to get a closer look and am confused. Threatbelows are resistant to aging, yet Omathis seems thoroughly old.

Without my asking (though he can likely sense what I'm thinking), he adds quietly, "It's not age or sickness that weaken me, Dear One. It's the state of the world. I'm tired."

He's lost hope. His only hope was me, and once I showed up, he'd decided hope wasn't worth having anymore. Once he met me, he gave up.

There's a tremendous crack, then multiple explosions rip through the air. The ground shakes and rumbles the way ground never should. The sky grows dark and thick with smoke and dust.

The dirt falls out from below my feet. I and everything around me plunge hundreds of feet in seconds. I am weightless; for a moment, disoriented, whirling downward through the air, it's like I don't exist.

Darkness, then a terrible, piercing light. What had been a field beside me is now the top of a cliff far above me. The river is now a waterfall.

I hear a distant rumble toward the ocean, a rushing hiss that chills me.

Many around me are groaning in pain, but most are silent, because they are no longer alive.

Mangled, buried. Dead. I know I'm going to die.

Or at least I want to.

There are tears in my eyes. I need this to stop.

"Omathis. I'm so sorry to ask this again and again. But you need to tell me about the flood. We need to talk about the Great Death. If I don't talk about what I'm seeing, I'll never be able to stop seeing it."

A wave—larger than anything I've ever seen, taller than the buildings that scrape the skies, almost as large as the mountain itself—rushing toward the city.

It crashes against the skyline. Towers are snapped in half, metal splinters, entire neighborhoods wash away. Miles of blue water stretch inland, taking wood and concrete along in a swirling vortex of destruction.

The streets are filled with Threatbelows who cannot outrun or outclimb the white frothy violence. The wave rises above, blots out the sun, throws their terrified faces into shadow. In an instant they are gone, erased.

Now I know how the Drowned City came to be.

Omathis can tell I'm on the verge of a terrible darkness, because we are in that darkness together.

"I have forgiven you for the past. I promise I have." I know instinctively that he wants to look me in the eyes, but he cannot. "I don't see why you must menace me with the memory of what you've done. What Mistersean has done. We've learned our lesson. We will obey. Why must you continue to remind me?"

I have no idea what he's talking about. Forgiven me for what? What lesson?

He continues. "I know that you want to explain yourself. That is why you broach this subject again and again. But I cannot bear to discuss it with you. I want to warn you: I love you. I always will. I have accepted what you've done as your right. Who am I to argue with you? Only equals argue, and I am not your equal. But I will never understand you."

"What do you mean? I haven't done anything."

He seems shocked.

But so am I. What is he talking about?

"You created us. And you slaughtered us. I have accepted it. I just never thought you'd want to discuss it."

106

THERE IS NO one I can talk to.

No one who understands the dark torrents that rush through my head. It's a lonely place to be.

Omathis heard me, but I can tell he didn't believe me. He said he did, but I know it wasn't true.

Omathis had spent years perfecting the masks, secretly, against Amp's wishes. They were meant to correct a flaw in the Threatbelow design, their one biological weakness: an inability to survive at higher altitudes. They aren't able to extract enough oxygen from thinner air to breathe. They'd tried following Mister Sean up the mountain but had suffocated as they passed the borders of Cloudline.

Sean Brathius had been working on a fix for this defect, but the project had run out of time. This is how he knew Mountaintop would be safe from the Threatbelows.

Omathis' mask pulled oxygen from the air in concentrated amounts, so the Threatbelows would be able to ascend and reunite with Mister Sean.

Amp tried to stop the Ascension. "No," he said, "Mister Sean doesn't want to see us. If he did, he would have come to us himself by now! Respect his silence. Accept his absence. Move on. We must scrape out what life we can have on our own."

But Omathis was resolute. "Without the Brathius, how can we call what we have a life? Cut off from him we are alone, abandoned. We are worthless."

Omathis gathered a horde of hopeful Threatbelows at the base of the mountain. All wore masks, their eyes fixed upward, excited to be reunited with their maker.

That's when the ground rumbled, the earth broke in two, and the ocean raised up high and crashed down over the city.

Afterward, Omathis believed Mistersean had unleashed his mighty judgment on the Threatbelows, smiting almost every one of them. A brutal punishment for the crime of attempting to visit him uninvited.

But that wasn't what had happened, I know. It was all a terrible coincidence. We have no technology in Mountaintop capable of a strike like this; we never have. Omathis might consider the Brathius gods, but we would never be capable of destruction on this scale.

"No! That's not what happened, Omathis," I protest, against the immovable weight of his certainty. He has it all wrong; they all do. "Earthquakes, floods—sometimes they *just happen.* No Brathius had anything to do with it."

I want to Soothe him, but since the dark visions have come I seem to have lost my power. I try, but nothing comes of it.

"Nothing *simply happens*. All is appointed according to the Brathius design. But although I may never understand this design, I know the Brathius heart is good. We've learned our lesson. There was a greater purpose that I cannot fathom, but our notions of good and bad, of love and hate, do not apply to you. All of us who live here in *Peccatum*, in the misery of the Drowned City, have accepted the judgment."

Omathis and his remaining Anaghwin decided they'd still love Mistersean. I cannot understand why. Of what use can it be to place your faith in a cold, distant murderer? Since ascending was strictly forbidden, they had simply decided to wait for their beloved.

Amp and his followers, however, were enraged by Mistersean's strike against the Threatbelows. "Amp has no doubt that you are his creator, his god," Omathis explained to me, slowly, as if speaking of such things made his throat hurt. "But he will never believe that you love him. The last thing he said to me, when I begged him to keep our kind united, was that only a fool chases the one who rejects him."

Amp and his Croathus have a saying, Omathis tells me, a rallying cry. No matter what Omathis has said or done to convince them otherwise, they will not abandon it.

"He hated us first, so we shall hate him more."

107

TORRAIN WANTED TO ignore Adorane's earlier advice about Icelyn, and studying the metal structure before him was a great opportunity to do so. In his living quarters, a hut in the middle of the village in the skyscraper, he reassembled it piece by piece. It distracted him from his constant flow of Icelyn-related obsessions.

What is wrong with her? Will she ever be well again? Is there anything I can do for her? Sometimes, when she's not overtaken by her visions, she smiles at me—really smiles, not just a fake smile where she's trying to be nice. Does she like Adorane better? I'm nicer to her. I'm sympathetic to her god complex and more caring about her suffering. In any case, once we get back to Mountaintop, Adorane will return to Catalandi, so Icelyn will have to pick me. Why did Adorane say she'll never like me? Has she told him this? I don't want to ask him—because I don't want to know the answer. Do Icelyn and Adorane have conversations about me when I'm not around? Do they laugh about me? Do they think I'm ridiculous? Will they ever call me Rainy?

His thoughts were exhausting.

Studying the straight lines of the metal antenna (something the Apriori used to capture invisible waves in the air that converted into pictures on their television) was a welcome relief. He knew there was no special technology within, no wires or circuitry like he'd found in the machines in the Apriori home he'd visited. It was just metal.

So how had it performed the magic he witnessed on that roof? The Threatbelows told him that it was one of the many waterbringers they'd found throughout the Drowned City. They relied on it for fresh water out here, where they were surrounded by seawater unfit to drink. He hadn't believed them until he tracked it down. They were right; the puddle below it was pure, drinkable, and delicious.

"How do you do this, you bunch of metal branches? How are you taking the salt out of the water?" Torrain cooed quietly to the structure, like a caretaker with a baby. "How can I coax these secrets out of you? How can I use you to bring water to Mountaintop?"

"Who are you talking to?"

Torrain turned and blushed. Icelyn was standing behind him. Torrain had been so lost in his study of the rusted antennae that he hadn't heard her enter the room.

"Sorry—I knocked first, but you must not have heard me. Ad told me this was where you were," Icelyn explained.

Torrain was happy to see she appeared less tormented. "Sure. No problem. Just trying to figure out…nothing. This thing is water-related…" Torrain trailed off.

Icelyn could tell he didn't want to explain any further. "Hey, if you want to carry on a conversation with towers of rusty metal, I'm not going to stop you." She smiled. "But why were you being so tender and kind to it?"

Torrain didn't want to discuss his flirtations with this inanimate object anymore, and being alone with Icelyn made him nervous. He couldn't think of a thing to say, except a half-hearted attempt at a joke that he didn't want to make. But after an awkward silence, it was the best response he had. "Well, I guess you could say it was love at first sight. I mean, can you blame me? This little number is pretty attractive." He held the antennae close, as if they were dancing.

Icelyn laughed, and Torrain felt a wave of relief. It was good to see her smiling. She'd been upset for a while now, losing herself in her dark visions.

"So did you just come here for a laugh? Jealous of my blossoming relationship here? Or was there another reason?"

"I was hoping you could help me find something."

108

THE IDEA CAME to me during another strained conversation with Omathis. He wasn't recovering from his weakness. I suspected he wasn't eating. He appeared to be wasting away to nothing, and I'd begun to be afraid he would die. From what? Heartbreak? Meeting-your-god-and-learning-she-is-only-a-girl-itis?

I couldn't bear the idea of this magnificent creature dying because I wasn't what he needed me to be. I knew, too, that he was the most sensitive canary in the mine. If he died, it was only a matter of time before the rest of the Anaghwin here in the Drowned City, Eveshone included, perished from a loss of hope too. Or worse—joined Amperous on the mainland.

"Please, Omathis. Eat something. You aren't well."

He sighed and continued staring into the distance. I followed his gaze, though I didn't have to. He was looking at Mountaintop, veiled by clouds. Just like he always did.

"What is it you want, Omathis? What can I do for you?"

"You are all that I need."

Omathis won't admit that I am a disappointment. He insists that I am everything he'd hoped I would be.

"When the Brathius descended, what had you hoped would happen? You have to tell me."

He continued to stare at Mountaintop, but didn't say a word. His eyes welled up with tears.

He wants to go to Mountaintop. *He wants to go to heaven, to live with his god forever.*

I suppressed my urge to tell him that he didn't want to live atop that parched rock, scraping out a life in monochrome—who would choose that? Compared to the lush valley, to the beautiful ocean, Mountaintop was no heaven. But he'd already lost so much of what he'd hoped was true—why ruin his dreams of paradise, too?

So I made a decision.

Going to Mountaintop was all this Threatbelow and his followers had ever wanted. It was what they'd tried to do before the Great Death stopped them. It was the gift they'd always thought their god would bring them.

So I'd lead them into Mountaintop.

That's what brought me to Torrain's room, to ask that he help me find the masks.

109

TORRAIN SEEMS TOO excited that I've asked him, and not Adorane, to help me. I hope he doesn't take it as a sign that he's winning this competition he and Ad are engaged in. I chose Torrain because Ad can't stand the idea that I am god of the Threatbelows. I can't imagine he'd ever support my plan to lead a group of them up to the top of the Mountain. I'll have to deal with all that later.

Well…to be honest, Torrain doesn't know why I want the masks either. He didn't ask, so I didn't tell him.

I want to find the blue-eyed masks so the Threatbelows can breathe in Mountaintop. I've had enough visions to have some idea of where they might be. Most were destroyed in the Great Death. But some still exist, in a great tall oval-shaped building where the Threatbelows gathered to outfit themselves before they embarked on their ill-fated trip up the Mountain.

What I felt of Omathis' memories of that trip is still painful for me. They were filled with unrestrained optimism, a group on the verge of finally entering their promised land.

There is nothing sadder than joy that collapses into misery.

Torrain and I study a map of the Drowned City, an artifact from when it was populated by the Apriori, before it was called *Peccatum*, when it had another name. The building that holds the masks, known as a stadium, was where the Apriori used to participate in physical competitions (much like prowess events up in Mountaintop). It doesn't seem to be far from the skyscrapers where the Threatbelows now live.

But looking out on the Drowned City, we cannot see it, only an open expanse of the ocean.

Torrain is the first to realize why. "It's underwater, Icelyn. It's got to be."

Of course. It's a tall building, but not as tall as a skyscraper.

He grabs my hand and pulls me after him, eager to get somewhere fast. "Oh, I know just what we're going to do."

I'm not afraid to admit that I love when Torrain acts like he's filled with unashamed wonder. Most of the time, he has an edge to him—quick to complain, or criticize, or act like he doesn't care. (Ad suffers from the same malady.) But right now all I see is unrestrained happiness.

"Where are we going?" I ask, as we turn a corner and reach a staircase.

"I saw some of those—what do you call them? Oh, what do you call them?"

"I don't know what you call them. I don't know what they are." I should be annoyed, but I'm charmed by him.

"To go underwater. To breathe under the water. Those things the Apriori used."

He wants to go *underwater?* Where those monstrous creatures live?

Poor Torrain. He had bad luck to be born into the Kith, I've realized. Nothing new has been invented in Mountaintop in the nearly three hundred years since the Ascension. Cognates make much of our intellectual abilities, but the truth is, all our learning is static and empty of real discovery or progress. The human compulsion to create something new—one that I recognize in Torrain more than anyone else—has been stamped out of our society. His dreams of scientific pursuit are always stopped cold by the hard wall of reality.

"Torrain, we can't go down there."

Torrain grabs my hands. "Of course we can. Come on—hasn't it been calling out to you since we got here? Exploring down there and getting to use more of the Apriori wonders? I've been working to fix them up. After three hundred years, of course, they've needed some care. But I've found a machine that can fill the canisters up with oxygen, and have been working to be able to power it. So now you've inspired me: I've just got to figure out the solar panels I've stumbled across on floor seventeen…" He rambles on, lost in his own world of technology. *Voltaic cells and nitrogen oxygen mixes and vulcanized rubber.* He might as well be speaking an obsolete tongue.

The original author of the Code, Mister Sean, knew the awful fruit invention could bear. We have, in our roots, an excellent reason to turn away from learning and forsake the creation of anything new. Inevitably, you'll regret shining a light on whatever darkness inhabits the shadows. Illuminate enough gloomy corners and you'll eventually find something deadly.

"I don't think it's a good idea," I protest.

"We're finally going to get to use them, Icelyn!"

We've reached a room that I've passed a hundred times. It's off a hallway that connects my part of the village with Ad and Torrain's. It's dark and crowded with discarded objects and parts, and I wonder how Torrain ever noticed the equipment he's currently rifling through. "You put this rubber attachment in your mouth, and then you can breathe in the air that's trapped in these tanks. This room was well-sealed all these years—you know, protected against the climate and moisture and elements." He rambles on further with technical details about how different metals and rubbers might have been preserved throughout the years. "…So a lot of the equipment is still in almost usable condition. I mean, it'll take some work on my part, but I think given a few days I can get some of them ready for us—"

"What are you guys doing?"

Damn! I was hoping to avoid Adorane and be off before he noticed. But now he's standing in the door. I flush with guilt, as if he's caught me and Torrain doing something far more intimate than preparing scuba gear.

"Nothing." I try to brush it off, but I know I sound unconvincing. "Just looking at some old Apriori technology." I stammer over my words.

Torrain looks ridiculous, somehow managing to smile with the rubber scuba gauge still in his mouth. "It's in surprisingly good condition," he explains, oblivious to the tension, "considering how old it is. But this room's uniquely ideal temperature and humidity levels shielded all this equipment from the harsh environmental conditions, so it makes sense."

I try not to roll my eyes in the darkness.

"Just getting together in a darkened room to look through ancient garbage? Was this spontaneous or planned? I mean, were you two just eating breakfast, then you decided to go digging through the depths of a cramped storage room together?"

Will both of them just be quiet?

"I'm taking her to look for something. But it's a secret. A secret from you, that is. She asked me to keep it a secret, so I can't tell you what it is. But it involves an expedition."

This is not helping.

Adorane can't hide his jealousy, and *that* I don't mind so much. He takes whatever we have for granted—as if it'll always be there, no matter how many times he dives into bed with Catalandi or brushes off my feelings because they confuse him. Perhaps it's not a bad thing for him to think he's not the only one I share secrets with.

"Is that true, Ice?" he asks.

Seeing how much it bothers Ad, all my objections over the trip underwater disappear. I nod.

"Well, then, I guess I don't need to know what it is you're looking for. But I'm certainly not going to let the two of you go anywhere alone."

110

WE SPLASH BELOW the surface. I'm mesmerized. In Mountaintop, the water was never deep enough to dive into (except when I fell into Waterpump channel, but that was traumatic—nothing like the peace I've found diving into this beautiful sea). From the Drowned City above, the ocean is a shining blue enigma; I am finally getting a chance to glimpse what lies beneath the waves.

I've suffered through a long wait for this. Every time Torrain seemed to be making progress, he'd test the renovated scuba gear and there would be a bubble, a leak, or even an explosion. "It's got to be perfect, or else we'll die," he warned in a tone so ominous that I didn't feel like I could rush him.

Finally, he let me know everything was ready. He made sure to impress upon me, multiple times, the difficulty of what he had accomplished. He wanted to explain why reviving three-hundred-year-old gear was so impressive and why it had taken so long. He insisted on sharing how he had done it—*every single step he had taken,* all the books he had read, all the research he'd done. I tried to listen, but he went through it in such dull detail that I finally cut him off with a congratulations and asked him to please stop talking before I fell asleep.

As it turns out, all Torrain's work was worth it. As we sink beneath the waves, we enter a different world. Every law of physics I've ever known doesn't seem to apply here. I float and sink and glide gracefully, holding onto the long rope that Torrain wisely tied to a skyscraper above so that we can't get lost.

Even though we cannot swim, it is easy enough to move through the water. We can drift, occasionally kick our feet (wearing the Apriori rubber flippers helps), and make progress. We're not going to set any speed records, but we're moving. In Mountaintop, water was for drinking and occasional washing. Never deep enough to move through *for fun*. (Adorane, of course, claimed he could swim as well as the Apriori could—but it's obvious that that was either a lie or wishful thinking on his part.)

The water bends sound, squeezing and molding it into something else. Ad's hair slowly floats above his head, gently swaying back and forth in the current. He looks hilarious to me.

The fish! They are a rainbow of colors like nothing I've ever seen, except maybe the flowers that grow Down Below: bright oranges, blues, and yellows. Belubus used to read me an ancient book, written for Apriori children, about a great hidden treasure guarded by a giant dragon. (I always loved that book.) These fish seem less like animals and more like that treasure, all its gems and gold pieces come to life. They move together, flashing and weaving, like they've spent their entire lives learning a grand dance and finally have an audience for their performance.

Bright rays of sunlight pierce the surface of the water and shine down until they are lost in the depths. I wish I could naturally breathe underwater, because I'd live here if I could. The terrible visions and thoughts I've struggled with haven't followed me down here.

I'm shaken out of my peace by Adorane, who grabs my attention through a series of overly complicated hand motions that I'm guessing mean *stop floating around and let's get going*. Ad bosses me around even when he can't talk. We swim after Torrain, who has already almost reached the stadium.

I'm glad that Adorane can't speak underwater. I know what he'd be saying. *I don't understand why you had to come with us, Icelyn. Torrain and I could have done this alone. But here you are just looking around like a wide-eyed baby, unaware of the dangers lurking beneath us. Now let's hurry up and get out of the water.*

Maybe I'm being unfair and he wouldn't be so tiresome. But one look in his eyes, even through the glass masks we wear, confirms my suspicions. Even when he's silent, he's too loud.

As we near the top of the stadium, I'm relieved to find that it's familiar, matching the one from my waking dreams—except for the years of coral growth, layers of barnacles, and swarms of fish that now make it their home. It seems to have been open to the air, a giant bowl that must have held tens of thousands of Apriori in its day. In this one stadium, more humans would gather to watch a silly athletic competition than are even alive today.

I scan the massive structure until I find what I'm looking for—a giant sign that says "Coliseum." At least it did in earlier centuries; now the C, L, and UM are all missing. I point toward it and we head in that general direction.

Before we dropped into the water, Torrain lectured us about the sharks (as if we could have forgotten the time they devoured an entire Croathus army all around us). I'm pretty sure he meant to reassure himself as well as both of us, but I had been trying to forget about them entirely, so he wasn't doing me any favors.

"Now, shark attacks on humans are historically rare," he started.

"Well, yeah, because we've all been clinging to a chunk of rock thousands of feet above sea level for hundreds of years," I joked.

"No," he cut me off. "Back when there were many humans, and they swam in these waters all the time. You know what I mean."

I did, so I let him continue.

"From what I've read, they don't *want* to eat humans. They prefer other animals. So chances are, even if we see one, it'll be uninterested in us."

Uninterested is not a word I'd use to describe any of the sharks I've seen.

"So chances are we'll be fine. They don't pose a threat to us."

"Excellent," Ad declared, hoping to bring the talk to a close.

I was also anxious to get into the water, and this was taking too long. Leave it to Torrain to somehow make diving into a sea of flesh-eating beasts boring.

But Torrain persisted. "However, it's worth bearing in mind that without humans, they've flourished. They're larger and stronger. There could be a hundred times more of them in the water, which increases the likelihood of an attack by one hundred times. Plus, it's not like they *never* attacked people before. Obviously, the Croathus weren't safe from them. But then again, those sharks were drawn to us and went crazy because of Eveshone's blood in the water." He adjusted his breathing hose, seeming to ponder this for a moment.

I'd heard enough. "Thanks, Torrain. I can assure you that whatever your goal was in telling us all this, you've fallen far short of it."

Now that I'm under the water, floating through this alien landscape, I hear Torrain's words ring in my ears. I struggle to control a rising wave of fear. If he hoped to make me paranoid about a shark attack, then he's succeeded.

With the glass diving mask, I can only see straight ahead. I have no peripheral vision. I feel blinded.

I watch sea lions play in the water nearby, as curious about our presence as the sturdy turtles are oblivious. Further off, a massive whale floats through the ruins of the city.

Without humans around to mess everything up, the animals have multiplied and thrived. I think about Ad's religion, and how it teaches that humans are stewards of the world, gentle caretakers who look out for the other creatures. It seems quite the opposite to me—all of the beasts have benefited greatly from our absence. The world seems better off without us.

We're getting nearer to the storage space that I know is located below the half-broken COLISEUM sign. I hate my lack of peripheral vision. With our forward-facing eyes, it's not like humans can see a whole lot on either side of us anyway, but having even that limited range taken away is disconcerting.

It makes me value one of the design upgrades Mister Sean made when he created the Threatbelows. Their eyes, I've noticed, are slightly wider set, and they seem to be able to settle back on an angle so they can become slightly more side facing when the moment calls for a wider perspective. Not enough to look like a freaky flounder or anything—it doesn't affect their general beauty, and I think it actually enhances it. But it's enough to be able to see something approaching from the side. I'd love a genetically enhanced pair of eyes right about now.

I know from my visions that Omathis stashed the excess Brathius masks in a room that the Apriori had used for storing snacks and souvenirs they sold at athletic events. Fortunately, as we swim past the giant O in COLISEUM (I'm tempted to swim through it but can't guide myself with enough precision), I see that the door to this space is wide open. I'd known my intuition could guide us there, but I wasn't sure how we'd unlock it.

It's dark inside, but Torrain has come prepared. He impresses me by producing a bright, piercing light that pours out of black cylinder. It must be an item he's found (and restored to working order—he really is something of a technical genius) while scavenging through the Drowned City. In Mountaintop, we had torches to light up our labs at night. But the Apriori had captured a spark of the sun itself, so that they could carry it and ignite it when needed. It could even go underwater without being extinguished! No fire or flame I've ever seen could do that.

How ridiculous that this room, which was once used to store hats and bags of snacks for the Apriori, now holds the Brathius masks—these relics so vital to the Anaghwin, the keys to ascending to their heaven and reuniting with their creator. I wonder what the Apriori working in this storeroom would have thought.

With the aid of Torrain's magical spotlight, it doesn't take long for me to locate them. I'm grateful when I do. This validates all of my visions. I saw these masks, this place, in my dreams—and now I've found them here in reality. I'm not crazy. I'm not just seeing things. A sense of relief and triumph washes over me.

They're beautifully crafted—*carved with love* is the phrase that comes to mind. Whoever made this, whether Omathis or some other Threatbelow, they clearly cherished the subject of their art: Mister Sean. In these masks, each slightly different, I sense an intense longing. It hurts to look at them for too long. Unrequited longing on this level is so painful, I'd like to pretend it doesn't exist. And this wasn't just unrequited—this was longing rewarded with pain, death, and disaster. Yet they continued to love, and for so long.

The Brathius mask's likeness is eerily accurate. When I hold it, I feel like I'm looking into a mirror. Not one that reflects only my face, I realize, but one that displays my essence. Whatever that means.

"These are what we need," I tell Torrain and Ad. Well, I don't say it —I gesture it with hand motions—but the boys understand. I'm sure Ad would be skeptical if he could talk, so I'm happy that he cannot. I gather the masks and stow them in the storage bags we've brought. Torrain pitches in immediately to help. Ad finally joins in, though I feel his confusion and reluctance. He's asked many times why we needed to make this journey, and I haven't dared shared the truth about these masks.

We carry little more than twenty masks between us—just enough to lead a group of Anaghwin up to Mountaintop. Just a small group would make up the first delegation—so as not to overwhelm

Mountaintop's citizens. Also, I didn't think we could transport any more without risking accidentally dropping some into the dark, deep ocean abyss.

We rise to the surface slowly. I hear Torrain's voice droning in my memory, about how we must be sure not to ascend too quickly, 'lest air bubbles form in our blood and sicken us to the point of death.' I have to laugh when he talks like this, using words like 'lest.' Once we get to the top, I'll have to remind him that he isn't still in elocution class back in Mountaintop.

I doubt that swimming to the surface could really be so lethal, but he's researched diving technology, not me (thank God). So Ad and I follow his hesitant lead, climbing the rope. I decide to enjoy the scenery one last time. Down here, you can see ancient water-logged cars and barnacle-encrusted road signs, along with quaint storefronts that now double as sea caves. This whole world the Apriori built over hundreds of years for their own use, now populated by fish and crustaceans and turtles.

And a shark.

Just one. Nothing like the frenzy Eveshone stirred up when we escaped to the Drowned City—but still the silhouette of a nightmare. I see the giant gliding slowly by, keeping a lifeless black eye on us.

I remind myself to breathe.

It approaches us. Ad and Torrain don't see it yet. I flail toward Ad, trying to get his attention. I don't want to be alone in knowing that we're seconds from death. He turns his head back toward me, annoyance in his eyes. What does he think, that I'm flailing around for no reason? But then he sees the shark, too. I can tell he's scared because of the air bubbles that erupt from his mouthpiece.

Because of those air bubbles, Torrain turns back and finally notices. He remains calm. In the past, I've been critical of Torrain's borderline-emotionless personality. Now I appreciate it.

Torrain motions for us to stop and freezes in place. He and the shark mirror each other's curiosity. He watches the monster, entranced by it. I don't like the way the fish continues its approach.

Without thinking about it—and certainly without deciding to do it—I find myself flailing toward and past Torrain to get away. My movements are jerky. I'm not a graceful swimmer (or a swimmer at all) in the best of situations, and fear has magnified my lack of skill. I need to get out of the water and away from this terror.

I tear my eyes from the bright surface above to look back and see with a flash of terror that my motion has drawn the shark's attention. It breaks from its docile glide and charges toward me.

I desperately swim for the surface above me, not looking back again. It's not far now. I can see the Drowned City buildings above the water, their lines waving and distorted by the slowly shifting surface.

I pull at the rope hard, one hand at a time. I know the shark cannot be far from me, but I can't look back. I don't want giant bloodstained jaws to be the last thing I see in my life. I focus on the surface. I'm almost there.

It's too late. The water around me is displaced with ferocity. I brace myself for the impact, followed by what I know will be tremendous pain. *This is the end of my life.* My last thought is a curious one: *I wish the* sharks *considered me a god.* That they were, by instinct, repulsed by the idea of digging into me with their hundreds of sharp, lethal white teeth.

The crash comes, as promised, and it's chaos. I'm lost in a churned-up mass of water, surrounded by air bubbles and bits of algae. My mask comes loose and water rushes in without warning, flooding my nostrils in a cruel attempt to infiltrate my lungs.

But I feel no pain at all. Am I numb? Am I already dead?

I'm grabbed roughly and yanked out of the water. I still can't tell where I am. I open my eyes.

I notice one sensation at a time. I'm lying on a firm, dry surface. A deck. The air feels like a gift as I breathe it in. I cough up the water still in my throat. The sun is warm on my face. I see Torrain and Ad, both hovering over me, concerned.

In terror, I prop myself up on my elbows, bracing myself for the sight of the mangled destruction the beast has left behind.

I see no blood. I still have legs. I still have everything.

"What happened?" I ask, my voice feeble and tired, just before I lose consciousness.

111

ADORANE'S MEMORY OF the attack was murky. He caught a flash of the charging shark and froze. He might as well have been a floating chunk of wood, because he'd had no ability to help Icelyn.

Had he been a coward?

Torrain put himself in the path of the shark in exactly the way Ad wished he had done. Torrain had been the hero Ad would have chosen to be, if he'd been given the option. Ad watched while Torrain swam between Icelyn and the beast and turned around to shield her. The shark's jaws closed on Torrain's metal scuba tanks, not flesh or blood, which released a chaotic swirl of bubbles, not blood, and the monstrous fish didn't like the taste. After an exploratory bite, it lost interest and swam away.

Icelyn looked at Ad as she realized that she was still in one piece. "What'd you do, Ad? How'd you stop that thing?"

He didn't know what to say. *Oh actually I didn't do anything, Ice! I just watched, paralyzed, waiting for you to be consumed. You're welcome!*

Torrain replied first. "It was a team effort down there, Icelyn. The important thing is that we're all here to talk about it."

Icelyn thought that Torrain was taking partial credit for something he'd had no part in, when it was the opposite. Adorane wanted to correct him and give him his proper dues, but he couldn't find the words.

Icelyn tried to stand up but collapsed midway. "Hold on," Torrain said, as he supported her. "You should rest. You rose too quickly from the bottom, you know. Plus, there was the shock of a shark attack."

"Right—a minor shock, hardly anything to be concerned about," Icelyn replied hoarsely, her face breaking into a smile.

Torrain gestured to Adorane to help him move her away from the water's edge. Ad complied.

Once they'd gotten her back to her room at the tower, Ad pulled Torrain aside. "Why didn't you tell her the truth?"

Torrain flashed a warm, confident smile. This was no longer the thin, arrogant grin he'd worn in Mountaintop. "I don't want an unfair advantage. No human being ever knows how they're going to react in a crisis situation. It could have just as easily been me who froze and you who helped—actually, I'm still surprised that's not what happened. She needs to choose me because of who I am, not because my adrenaline ducts opened a little wider than yours."

Ad was taken off-guard by Torrain's reasoning. It seemed so unlike him. He responded slowly, searching carefully for the words. "Yeah, but you really did spring into action. I think she should—"

"You know what I think, Ad? I think friends spare each other as much embarrassment as possible. That just wasn't your best moment. It didn't represent who you are. So why shine a light on it?"

"Well, thanks…Rainy." Adorane said.

"No problem, Addy," Torrain answered, smiling, and put his hand on Ad's shoulder, as if to say the conversation was over and the matter settled. Then he left to check on Icelyn.

Ad hoped Torrain was right. He didn't want to be defined by his brief moment of inaction, either. But a feeling he'd never experienced before had begun to creep up inside him—the cold fear that maybe he wasn't as brave as he'd thought.

His thoughts were interrupted by a shriek of anger from Icelyn's room. Then the bang of a violent crash—and Icelyn's tired, muffled scream in protest.

112

"MY PROMISE TO spare you from the Fury no longer applies when you put her in danger!" Eveshone shouts.

I fear Eveshone's jumped into the River Fury, and her feet no longer touch the ground. She's more beast than anything else now, and she's focused on Torrain.

Torrain slumps against the wall where she's tossed him. "No. Stay there! Stay back," he stammers, too weak to flee. Poor guy—he walked into the room unaware of her rage. He hadn't known that I'd told her about our expedition under the water, or how furious she'd become at Ad and Torrain for allowing me to go under the surface.

"Listen to my voice, Eveshone! Hear me!" I try to shout, but I'm exhausted from the trip underwater.

I am relieved to see that she hears me anyway. But her face remains livid. "They risked your life. They could have led you to your death." Tears threaten to spill from her eyes. She continues to move toward Torrain, coiled to strike.

Ad enters and rushes across the room. He puts himself between Eveshone and Torrain. *Great. Now they're both at risk.*

"Eveshone! Do not hurt them. Back away."

"I am the only one who cares to protect you," she says, hurt.

As much as I love her fierce loyalty, and hate yelling at her like a dog, this is getting tiresome.

"Eveshone, you *need to stop threatening them.* This was *my* choice. I forced them to come along, not the other way around." I rise, with difficulty, and approach her. To my relief, I can feel a shift inside of her. The kind soul I've grown to love is back in control. I put a gentle hand on her. "You know I appreciate you and your unending care for me."

"I want what's best for you," she answers, as a chastened explanation for her violence. "I will give anything, including my own life, to protect you."

"I know you'd give anything to save my life," I reply, and am relieved to see her start to calm down.

Suddenly Ad shouts: "Yeah! You don't have a monopoly on saving Icelyn's life, you know!"

Be quiet, Ad. You're not helping. And am I so weak that saving me is some kind of organized competitive event?

"Right, Torrain?" Ad persists. "Back me up on this!"

But Torrain doesn't answer.

When I look at him, I can see why. He can't answer. He's unconscious—and lying in a puddle of blood.

113

AD AND I work to staunch the bleeding, and Eveshone even helps by stitching up Torrain's wounds. The bleeding isn't from her tossing him across the room, as she is quick to point out, but from a series of gashes he's suffered along his shoulder blade.

"The shark bit him. I guess he didn't want to complain, so he hid it from us," Ad explains in grudging admiration, as if he's wishing the shark had bitten him instead.

I stop before I ask my next question—how did the shark bite Torrain if Ad was the one who shielded me from the attack?

Then I realize that I know the answer. Ad didn't save me down there. Torrain did.

No need to shame Ad by discussing it. (See? I can be sensitive.) But I wonder what Ad was doing while Torrain was jumping in front of the jaws of the shark. I suppose I'll never know what happened down there—but it's good thing Torrain was around, or I'd be dead.

Once Torrain is nestled into bed, patched up, and looking as good as one can after being bitten by a shark and then thrown into a wall by a lethal beast, Adorane and Eveshone both drift away and leave him alone. I mean to leave him to his rest, too, but for some reason I can't.

I sit next to his bed and watch his face. I try to parse my inconsistent reaction to it. I'm not repulsed by his face anymore—it's a pleasant face, I guess. Even handsome. I'm not sure why I've never realized it before.

It's a heady experience, being able to look at him long enough to *really see him* without fearing he'll get the wrong impression. Normally I'd have to steal glances and look away as soon as he noticed. I'm not sure why I am so drawn to his face—except that I worry I'm not actually sure what he looks like, and it's suddenly incredibly important to me that I do.

Ever since Ad stole kisses from me on the beach, I've been determined to return the favor, on my terms. I'm tired of thinking about that messy encounter and want to put it to rest. If I can go into the moment with eyes wide open, then I can figure out how it feels and whether I like it or hate it.

Watching Torrain's peaceful face, I decide that Ad can wait. For now, I want to kiss my Intended(?) for once. Whatever becomes of us—probably death, or at least a breakup from an ill-advised Intention, it'd be embarrassing if we didn't kiss at least once anyway, right?

I lean over and touch his cheek with the back of my hand. It's smooth, like a girl's cheek. I'm sure he wouldn't want me to think that, but it's not a bad thing. Ad's face had been rough, and it scratched mine when he kissed me.

I lower my face toward his and see his eyes slowly flicker open slowly. "What are you doing?" he asks. His voice is hopeful.

I press my lips against his, and am surprised when a sensation that no word can describe passes between us. I thought this would be some kind of clinical experiment, but I am surprised to find feelings—a rush of excitement, confusion, electricity, almost the same as the feelings I had when Ad kissed me.

I pull away. Torrain's eyes are now open as he studies my face. He looks like he's wondering if he's dreaming. "Why are we kissing?" he asks.

"We're not kissing. I'm kissing you, and you're being kissed." I say it all a little more forcefully than intended.

"That sounds…good," he answers, confused.

"I just…I decided to kiss you."

"No complaints," he replies. "So, does this mean that you and I—"

"This doesn't mean anything." I kiss him one more time, hard, to shut him (and his expectations) up, and then leave the room.

114

IT'S TIME TO talk to Ad about the masks.

I need an excuse to fight with him anyway. The kiss with Torrain was better than expected, but I'm left with aftershocks of regret. I feel dirty—like I rolled on the forest floor and now I'm caked with dirt, twigs, and leaves. Or something like that.

I wish I hadn't done it. It's *Torrain*! I've spent years loathing his face, his touch, his every word. And now I'm giving in to what my parents expected of me—complicit in this terrible Intention?

But then again—things are different now. And Torrain saved me.

What would Ad think? I don't want him to ever know.

But how unfair! I know that Ad has kissed Catalandi, and with more vigor than I just kissed Torrain. I've seen that with my own eyes—and he expected me to act as if it were no big deal.

So why do I feel like I just did something wrong? I didn't. Torrain is my Intended, just like Catalandi is Ad's, and Adorane Hailgard and I don't owe each other anything.

Arguments with Ad are tiring even when he's not present to participate in them.

I am enraged at Ad's very existence, seized with the instinct to have it out with him and end this thought cyclone once and for all. Since I can't talk to him about the actual kiss, I decided to air my grievances about something else: the certainty that he's going to hate my plan for Mountaintop, the Threatbelows, and the fate of the entire known world.

"You and Torrain keep carrying on about us needing to return to Mountaintop," I say as I burst into his room.

Ad's throwing shards of broken seashells out a window into the water and watching them sink until they're too deep to be seen. He looks up at me as though I've lost my mind.

The truth is, they actually haven't been talking about this much, though I know they've wanted to. I can sense that they've both been looking for the right time to broach the subject, walking on eggshells—because the last time they tried to suggest we return, I shut down the conversation with an angry, fearful, and intense overreaction. I realized I was being selfish, that the three of us couldn't stay here in the Drowned City forever – but the idea of leaving Eveshone and the other Anaghwin to go back to Mountaintop, that cold place where everyone had turned their backs on me, made me nauseous. I couldn't handle deciding how to solve that problem then. Even the thought brought me a misery I couldn't yet bear.

Ad proceeds with care. "We've been here too long. Think of everyone up there. They've got to be running out of water by now, and they probably think we're all dead. Torrain thinks he's figured out some innovation, if you can believe it—evaporation and condensation, drawing the water out of thin air. I have no idea what he's talking about, but he thinks it'll work." Adorane is tired of giving Torrain credit, but Torrain keeps earning it. "So, yes—I think you're being…"

"Selfish?" I offer, knowing he doesn't want to say the word. He nods.

He continues to tread carefully, but passion rises as he speaks. "…Keeping us all here just because you don't want to go back. I've tried to be patient—"

"Calm down, Ad. I agree with you now. We should go."

I pull out one of the masks that we retrieved from under the water. I adore studying it. Whoever made it loved the subject through and through, and that affection shows in each carved groove. If Ad could only see this mask the way I do, he'd understand why I care for these creatures.

"This is their technology, Ad. It concentrates the oxygen at higher altitudes. So they'll be able to breathe, even up there."

"What…what are you talking about, Icelyn? Why did we get these?"

Ad asks. From his tone, I can tell that he already knows the answers to his questions—and hates them.

"We'll go—but I can't leave them behind."

"Never! Are you insane?" Ad throws the blue-eyed mask onto the floor and it shatters.

If it's a fight I wanted, I think miserably, *then I've done well.*

"That's why we went down under the water?" he explodes. "To get *these?* So that you can lead these *monsters* up into Mountaintop?"

I welcome his anger. It feels right, and it lessens the guilt I've been carrying since the kiss with Torrain.

"I owe this to them, Ad. You look forward to a day when your god returns to whisk you away. What if your god showed up—and then decided that, upon closer inspection, he didn't want you in heaven after all?"

"Don't compare whatever you're doing with *them* to *that*. You're not a god! Do you really believe you are? You're Icelyn, the girl I grew up with. Human. Just like me."

"No, no, think about it. I am *their* god."

"Stop. You're not all-powerful. Or all-knowing. Or, even half the time, good at all. What kind of god would *you* make?"

"Oh please," I retort. "All those things were added to mankind's conception of God late in the game! The part about being good, especially. For the longest time, the relationship was filled with fear, exasperation—and maybe, if you were lucky, a trace of comfort. That's it. Not far off from what I provide. I think I'm giving them more hope than your average god."

"We *are not* inviting the beasts that slaughtered all of humankind into the last safe haven on earth to satisfy your delusions of divinity. No, Icelyn. *No.*"

We are all going to ascend together. That much I know. Omathis, Eveshone and the other Anaghwin here in the Drowned City will see their Promised Land. I have to prove to them that I didn't send the flood. Adorane might pretend that he can stop my plan, but we both know he can't.

With the might of the Threatbelows obedient to my command, how could he? How could anyone?

"I knew you would disagree, Adorane. But I just wanted to tell you, as a courtesy. They are coming with us to Mountaintop."

I dreaded telling Ad about my plan to return to Mountaintop with the

Anaghwin who love me. But even more, I looked forward to sharing it with Omathis.

And the truth is, it went even better than I'd hoped.

When I arrived in his chamber, in the old cage that had once held him captive, he already knew. Telepathic communication (or whatever it is we share) really doesn't work when you've got something to hide. (Though it can be done, you need to constantly guard your thoughts, which is easier said than done.) But when you've got news worth treasuring, there's no better way to share it with someone else. Normally, when you share an exciting thought or story that you're hoping a loved one will enjoy as much as you do, you can't be sure they do. They can give you clues, like a smile or a tear, but everyone knows those things can be faked. You can never be *sure* that they appreciate what you cherish as much as you do.

But when you can share it without words, you can feel the love they have as strongly as you feel your own.

Omathis looks at the mask, and he feels no fear, as I worried he might (since it's another instance of me harkening back to the Great Death). Instead, it confirms what he'd picked up from my thoughts and had hoped was true.

"Dear One. Lovely. I—"

As I watch him, centuries of burdens fall to the ground. I knew this would be the only way to prove to him that Mistersean and I didn't purposely unleash the Great Death on our creation. The only way he could believe that we wanted him with us.

"Gather all those who still love me, Omathis. I'm bringing you home."

Part Four
Coming Home

115

AMPEROUS HATED WHAT he was feeling. Something significant was being born in the Drowned City of *Peccatum,* but the details remained a mystery. Something was stirring, he knew without a doubt. He just didn't know what.

His brother was planning. But even worse, his brother was *hoping*. He'd not felt the pull of Omathis' vast reserve of optimism for hundreds of years, but now that terrible sensation was beckoning again. It was worse than he'd remembered. Harder to resist.

He wished he had spies in the Drowned City. He needed to know what was going on. But his Croathus were instinctively afraid of the waters around the place. It was born of the Great Death, and existed, they feared, to finish what that awful day had started. None in Amperous' ranks would dare visit the Drowned City, let alone embed themselves in society there. They considered it haunted.

Amperous had always despised this superstition, but he wasn't immune to it. The one time he'd been able to rally his followers and pursue the human party into the ocean, they'd paid the price with the worst massacre since the Great Death itself.

The sounds of mourning hadn't let up since. As much as he hated to hear the pain from those he'd promised to lead and protect, Amperous didn't want to tune it out, either. He needed to hear it, to build his resolve—for himself, first, and then for all the others who he needed to follow him.

He needed the strength—because whatever Omathis was planning and hoping for, Amperous knew he had to destroy it before it destroyed them.

116

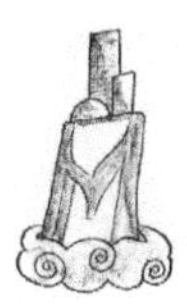

MARJAN COULD MUSTER no desire to leave the tower anymore. When she did, she had to face the angry Veritas who were unhappy with Nicholas' leadership. She had no desire to answer for or defend him. She wanted to shout that she had nothing to do with Nicholas, that if she never saw him again she would be no sadder. (It was impossible to be any sadder, anyway.)

Istoch cared for her. Her heart was too numb to realize it, but she appreciated having him there. When she was thirsty, a glass of water would appear beside her bed. When she was hungry, there would be a prepared meal of acorn meal and ultralion (her favorite) on the table.

It was as if he knew what she needed and when to have it ready for her. But he kept his distance at the same time, never hoping to speak or even sit together in silence. Even in this way, he knew exactly what she needed: solitude, with a trace of companionship.

She took a bite of the ultralion filet. She wasn't sure where Istoch was, but she was sure he was nearby. "Thank you," she called out softly. She wanted to say more, but she didn't have the energy.

As much as she despised Nicholas' recent decisions, his choice to bring Istoch into their home was the exception.

Nicholas sensed he was making a bad decision, but didn't know what else to do. Icelyn was dead, Marjan had frozen him out. He had no one else to ask. There were no options.

Tranton answered the door and appeared glad to see him. "Nicholas! Come in—let's solve the world's problems together."

Nicholas decided perhaps he'd misjudged Tranton. His trusted advisor was the only one who still supported him. That couldn't be ignored. Regardless of any bad decisions Tranton had made along the way, he was only trying to do what was best for all of Mountaintop, and Nicholas in particular.

"Yes," Nicholas agreed. "Tell me. How can we make this right?"

117

THEY WAITED UNTIL Icelyn was asleep.

Torrain and Ad had solid reasons to justify their actions. They had to ensure Mountaintop's safety, because the very survival of humanity depended on it. But still, they knew they were betraying her.

Not that they were doing anything yet. But even talking about it, preparing for it just in case, felt wrong.

Once they had reached a darkened, abandoned platform, far from their sleeping quarters and any Threatbelow who might hear or see them and report back to Icelyn, Ad spoke. "It's not like she's really a god. We don't have to obey her."

He was aware of how pathetic this sounded as soon as it left his lips. His protests proved that they were doing something that made both of them uncomfortable.

"Maybe she's not a god. But she is special. And she would hate us for doing this," Torrain replied.

Ad didn't argue.

Torrain produced one of the blue-eyed masks from his bag, focusing on the science to forget his emotions. "The way it works, I've figured out, is that it concentrates whatever gases are in the air around it. So when the Threatbelows put it on, it draws in enough oxygen so they can breathe, when normally they wouldn't be able to get enough."

He fastened the mask to his own face and inhaled. "So right now, I'm getting a huge rush of oxygen. About four to five times the amount I'd normally take in. It's actually pretty exhilarating—do you want to try it?"

Ad shook his head, declining. "So how is this a failsafe?"

When Ad had originally shared his concerns about Icelyn's plan to bring the Threatbelows up to Mountaintop, Torrain had whispered back, "I know. But I've figured out a way to protect ourselves with the masks. Should anything go wrong."

As Torrain explained how the masks could be used against the Threatbelows, Ad settled into a deep sense of comfort. Torrain was right. It was a brilliant plan. The Threatbelows would not be a threat up in Mountaintop. Ad and Torrain could make sure of that.

Adorane tried not to think about Icelyn. As much as he didn't understand it, he knew the love she had for these creatures was real, and that it was intensely strong.

They were going to break her heart.

118

ONE ASPECT OF my plan concerns me: Mountaintop is anything but heavenly. Once Omathis and the others get there and finally see the paradise that's been obscured by Cloudline for hundreds of years, they're bound to be disappointed. It's a world of crumbling stone and dust, somehow sterile and dirty at the same time.

I want Omathis to hold onto his hope, but maybe he needs to understand that the better world might be the one he's living in already. While Mountaintop was safe, it was also dull and ugly compared to life Down Below. I suppose most refuges are. I wouldn't wish that on anyone.

"You know—I just need to say that it's not so great up there, Omathis. I'm serious. There isn't much going on. It's all different shades of brown and gray. I'd hardly call it a paradise." I feel like I have to warn him, so that he has the chance to bear the letdown in small amounts, not all at once.

"If you're there, it's paradise. It could be a dark, dusty hole in the ground, but if it's the home of the Brathius, it's where I belong. To sit with you on my left and Mistersean on my right—I could think of nothing better."

Oh...Mister Sean.

I hadn't thought about that, either.

* * *

We pack masks into the boats, one for every Anaghwin who will ascend with me. I'm surprised that Ad has given up protesting. Torrain hasn't tried to dissuade me, either. By now, they both know I can't be convinced otherwise. But I still expected them to be petulant, or at least quietly mumbling their objections. Instead, they almost seem guilty around me, like *they're* the ones forcing *me* to go.

I'm not complaining. It's one less obstacle to overcome. I'm glad I don't have to debate with them, because I know that my reasoning for taking the Threatbelows to Mountaintop isn't rational. I feel compelled to do so. It needs to happen. And once we get there, I suppose I hope that the Kith will embrace me and my children, and we can all live together as a new, stronger, united community. It seems unlikely, I admit, but it's how I see it needing to be. That's the beginning and end of my argument.

Omathis has rallied the entire village, and the general mood is festive. Everywhere I go there are songs being sung, and joy is contagious.

I sing along at one point, because the Threatbelows are watching me and I can feel their desire that I join in. *"Then we will be together, the love that was born inside us finally freed!"*

I catch Ad's glance—he's looking at me judgmentally, like he finds me ridiculous.

"Oh, come on. You of all people should understand why this is a wonderful moment. Don't you look forward to the day that your god comes back for you? Sing with us!"

He doesn't. I laugh, because he's so serious, and for some reason I can't help but needle him. "You're jealous, admit it! Because their god came back first."

"You don't count as a god, Icelyn. So no, I'm not jealous."

"Well, maybe I'm just the first god who wasn't so afraid of her creation that she actually came back for them. That's probably the problem, you know—why your god is taking so long, staying up above the clouds in heaven. We're awful down here. Brutal, rude, deadly. Why would he come back? Maybe he's terrified of us, just like the humans hiding up in Mountaintop for the past three hundred years."

"My god's not scared of us, Icelyn."

"I'm just saying it's a possibility. We can be pretty scary sometimes." I lift my arms and make a fearsome face.

He grins despite himself. "You're such a clod of dirt, Ice."

"A *divine* clod of dirt."

Omathis summons me. He's lost the joy he had earlier. I'm afraid he's figured out that Mistersean has been dead for a long time.

But it's worse than that.

"There are thousands of them—and more coming every day."

He hands me a tool from the time of the Apriori called *bino culars* that let you see into the distance as if you're close up. Another miracle, another divine power that they probably accepted as nothing special.

Adjusting the lenses, I see Croathus massing on the shores. Even miles away, we can hear them bellowing and roaring. I can feel their dark hunger—the same inner hell I'd experienced when reliving the massacre of humanity through Omathis' memories.

I can't believe how many there are. They cover the beaches and swarm the mountains and fields. I shudder, almost dropping the binoculars.

"Why are there so many of them, when there are only a handful of you living in the Drowned City?"

"It's easier to hate than to hope. Hope hurts. Rage tastes better, even though it's poison."

There are no young Threatbelows in the Drowned City. Omathis once told me that he'd forbidden procreation after the Great Death. Why bring more Anaghwin lives into this sad, lonely misery? But there are young Croathus among the adults on the shore. It seems Amperous doesn't see any problem with adding children to his swarm of hatred.

Omathis looks defeated. "Amperous has sensed my excitement. And he's come to stop the Ascension."

He says it as if Amperous has already succeeded.

I can't sleep. I'm worrying too much about the toll my plan's collapse has taken on Omathis.

I tried to tell him we didn't have to give up hope. He asked me if I could move the earth and clear Amperous and his horde from the shores, but without killing them, as I'd done the last time.

For the hundredth time, I told him I'd had nothing to do with that. He replied that he knew, of course, that I was right—but it didn't seem like he believed it. He asked if Mistersean could make the ground rumble, then.

I'm trying to rest in a hut at the edge of the skyscraper with a view of the water below. I watch the waves lap against the buildings, and in the darkness, a sudden movement catches my attention.

I see a boat traveling toward shore. Threatbelows use the vessels to catch fish and gather other supplies from the waters, but never at this hour. There's only one in the boat, standing and rowing away from the Drowned City.

"Omathis!" I shout. If he hears me, he doesn't turn.

I spring from the hut and rush across a bridge and down a flight of stairs to get closer to where his boat is passing by. "Omathis, where are you going?"

He ignores my shouts until he's too far away to even hear them.

What is he doing?

119

OMATHIS PULLED HIS boat to the shore. He'd considered leaving it anchored far from the beach and swimming in, concerned that Amperous might use it to infiltrate the Drowned City, but he could feel his brother's—and the other Croathus'—fear of the waters was still very strong. They associated these waters with the Great Death, and their terror had only grown more intense since the feeding frenzy they'd suffered when chasing Eveshone, Lovely, and the two humans. They'd had hundreds of years to build their own boats and had never made even one attempt; chances were his boat was safe on the shore.

"You can come out of the shadows, my brother," Omathis said.

Other than the waves crashing into the shore, silence.

A shadow emerged from the nearby trees. Amperous approached Omathis with a regal stride.

"Send the others away. I mean you no more harm than you have planned for me."

Amperous split the air with a graceful swipe. A hidden mass of Croathus surrounding them appeared and just as quickly cleared away from the beach.

It was their first time facing one another in ages, these brothers who had known each other as long as they'd known anything at all.

"When we arrive tomorrow, let us pass through unharmed."

"You can't stop the rain from falling, Omathis. Neither can I."

Amperous already knew what Omathis wanted. The answer was no, but he knew the question still had to be asked.

"Come with me," Omathis said urgently. "You belong with him, just as I do. We should be together."

Omathis could feel the pull on his brother's heart. *Yes, you remember Blue Eyes. You are still a Anaghwin deep inside.* He watched Amperous, and for an instant he believed his brother would turn—but then Amperous' expression hardened as he flushed any nostalgia from his memory.

"Go back to your Drowned City of Death, Omathis. Stay there. Don't add more blood to the ground; it's been soaked with enough already. Any Anaghwin who reach this shore will die."

Omathis had sensed a softness in his brother. It was gone now, but it had to be in there somewhere. "We can still have everything we deserve. Everything we've ever wanted."

"You and I have never wanted the same things, brother," Amperous said bitterly as he turned and walked off toward the darkness.

"My brother! Come back!" Omathis shouted, his voice raw. But Amperous disappeared into the shadows.

The howls and the screeches from the Croathus guarding the base of the Mountain grew louder.

120

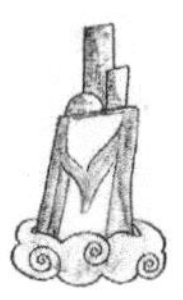

THE SUMMONING BELL cut through the cold air. The surviving Kith —Tranton put their number at only sixty-two—shuffled toward Kith Hall. Nicholas was relieved to see them, as pathetic as they were. He'd feared no one would bother to attend.

"When people have lost everything, you don't have to give them much to win their loyalty," Tranton had explained to Nicholas. "It's the people who have loved ones, values, a water supply, who still have things they care about—they're the ones who will call for revolt. But once they've lost all they have, it's too late. They'll take whatever they can get. So if you give them anything, you'll emerge as a strong and benevolent leader."

Tranton and Nicholas had choreographed and refined the speech. Nothing was left to chance.

Nicholas scanned the gathering and felt guilty at what he saw. Sunken eyes and paper-thin skin stretched tight over unhappy faces. Maybe he should suggest that they all line up and jump from Cliffside. It'd be a mercy to put humanity out of its misery.

Tranton gave Nicholas an encouraging nod, refocusing him. He was going to lead them out of here.

"I have asked you to all come here, first and foremost, to apologize. For everything we've suffered through these past months. For the bad decisions, the overuse of force, for what we've all become."

His words captured the Veritas' attention. This was unexpected.

"I am the Chief Cognate of this great people, and I am reasserting that position. Mistakes must have consequences. I am stripping Tranton of his duties. His intentions were good, but he has hurt every one of us."

The Tarlinius grabbed Tranton as if he were a prisoner, and he played the part with conviction. Shocked! *What is the meaning of this?*

Gasps arose from the crowd. They looked surprised, but not upset. Tranton had no allies among the Kith.

Nicholas' voice grew clearer. "This is not the Kith my forefathers envisioned when they rose above the Threat Below and built this grand city, refined by sacrifice and survival. We will ascend again, fulfilling the promise of our great destiny, not succumbing to the weighty gravity of our worst fears."

The Tarlinius dragged Tranton into the center of the stage and tore his vestments off.

Nicholas could sense the Kith's spirit swelling. "Help us cleanse the Kith of the despair that weighs us down!"

The crowd surrounded Tranton and joined in his defrocking. They took his crimson robe, exclusive to the members of Council of Ultracognates. They stripped off the purple belt that signified his advisor role. They even took his ancient cotton overcoat. A relic of life Down Below, the coats were standard issue for all Cognates, but were not provided to Veritas because there weren't enough to go around.

The Tarlinius dragged Tranton out of Kith Hall.

Nicholas faced the enlivened Kith. Now he only had to execute the final act, to seal the work.

"Thank you for helping me rid the Kith of this sickness. Now please, I implore each of you—join me in honoring the sacrifices our brave Veritas have made." He paused, as if to hold back years, his voice broken with emotion. Then he gathered the strength to finish, inspired: "Let's build the Kith into something greater than we could even imagine."

That was how Nicholas regained the favor of a broken people. It was how Tranton maintained complete power over a community on the verge of death. And it was how nobody thought to ask Nicholas where they were going to find more water when their dwindling supply trickled to a halt.

121

I DON'T KNOW what to do.

Omathis has returned despondent from his mysterious trip to the mainland. I know he met with his brother; he didn't tell me, but I know. He's abandoned his dream of visiting Mountaintop, resigned in the face of the numbers. A hundred versus hundreds of thousands—and growing.

"Isn't there some way?" I ask him. "We have to at least try." We can't just stay in the Drowned City forever, I think, beginning to panic.

"Life is exactly what it is, and nothing more," he replies sadly and enters his old cage.

I hate that old cage. Someday I'm going to smash it into pieces. Not today; it would probably kill Omathis if I did. But someday.

I need to talk to someone. But Ad has heard whispers already that the trip to heaven has been canceled and has been walking around with a hint of a smile on his face. I have no desire to see him gloat. What makes his satisfaction all the more galling is that the poor Anaghwins' joy has been snuffed out by the same rumors.

I find Torrain in his makeshift lab, a hut the Anaghwin had abandoned so he could finalize what I call his Condensation Tree. It's a fine idea, and I know it'll work and provide water up in Mountaintop—he's demonstrated it to me many times—but I'm bored by his extended explanation, which he's droning through again.

He can tell. "Sorry, I know I can get caught up in the details."

I shake my head, as if to say *no, your boring conversation isn't the problem.*

Torrain has probably heard that my plan has imploded. I wonder if he wants to talk about it. I wonder if I want to, too.

"You know, when the Threatbelows first told us about their fresh water supply out here—the puddles scattered throughout the Drowned City that led me to these antennas—"

I give him a tired look. I honestly can't believe that he's going to talk about the Condensation Tree again.

But he persists. "No, listen to me. This isn't the same boring subject matter."

I roll my eyes, but I listen.

"Do you remember when they told you that the puddles of water all over the Drowned City were gifts from Mistersean? Little pockets of fresh water, proof that he loves them."

"Yes, Torrain—" I start. Is he really about to go on a tirade challenging their entire faith, Ad-style, because of this slight misconception?

"Stop. I'm not going to try to say you aren't their god. I don't care—except that you do, so I do care, and I'm fine with it. But remember when I tried to get you to tell them about the science of it all? How it worked, and how they could make their water gathering easier by moving all the antennas closer to where they lived? They couldn't understand what you were trying to say. 'No, we can't move it! Mistersean put the puddles where the puddles belong. Who are we to move them?'"

"I get it. You think they're stupid."

"No, not at all! God, *listen* to me. It's made me realize: *We're* the stupid ones. Humans. Because when we come across things that are exactly where they should be, we rearrange them. We've moved rivers, oceans, mountains, forests. We look at all these systems, perfectly set up by nature, and we think, 'Oh, how can we alter that?' We're ridiculous."

It's funny how talking with other people works. Torrain's point about the stupidity of humanity has sparked an idea in me that I would have never had any other way. Yet Torrain wouldn't have come across this idea he's sparked in me on his own, either. It was born at the intersection of our ideas, and it couldn't have been unearthed without our overlapping.

Cognates claim that humans are special because they're smart, while Veritas value humanity's physical abilities. We've always assumed that one of these traits or the other was the root of our superiority. After all, how else would we have become so dominant on this planet for so many centuries?

But what if it's *neither?*

What if it's just that we're stubborn? Rebellious. Unwilling to accept reality. Defiant fools who want our own way.

All other animals obey the laws of nature without question. Dolphins swim; they never wonder if they could figure out a way to walk on land. Birds catch worms; they never question why or consider whether something else might make for a tastier meal. Bees build hives. Beavers construct dams. They do what they do, and what they've always done, without question.

Humans are the only creatures that have impossible desires—Let's breathe underwater! Let's fly in the air! Let's raise towers hundreds of feet high!—and believe they're actually entitled to them. They believe they can remold the world, disrupt all order, and create chaos until they get what they want. We steal fire from the gods because we like its warm glow, we eat the forbidden fruit because we want to know what it tastes like, and we wrestle with the gods until they give us a blessing we demand but don't deserve. We may be ridiculous, but we hammer away at the world until we get what we want. (Even if what we want ends up killing us.)

The Threatbelows here in the Drowned City don't share this trait. They've accepted the world they've been given. Everything is where it belongs. Keep the puddles there, because that's where Mistersean put them. Stay down here, even though all we've ever wanted is up there, because this is the fate we've been handed.

"Life is exactly what it is," Omathis had said to me, before he crawled back into his cell and curled up into a ball, "and nothing more."

No, Omathis. There *is* something more. You can seize your life and alter it; you can shape your circumstances until they're much more than you ever thought they could be. That's the gift I'm going to give you. I'm going to teach you how to steal the fire. I'm going to show you how to batter and break reality until it bleeds out what you want.

122

THE BROILING SWARM grew restless. By now, Amperous didn't recognize most of the Croathus who'd joined him on the shore. He knew they were from deep inland, a week or more's journey away, where offshoot batches had spread centuries ago. Some wore the skins of beasts unfamiliar to him—pure white bears, creatures with great curved horns, and giant cats streaked with stripes. But they all fell under his leadership as soon as they reached the shore. Even though this was their battle, it was his most of all.

But they did not wait peacefully. Their hunger for violence was loud and thick. At one point a bear wandered out of the woods, and barely a minute elapsed before it was torn to pieces and consumed.

A distant blip in Amperous' mind registered concern that Omathis would become reckless and lead his followers into this churning death trap.

No, Omathis would never do anything so foolish. And if he did, then he deserved death for following a foolish dream. As sad as he would be to see his brother's life taken, the hard reality was that he could never extend enough mercy to shield Omathis from the consequences of his actions.

As his ranks swelled, Amperous began to feel the inklings of destiny

—pricks behind his eyes at first, which soon crystallized into thoughts and plans.

There were so many Croathus in the world now. He hadn't realized how much they had multiplied. And all of them were unified in their hatred for those that lived up above.

He hadn't figured out how yet, but he now knew what they were all going to do—why they had all gathered here as if by instinct. He was going to lead them up to the top of the Mountain—and finally, the world would belong to them alone. Dark memories, bones, and bloodstains would be all that was left of the humans. They'd finish the slaughter they started centuries ago. And at that point, with all their painful, empty Brathius hopes extinguished, he and Omathis could finally make their peace.

The destiny that played out in Amperous' mind made his heart swell. This day, this entire three-hundred-year struggle, would have a happy ending.

And then he saw the boats.

123

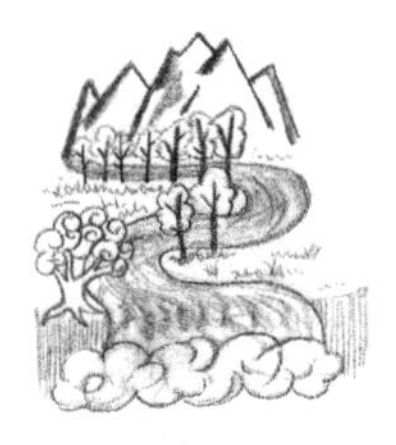

SIX VESSELS FILLED with Anaghwin sailed toward the mainland. Thousands of Croathus awaited their arrival. Not one brave Anaghwin suggested they turn around and retreat to the Drowned City. They held their spears tightly and prayed they'd have the strength to survive long enough for the plan to work.

In the Drowned City, as they'd loaded into the boats, one had asked Icelyn if they'd ever see her again.

"If our hopes are fulfilled," she responded.

"But what if we die?" the creature persisted, even though everyone knew it was not *if*, but *when*.

In response, Icelyn only kissed each of them on their foreheads.

As Icelyn and the others in the Drowned City packed their supplies, she'd obsessed over whether she'd made the right choice. She hadn't asked the courageous Threatbelows to embark on their suicide mission. They'd sensed it was needed. The plan she'd sold to Omathis and Eveshone—exactly the kind of ridiculous impossible human idea that was better left unthought—hinged on sacrificing a large number of those who had been loyal to her for the past centuries.

Omathis protested. "How could we ask those we love to plunge headfirst into death just so some of us can reach the top of the

Mountain? No, no, it cannot happen."

Icelyn had immediately agreed, feeling an unexpected sense of relief. Of course, her plan wouldn't work.

But then a group of Threatbelows had approached her and Omathis. They'd felt what she'd needed, though she hadn't made the request out loud.

"Let us go," they begged. "You'd never ask this of us, but we want to do it for you."

She had agreed, drawn by a feeling that this was their fate, that they had to do *something*.

As she packed, though, she wondered if she should have worked harder to forbid them.

Icelyn noticed Torrain and Ad packing three metal cylinders, like the ones they'd used to breathe underwater. In response to her questioning expression, Ad answered, "Just in case."

Torrain avoided eye contact.

Icelyn was beginning to harbor misgivings about Ad and Torrain's recently forged friendship. She appreciated that they were getting along better; it made things easier for everyone involved. But trios are always confusing. It seemed like two out of the three couldn't grow closer without the third being excluded, even if just a little. She felt shut outside of their friendship. It was probably all in her mind, Icelyn told herself. Both would jump at the chance to become her lover, if she ever made a decision in that regard, she told herself.

The Anaghwin who prepared to ascend to Mountaintop—twenty of them, including Omathis and Eveshone—loaded into two boats. With their peculiar grace and statuesque build, this gathering seemed ceremoniously important, as if their movements and placements had been choreographed by experts and rehearsed to perfection. They wore their Brathius masks already, for Omathis had explained that it would take time for them to mold and fit onto each Anaghwin's face.

Icelyn had to fight back tears. These beautiful creatures were born of her. It was as if she were watching the best parts of her soul, made physical and pure, on display.

She felt like she should make an inspiring speech. Before she could even figure out what those magical words should be, she started speaking. Sometimes you just have to jump and trust gravity to take you where you need to go.

"My children," she proclaimed, "the great day has arrived! Come with me to the place that was promised to you long ago. Together, we'll take back the home you've desired for centuries."

While the two ships sailed through the channels of the Drowned City, out toward the open ocean, Ad asked: "You said they were going to *take* the home, Icelyn? Not *visit*, but to *take*? Is this a visit to heaven or a military operation?"

Icelyn didn't know the answer. She wasn't sure why she'd said what she said. "Just a visit. Allowing the long-suffering ones into paradise for a peek."

Ad watched the hopeless Threatbelows stretching off into the distance, cutting through the water toward the Croathus. "This is a very high cost for a peek," he commented.

Icelyn knew he was right, and again wondered if she was making the right decisions. Yet there was a part of her, quiet but forceful, which calmed her down. Though she wanted to stop what was about to transpire , she couldn't shake the notion that this needed to happen, fated and destined, regardless of what she wanted. Maybe this was what Omathis and Amperous needed to reconcile. Perhaps the Croathus and the Anaghwin would finally be one again when forced to face each other.

Ad took a long look at the Threatbelows packed into the ships, all twenty of them. Tall, strong, vicious, and lethal. "If you needed an army, this would be ideal. Are you sure you aren't leading an army into Mountaintop?"

Icelyn didn't respond. For a moment, she enjoyed the image of Tranton and Father stepping forward to command her, then noticing the terrifying creatures under *her* command. What could they do then? The bars on her bedroom windows, Tranton's velvet tongue, Father's authority—what use were they against her and her loyal children?

She indulged for only a second, then banished the thought. It scared her. She knew that she'd loosened the flow of a river that couldn't easily be dammed. She hoped she could maintain control of the current, but she had to be careful not to be swept up in it too.

Omathis and Eveshone navigated out of the Drowned City and north, moving up the coast, away from Amperous and the bloodbath that would soon commence on the shore.

As the other hapless Anaghwin distracted the Croathus, their group would approach the mountain from the water, making landfall at an area called the Northern Daggers. It was a terrible plan. Massive waves crashed into and pummeled the mountain amidst jagged towers of rocks that jutted from the ocean. No one navigated the northwest side of the mountain, and for good reason: It couldn't be done. Their boats wouldn't survive. All they could do was hope.

At least their chances were better than those who were heading toward the shore.

124

AMPEROUS TOOK NO joy in their death. They represented all that he had grown to hate—blind hope, weak reliance, cherished delusion. Wiping away this viral strain of belief would make his species stronger, he knew.

But that didn't mean he enjoyed it.

How could Omathis be this foolish? Had his brother hoped that Amperous would find mercy and let them pass? No. Omathis knew Amperous wouldn't let them through. Despite centuries of estrangement, they were still close enough to know where the other stood.

But Amperous knew that desperation is the root of insanity. Yearning to be with the Brathius had rotted these Threatbelows from the inside out. This poor remnant would receive mercy from his army—by being put out of their misery.

Amperous was the leader of the Croathus army, so he made the first strike, as expected. As was tradition.

The first Anaghwin to emerge from the waves onto the sand was an easy target. She fought back, drawing blood, but it didn't take long before she was subdued. She didn't beg for her life, facing her end with bravery. Amperous felt a curious amount of pride for his brother,

Omathis, that a follower of his would accept death with such dignity.

He gashed at her exposed abdomen and split her open. As he did so, he felt a rush of pain and grief. He had never hated the Anaghwin like he did the humans. He turned his eyes up to the approaching boats with a heavy heart.

125

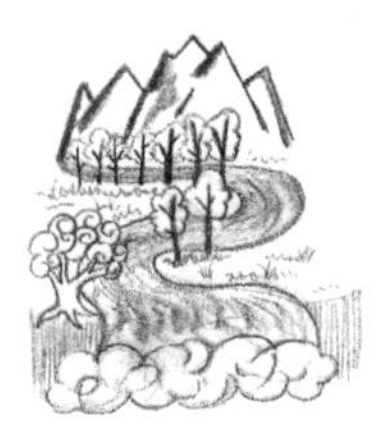

I'M STRUCK WITH a force so strong that I slump over and nearly collapse overboard before Eveshone catches me. Nothing has hit me, though—at least nothing that is outside of me. This violence comes from the inside. I house a distress so mammoth that I fear it will tear me into pieces.

"What is the matter, Lovely?" Eveshone asks, her concerned eyes searching my tortured expression.

What I feel is the opposite of a Soothing. There is not an ounce of peace, or warmth, or comfort. Only cold desolation.

I turn and look back toward the shore, and I know why.

They are dying. My children are being slaughtered.

"Be my strength, Eveshone," I plead.

She holds me.

I sense as each one dies and slips from this world into somewhere else. I feel their last exhalations, their last views, their last acts of bravery, their last pangs of fear—each one of them, exploding through my chest.

They perish while loving me. This only makes their deaths hurt more, for me and for them. It's better than dying without any love at all—but oh God, the pain.

I collapse to my knees, holding Eveshone as I howl.

126

AS THE REST of Amperous' army descended on the Anaghwin from the Drowned City, he bounded away from the massacre.

He didn't want to slaughter Omathis. Even though he knew that killing his brother was necessary to move the Croathus forward into greater strength, to sever the last tether to their humble origins, he didn't want to be present when it happened.

But then he stopped. He tuned out the bloodbath on the beach and focused on a smaller, quieter notion somewhere behind his eyes—almost too muted to be heard.

Omathis wasn't here.

Omathis wasn't in the Drowned City either.

Amperous rushed toward higher ground, scrambling toward a cliff that jutted out into the waters, a point that afforded a view of the coastline for miles north and south.

He fought off a steady drumbeat of panic. There was something he hadn't accounted for; something else was happening. The last time he'd felt this way was as a child, in the lab with Mistersean. When the lifetime of love and nurturing he'd known was wiped away by the knowledge that he and Omathis were about to be exterminated.

Not knowing what is truly going on is the worst kind of blindness.

Amperous ran faster and faster, bounding over rocks and up sheer cliff faces, the terror inside him mounting.

Where was his brother?

127

OMATHIS WARNED ME. I shouldn't be surprised by the violent waves and chaotic currents ricocheting between these stone pillars shaped like scythes. But God, there are places in this world where no living creature is meant to survive—and this is one of them.

He and Eveshone watch me closely. I know they're wondering if I'll decide we should turn back. It's easy to be brave when hearing about danger, but seeing it firsthand and still moving forward takes a different kind of courage. We could turn back toward the Drowned City now and save ourselves.

But I can still hear the distant cries from the shore. What's worse, I continue to feel their deaths in my chest, searing and immense. The Anaghwin have laid themselves down for us. To turn back now would mean they sacrificed in vain.

"We'll make it through," I declare, making it sound like there's no reason to think otherwise.

Adorane smirks at me, as if to say, *oh look who's the nautical navigation expert now,* but he stays silent and places a steady hand on my shoulder. I appreciate this. If these are our last moments alive, I'd rather spend them touching than joking.

Both ships plunge into an eddy. "Pull!" Omathis shouts, and as a team we work the oars to evade a twisted stack of rocks. He guides the ship, controlling the rudder, screaming instructions out of necessity—the rush and crush of the surf is deafeningly loud—rather than passion.

We last longer than I expected. I even begin to harbor hopes that we'll make it through. The mountain grows tantalizingly near.

But then Omathis shouts again. We pull on the oars as a tall stone spire rises ahead on our right side, blotting out our view of the mountain or anythings else. I lose my sense of direction, unsure which way is up or down, forward or back as we're tossed violently into the sky and then sucked into the greedy, hungry sea.

I hear Eveshone cry out; I see Torrain's face contort with effort as he pulls his oar as hard as he can.

I hear the ear-splitting rush of a wave breaking over the ship's bow as the floor lurches beneath my feet.

Adorane does his impressive best to navigate through the gauntlet of eddies and wicked currents, but it's an impossible task.

We smash into the rocks.

128

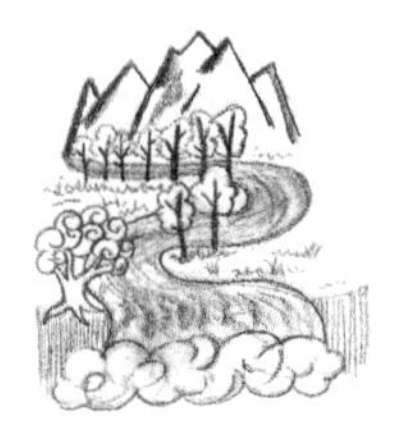

AMPEROUS SCANNED THE horizon, working to regulate his breathing. *Don't succumb to desperation,* he told himself. *Everything can be controlled, and everything will.* He wouldn't listen to fear. Fear encouraged you to look to others for help, protection, and safety, instead of yourself. Fear made you weaker.

He peered through the ancient *bini ocularis,* a metal and glass relic left over from the Apriori.

Now he saw them.

Omathis, what have you done? Even worse, what are you trying to do?

Two boats, battered and broken, were caught in the whitewater between the Northern Daggers.

Desperation is the seed of insanity.

Anaghwin spilled from the ships and struggled to stay afloat in the angry surf.

They will die, Amperous reasoned. *They have chosen suicide—like those on the beach, though by different means.*

He didn't want to watch, and he began to turn away and leave them to their death. But then he noticed something that made him raise the bini ocularis again. The Anaghwin in the water were wearing the cursed blue-eyed Brathius masks—those harbingers of the Great

Death.

And in the waters with them, struggling to keep their small heads above water, he spied humans.

What is going on here?

By the time he was galloping down the incline toward the beach, bellowing toward his followers to abandon their lopsided battle and follow him, he'd figured out exactly what was happening.

He cursed himself for being fooled.

These Anaghwin being slaughtered on the shore were only a diversion. Their pointless deaths were certainly a human strategy—no Croathus or Anaghwin would ever value a life so cheaply—but the sacrifice had worked. While he and his army attacked the boats, Omathis and his followers were trying to take another way up the mountain, where they would either be reunited with their maker or incite his murderous rage once again.

Either way—whether by reestablishing subservience to a god who had abandoned them or by inviting an event more lethal than the first Great Death—Amperous feared his brother was about to betray their kind forever.

Amperous began commanding his army to fell trees and carve them into boats. Their superstitions about the Drowned City and the oceans had to be placed aside, because they faced a greater threat. They needed their own supply of Brathius masks.

Not for worship, but for warfare.

If Omathis survived the turbulent waters, Amperous and his army would follow him up the mountain. And when they got there, they would destroy their creator once and for all.

129

I STRUGGLE MY way up from underwater and have only seconds to look around before I'm sucked back down below the surface. The weight of the water pushes at me from unpredictable angles, and my body is thrown over and over again into the unforgiving rocks. I shield my head with my arms. I can't see anything. I can't breathe. Pain racks my body.

I catch glimpses of total destruction while my head is above the water. Adorane and Torrain are nowhere to be seen, and I fear they've died. The Threatbelows manage the waters better than I do—they are stronger and sturdier, and I can see that many of them have already reached the shores. I shout to them for help before I plunge beneath the surface again.

I hit a rock pillar, one of the daggers that gives this death trap its name. I see a Threatbelow dive below the waves to help me, but a massive wave lifts it up and crushes it against the rock wall without mercy. I cry out beneath the water as my heart tears open—another one dead.

I try to pull myself up onto a shelf carved into the rocky wall but fail. My punishment is another trip into the brutal deep. I'm tempted to give up and let the waters take me. Replace this torture with numb silence. Unending darkness is a tempting trade for my suffering.

But it's not fair to Omathis and Eveshone to be a god *who dies and stays dead.* I won't do that to them. I break through the waves and breathe. This time, I'm able to hold onto the craggy shelf and cling to it against the crashing surge of water.

I pull myself out and huddle into a depression in the rock. From here, I can see how everyone has fared.

How can this be the same peaceful blue ocean around the Drowned City? Threatbelow corpses are thrown and buffeted by the waves all around me, as if the ocean hadn't already hurt them enough.

I feel the loss of every one of them, each one a hook sunk deep into my heart, always pulling downward. I think tears are filling my eyes, but I'm so soaked already that I can't be sure.

My heart swells with relief when I see Omathis and Eveshone, both safely squished into a half-cave carved into the rock wall. I carefully climb toward them, making sure to stop and brace myself against the crashing waves. I also spy Torrain, bloodied but climbing toward safety. He's going to survive. I'm surprised at how much joy this makes me feel.

Then I see Ad, floating face down.

No, not Ad. Ad can't die. I scream toward him, but he doesn't move, except with the water's currents, like any floating object would. I'm not sure what I can do for him, but I try to jump from the rocks back into the water to save him.

But I never touch the water.

Omathis catches me and keeps me from falling. I struggle against him, commanding him to let me go, but he either can't hear me or won't. And I can't pry myself from his strong hold. I'm desperate. If Ad's still alive, I need to save him. And if he's not—then I want to be dead too.

"There's nothing you can do," Omathis shouts over the waves.

"You're wrong!" I scream, sobbing. "There's always something you can do. Always! Let me go!"

"Everyone who's going to survive has survived. The tide has come in; the ocean grows angrier." He's right. The waves are larger and the currents are worse. But none of this means anything to me.

Then I see Ad move. He lifts his head just far enough to sputter and cough before he's face down again. *He's not dead!* This time I manage to twist out of Omathis' hold.

But Eveshone blocks me before I can leap into the waters below. She shoves me back into Omathis' arms and jumps in instead. I slip on the wet stone and feel and my head slam against the rock wall of the cave.

As I begin to lose consciousness, all I can think is: *No, this is terrible! I can't lose them both.*

...And why would Eveshone save Adorane?

130

ADORANE'S BODY HAD given up on him. He hadn't been weaker than the rest, just unluckier—the waves that caught him repeatedly slammed him into the stone stacks instead of pulling him underwater. He'd hit the daggers one too many times and swallowed too many gulps of seawater.

Eveshone hadn't thought; she'd just acted. She couldn't allow Icelyn back in the deadly waters. The only way to keep Icelyn out was to be the one who entered them instead.

Eveshone was a strong swimmer. She'd grown up with river currents, which flowed in one general direction, according to predictable patterns, unlike this underwater chaos. But she still had an advantage in the water, knowing when to fight against the forces and when to coast. Before too long, she made her way to him. She held his limp body against her own, shielding him from harm, as the waves crashed her up against the rocks.

Adorane regained consciousness, but he couldn't tell if he was dreaming. *Eveshone? But…she hates me…*

Eveshone experienced a surge of *something* for this weak creature—protectiveness, pity, care. Was this what Icelyn meant when she'd talked about being a mother? This feeling of wanting to keep a weaker creature safe? She fought through the choppy waters, taking care to keep Adorane's head above the surface. No, she didn't feel like she was Ad's mother. But she did feel something. He was pathetic, and he needed her.

As she reached the cliff and held Ad up so that other Threatbelows could lift him into the sea cave, she was sure of it.

For the first time she could understand, even on a small scale, why Icelyn was so bonded to this creature. She finally felt something for him other than what pure instinct dictated. She finally felt something other than hate for him.

131

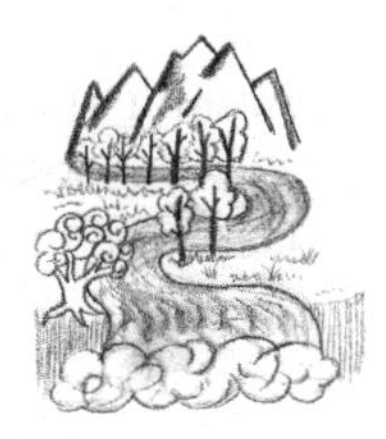

WE SPEND THE rest of the day climbing away from where the ocean punishes the cliffs. This would have been impossible for me and Torrain (and Ad, in his injured state) without the help of the Anaghwin. They are built for this kind of activity; we aren't.

Of the twenty Threatbelows who journeyed with us from the Drowned City, four died in the Northern Daggers. I feel a flash of guilt for thinking it, but sixteen Threatbelows still make for a stronger force than anyone in Mountaintop could ever hope to oppose.

Once we reach Mountaintop, it will be mine.

Is that really so wrong? I argue with myself. *After all, Tranton killed Torrain's mother. Mountaintop is corrupt. In need of cleansing.*

"Hey, Torrain," I call out to him. "Your mother's death will finally be avenged." I guess I'm trying to get his support for a plan I won't even admit I have, but Torrain doesn't seem to want to talk about it.

"Let's just get there first, Ice," he responds, eyes cast downward.

The sun is setting, bathing the Northern Daggers below in purples and golden orange. Contradictions are the foundation of this world, I realize. The most beautiful places are also the most deadly. The most peaceful scenes harbor chaos and destruction below the surface. The Threatbelows, Adorane, Torrain, myself—are we any different? We are all good—but oh, what terrible things we are capable of.

The Anaghwin busy themselves preparing a meal. I wouldn't call it a feast, but it includes roots, leaves, and even some small animals they've managed to snare, and the smell of it makes me crazy with anticipation. Adorane, Torrain, and I retreat to a small overlook, because waiting nearby is too difficult.

Watching the sunset with these two and having survived what we did today makes this a moment I both cherish and want to end. I'm on the verge of tears. I want to tell them I love them, to thank them for following me here, but I'm afraid to say the words aloud. We all should have perished today. Ad especially.

"We could have drowned today," Torrain says dully, staring out at the ocean.

Guilt and fear wash over me—for this whole crazy plan, for the dead Anaghwin, for the friends I came so close to losing. I don't know what to say. At a loss, I try to make light of the situation. "Oh, come on, Rainy. Don't exaggerate. I was thinking of going for another swim right now. It was no big deal."

(Ad told me that it would please Torrain immensely if we called him Rainy now and then. Torrain is strange.)

Torrain gives a wry smile. "Yeah, well, we should probably ask Eveshone to join us. Wouldn't want to go too far without Adorane's babysitter."

I'm not sure why, but that breaks the dam of emotions. I explode into laughter, and I can't stop even when my stomach hurts. Torrain does too. Adorane seems not to get the joke, protesting loudly that we aren't funny.

It's dinner time anyway. I stand and say as much. Torrain and I head towards the fires, and leave Adorane to his awkward, sullen silence.

When I first see the fires the surviving Anaghwin have built, I'm frozen by a jolt of emotion. The holes in my heart, one for every Threatbelow who died on the beach or were crushed into the stony pillars of the Northern Daggers, are still raw and painful—and yet I don't only feel sadness and grief.

I feel *them*. Every precious fallen Anaghwin. Each of them individually—their smiles, their voices, their passions, their fears. All of them. I can still sense them in sky above, in the air I breathe, in myself. Not only the *memory* of them—but *them*. Not in the same way I did when they were alive, but closer to that than to nothing.

I will never say this to Adorane, because I don't want to get his hopes up—but it's as if, even though dead, they persist. Or—*persist* might be too strong a word, but at least where or whatever they are now is not completely barren. They are swaddled in sadness, yet not entirely devoid of joy.

Not quite life, but not nothing, either.

I can feel that.

Not nothing.

Dinner is even more delicious than I expected. Maybe it's because I almost died today, so any pleasure feels stolen. Or maybe it's just because I'm famished. Either way, it's one of the best meals I've ever eaten. Better even than the ultralion festivals we'd have once a year up in Mountaintop. (And that's saying something.)

Halfway through, I realize I am no longer angry with Ad. I'd worked through whatever conflict we had earlier in my head, without his involvement. This is the way most quarrels with Ad are, actually—completely in my head. Born there, suffered there, and resolved there. I suspect it's the same for him. He and I even share a few laughs while we eat.

After the fires have been put out, and everyone has laid down to rest before our ascent, I hear Adorane rise from his earthy bed and walk into the darkness.

I want to follow him. Ever since I saw his body floating helplessly in the waters and thought he had died, I've wanted to hold him close to me. I haven't been able to yet. Arguments, propriety, and Torrain's presence all got in the way, as they tend to do.

A dark, remote area with Ad, far away from everyone else. That seems like the perfect place not to have to worry about petty fights or acting according to the Code. It takes me a while to work up the courage, but eventually I slip from my own uncomfortable spot on the ground and trail him.

When I finally reach him, he's sitting on an outlook that provides a view of the whole coast, even the Drowned City. The bright moon silhouettes the skyline out on the horizon, and the flat sea mirrors a thousand stars.

Adorane is talking to someone. He sounds comfortable and relaxed, as if he's speaking to a best friend. I can't tell who it is. Torrain is the only eligible candidate, and I left him behind in the camp.

As I get closer, I feel a jolt of shock.

Ad is *talking* to Eveshone.

And she's talking back.

I've spent months in the Drowned City trying to teach the Anaghwin and Ad and Torrain how to communicate with each other. I've repeated our telepathic shared thoughts out loud for the boys, sung at the top of my lungs to show the Anaghwin how beautiful their thoughts sound in our Kith language, translated Ad and Torrain's monologues into messages for Eveshone and Omathis and vice versa. Throughout it all, I've dealt with either apathy or unveiled hostility; I never imagined it had worked. Apparently many of the lessons have sunk in, despite their protests..

This is what I've wanted all along—the two of them interacting as if they don't want to murder each other. They're so comfortable, and their conversation sounds intense. Deep. The kind of talk that Adorane and I have had only a handful of times. The kind of talk Eveshone only has with me.

I crouch in the shadows and eavesdrop.

Adorane is talking. "I look at the world, and wherever there is hunger or thirst, there is something to fulfill it. It's just how things work here. My tongue is dry, water exists. My lungs yearn for oxygen, and there is air I can breathe. I need to be loved, and there are lovely people."

"Even if they don't always act so lovely to you," Eveshone adds. They both laugh.

Was that a joke? Eveshone doesn't joke. Wait—was that a joke about *me*?

"Exactly. Even if. But my point is, there isn't one desire I have that doesn't have some kind of fulfillment," Ad continues. "When I want adventure, there are the woods I can explore. If I want speed, there are vast spaces I can run in. For me, the existence of desire is a clue—or at least a hint—that what is required to satisfy it exists, somewhere out there."

"I like that, Adorane. That makes me feel better."

What's this? What is Eveshone worried about? It almost sounds like Adorane is reassuring her.

"I want to believe that she's telling me the truth, that she is who she says she is and is taking us to where I hope she is. But sometimes it's difficult. Sometimes I'm afraid she doesn't have any idea what she's doing."

Tears sting my eyes. They *are* talking about me. Eveshone doubts me. I never had any idea her unconditional trust was at risk.

"If you desire a god, if your heart feels incomplete without a heaven, if you feel there's something calling you from outside your everyday life—then I believe that all that exists. That's how it works. Veins need blood, blood exists. You need Lovely—so she exists."

I've never appreciated Adorane more. He's supporting me—helping Eveshone out of her crisis of faith. And he doesn't even believe I'm a god.

Who would have thought that this boy who used to catch beetles and fling them in my face would turn out to be such a deep thinker? I can tell that the ideas he's discussing haven't been handed to him, accepted by him without question. He's come up with them on his own—invented them out of nothing but his own observations, feelings, and longings. He thinks about all this more than I do. No matter how he acts on the outside, his inner world is rich and inventive.

There's a part of me that wishes, if only for him, that it were all true.

All this talk of his desires makes me aware of my own. I emerge from where I'm hidden. I know I should let them talk longer, but I want to be alone with Adorane.

"Wow! The two of you together, and no need for restraints." I mean it to sound like a joke, as if I've just casually happened upon the scene —but I realize that hurt and jealousy sneaks out in my voice.

Eveshone mumbles that she needs to attend to Omathis and hugs me quickly before she darts away. Adorane takes a moment to collect himself before he explains.

"You're probably wondering…she's not as bad… I mean, you're right. She's special, and—"

I don't want to hear why they've started talking. Normally I'd be interested, but not right now. Ad's generosity, his love for the world, his body—all these feelings are swirling inside me, making the air around me crackle with life. I lean into Ad and pull his face toward mine. I kiss him on the lips.

But it's all wrong. He wiggles from my embrace like a frightened animal snared in a trap.

"Icelyn! What the hell?"

What the hell? I don't have an answer for him. This isn't how I envisioned this at all. Now that the spell has been broken, what I just did seems ridiculous.

"I thought you wanted to—I mean, I thought you wanted to again. I thought I was the one holding it up—"

"I did, Icelyn. But…I'm sorry…it's just…there's a time and a place. This is neither."

I did not know there was a time and a place for Ad. I thought the time was whenever I was willing and the place was wherever I was.

"I'm…I'm sorry. I must have been confused. I'll leave you alone—" I stand abruptly, my cheeks stinging with shame.

"No, I don't want you to leave. Please," he grabs hold of my arm. "Please, sit back down."

Now that I'm closer to him, I can tell that Ad is in his brooding, deep, complicated mode. This version of him makes me uneasy, but it fascinates me, in the same way looking at the Northern Daggers would.

"What are you thinking about?" I ask as I sink down beside him. I will myself to push aside the shame of having my affection rejected.

"My father."

132

AMPEROUS BROKE THROUGH the crimson waters first, gasping, and helped the other Croathus into the boat. They loaded the Brathius masks into the vessel, desperate to escape the deep.

If they were humans, they'd term this mission a success. They had gotten what they'd set out to find and only suffered four casualties. Amperous was disturbed to find that he was now thinking this way himself—that the loss of a few lives was worth the ultimate goal. He fought down a wave of disgust with himself. He vowed not to succumb to this dark human thought process any more than needed in his mission to wipe away humanity.

They'd managed to avoid the Anaghwin left behind in the Drowned City. That was an achievement. He had no desire to slaughter anyone else—and certainly not those that had stayed where they belonged, exiled to this desolate place.

They began to row. Their boats cut quickly through the water, directly toward the mountain.

133

"IT'S CRAZY, IT'S like all the good fathers die, and the horrid ones persist…"

I've been sitting beside Adorane for a long time now. Eventually the silence made me uneasy, and I began to talk. For some reason I thought the empty spaces would be better if filled with my words and ideas, but now I realize how foolish I sound. "Never mind," I backtrack. "I just…I'm sorry. I don't know what to say."

My words hang in the air. Adorane's silence is worse than any reply I can imagine. I want him to speak.

But he doesn't. He continues to stare down toward the ocean and the horizon, as if he can't hear me at all.

I watch the waves below, which look like they're crashing in slow motion from up here. Another stretch of time passes. Finally he says, "Do you think I'll see my father again?"

He doesn't sound argumentative, he's not gearing up for a debate. His voice is plaintive, needy, like an exhausted child asking for a goodnight story.

I don't know what to say.

His voice is more assertive. "You believe I'll see my father again, don't you? I mean, I will see him again. Tell me I'll see him again."

I'm flooded by his words and the emotions that power them.

He continues, louder, before I have a chance to formulate my thoughts. "You don't believe it, do you? Well then—where is he, Icelyn? All that he was, all the dignity, warmth, bravery, and goodness—you think it was just a…fortunate collection of molecules that has now dispersed? Is your world that hollow? That my father was a happenstance that happens to stand no more? *Where is he*?"

What does he want me to say? I feel as though I'll be killing his father all over again if I state my usual views. I know I should just agree—that he needs me to agree—but I've never been able to lie to Ad. My words would be hollow and false.

Eveshone. I wonder if she picked up on how I still feel the essence of the dead Anaghwin and told Adorane. If she did, that was a mistake. I don't know what all that meant yet. I don't think my connection to the Anaghwin, even those deceased, is any kind of proof of the heaven found in Adorane's hopes and dreams. I pick up a rock and toss it over the cliff, agonized.

"Say something, Icelyn."

"I don't know. I—I hope it's true. But I don't know, Ad."

Ad is energized by my statement, like he's been itching for a fight. It's as though he's trying to convince both of us that his vision is true. "It's not like I'm just coming into this with absolutely nothing, and projecting what I want without any precedence! I mean, if we had nothing, no consciousness, no waterfalls, no green, no red, no color at all, no sound, laughter, no people, no sky, or sun, or song. If there were nothing at all, and I came to you, if there was even a you who could perceive it, and a me who could speak, and I talked about hoping for a world where we had all those things, and I was making it all up based on nothing anyone had ever seen, ever, I think you'd be justified in saying, 'Well, of course that's what you want, but that's not what there is.'"

I don't know how to respond, but I doubt Ad wants a response anyway, because he continues. "But we already have all those things, Ice! They are here, we don't need to hope for them. No one disputes that they exist. We already live in a world where we have love, anger, stones, gold, flowers, snakes, and any number of unbelievably magical things that you'd probably think were too incredible to believe in if they didn't already exist. Excitement and disappointment, canyons and oceans. If all we knew was a black void of nothingness and I managed to tell you about a world where there were waves and rainbows and

Drowned Cities, then of course I'd see the reason in you saying 'Bah, that's a delusion! We have nothing! Nothing is all we've ever had! All of your wishing won't make it any different. It's all too good to be true. That's not possible!' But, we have all of that and more. All of these impossible magical things, they're here."

Ad is a mystery I'll never solve. All these thoughts he has jammed up inside of him. Are they always there, swirling around? I start to speak, but he cuts me off. "You accuse me of wanting an impossible miracle. Heaven. But Icelyn, we already have our miracle! The impossible has already happened. Again, pretend we're in that dark nothing room. Which would be harder to believe – going from absolute nothing to the world we have now? Or going from the world we have now, and tacking on an afterlife, a place where my father still exists, too? I'm just talking about a little bit more, Icelyn. The hardest reality to believe in is the one that's already here, I'm just extending it out a little further. It's not ridiculous. If I sang you a song, and ended mid-phrase, not even halfway through a chorus, you'd ask me why I stopped. You'd want to hear the rest. That's all that I've done, Icelyn. I see this world, and I think it ends mid-chorus. Father's life ended mid-chorus, and I want to hear the melodies that are queued up next. It's not like there's no song, no such thing as music, and I'm wishing that there was. We all agree there's a song. I just think there's more to it. It makes sense to me that there's a little bit more."

I don't think he even took one breath.

Up until a few months ago, I didn't even know what a song was, so Ad's analogy rings hollow for me. I have the sad thought that sometimes the song just ends before it's supposed to. I'm glad Ad can't read my mind, as Eveshone can.

I hold his hand and stare at him until he looks up from the ground, his eyes wild.

"I want to believe in all of this. For you. I want you to see your father again. I hope more than anything that you can."

Ad slowly nods, looking back out to the horizon. "Thank you, Icelyn. I just—" Suddenly he stops talking. His hand grips mine harder —so hard it hurts.

No. We see them, at the same time, moving silently through the moonlit water below.

"We have to go. Now."

Adorane and I rush to awaken the camp, but we find that none are sleeping anyway. They are packing the supplies, clearly disturbed. Whether they read my thoughts or feel the approach of the Croathus on their own, Omathis and Eveshone and the others know we need to continue our ascent, right away, or risk being overtaken.

I don't have time to be impressed by my ability to keep pace with Adorane and Torrain while we rush upward, upward, always upward.

"How many were there?" Omathis asks me, though I sense he knows the answer. Maybe not the exact number, but he can feel that there are more of them than us.

I didn't have time to stop and count, but I think back. Four boats. About ten per boat.

"I'd guess around forty." I'm panicking inside. There are forty hostile creatures heading up to Mountaintop. More than two for every one that will protect me.

I thought I'd take an army, *my army*, and seize power from Tranton and Father. (I'm now admitting this to myself, at least, even if I won't to Ad. This is one of the reasons I'm leading my followers into their heaven.) Instead, I've found myself being pursued by a larger and more murderous force. This could be the end of my dear Anaghwin followers and what's left of humanity—all in one terrible day.

"And they were wearing the masks. You're sure of it?" Omathis' face twists in disgust, like something deep inside him physically hurts at the idea of Amp and his followers bearing the likeness of the Brathius.

I don't answer. I don't need to. *Yes. So they'll have the ability to breathe at the top of the mountain.*

"So there's nothing to stop them."

134

"I FIGURE WE'RE about twelve hours ahead, depending on how long it takes them to make landfall. We're moving at a steady rate of four miles an hour, even though the grade has increased to fifty-five percent —"

Torrain is a bundle of frenetic excess energy. I can't understand this, because I need every ounce of strength I have to keep moving up the mountain. How can he waste so much on all this talking?

"They won't bother with the Northern Daggers, because they don't need to, like we did. I can't be sure we're making better progress than they are, but we're not flagging. So once we get there, we'll probably have about half a day to fortify Mountaintop and prepare for the attack —once you convince your father and Tranton to trust us, that is. That might take a while."

"Torrain, *please* stop talking." It's tiring just listening to him.

I can tell he's afraid, like we all are. He works through his fear by creating a tidal wave of thoughts and ideas. Ad trudges along in silence. I'm somewhere in the middle.

"Sorry, I know that I'm saying a lot. But just one more thing. I have to say it."

I sigh, but indulge him. "What?"

"We might have something that will help," he whispers. I'm not sure why he feels the need to be so discrete. "It's a secret weapon."

God. Has Torrain grown delirious? His face is the color of a rose, and his eyes can't seem to focus on any one thing.

"Secret weapon? Torrain, drink some water."

Ad overhears me and his interest is piqued. "Torrain, what are you talking about?" His tone is so accusatory that I feel guilty for our conversation, though I have no idea why I should.

Torrain looks straight ahead and tries to act as if he didn't say anything. "Never mind. Nothing."

I look over at Ad's face, hard eyes staring at Torrain, and now I know it's not delirium. Torrain was about to tell me something that Ad didn't want him to share. But an unspoken threat has passed from Ad to Torrain and silenced him.

What's going on?

135

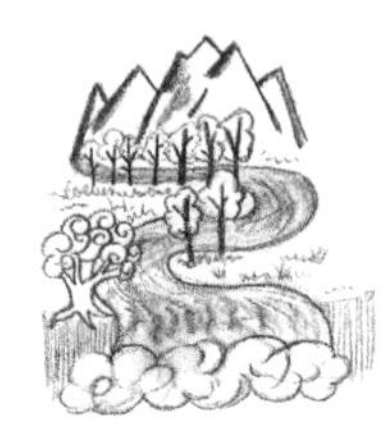

AMPEROUS DOESN'T NEED to inspire his group to move any faster.

They've picked up their pace, and now they're close enough to sense the fear from Omathis and the Anaghwin. It cascades down the Mountain, heavy and intoxicating, beckoning the Croathus to push through their exhaustion, strengthening and emboldening them.

No one stops to catch a breath. They find one cache of untapped energy after another.

This is the heady rush of being the predator, Amp thinks, as he leads the bloodthirsty group upward. The advantage given to those who chase over those who are chased. The prey rarely escapes for good; they can only delay the inevitable. It's only a matter of time before the hunter catches up.

136

WE REACH CLOUDLINE so quickly that it surprises me. This means we're making excellent progress, but my mind is too fragmented to be encouraged. How can we defend Mountaintop? What was Torrain talking about? What have I done?

I'm still a kid, I silently shout to myself, or maybe the universe—hell, if Ad's god can hear me, I won't complain. I want the attention of anyone big enough to hear and be able to do something about it, even though I'm sure there's no one that fits that description. *How could my decisions have such immense consequences? A seventeen year-old girl should not be able to end the world. There's a flaw in the fabric of reality.*

No one stops to celebrate the milestone that Cloudline represents. We stand on the edge of the shroud that's separated the Anaghwin from their heaven for ages, and we don't have time to do anything but continue our dogged climb.

I warn Omathis about the ravenous, sick Threatbelows that occupy the white blindness, making sure to keep my voice low so Ad cannot hear. I don't want to remind him of his father's death.

"We know already, Lovely. We've been able to smell the Cloudies for at least two miles now."

Oh, great.

We move into the soupy mists. I make sure that Ad, Torrain, and myself are completely surrounded by the Anaghwin.

We continue our ascent.

I remember the girl who took this same deadly trip downward. The days have bled into weeks, which have stacked up so high that I don't know if I've been away three months or six or more. I'm lifetimes different now from that girl who escaped the Mines and walked defiantly into Cloudline. If I could see her now, she wouldn't believe anything I had to say.

Except for the fact that we're being pursued by Amperous and his murderous clan (whose presence both the Anaghwin and I can feel by now), the trip through Cloudline is easier than the massacre we suffered on the way down. Those airsick Croathus who are foolish enough to charge us are destroyed by my Anaghwin, who are healthier, stronger, and fortified by the oxygen masks.

I trust the Threatbelows who worship me, but watching the violence they unleash to tear our attackers apart unsettles me. That same ferocity, doubled in numbers and stoked into white-hot rage, is pursuing us too, barreling up toward Mountaintop.

"You don't have to worry," Eveshone tells me, reading my thoughts. "Amp and his followers would never carve you up. It's sewn into our natures—we can't just *kill* a Brathius, even if we wanted to. Omathis, me, Ad, Torrain—we will all likely die. But you should be fine."

Perfect. Thanks for the encouragement.

"I won't be fine if you're dead, Eveshone. I'd never be fine again. Do you understand that?"

"That's how I'd feel if you died—though I know, of course, that gods can't die." She stops suddenly, as if a thought is hitting her for the first time. "Or wait—*can* gods die? And then not be dead anymore? Ad was telling me something that confused me—"

"Oh, don't listen to Ad so far as gods are concerned." I feel a flash of annoyance. Ad shouldn't be telling Eveshone about his god who died (or whatever he did). She's got a god already: me. She doesn't need his. He's only confusing her. "I'm not going to die."

"Good," she exclaims, relieved. "But if you did, I'd feel the same way. I could be safe and comfortable for an eternity, but I'd never be fine. I'd rather die than have you die."

Eveshone's belief that the Croathus would never kill me gives me an idea. I should go and speak to Amperous alone. I've convinced many Anaghwin to behave counter to their human-slaughtering instincts.

Perhaps I could save Mountaintop.

Omathis, Eveshone, Adorane, and Torrain won't even let me finish the proposal. I don't believe those four have ever agreed about anything, but they are unified in their refusal to let me go.

"My brother may not be able to slaughter you directly, but he was trying to poison you up in Mountaintop. And who knows—perhaps he's reached the point where his Fury could overcome what's left of our kind's natural love for the Brathius," Omathis insists. "I'm not so sure he wouldn't murder you."

137

I WAIT UNTIL Adorane is occupied with Eveshone. The two of them talk often now. I'm not sure if I'm jealous, or if I am, *which of them* I'm jealous of. I always thought I wanted my friends to like each other, but now that they do, it only makes me uncomfortable. They seem to be talking about a defensive strategy once we reach Mountaintop, which is fine—I guess.

I walk beside Torrain, determined to squeeze him until he gives up his secret. It's obvious that he has one. He and Ad have been acting too strange for there to be *nothing*.

Belubus' words echo in my mind. *You may be forced to be a worm at some point, but at least try to be an eagle first.*

"You're going to tell me, Torrain. I could try to trick you into telling me—but I'd rather you just be honest with me, since we're friends. Let's look out for each other. I need to be able to trust you. What did you mean by 'secret weapon?'"

The way of the eagle works sometimes—and it feels much better than the way of the worm. Torrain, once he's sure that Ad won't overhear, tells me everything.

But dear God, if he was trying to put my heart at ease, he fails. What he tells me does the exact opposite.

138

I'M HOME.

Not in a good way, the way many people mean when they say *home sweet home* or *home is where the heart is*. My heart feels heavier the closer we get. I notice the scent more than anything—it smells different this high up the Mountain. Colder. More sterile. Sharper, like it might stab me if I'm not careful.

We're still far from the Wall, but as soon as we leave Cloudline I'm struck by how constricting and small this place seems. Down Below is filled with deadly creatures, rage, and danger, but it also feels like life itself. This just feels like an empty prison.

Unlike Omathis, I find no comfort in returning to the cage of my childhood.

We're still a few hours from the Wall, but the Threatbelows fall silently into formation behind me. We haven't discussed our approach, but this is exactly how I'd envisioned it. A god leading her people. A general backed up by her army.

It won't be long. I have no idea what's in store for me, for my followers, Mountaintop, Father and Mother, Torrain, Adorane—any of us. But whatever awaits, no one will have to wait long before it's revealed.

139

ISTOCH HAD TAKEN to exploring the outskirts of Mountaintop early every morning. He wasn't sure what he was looking for. But hanging around Brathius Tower had become unbearable; it was all stone and silence, and he had nothing to do but replay painful moments in his mind. All he wanted to do was get as far away from there as the Code allowed.

His last discovery had brought pain to everyone in Mountaintop, especially Marjan. He hoped his next might bring balance.

His friends were no longer his friends. They only mocked him—if they bothered to talk to him at all. They teased him because he cried daily, and laughed at him because Marjan dressed him in the refined outfits of a Cognate—he'd heard them call him *Cry-boy* and *Frilly-Fo*.

But mostly he suspected they feared him because he'd killed someone. He couldn't blame them and he didn't care. What was he supposed to do? Play children's games all day, as if all of their lives hadn't been changed forever? He'd always been a serious boy, and now he could no longer keep up even a pretense of being anything else.

The first time he'd journeyed this far down the Mountain, he'd experienced a thrill from the danger, which broke through his deadened shell. It felt good, like maybe there was a chance he could be human again. He now walked the perimeter of the Wall as part of his routine. Sadly, though, he'd grown used to the place and no longer experienced any jolt from it.

That was how he saw her: far off below, coming toward Mountaintop like a ghost, flanked by her army of horrors.

He took a second to verify that his eyes weren't playing cruel tricks on him before scrambling back to the village.

In one form or another—alive, dead, or come back to life—Icelyn was back. Nicholas and Marjan needed to know.

140

MARJAN DIDN'T BELIEVE the boy. Nicholas couldn't blame her. What Istoch had promised was exactly what they both wanted to be true, but was impossible. They'd worked so hard already to accept that Icelyn was dead.

Yet Istoch swore he'd seen her. And she wasn't alone, he said.

Marjan was so cruel that Nicholas was concerned about her state of mind. When Istoch insisted, it pushed her to the edge. "Stop saying that! Choke on your cursed words, boy, and die so I'll never see you again."

Istoch's eyes filled with tears. Nicholas tried to grab hold of him before he ran from their tower, but Istoch slid easily from his grip and was gone.

Nicholas knew it wasn't in Istoch's nature to joke about such matters. What if he *had* seen Icelyn? What if the evidence of her death had been some sort of mistake?

Despite knowing how foolish he was, Nicholas sprinted toward the Wall.

"Why are you crying?" Tranton stopped Istoch, who was running from Brathius Tower.

"It's nothing, sir."

But Tranton had heard from a Tarlinius that the boy had been out of sorts, and maybe even kicked out of Brathius Tower. Tranton had sent for Nicholas, curious, but had been told Nicholas was not at home. No one could account for his whereabouts.

Tranton held Istoch firm by the shoulder. "I need you to tell me what is going on. As your elder, I command you."

But Istoch didn't care anymore. While he was sure that Nicholas and Marjan had all but disowned him, had still no desire to betray anything to Tranton.

"Tell your Tarlinius to shoot me in the head, then. It'd be a mercy."

Tranton knew the boy was hiding something for Nicholas and Marjan. And Nicholas and Marjan only cared about one thing enough anymore to keep to themselves.

This had to do with Icelyn.

"Where is she, boy? In Mountaintop? Tell me, or I'll have a Tarlinius ask Marjan. You'll force my hand."

While Istoch didn't care what happened to him, he didn't want Marjan to come to any harm.

141

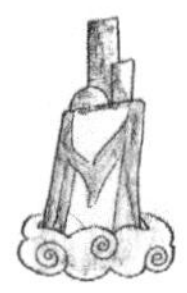

I'VE IMAGINED THIS moment so many times since leaving.

I know how I want it to play out—Father and Tranton both helpless against me. Before, Father had the option to agree to my demands out of reason and respect for our relationship, but he didn't. This time he'll have no choice. I'll take control of Mountaintop and finally fix the mess he's made by deferring to Tranton.

When we first see the Wall from afar, I'm amazed to see that *they* stand atop it. It's as if they've been waiting for me. I rub my eyes to clear away the sweat. How did they know I was coming?

I ask my followers to stay behind and hide in the underbrush. As I approach the Wall alone, the Tarlinius have the gall to train their guns on me.

"You will lower your guns and allow me back into Mountaintop," I declare loudly. "But not as a chastened, wayward child."

I notice that Father avoids eye contact with me, and his are filled with tears. He looks happy to see me—and at the same time, ashamed to look at me, feeling the weight of his betrayal.

"You are to welcome me as the new Chief Cognate," I finish.

Father chuckles, hoping that this is a joke that I'm making, a peace offering. But I stare at him, my eyes hard.

A look of horror crosses his face as he realizes I'm serious.

Tranton speaks like he's explaining why one must always clean up after oneself to a messy child. "Icelyn, do not be ridiculous. You'll be lucky if we allow you back into the Kith, and you'll be grateful for whatever scraps we deem appropriate for you."

I raise my arm. My army walks out of the underbrush, backing me up with an impressive formation.

I watch Father's eyes as he takes in the terrors that I command. Tranton, too. They are not just surprised, but afraid. Horrified. Father looks at me as if he doesn't understand what I've become.

An antsy Tarlinius fires his gun, striking Eveshone in the shoulder. She doesn't even cry out in pain. Bullets have little effect on her kind. Before I can react, Eveshone charges the Wall in anger. Pathetic sprays of badly aimed gunfire do nothing to stop her. She scales the Wall and lifts the offending Tarlinius high above her, a sharpened talon ready to slice him through. Father and Tranton back off in horror.

"Stop! No bloodshed! Unless that's what Father and Tranton desire —then I cannot be held responsible for what will happen."

I stare up at them. They used to lord their authority over me. I watch as they realize that they no longer have any.

"I will be the Chief Cognate of Mountaintop, or Mountaintop will no longer exist."

I catch a glimpse of Adorane and Torrain standing aside the Anaghwin. I'm hoping to see pride or excitement on their faces. Instead, I see that both are staring at me in horror. I push away the hurt I feel.

Father gestures, and the Tarlinius drop their weapons. The mantle of leadership has been transferred to me.

I've looked forward to this day longer than I can remember.

Why does it feel like I've made a terrible mistake?

142

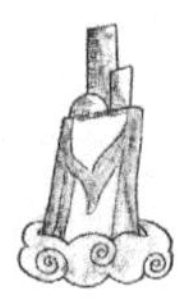

BY THE TIME we arrive, word of our return from Down Below has spread. Charnith Hailgard runs from her round out to the edge of town to smother Adorane with a welcoming embrace. Catalandi makes sure to grab him, too. I wonder if he'll tell her that he's tasted my lips since seeing her last? For all Torrain's talk about how awful his father is, even Marcel is jubilant.

Everyone thought we were dead, but we are unexpectedly alive, and that gift has buoyed many. Curious Kith emerge from their rounds and labs to see us for themselves. I hear Torrain excitedly explaining his Condensation Tree solution, and how it will provide the water Mountaintop desperately needs.

From my place behind Ad and Torrain, I can already see that there is no party waiting to greet me. Once we reach the outskirts of town, I stand a good distance away from the reunions and merriment. I don't want to terrify the innocents with my army.

My face grows hot, and I try to blink tears from my eyes. Where is Mother? Is Father really so upset that he will not even come to greet me? I've missed them—God, I had no idea how much.

Stop it. I try to gather myself. What was I hoping? That they'd scoop me up in their arms? Stupid. I am no longer a girl; I am a conqueror now. My people are the Anaghwin, not the Kith who raised me.

I've stayed back long enough for Adorane and Torrain to enjoy their loved ones undisturbed. The Threatbelows and I must now enter Mountaintop.

Any joy from the reunion abruptly ceases when we appear. I hear screams. I see women, children, and even some men flee.

"I never imagined this is what it would look like," Omathis whispers. To my surprise, he sounds more awestruck than disappointed. I shake off my feelings about Mother and Father and focus on the Threatbelows. Seen through his eyes, I suppose Mountaintop might look fantastic, with its severe drop-offs and view of Cloudline from above. Kith Hall and Brathius Tower jut from the peak into the sky above, intact and almost new compared to the ruined skyscrapers in the Drowned City. Labs and rounds line the streets all the way to Waterpump.

"Yes, here we are. The highest point in the world."

I grab hold of Eveshone's hand with my left and Omathis' with my right. "Let's head toward Brathius Tower. That's where you'll stay." I say it loud enough that Father, standing on the outskirts of the crowd, can hear me. I'm not sure if any of the decisions I'm making are right anymore, but at least he won't be able to ignore me.

I knew that the name alone of my home, *Brathius Tower,* would excite them. All of the Threatbelows are so thrilled to be here with me that they don't seem to notice how much they terrify the Kith, who cower and hide while we walk through town.

I hear whispers of horror among the familiar faces of the Kith.

"How dare she?"

"What could she be thinking?"

"She's betrayed her own people!"

"Everything will change."

I would explain, but no one even bothers asking why I'm doing this. No one is happy to see me.

One boy approaches me. Though shy, he's brave enough to face the Anaghwin that surround me. "Hello, Icelyn. I'm—"

"Istoch," I finish. "I remember you."

He seems pleased that I do. "I'm very happy to see that you're alive."

A wave of tenderness flows through me, threatening to bring tears to my eyes. At least someone feels that way. These are my people. My whole life, I believed they loved me. How wrong I've turned out to be.

"May I walk with you, Icelyn? I live in Brathius Tower now, too."

"You do?" I'm surprised.

"Yes, ever since my parents were both killed."

Oh.

Mountaintop is not doing well. As my eyes glance over the Kith, I see that they are hungry and exhausted; many look near death.

Why can't they see? *This* is why I've come here with my Anaghwin. To rescue them from their suffering.

We reach Brathius Tower. If Mountaintop is heaven, I suppose this is God's throne room. I turn to Eveshone, Omathis, and the rest of the Anaghwin.

"On behalf of Mistersean, I, Lovely, now invite you into your rightful home."

They're like children let loose at playtime once inside Brathius Tower. They scramble from room to room and up flights of stairs, trying to reach the top. I laugh at their unrestrained glee. Omathis looks young again. Bringing them here was the right decision.

I let them explore the Tower on their own. Omathis finds many relics from the Ascension, possessions of Mistersean. All are meaningful to him. "Look, here's the ball he threw to us! And here are the outfits we wore to our first exhibition. Here are our first attempts to write our names."

I've looked through this chest of relics before and wondered why anyone would bother keeping them. Now I know. I am glad Mistersean saved them.

I need to find Mother. I go to my room and find that the door is locked. I knock on the door.

"Go away, Nicholas." She sounds broken, bent, like she's been cracked in half and emptied out. My heart is seized with pain.

"Mother, it's Icelyn."

I hear a gasp, and not even a second passes before the door flings open.

She looks at me with cautious eyes. She's afraid to believe what they see.

"How is this…? Where did you…?"

"I'm back."

The tears overtake her, and she collapses into me. I hold her, and our tears wet one another's hair.

* * *

I find him outside, near Talmer's Folly. I'm not sure if I was looking for him, or if I only wanted to see Mistersean's grave after everything I'd learned about my ancestor, or if somehow Omathis himself had called to me without words.

Omathis sits in front of Mistersean's grave. I read the engraving aloud:

Sean Brathius.

Born 33 years before Ascension.

Died 43 years after Ascension.

The greatest pain is the love you leave behind.

I haven't told him that his God, his father, his creator, had died. I didn't know how. Now it's too late.

I sit beside Omathis, and no words seem appropriate, though I'd love to say something. He's crying. I wonder why Sean decided to include this feature in his design for the Threatbelows. How do tears help make a weapon more lethal? Then again, I realize, Sean didn't see Omathis, Amperous, and the Other Batches as soldiers and nothing more. He loved them.

For the first time in a long time, I feel a Soothing pass between myself and Omathis. He holds me close to him and whispers: "This stone is a lie, Lovely. You are proof that he never died."

Omathis is right.

I reply, not sure whether the words come from me or Mistersean speaking through me: "No matter how big you get, you'll always be small enough to be held. Still enough to feel my heartbeat. Warm enough to face the cold stares from all others. Yes, you are mine, aren't you?"

"Yes, Mistersean. Yes, Lovely. I am yours."

"And I am yours, too."

143

WE GATHER IN Kith Hall, and I call the meeting to order as my first official action as Chief Cognate of Mountaintop.

Adorane, Torrain, Eveshone, and Omathis sit alongside me. I've summoned Tranton and Father, and they were wise enough to attend. I'm glad. I didn't want to have to send out a Threatbelow to hunt and retrieve them. (Well, in Tranton's case, maybe I would've enjoyed it a little.)

"They're coming. We must be ready."

I explain to Father and Tranton that Amperous and his forty beasts are ten hours away at most. I tell them how we've ascended with the Threatbelows loyal to us to defend Mountaintop. As I speak, I see Father's face soften—I might even detect a trace of gratitude—while Tranton's becomes more and more alarmed.

I don't mention that we ascended first and Amperous followed us—that I opened this box of death in the first place. Adorane, Torrain, Omathis, and Eveshone all know the truth, but no one gives me away. I'm embellishing, making myself sound better, to make things easier—but also, I realize, to make Father and Tranton like me again. I wonder why I care.

I've already spoken with Adorane and Torrain about the best

defense strategy for Mountaintop. I go over the plan. We'll post the Threatbelows along the perimeter of town. What high ground there was could provide an advantage. All the Kith would lock themselves inside Kith Hall for protection.

"Huddled together in one place? So they can more easily be slaughtered?" Tranton interjects. As if he has any expertise when it comes to the Croathus.

"No," I argue, "so we can more easily be protected—"

"No. The Kith need to scatter and find hiding places—" Tranton interrupts.

I cut him off. "You don't understand. There *are* no hiding places. The Croathus enjoy hunting us. They can smell us. They can sense us wherever we are. At least here, we'll have some protection."

I don't mention that the protection comes courtesy of creatures that would gladly eviscerate the Kith, if not for me.

"They're superior predators, and they outnumber our beasts two to one—and yet we're going to rely on this feeble protection. This is the best plan you've been able to come up with? We will die. All the Kith will die!" Tranton's voice rings through the hall, rising in panic.

"Tranton, be quiet! Or I will have one of my children rip the throat from your neck!" I've lost my patience. I've forgotten how much I hate Tranton.

After my outburst, the room is silent. Eveshone sits up straight in her seat, hopeful that I may follow through on my threat and let her kill Tranton. She doesn't like him either. I shake my head and she sits back, let down.

"Alright. One more question—if I'm allowed, without you threatening more violence?" Tranton sounds chastened, yet arrogant.

I nod.

"Is there no weakness in these creatures that we can exploit? Ask your beasts here. They should know. Every living creature has a flaw."

Torrain speaks up, as eager and clueless as a puppy: "Actually, there is one—"

"No, Torrain," I cut him off, furious. The terrible plan he and Adorane hatched is not an option. "Tranton, this is the best course. Gather the Kith and lock them in the hall. Any who decide to flee will be outside of my protection, and they will be slaughtered."

As we exit Kith Hall, Torrain attempts to earn my forgiveness. "Please, Icelyn, I wasn't thinking it through. I wasn't saying that we should *do* that…it's just that he asked, and I knew the answer to his question."

I know Torrain isn't being malicious, but sometimes being oblivious is even more dangerous.

My Threatbelows busy themselves shifting the earth into defensive mounds all around Mountaintop. They pull bushes and brush from the ground and create barricades of brambles. Some salvage material from the ruins of Talmar's Folly to bolster their defenses with cracked stone and old beams of wood.

Most of the Kith gather in Kith Hall at the sound of the Summoning Bell. I'm not sure what Father and Tranton have told them, but they don't seem to want to hear anything from me. Some of us begin fortifying the Hall by stacking rock and dirt around its walls. My goal is to have the Hall buried to the roof by the time Amperous arrives.

Some of the Kith have fled, I am told. They do not trust that I mean well for Mountaintop, and they want nothing to do with this coalition of Threatbelow and Human. They will be the first to perish. I'm not being cruel—but those who desire to live outside of my reign will certainly die there. That's just the way it is.

Adorane has been silent since the meeting, which worries me. It occurs to me that we may be living our last hours together. I probably won't die in this siege, but he and Torrain could. I surprise them both, hugging Adorane close first and then Torrain. For all their faults, they're the best humans I know. I wish we could live together forever.

"Adorane, get your Veritas to pray." It seems like a good idea. Who cares if it's not real? If it makes them feel better, then it's real enough.

He smiles and gestures for me to listen. I hadn't had to say anything; they've already thought of it. I hear their songs escaping through the walls of Kith Hall. The melodies are beautiful. If Ad's God existed, he'd probably like them very much. I hope someday my Threatbelows sing songs like these for me.

144

I'D HOPED THAT Father and I would have a moment like the one I shared with Mother. But I didn't want to be the one to ask for it. Children shouldn't have to beg their parents for a close relationship. Then it doesn't count. It's like asking for a surprise. Almost by definition, if you have to ask, then it doesn't exist.

I didn't ask, and he didn't offer, so we never had our moment. I saw him shuffle into Kith Hall without even a wave.

I understand Ad's metaphor about the song that was cut off mid-chorus now.

I can feel their approach. It won't be long now.

Mountaintop is unrecognizable, engulfed in defenses and swallowed by briar, stone, and dirt. It occurs to me that to be invulnerable, something must become ugly.

My Threatbelows stand on the tall earthen berm that's been built around the town, awaiting battle. Ready to die, if that's what I ask.

Adorane and Torrain refuse to stay in Kith Hall with the other villagers. I'm not surprised. They've been through too much to join the ranks of the normal. I'm not sure what they'll be able to do against Amperous' forces, but I won't order them away.

Adorane has been vital in the hours leading up to this moment. The Threatbelows, while outstanding warriors and hunters, have never had a need for military strategy. Hunting down and destroying humans, even against advanced human technology, has always been easy for them. They are too fast, strong, and lethal; they've never been over-matched.

But Threatbelows have never fought against other Threatbelows. Until now.

If a weaker force is to destroy a stronger one, though, they need a strategy. Adorane has always been an avid student of ancient military tactics. I'm thankful he's learned how to communicate with the Threatbelows. As I pass by, directing the preparations, I hear him imparting brilliant military concepts to them. I hear him shouting about guerrilla tactics and awareness. It occurs to me that we may stand a chance of survival.

Then I begin to hear the screams of those Kith members who decided to flee Mountaintop and hide. They are being slaughtered.

Amperous and his forces are inside the Wall.

145

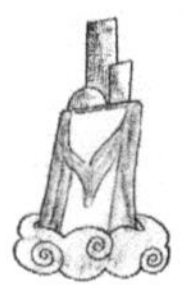

TRANTON KNEW THAT Torrain and Adorane were hiding something. They had discovered a way to defeat the Threat Below. They knew how to destroy this terrible menace, and yet they remained silent out of loyalty to *her.* What fools they were. He only wished he could have gotten to them in time.

While trapped in the buried Kith Hall with the rest of the Kith, Tranton's mind raced. He could taste it. He finally had the chance to avenge his great-great-great-great grandmother's murder—the first crime these vile beasts ever committed against humanity. He could be the Nilsing who finally lived up to Travis' vow.

Tranton knew the secret history of Mountaintop that his family had passed down over the years. He'd learned it from those dusty volumes he'd found in the cave. He could never forget it. And now he was going to become a vital part of that history.

He knew why the Nilsings were the true leaders of Mountaintop.

Only the Nilsings had been brave enough to fight back. Only the Nilsings had possessed the strength to deliver a blow that kept the Threat Below from trying to ascend the Mountain centuries ago, with an attack so lethal it had left them afraid to disturb Mountaintop ever since.

Now Tranton could wipe them all out. He could finally put this ancient war to rest. He knew it. If only Adorane or Torrain would tell him how.

"You'd let the whims of a seventeen year-old girl threaten our survival?" he'd shouted at them as Icelyn ordered him dragged into Kith Hall.

But yes, they would.

146

I BUCKLE UNDER the strength of a Soothing that flows from me into Omathis and all of the Anaghwin who stand on the perimeter to guard me and the Kith. It's a flash, over before I realize it's begun, but more intense than any we've ever shared before.

One last chance to show them how much their mother loves them.

I adore these creatures. If they die, I hope I die with them.

Mountaintop fills with an eerie silence. I look at Torrain, fearlessly waiting atop the berm to my left, his eyes scanning the horizon. I watch Ad pace behind the Anaghwin to my right, his eyes darting to and fro. I look at Eveshone, who stands by my side on the berm, talons drawn. The only sound I can hear is the pounding of my own heart.

We hear the lethal force approaching. A thundering through the trees, a mighty wind rushing through this place I've called home. Their darkness threatens to swallow us whole. I can't keep it away. I remind myself to breathe and keep my eyes open, wide open, though I experience a deep longing to close them so I won't see what's approaching. I promise myself that I won't be overcome by the sound of my own heart beating. I feel myself on the edge of fainting, but vow to stay alert.

I can feel the constricting force rising up the Mountain, crowding us, promising to overrun us, to blot us out, to finally erase us from this world. If there were any other plan—any *better* plan—available to us, it no longer matters. It's too late now.

They are here.

147

AS THE CROATHUS approach, a terrible roar rises in the air.

Adorane barks orders as he runs the circumference of Mountaintop. "Do not give up your advantage! Wait until they are near, and then strike!"

My Threatbelows hurl stockpiled boulders and downed tree trunks. Though massive, these projectiles don't create an impact powerful enough to kill any of our attackers, but they do slow the advance. To kill them, the Anaghwin must get closer.

When Anaghwin and Croathus meet in a devastating clash, it feels as if the earth itself rumbles below my feet in protest. The Croathus hurl themselves over the barriers, meeting Anaghwin in a whirlwind of claws and screams.

I don't know what to look at or listen to. I'm surrounded by a whirl of violence, and I can't focus on any of it. My Anaghwin have the higher ground perched atop the berms and use it to their advantage. I want to look away but cannot. I'm forced to witness these magnificent creatures grapple, slice, bite, and fight with beastial ferocity.

Part of me knows this is what these creatures were created to do, to battle and rip enemies apart, to kill and slaughter, but it tears my heart in two watching them unleash themselves on each other. I whirl around and around as the hateful scene assaults my eyes. I can't tell if we're winning. Already the dead pile up on and around the dirt mounds. I note with grim optimism that most of the dead are Croathus.

Eveshone knocks me to the ground as a shadow rushes overhead. "Pay attention," she scolds, as hard an admonishment as Eveshone could ever deliver to me. "He wants to claim you as a prize."

I rub the dirt from my eyes to see who she's talking about. Amperous has broken through our line of defense and would have pounced on me if she hadn't shoved me out of the way.

My Anaghwin turn their attention to Amperous, who is terrifying. He's possessed. I watch him cut through two of my Threatbelows, Yeorn and Pitchkov, and feel my own heart searing with pain. Amperous moves past the other Threatbelows on his way to a confrontation with Omathis. I fear he is changing the tide of the fight on his own.

Amperous has blotted out the blue eyes on the Brathius Mask he wears. I note with horror that all the Croathus have replaced the icy blue with angry black and red slashes. I fear they plan to do the same to my Anaghwin—and me, too.

Amperous strikes out and Omathis falls back, wounded.

"No!" I shout.

Though my voice is feeble, it freezes Amperous for a moment.

I don't know what to do next. I can't watch Omathis die.

But before I can see what happens next, I'm jerked down from the berm where I stand.

It's Eveshone again. She holds Adorane—against his will—in one arm, and me in the other, and shouts, "We're being overrun!"

Amperous and his Croathus breech the berm and converge on Kith Hall. My Anaghwin (including Omathis, who's still alive, to my relief) gather to defend it.

Eveshone places me and Adorane on the peak of Kith Hall, at the apex of the battle, where I am surrounded by defending Anaghwin. Another Anaghwin, at Eveshone's command, places Torrain beside us.

Amp's Croathus begin digging into the dirt we've used to bury Kith Hall.

They can sense humans below. They want to kill them.

"Stop them! Don't let them dig," I plead, and my Anaghwin do their best, but it's not enough.

I grab Adorane and Torrain's arms desperately. "My God, what can we do? What are we going to do?"

Neither of them say anything, because there's nothing to be said.

The protective dirt is now riddled with holes and tunnels. As soon as an Anaghwin stops one Croathus from digging, another two start burrowing.

I hear a human scream.

I turn around to watch a Croathus pluck a terrified man from inside Kith Hall. I recognize him as a Cognate named Plythius. He doesn't suffer for long.

Everywhere I look, Amperous and his beasts slaughter more of my Anaghwin. I've lost count of how many, but can feel each of their deaths. My senses have hit their limit; my vision blurs as I bend over, crippled in pain. We're outnumbered and now without any tactical advantage. The smell of blood in the air enlivens the killers. The dirt they dig up is saturated, muddy with blood.

I watch Eveshone push back the advance as well as she can, even for a second, but she can only do so much, and I lose sight of her while she's swallowed up into the battle. I realize that Adorane and Torrain have disappeared from my side, too. I cannot see them anywhere. Panic chokes me, strong and unyielding, and I begin to scream. I am alone, surrounded by carnage.

We are doomed.

148

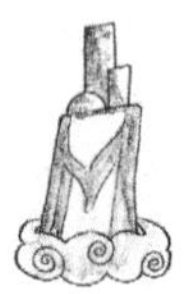

ADORANE AND TORRAIN had hoped it wouldn't come to this. They could still hear Icelyn screaming their names, and both felt a stab of guilt over abandoning her at the top of Kith Hall. Hopefully someday she'd understand why they were doing this.

They'd denied Tranton the explanation he wanted in hopes of avoiding what they now needed to do. But they'd promised one another: If the survival of humanity was threatened, they'd be strong. Now Kith Hall was breeched. As soon as they saw the first human carved in half, their eyes met, and they started running. They had no choice.

They both knew Icelyn would never forgive them. She played the part of the loving god. That's what she had promised to her children; that's who she had led them to believe lived here in Mountaintop. A *loving* God.

But long before gods were loving, they were full of wrath, Adorane knew. Long before gods bestowed life, they took it.

Adorane and Torrain dug up the canisters they'd stashed in case desperation demanded them. The canisters Torrain had worked over obsessively and restored to working order. The canisters he'd been able to fill only after completing weeks of research and experimentation—

trial and error to uncover an ancient technology. Even Adorane had to admit that Torrain had a special gift for Apriori wonders, a knack for achieving the impossible.

And now, though neither had wanted it, they would become the vengeful gods.

The Brathius masks concentrated oxygen so the Threatbelows could breathe. But, Torrain had discovered, they could also concentrate other gases. Even toxic ones. To lethal levels.

Everyone who wore the masks would die from the poisonous gas Torrain had captured in the canisters. Amperous and his deadly army were the targets. But Omathis, the loyal Anaghwin, and—though it pained Adorane to think about it—even Eveshone all wore the masks too. It was unavoidable.

They prepared to release the toxin. Adorane hesitated.

"We have no choice," Torrain shouted. His eyes searched Adorane's face, hoping Adorane might be able to convince him otherwise. But they had no choice.

Before Torrain could turn the handle, Adorane stopped him. "Wait!"

Adorane ran through the turmoil until he found Eveshone, who was slicing through a defeated Croathus. "You must flee."

She was confused. "I could never abandon—"

"Lovely commands it!" Adorane screamed, tears in his eyes. "You have no choice. Leave! Run back down the mountain. It is Lovely's will!"

Eveshone didn't want to leave. But something about the way Adorane looked at her made her believe that he wanted the best for her, that he could be trusted. She couldn't disobey Lovely. Eveshone stepped in the direction of Icelyn, to hear the command from the source, but Adorane grabbed her.

"No. There's no time to say goodbye. Go now! It is her will!" Adorane shouted.

Eveshone jumped from the roof of Kith Hall and disappeared beyond the berms.

149

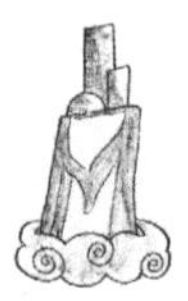

JUST WHEN EVERYTHING seems destined to collapse into death and bitter memory, I experience a warm cavernous love. An ocean of clear blue a trillion miles deep.

Amperous and his murderous horde.

I see them not as blood-soaked shadows, but as bright shining stars, a brilliant constellation more stunning than a handful of diamonds. I see them not as they are, but as they could one day be. As what they are destined to become.

Time slows down and I feel each of them in my heart. I want them to stay there forever.

I feel a perplexing love for each of them, even while they bear down to kill us.

Maybe this is how it feels to die: bliss, then release. Even when it makes no sense.

I love them. Even the evil ones. Even the ones who hate us and want us dead.

I watch them perform vile, monstrous acts, and beg them to stop. *Stop murdering them,* I plead—for the poor Kith who are dying, of course, but even more for their own sakes. *This isn't you.* The Croathus are better. They are meant to be gorgeous, powerful, the pinnacle of perfection.

I desire them. I ache for them. I need to set them free from themselves so they can become who they are.

Every single one of them.

150

AMPEROUS SHUDDERED AND collapsed, though nothing had touched him.

What is this? It was an old feeling, one he hadn't experienced in ages. Just as he was ready to finish this, to claim her, he'd been stilled. He couldn't move.

He didn't want to move, even if he could.

Everything felt warm and wonderful exactly where he was right now. He didn't want to shift even an inch to the right or left if it meant this sensation would end.

He had gotten so close to reaching Lovely herself, so close to capturing her (though he knew he could never kill her) and squelching Omathis' hope forever. But now all he wanted to do was look at her and feel her pulsing through him.

Her beautiful blue eyes locked onto him—and once again he felt small, in a good way, comforted by Mistersean's blue eyes.

He looked up and saw Mistersean standing before him. He suddenly understood how much his maker truly loved him. Amperous' heart was stilled. His breath was calmed. He was tiny again, cuddled up against his brother, floating in a sea of unquestioned calm.

He never wanted her to look away.

151

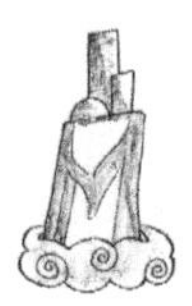

I'M SOOTHING THEM. Each and every one. They freeze and fall all around me, paralyzed in their peace. My Anaghwin pounce, taking this advantage to kill.

"No!" I shout, commanding them away. "Leave them be!"

It sounds like an idiotic command, I realize, but they follow it.

I Soothe them. What I feel for each of them is strong and heavy and exhausting. But I am motivated to continue by the excitement rising in my throat. *I can turn them.*

I love them.

They can love me, too.

All of my children can be a part of the family.

Love will win.

I see a vision of the world not as it is, but as it could be, a world I'm meant to mold into reality. I don't see this world of bloody mud and slaughtered Kith around me. Instead, I see the Anaghwin and Croathus living together again. I see the brothers reunited, all in harmony with the Brathius, their creator. I see the humans leaving Mountaintop, stretching their legs and cherishing their freedom to explore the world once again, woven back into the grand tapestry of earthly existence. All because of my love.

I see the Croathus falling all around me, as if in worship. Their bodies, normally coiled and ready to strike, are resting peacefully. Maybe Mountaintop truly can become heaven. This could be a paradise for us all.

Then I hear a hiss.

152

EVERYTHING SMELLS OF choking rot and sharpened decay. The thick scent of sulfur surrounds me—which is appropriate, because I'm in hell.

They're dying. All of them. I Soothed them, and now they're dying.

Foam spills from their mouths as they cough and choke. Their bodies spasm. *What is happening?*

Then, as I watch a Croathus clutch at its Brathius mask, trying unsuccessfully to tear it off before slumping over in the mud, I know.

Adorane and Torrain.

What have they done? I turn to see them standing there with their accursed canisters, the ones they brought *just in case*. Tranton struggles to join them, emerging like a worm from one of the tunnels into Kith Hall.

"No! Turn it off! I was stopping them!"

Adorane and Torrain's faces flash with regret. Realizing their mistake, they both go for the knobs to turn off the murderous gas, but Tranton grabs one of the canisters. He tosses it toward the Summoning Bell, and it lands there, wedged beyond reach, releasing death on the creatures below.

The berms are covered with the dead and the dying. My children, each plucked from life with choked cruelty, tortured and struggling for air. I shake my head, trying to dislodge the memory before it sticks, but I already know I'll never forget. Even though I breathe in unconcentrated amounts, the gas feels like shards of glass in my throat and lungs. I can only imagine the agony they are in.

I'm crying. But it gets worse.

Where's Eveshone?

Oh, please, where is Eveshone?

Dear Lord, Omathis is convulsing before me.

I rip Omathis' mask off of his face, and he struggles for air. I press my lips to his mouth and share the air I have. He takes a deep draw, and I pull him to his feet. He can't survive for long at this elevation without the mask. I desperately turn to my left and right, searching for Eveshone. I can't leave her. She must come with us.

"Eveshone, where are you?" I shout, but all I hear in response are sputtering groans and rasping, broken inhalations, the discordant death song of my suffering children.

I sprint across the berm, searching for her among the fallen. I can't find her. My throat is raw from screaming her name. "Eveshone! Eveshone! Do you hear me?" This cannot be. She cannot be dead.

Omathis stumbles in my direction, reaching for me. "Dear One, I—"

He collapses to one knee, and I again press my lips to his to fill his lungs with oxygen. I turn and resume my reckless charge atop the berm, looking again for Eveshone. I try to leap over a fallen Croathus, but his large frame clips my foot and I crash headfirst onto the ground. Before I can rise to continue my search, I'm lifted out of the dirt.

It's Omathis. He's carrying me. "What are you doing, Omathis? Eveshone needs—"

"You are not safe here." He sounds determined, like he knows something that I do not.

"I don't care about my safety! I need to find her!"

Omathis' eyes flutter closed, and I know he'll expire if he doesn't descend soon. I press my face to his and give him another shot of air. "Leave! You run. Get out of here. Down the mountain! We'll meet you."

Omathis appears frightened anew, jolted with fear, like he's been reminded of an imminent horror. "My brother's Fury is aimed at you. You're leaving with me," he murmurs. He lifts me beneath his arm and carries me down the berm, against my will. I hit at him desperately.

"I'd rather lose my own heart! Eveshone! If she dies, I'm dead already! Leave me. I command it!" I scan the bodies and shout her name over and over, but there's no response.

"My apologies, but I must take you." He says it calmly, as if my entire life isn't breaking into sharp stabbing pieces and collapsing all around me.

Though he's terribly weak, he manages to hold me fast and shuffle away from the battle. I flail at him, grabbing and scratching and doing anything I can to slow our progress, but he carries me away. Away from Eveshone.

I take one look back at Kith Hall as we head out of Mountaintop. Adorane is climbing to the top of the Summoning Bell, trying to get the canister. But the damage is already done. On the dirt hill built to bury and protect the hall, I see the bodies of loyal Anaghwin, enemy Croathus, and my fellow Kith ripped into pieces and strewn across the earth. I loved them all. And they are all dead.

Those Kith fortunate enough to survive emerge from the tunnels, grateful to be alive. Mountaintop is saved. That's the choice Adorane and Torrain made.

They will be hailed as heroes forever. *Good for them, they'll be so proud.*

As Omathis and I hurtle toward Cloudline, I scream, empty, defeated—and filled with unending fury.

153

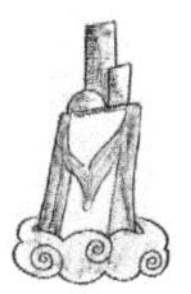

AMPEROUS STRUGGLED OUT of his mask and embraced the pain in his chest. He found a hardened, dead strength there, an ugly weapon forged in the tortured fire.

He refused to die like this.

He'd been fooled again. He'd felt the love and trusted it. He'd let it still his heart and calm his Fury. He'd entertained hope. All of the temptations he'd held fast against for centuries had rushed back, and he'd allowed his heart to be captured by a Brathius.

He'd believed in her.

That's what humans do. They pretend to love you just enough to draw you close and expose your soft underbelly. Then they stab and twist and hack away until you die. He'd learned this lesson before—yet he'd fallen for the ruse *again*.

He'd let her Soothe him. She'd Soothed all of them. And now they were all dead.

It was the only skill humans possessed—their sole talent. But he would not let himself die at the hands of their deception.

He stood and staggered into a run, dimly trying to follow *her*.

The *murderer*.

154

I AM NUMB. Even when I move, I am frozen in shock. I am a tragic ghost haunting the woods. I am sadness. I am the farthest edge of despair. I am an uncontrollable aura of grief drifting after Omathis. *All those Anaghwin, departed. And Eveshone. Where is she?* I can't bear to think about it. She must be dead by now. I want nothing but to join her.

I remember Jarvin, and Eveshone's father—their hollowed-out bodies strung up for all to see. That's how I feel now. All that was good carved out of me—yet somehow, through a cruel trick, still alive.

I move out of habit more than will, barely inside my own body, as if I'm watching someone else do what I do. I watch myself give Omathis another gulp of air and hear us determine he can wear his mask again, because we're far enough away from the poison now. *The poison that took my Eveshone.* I see myself pause to look back at Mountaintop. I feel myself thinking about how in this past day, before the attack, I've realized that I do love the people who live here. Mother. Even Father. Istoch.

But I am leaving, and now I can never go back.

Torrain's Water Tree will save them. Adorane has destroyed the danger posed by the Croathus, even if it meant murdering my Anaghwin children in the process. Even my dear, loyal, innocent

Eveshone.

Adorane may not realize it yet, but he sacrificed me, too. I'm worse than dead. And so I have no place here anymore.

Omathis stares back at this village he'd always considered paradise.

"I'm sorry heaven wasn't what you dreamt it would be, Omathis," I say, my voice flat and dull.

He doesn't answer.

We trudge through Cloudline, and though Omathis remains vigilant, I'm blind to everything but my own wounded heart. I'm a jumbled mess. I want to curse him for taking me away from Eveshone. Yet I'm unspeakably grateful that he's still alive and by my side. I don't know how I feel; I don't even know what's real anymore.

"Be still, Lovely," Omathis whispers, stopping me with a strong arm.

I hold my breath and hear the noise that has him worried. There's a crashing through the underbrush, far off but growing closer. I dimly mull over what it could be, and resent whatever animal might be alive and running while Eveshone and my other children molder lifeless up in Mountaintop. If such beautiful creatures are denied life, then no one should be allowed to partake in it.

"It's not an animal," Omathis observes, reading my thoughts. "Not human, either."

Omathis tries to shield me from the yellow blur that emerges from the white clouds, but it's too late. Before I can say anything, I'm flat on the ground, too tired to scream, just hoping it will be over soon.

155

"YOU ARE SAFE, Lovely? You are well? No wounds that cause you continuing pain? Why are you crying, then? Why all the tears? Tell me, where is the blood? I will bind you together. Just tell me where you hurt."

It's Eveshone.

Relief floods through me. I cannot contain what I'm feeling, so it all spills out in sobs and tears and even some laughter. Unable to speak at all, I can't answer her avalanche of questions, which only further convinces her that I'm mortally wounded and in urgent need of her care.

I am grateful beyond measure that my child has returned from her lonely grave. I've never been happier than to be her mother again, inhaling her scent, feeling her skin against mine.

As the tears stream down my face, I realize I don't know if I can be a mother anymore. I want to, with all my heart, but fear I cannot handle it.

It's all too painful. When I believed she was dead, every ounce of color and life drained from my body. I don't know how I can bear her moving through this world, vulnerable, every day holding another opportunity to take her away from me.

I can only cry.

I have a fleeting thought. Is this how Mother felt about me? Did she miss me this much? Was she this bereft, this empty when she'd believed that I'd died? *Father, too?*

I didn't know life could contain such depths of anguish. Thinking of them feeling so terribly makes the tears flow even hotter. I grip Eveshone as hard as I can.

How are you here, Eveshone? Omathis wants to know.

"Lovely commanded it. She told me I had to leave," she insists.

"Who told you that?" I find the words to ask, incredulous.

"Adorane. I tried to find you, Lovely, but he shouted at me with such conviction."

He spared her. I am still angry at him—angrier than I ever thought I could be with anyone—but I am grateful. I couldn't have faced my life without her. I reach out and grab Omathis and hold both of them close to me.

I belong with them. Even more so, I belong *to* them. I miss Mountaintop, Adorane, Torrain, Mother and Father in a way that hurts with every breath. But I can never abandon these two. They are the only two who have not betrayed me.

Down in the lush, green valley, we find that Amperous' raging horde has dispersed. Perhaps they've sensed that it's over and returned to their homes to figure out what to do next.

It's over.

Whatever we've just lived through, one thing is for sure. One age has ended, and a new one is about to begin.

We find one of the boats Amperous and his ascending army used in their pursuit. We load in and shove off into the vast ocean. I feel freedom in the wind and the unending blue and the sound of the crashing waves.

It's time to go back to the Drowned City—to join those Anaghwin who didn't make the ill-fated journey into paradise and figure out what we want our world to look like.

I grasp Omathis' right hand, an urge to reaffirm our bond rising in me. "I'm so sorry you lost Mistersean, Omathis. And now heaven's been stolen from you, too. But I promise that you still have me. You will always have me."

Omathis looks over my face with careful deliberation, like he's cherishing every inch, every freckle, every wrinkle. I stare back at him, unembarrassed. He turns and looks back at the mountain, still shrouded in clouds, then fixes his eyes on me again.

"You're enough, Icelyn Brathius. You're more than enough. I will always miss Mistersean—but one out of two gods is more than most get, isn't it?"

"Yes, it really is," I agree.

"And you know, Lovely—heaven was only a paradise for us because the Brathius lived there." He sighs. "So Mountaintop is not our heaven anymore."

Eveshone nods. "It's time we find a new one, then," she adds, with a hint of excitement.

"Yes, let's find a new one," I respond, grabbing hold of her hand too.

We glide toward the Drowned City, through the waves and into the wind. Together, we'll face whatever this new age holds.